JENN

THANKS FOR ALL

THE HELP.

# BOXCAR BLUES

# BOXCAR
# *Blues*

# JEFF EGERTON

JAMES A. ROCK & COMPANY, PUBLISHERS
ROCKVILLE • MARYLAND

*Boxcar Blues* by Jeff Egerton

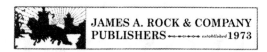

JAMES A. ROCK & COMPANY, PUBLISHERS

*Address comments and inquiries to:*

James A. Rock & Company, Publishers
9710 Traville Gateway Drive, #305
Rockville, MD 20850

**E-mail:**
jrock@rockpublishing.com    lrock@rockpublishing.com
Internet URL: www.rockpublishing.com

Trade Paperback ISBN: 978-1-59663-566-1

Library of Congress Control Number: 2007923813

Printed in the United States of America

First Edition: 2007

*This book is dedicated to my mother*

*Ruth Egerton*

*Through several years of rejections,*

*her support for a fledging writer*

*never wavered.*

*Thanks, Mom.*

## Acknowledgments

I'd like to thank everyone in the James Rock family of publishers, who accepted, then produced and published *The Boxcar Blues*. My family, Diane, Donna, Kevin and Kelly have been behind me all the way and support is the best thing an aspiring writer can have. Merlyn Faye put up with my indecision long enough to provide the author photo and book cover. Scott Caldwell's help on the web site was invaluable.

# Prologue

In the early 1930s men moved across the land like an endless trickling stream of humanity. They traveled on foot, a few by car, but most by rail; inside and on top of boxcars. Most often they didn't know where they were going, but kept moving. It wasn't determination, it was desperation. There had to be a better life out there somewhere.

The migrant army was predominantly men, but occasionally women and children tagged along. They could be just as hungry as the men; they could show you the idle stare of hopelessness, same as the men. They could suffer as easily, most of the time more easily. Everyone was different, each suffering in their own way, and yet everyone was the same—all cut from the same worn and ragged fabric.

The stream moved in every direction at once. Men heading north to seek work in the auto factories; south to find work picking cotton; east to the tomato crop in New Jersey; west to the hay fields of Imperial, or apple orchards of Washington. The hell of it was, most of the time, once you got there the work was over. Again you had made the trip for naught. You were turned away, usually by armed guards who let you know you weren't wanted. "Ain't any more work, get the hell out of here."

So, you got the hell out of there, maybe found a hobo jungle or the cardboard shanties of a Hooverville. Then you sat and you thought the same thoughts you struggled with in Amarillo, in Birmingham, or Yuma. You pondered your fate at every stop and came up with the same solution, you had to keep moving. Work wasn't going to come to you. Nobody ever walked into a hobo jungle and offered you work, 'cause there wasn't any work. And, even though there wasn't any work, you had to look for it. All of those rumors of work couldn't be wrong.

When you couldn't find work, you still had to eat, so you begged and if that didn't pay off, you stole. The great lesson of the depression was—you can get used to anything. Life, such as it was, had been reduced to its simplest terms: do what ever you can to stay alive.

The Great Depression—nothing great about it.

1

# Chapter One

August, 1932. Dakota Springs, Texas

✦ ✦ ✦

From his hiding place in the tall field grass, Luke Jackson watched the stranger saunter down the dusty gravel road with small brown clouds following his footsteps. The guy continued past the farm house, then stopped and ducked into the corn field and disappeared.

A minute later, Luke heard the rustling of corn husks. He saw the stranger hunker down in the grass twenty feet from him. He was certain the guy's intention was the same as his. The guy had heard the familiar clucking from a well stocked hen house and was planning on getting himself a chicken dinner. He had to beat him to it.

✦ ✦ ✦

Curly Levitz settled down in the grass and watched for any activity around the farm house. He was deep in thought about a plump pullet when the voice scared the hell out of him.

Luke yelled in a whisper, "Hey kid, wha'chu doin'?

Curly saw a dark face staring out of the field grass. Not knowing what to make of the guy he looked back at the house.

Luke tried again, "I said, what are you doing? Are you planning on hitting that hen house?"

"Yeah, what's it to you?"

"I was here first, that's what."

✦ ✦ ✦

Curly saw big dark eyes staring out from under a worn fedora. One cheek had a burn mark on it; buck teeth glowed against the dark skin like a candle in a cave. He said, "I don't care. I'm going after one of those hens."

Luke's last meal of two stale tortillas was two days ago. He countered, "You stay put. I'm goin' first."

Curly wasn't about to give in. He said, "The hell if you are. I ain't waiting for no one."

Luke had sized him up. The kid was smaller than him, but had that tough look about him that anyone on the road quickly acquires. If it came to a fight, Luke thought he had the edge.

He broke for the house. To his chagrin, the kid jumped up and ran beside him. Luke said, "Get back in the field, kid. I'll get us some chickens."

The kid didn't listen.

Luke stopped beside the farm house.

The kid, right behind him, said, "What's wrong?"

"I'm just making sure there ain't no one around."

On his hands and knees, Luke crept past two windows. He didn't hear any sounds coming from the house and hadn't seen anyone. It was looking better all the time, except for the pest that wouldn't go away. He tried to scare the kid. "Farmers have been known to shoot at chicken thieves. You sure you wanna do this?"

"You ain't gonna scare me off, fella. I'm just as hungry as you are."

Luke cursed to himself. He wished the kid would have waited in the field. He said, "I don't think there's anyone in the house. You ready?"

"Hell yes. Let's go."

Luke thought about the racket chickens made when you grabbed them. He hoped the kid knew enough to wring their necks to shut them up. He took off for the hen house with the kid right behind him. As soon as they ran through the door, the resident hens started making a ruckus that could be heard in the next county.

Luke grabbed the first pullet he could catch. He started to wring its neck to shut it up, then saw an axe and chopping block. He laid the bird on the block and whacked off its head.

Curly grabbed two pullets. He struggled to behead one while holding the other.

Luke yelled, "C'mon, kid. Don't take all day."

The door to the farm house flew open. A farmer looking down the barrel of a shotgun rushed toward them. He was tall, madder than hell and yelling in a deep voice, "Put them birds down, you theivin' bastards!"

The guy meant business. The boys stopped and dropped their birds. As if to emphasize their death, the headless chicks flapped aimlessly around in the dirt.

The farmer looked at his dead birds, spewing out their lasts drops of blood, then back at the boys. He roared, "Already kilt 'em, hunh? That's what I ought to do to you two, is take an axe to your necks."

The boys backed cautiously away from the enraged farmer. Luke said, "Mister, I ain't eaten in two days. I'll do some work around here to pay for those chickens."

Curly picked up on the logic, "Me too, mister. I don't mind doing some chores."

The farmer never softened his demeanor. "I don't want your kind around here. Get your low-down hides off my property and don't come back."

Luke and Curly backed away a few steps, then turned and ran to the field. They picked up their bindles and looked back at the disgruntled farmer. He was watching them with an icy stare; the shotgun in one hand and two dead chickens in the other.

Curly said, "I feel sorry for the next hobo that hits that hen house."

Luke said, "Thanks to you, we didn't get nuthin'."

Curly shot back. "God damn it, it wasn't my fault."

"I could 'a made it out of there with a nice fat pullet if you didn't take so long."

"I was trying to get us another bird."

"You ain't any good at stealing chickens, that's for sure."

"Shit, I stole more chickens than you've ever seen."

"You sure talk big."

Silence prevailed for the next five minutes. The boys knew there was no point to arguing. They were without a meal and the reason didn't matter. In the distance a train whistle cut the late afternoon heat. They both looked toward the sound that pulled at them like an invisible shepherd, guiding them toward the tracks that stretched unerringly into the future.

Luke said, "You gonna catch out?"

"I don't know. I might hit the stem first; see if I can get a meal."

"I don't do no begging at houses unless black folk live there."

"White people don't give you food?"

"Not very often."

"There's some houses up ahead. You wait out of sight and I'll see if I can get us something."

"I hope you're better at putting the arm on people than you are at stealing chickens."

"You just watch. I'll talk them out of their gold fillings."

"You sure talk big."

✦ ✦ ✦

From the cover of a corn field the boys looked over a recently painted house with a two year old Ford Model A in the driveway.

Curly said, "This is as good a chance as we'll find today," then left to redeem himself. He approached the house and saw the man of the house in the front window lighting his pipe. Perfect. Right after dinner was the best time. He headed for the back door to catch the lady of the house cleaning up. If he was lucky he'd get a warm meal. He always offered to do some work, but most often they'd give him something just to get rid of him. They didn't want no hobo hanging around, even if he was just a kid.

Hat in hand Curly approached the back door. He knocked softly and a lady answered. With a sorrowful look he stood back and said, "S'cuse me, ma'am. I was wondering if you had any work I could do in exchange for something to eat. I don't need much, just a piece of stale bread or something, an' I'm real good at painting. I'll put a fresh coat on that shed in an hour."

A plump, gray haired woman wiped her hands on her apron, and said, "Oh, you poor dear, you're just a young boy. Wait here."

Curly sat down on the stoop. From the smell, he thought he'd be feasting on pork chops and potatoes, maybe even a piece of apple pie. He'd make that black kid eat his words.

His thoughts of a warm meal disappeared like smoke in a breeze when he heard the old man's voice, "Martha, was that someone at the door?"

From his tone Curly could tell the old fart wasn't in favor of hand-outs. The wife said, "It's just a young boy. I was going to give him a pork chop and bread."

"The hell if you are. He can go somewhere else for his handouts. I work too damn hard to be supporting every vagrant that knocks on the door. Word gets around we're handing out food and they'll be lined up down the block, trying to eat us out of house and home."

Curly had heard this song before. He was long gone when the guy threw open the door.

❖ ❖ ❖

He walked back to the field, knowing what the black guy was going to say.

Surprisingly, Luke said, "I knew that house wasn't no good. They got a new car, curtains on the windows and fancy shutters. Ain't no way they're going to give nothing away. Rich people hold onto their fixins like it's life or death. They don't know about bein' hungry."

"Yeah, I can't argue with that."

The boys walked toward the tracks, watching for another house that might be worth a visit. Every house they passed looked as if they were long deserted; no lights, screens torn, shingles falling like snow-flakes. A sad reminder of transient times when people lived somewhere until the rent was due, then left town.

A quarter mile from the tracks they saw a pear tree that hadn't been picked clean yet. Luke scrambled up the tree and filled his pockets with ripe pears. A block later they sat down under the portico of a closed Standard Oil station and ate most of the pears. Curly said, "Pork chops would have been a lot better. I hope the guy back at that house chokes on his next meal until his fat ass quits breathing."

Luke looked off in the distance. He didn't care if they guy choked or not, he was thinking about his future. He asked, "Where you going next?"

Curly grabbed handful of pebbles and tossed them one by one at a faded sign. "I don't know. I guess I'll catch out and see where I end up. How 'bout you?"

"There ain't no point in staying here." Luke stood and looked toward the tracks. "We might as well travel together for a while. What's your name?"

Curly held out his hand and said, "Abraham Levitz. Most people call me Curly."

Luke shook his hand and smiled, "Luke Jackson and everybody calls me Luke."

"I kind of like traveling with someone. Don't do it often. Most of the time I stick to myself."

"That's why you ain't eaten in so long."

"Wha'dya mean, Luke?"

"You're the worst chicken thief I've ever seen."

# Chapter Two

An hour later Luke and Curly hopped into a boxcar on a west-bound freight train that was just gathering steam. Out of habit they looked to see who else was in the car. Once the train was under a head of steam it would be going too fast to jump off and they'd be trapped with their fellow riders, good or bad.

At one end they saw a few men who gave them a cursory glance, then went back to sleep; those weren't the ones they worried about. They were looking for the men who stared at them, sizing them up for robbery or other violent act.

Luke was searching for the look of those who carried a hate for black people with them. They weren't hard to spot because they never hid their hatred; in most cases, they wore it like a badge.

They didn't see anyone who looked troublesome, but still Luke decided to hide out in the end of the car that was filled with packing paper. He said, "I'm getting some shut eye under this packing paper. Wake me if you decide to drop off."

"O.K." Curly gathered some paper for padding and sat down near the doorway. As the rhythmical clicking of the wheels increased and the swaying of the boxcar became more erratic, he lowered his head and thought of his family back in upper New York.

His Dad would be working the fields seven days a week, trying to raise enough produce to feed the family and sell what was left over, if there were buyers with cash. His brothers were too young to leave home, but had wanted to go with him rather than live with the bitch his father had married. She'd moved in and turned their life into a living hell. An ex-school teacher, she'd taken to whacking their hands with a ruler when the chores weren't done to her satisfaction. The last straw had been when she grounded him because he wasn't paying close attention to her tutoring. He'd complained, but his father said the extra schooling was good for them and they should be grateful for her help. Curly countered with, "It's her or me. If she stays, I'm leaving."

His Dad said he loved this woman and she was staying. He warned his son there wasn't much work to be had. Undaunted, Curly packed his bags and left that afternoon. Since then he'd traveled over a thousand miles looking for work. Every time he was turned down for a job his Dad's words rung in his ear. He was thinking about finding work when sleep came.

◆ ◆ ◆

Curly woke with a start when he sensed someone near him. Before his eyes could focus in the blue-black light of the approaching dawn, he smelled them; there was no mistaking the gamy scent of hobos. He saw a dirty, tattered man sitting a few feet to his left, between him and the doorway. Dark eyes stared at him from under a worn fedora, but the voice came from his right, "Don't be afraid, boy. We want to give you something to eat."

Trouble! Nobody ever offered you food in a boxcar. Curly turned his attention to the speed of the train—was it slow enough to jump off? No, the engine was under a full head of steam and he had no idea how long before there'd be another water stop. He had to bluff.

In his huskiest voice, Curly bellowed, "I don't want your fuckin' food! Get the hell away from me before I throw you off the train."

"Whew-we," the one on his right said. "We got us a tiger, Gene. He's gonna throw us off the train."

Curly's head spun as he looked around the boxcar. Deserted. He wondered if Luke was still sleeping in the packing paper. Then he calculated his chances of surviving a jump from the fast moving train—not good.

The man on his left pulled out a knife. The other one laughed, "He-he, you still gonna throw us off the train, sonny boy?"

Curly thrust his hand in his jacket pocket and screamed, "I'm packing a rod. Get the hell away from me or I'll shoot!"

"Uh-oh, he's got a rod, Gene." With astonishing quickness, the man on his right grabbed him by the crotch and laughed, "Where you got that rod boy? You got it hidden down here by your little pecker?"

Curly threw a forearm into the one who'd grabbed him and tried to scramble to the other side of the boxcar. The guy with the knife grabbed his collar and threw him to the floor, slamming his face into the wood. He felt blood on his cheek, and the tip of the knife sticking him below his ear. A threatening voice said, "Don't make a move, kid."

"You ain't gonna to be throwing anybody anywhere." The one who'd grabbed his crotch was fumbling with Curly's belt buckle. When it was undone, he tugged Curly's pants down.

Curly shouted, "You God damned queer bastards. If I get my hands on you, you're dead!"

A fist to the side of his head, then, "Shut up, kid!"

Curly grit his teeth, steeling himself. His urge was to struggle, but the knife point in his neck stilled him. He was prepared for the worst, when he heard Luke's voice bellow above the din of the train. "You two, leave him alone."

Both men turned toward the voice. Curly drove his feet into the guy's crotch. Hearing a loud scream, he scrambled away and pulled up his pants.

One guy yelled, "Com'ere kid, I ain't done with you."

Luke stepped out of the shadows. The guy with the knife turned toward him and attacked, slashing wildly. "Get outta here nigger, this ain't none o' your business!"

With astonishing quickness, Luke grabbed the guy's wrist and wrapped an arm around his neck. The hobo struggled, but Luke twisted his arm until a bone cracked. The hobo roared in pain and dropped the knife. Curly grabbed it.

Luke threw the guy out the door. A scream followed the hobo. He pointed to the second guy and said, "You want to take care of this one?"

"Yeah." Curly held the knife to the cowering man's throat and screamed, "You queer son of a bitch. I ought to dress you out right here."

The man cried, "Look kid, we was jes' havin' a little fun. I wasn't gonna stick it in ya'." Wide, terrified eyes searched Curly's face to see how much hatred was in the boy. He muttered, "What-What're ya' gonna do?"

"I'll fix you so you won't be able to fuck anybody ever again."

The man cried, "No, no, wait a second, kid!!"

Luke said, "You better not cut him or he'll die for sure."

"You just broke a guy's arm and threw him off the train."

"Yeah, because they were gonna hurt you. This guy ain't so dangerous now."

The cowering hobo picked up on the logic, "Yeah, kid, listen to the nigger. I ain't gonna do nothin' now. There ain't no use for you to hurt me, we can forget about this."

Curly kept the pressure on the knife and told the man, "Mister, you've got ten seconds to get off this train or I'm gonna cut you long and deep."

"Wait, I gotta get my pants on."

Curly threw the guy's pants to the end of the boxcar, "Move it!"

"But wait, kid, I can't … ."

Curly jabbed the big steel blade at the guy until he jumped out the door.

With his heart racing, he stood in the doorway of the rocking boxcar. He felt several years older. He said, "Thanks for the help."

"That's O.K. Now that we got rid of them, we better drop off, quick."

"Why?" Curly didn't understand the urgency.

"'Cause, if either of them two live, they're going to be screaming about a white man and a Negro that threw 'em off the train. Word's gonna go down the line and the law will be waitin' for us at the next stop. They'll just throw you in jail, but they'll sure as shootin' lynch me."

Curly leaned against the swaying wall of the boxcar and said, "Are you serious?"

Luke asked, "Curly, how long you been on the road?"

"A month or so. Why?"

"Well, you sure ain't learned much. I'm surprised you lived this long."

"Wha'dya mean?" Curly shot back. "I can take care of myself!"

Luke snickered. "You sure got a short memory."

Curly reacted, defensive, "Yeah, well that guy had a knife."

"We're slowing for a grade. Let's ditch this westbound and catch out on an eastbound. They'll be looking for us at the stops west of here. Our best bet is to head back east for a few hours."

"Do you mean the law will be looking for us?"

"They might be. We'd best avoid them."

"That means we can't show our faces around here, right?"

"That's right."

"Shit!" Curly yelled. "If we can't show our faces, how the hell are we going to get anything to eat?"

"I don't know, Curly. I guess we don't eat."

# Chapter Three

When the train slowed, the boys jumped onto the cinder siding and rolled into the tall grass. They walked along the tracks until a water tank appeared in the distance, which they approached cautiously.

Luke said, "Go way back in this field. Some of the railroad bulls in these parts carry shotguns. If they think someone is waiting to hop a train, they've been known to fire a few rounds of buckshot into the field."

They ran into the field and laid down. Curly asked, "What if the bulls kill someone by shooting into a field like that?"

Luke answered, matter-of-fact, "Someone gets killed, most likely they dig a hole and throw him in it. Since I been ridin' the rails, I've seen hundreds of guys die out here."

"All of 'em shot by the bulls?"

"No, most of 'em are killed getting on or off trains. Guys make the mistake of ridin' the blinds between passenger cars, or they ride the rods below boxcars. They're both dangerous. Saw a kid last week, sittin' the doorway of boxcar swinging his feet when the train went by a switch. The switch caught his feet and took him clean out of the car. 'Nuther guy tried to catch out, but the train was goin' too fast. It threw him right under the wheels—cut 'im in half."

"Holy shit." Curly said, thinking how lucky he'd been so far. They turned toward the mournful whistle and unmistakable chugging of an approaching train. Knowing the brakeman would be looking for hobos, they waited in the field. After the train took on water, they heard the two short whistle blasts that signaled the engineer was about to blow down the boiler. Once the tall driving wheels started to turn, they sprinted for the train. Luke saw Curly heading for the front ladder on a closed boxcar. He grabbed the rear ladder and climbed to the top of the boxcar.

Once on top, Curly slowly walked the catwalk toward Luke.

Halfway there he saw Luke waving and shouting, "Get down, Curly, get down!"

Curly lay down.

Luke ran toward him and said, "Don't you know nothin'?"

"Wha'dya mean?"

"Don't walk a boxcar with your back to the engine; that's a good way to get killed." As Luke said this, an over-hanging signal arm whizzed by, barely four feet over their heads.

Luke continued, "See that? If you're standing with your back to the engine and one of them, or a bridge comes along, you're dead. You always walk a catwalk facing the engine."

Curly said, "O.K."

Luke handed Curly his belt. "Here, we'll sleep in shifts. Tie yourself on and get some sleep, I'll enjoy the scenery."

"OK. Thanks, Luke." Curly wrapped the belt around the catwalk and laid his head on his bindle. He said, "Hey Luke, I just thought of a nickname for you."

"What's that, Curly?"

"After seeing you run that catwalk, I'm gonna call you, Catwalk. Catwalk Jackson. How do you like it?"

Luke grinned and said, "Yeah, I kinda' like it. Curly and Catwalk— ain't we a pair?"

◆ ◆ ◆

The second hobo who'd been thrown off the train, struck a crossing signal that inflicted severe internal injuries. Before he died he told his story to a citizen waiting for the train to pass. "Me an' my friend was riding in a boxcar, going out to California to look for work. These two young guys jumped us, a tall nigger with a burn mark on his left cheek an' a white guy with real curly hair. The nigger had a big knife. They beat my partner bad an' did all sorts of perverted things to him before they threw him off. When they took my pants off, I knew they was goin' to rape me too, but I made it to the door an' jumped. Ya' gotta tell someone about these guys. They ain't very old, probably in their teens, but they're meaner than hell."

The motorist drove to the nearest police station and reported the incident. He then told everyone he saw about the meanest desperadoes since the James gang.

◆ ◆ ◆

Watching the clouds drift by, Catwalk thought of his family back on the farm in Mississippi. He worried about his Momma trying to feed eight kids when only three of them were old enough to work the fields. She always made do and never complained, but it was hard on her. More than anything else, he wished he could find work and send her some money.

Since he left home there had been occasional work, but he wasn't sure if the money he'd given to people ever reached her. Most likely it had been stolen. Now that Curly was with him, he could help write her a letter and send her money themselves. This brought a smile to his face. His smile disappeared when he thought of the trouble they were in. They had to avoid the police and the railroad bulls. He didn't know if the hoboes had talked, but knew how life worked on the road. If the hoboes had talked, it would be remembered that a black man threw a white man off a train. That was grounds for hanging—period.

If they were successful at avoiding the police and the bulls, they still had to find work, and that was almost impossible. Now, more than ever, he was glad he had a friend with him.

Catwalk saw the terrain rising. He nudged Curly. "Comin' to a grade, time to drop off."

"You think we're far enough away yet?"

"I hope so. Anyway, we better get off before some other 'boes see us."

◆ ◆ ◆

Ten minutes later their worn brogans shuffled through the hot gravel as they walked down a Texas farm road. The midday sun was blistering, white hot and hard as steel, but the boys seemed immune to discomfort.

Curly asked, "Catwalk, were you serious about them lynching you?"

"Sure was, Curly. Don't you believe me?"

"Well, why would they? They don't know it was you that threw him off the train."

"Curly, where you from?"

"Norwich, New York. That's in upstate; we had a farm about ten miles outside Norwich."

"There any black folk up there?"

"A few. Old man Sachs had a couple worked for him. Why?"

"Curly, there's plenty o' places in this country where white men don't even think twice about hanging black men. My Momma told me some of 'em do it jus' 'cause they're mean."

"Holy shit." Curly said. "That don't make any sense."

"Well, they think 'cause they're white and we're black that they can do it. An' most people don't care about it, except they don't want to lose a good worker. Some people treat us real nice. We worked two seasons for Mister Slade an' he was a real kind man. He even brought a doctor out when Daddy took sick. When Daddy died they had a nice box with flowers for him and a preacher to read over him so he'd go right to heaven. There's other people who are just looking for somewhere to use their hate. Like those two back in that boxcar, they'd just as soon stuck that knife in me as look at me. I can tell the ones that got the hate in them."

"There's some people who don't like Jews, but they don't hang 'em. At least I never heard of anyone doing it."

"Are you Jewish?"

"You kidding, with a name like Levitz?"

"I don't know what's a Jewish name, 'cause I never knew anyone Jewish. The only people I knew were the people on the farm where we lived."

"Didn't you ever go to school?"

"No. I had to work since I was little. My Momma taught me reading letters some."

"But you seem smart to me, and you talk like you're smart."

"My Momma used to spend hours teaching us kids to talk proper. She'd say, 'Luke, just 'cause you work as a cropper, don't mean you have to talk like a cropper. Some people might not like you 'cause you're black, but for the ones who don't hold that against you, if they hear you talk proper, they'll be more likely to take your side. And, that will help you get good jobs.'"

"Your Momma sounds like she's pretty smart."

Catwalk smiled with pride, "My Momma's the smartest lady in the world. She used to read to me, every night after work. She'd say, 'Luke, since we're poor and you can't travel, you can see other places through books. I miss that most of all, hearing my Momma read to me."

Curly slapped his friend on the shoulder and said, "As soon as I find something, I'll read to you, Catwalk."

"Do you know how to read letters, Curly?"

"Sure, I made it through the seventh grade, but then they closed our school. Why?"

"Well, I want you to teach me how to read and to write too, so I can write to my Momma. If we can find work, I'll send her some money."

"Sure, I'll teach you."

Luke smiled, knowing how his Momma would feel if she got a letter from him.

"Is that why you're on the road, 'cause your Daddy died?"

"Yeah, my Momma had too many mouths to feed."

"How long you been out here?"

"Oh, I don't rightly know; I reckon it's eight or nine months now."

"You ever had anybody do anything to you, like those two back there?"

"No, but I'm real careful and good at staying out of sight. Nobody sees me unless I want them to. I don't go to no hobo jungles or Hoovervilles unless there's other black folk there."

Curly saw a dust cloud down the road, and said, "There's a car comin'."

"Get in this field, fast."

They jumped a fence and ran into the corn field, not stopping until they were far into the field.

As they ran through the corn, Curly said, "Do you think the people in the car are looking for us?"

"They could be, Curly, but we don't know. We better stay out of sight just in case."

# Chapter Four

"Did you see that, Sheriff?" Deputy Alton Jones asked Sheriff Wendell Tyler. "Two men. As soon as we made the turn, I seen two men walking down the road, but they seen us and ran into the field."

"So?" The sheriff said, "There ain't no law against running through a corn field."

"It could be the two killers we heard about in that telegraph message."

"Are you sure you saw someone?" The sheriff hoped his deputy would get the hint that he enjoyed driving his new Nash police car more than chasing some damned hoboes.

The deputy wouldn't be put off, "Just as sure as I'm sittin' here, Sheriff."

The sheriff countered, "Nah, it couldn't a' been them. Hell, the message said they were searching for those guys over west of Bailey's Junction."

"Yeah, but they could've doubled back. Stop the car. I want to see something."

The deputy walked to the edge of the field and scanned the soil. "There's fresh foot prints of two men in the dirt. They're hiding in the field."

The sheriff said, "Those prints could have been left there by the men working the field."

"Sheriff," the deputy pressed, "We had a hell of a rain two nights ago. Any prints that're visible have been made in the last day or so. Someone in that field is running from something."

The sheriff drove away. There was no getting out of this, but if it was the killers, he wanted more men. He said, "I'm going to stop by Chet's house to warn him. Then we'll go round up some help. If it's the same ones who threw them guys off the train, they're dangerous."

Excited about seeing some action, Jones said, "That's agreeable to me, Wendell. I know it's those two and we're gonna nab 'em."

✦ ✦ ✦

Curly and Catwalk waited behind an oak tree in the middle of the corn field. Catwalk carefully peeked around the tree and saw the white star on the door and whispered to Curly, "It's a po-lice car and one of them is looking around at the edge of the field."

"He's looking for foot prints." Curly whispered back.

"What if he sees our prints?" Catwalk asked. "Do you think he'll come after us?"

"I don't know, but we'd better head for the other side of this field. C'mon."

The boys quietly moved down the corn rows, then came to a dirt road. Curly said, "Let's head down the road. We'll stay close to the field, so we can duck back in."

Catwalk looked apprehensive, but said, "I guess that's O.K.. Wouldn't hurt to get out of this area as soon as we can."

"It wouldn't hurt to find something to eat. I'm about ready to chew on this field corn."

"Are you crazy? We can't go begging for food with the police looking for us."

"Well, sooner or later, we gotta eat or all they'll find is our carcasses."

❖ ❖ ❖

Sheriff Tyler drove to Chet Parker's place where they found the old man tending a vegetable garden. He walked over to the patrol car while wiping his brow. "Mornin' Wendell. It looks like you got yourself a new police car."

"Sure did. Picked it up at Recker's dealership two days ago. He claims she'll do over sixty, but I hain't tried it out yet 'cause I gotta break it in first."

The deputy couldn't care less about the patrol car. Itching for action, he leaned over toward the driver's window, "Chet, we stopped by to warn you about a couple of mean hombres that might be in Morton's field. They're young guys, but they're meaner'n hell. They killed and raped a couple hoboes over toward Bailey's Junction. One of the guys lived long enough to identify his killers—a nigger about six two with a burn mark on his cheek and a white kid about five ten with curly brown hair. Keep a gun handy and if you see 'em, shoot 'em on sight."

"Damn it, Alton, we ain't shooting anyone." Sheriff Tyler tried to temper Jones' lust for violence. "Chet, we wanna pick these guys up, but we gotta make sure we got the right guys. If you see 'em, let us know. We're going over to the Puckett lady's place to warn her now."

The farmer said, "I'm going over there. I can tell her about these guys."

"Thanks Chet. Tell her they're dangerous and she should keep her doors locked."

◆ ◆ ◆

While the sheriff drove back into town he thought about his deputy's attitude and hunger for a confrontation. Jones was a member of the local Ku Klux Klan, but his Klan activities and personal prejudices had never been an issue in his job. The Sheriff saw the Klan as a bunch of local boys who just wanted to get drunk and raise a little hell. Now, he thought, if his deputy came across the two men, he was liable to shoot first and ask questions later.

The two lawmen walked into Clark's Mercantile and greeted four men sitting around a card table. The Sheriff asked for a cold soda. The proprietor asked Jones if he wanted anything. Jones said, "Nothin' for me, Ray. We're goin' after a couple a' mean hombres that we saw duck into Morton's corn field."

This comment brought up several questions and the sheriff addressed them, "We're not sure who we saw. Alton saw somebody run into the field and now he's jumping to all sorts of conclusions that it was the same two as we heard about in a telegraph message."

Jones said, "I'm betting it's the same two, Sheriff."

The Sheriff shot a scowl at his overzealous partner, then said, "We got a message about a nigger and a white guy that assaulted a couple of hoboes and threw them off a train. One of the bums described his attackers. He said they're armed with knives and very dangerous."

Again the deputy spoke up, "They're the queer type too because the nigger fucked both the hoboes before he killed them."

"Alton, we don't know it was the nigger that did the rapes. All it said was that these guys were raped before they was killed, but we don't know who did it."

"C'mon, Wendell, you know damn well, ain't no white guy gonna rape another white guy. It had to be the nigger. The big buck couldn't wait to find his self some pussy."

The Sheriff was clearly tired of his deputy's ranting. "Alton, shut up for a minute so I can talk to these men. I need volunteers for a posse, and I'll need one of you to drive his car. The county will pay for your gas and ammunition."

All four men volunteered. Going after hardened criminals beat the boredom of playing cards for match sticks. They left to get their guns.

# Chapter Five

After walking for thirty minutes, Catwalk and Curly saw a farm house in the distance. They ducked into the field and approached the house from the cover of the corn. Their hunger prompted talk about begging for a meal even though it would expose them.

"Catwalk, I gotta get something to eat and most farm houses have plenty of food. Hell, they probably even got a vegetable garden."

"I know that, Curly, but if you go to that house, they can identify us. If anyone comes looking for us, we're gonna get arrested."

Curly considered this, but hunger was over riding his apprehension. He said, "Here's what we'll do. I've got a better chance of getting a handout than you do. Stay hidden and I'll try the house. If I get something to eat, I'll go down the road and you meet me when we're out of sight of the house."

"O.K. If anyone comes looking for us while your gone, I'm gonna hightail it for the tracks and catch out on an eastbound."

Curly said, "Don't worry; I'll get us some grub."

◆ ◆ ◆

Curly ran across the road and approached the house, while looking the place over. He saw a two story house in need of paint and some old plows and manure spreaders sitting in the remains of a shelter. Beside it another shed had collapsed until it was nothing more than a pile of weathered lumber. In spite of the signs of despair, someone had put some work into the place. They had a large vegetable garden, encircled by chicken wire and a new chicken coop, which sounded as if it housed a couple dozen hens. The barn had been repaired and beside it a few head of Guernsey dairy cows lay in a corral. Nearing the door he felt his chances were pretty good, but that's what he'd thought at the house back in Dakota Springs.

Curly took off his hat and gently knocked on the screen door. He heard nothing and knocked a little harder. To his surprise, he heard a pistol being cocked behind him and a female voice said, "Hold it right there."

Curly froze. He never thought he'd never be apprehended so quickly. Running away crossed his mind, but the pistol said otherwise.

The voice said, "Turn around."

He did and found himself staring at a tall red-headed woman holding a Colt Forty-Five that looked like a cannon to him.

Maxine Puckett wore bib overalls and a gingham shirt. Her long red hair was wrapped up, on top of her head; sparkling green eyes sized up Curly, "Christ, you're just a kid," she said as she lowered the pistol. "I thought you were one of the desperadoes they warned me about."

Curly said, "Um, how do, Ma'am. I'm just looking for a little work so's I can get something to eat. I'd be glad to clean out that barn, or milk your cows."

"What's your name, boy?"

"Abraham, Ma'am. Abraham Levitz, but most people call me Curly."

"How long since you ate?'

"Ah, it's been two days, since we ate—I mean, I ate, Ma'am."

"Well Curly, I just cleaned and cut up a couple pullets. You think you could stand some fried chicken and biscuits with gravy?"

Curly's mouth started watering at the thought of such a sumptuous meal. He stammered, "Yes Ma'am, I sure could, and I'll be glad to work to earn my meal."

"You say you can milk cows?"

"Sure can, yes Ma'am."

"O.K., Curly, my name's Maxine. The milking stool and bucket are just inside the barn door. Give those cows some attention and you'll have fresh milk with your dinner."

"Sure thing, ma'am."

While milking, Curly thought of how he could take some food to Catwalk. He didn't want to blow the deal by telling the lady he'd rather take the food with him instead of eating here. He was on the last cow when he decided he'd eat here, and then tell her he'd do some extra work if he could take something with him.

When he carried the milk to the house, however, he found his worries were unfounded. Maxine was sitting on the back stoop smoking a cigarette. She asked him, "You want a smoke?"

Curly answered, "That sounds good. Ready-mades are hard to come by on the road."

Maxine handed him a tin of Chesterfields and asked, "Where's your friend?"

Curly coughed. "Beg your pardon, ma'am?"

"Your friend, the one traveling with you, where is he?"

Curly hesitated, but then decided to come clean. "He's waiting over in the corn field."

"Not many people travel alone these days. Go get him. I've got enough for him."

"I appreciate this, Maxine. I'll be right back."

Curly ran across the road and hollered for Catwalk. He'd yelled three times when he heard, "I hear ya', Curly. Quit makin' so much noise."

Curly tugged at his friend's arm and said, "C'mon, the lady that lives here is real nice and she's fixin' a fried chicken dinner, with biscuits for us right now."

Catwalk shot Curly a troubled look and asked him, "Are you sure we should eat here?"

"Whad'ya mean? Of course we should eat here. She's fixin' fried chicken with biscuits an' gravy. We ain't gonna get a better offer than that in a year."

"Well, O.K." Catwalk still sounded apprehensive.

"What are you worried about?"

"It could be a trap. As soon as we sit down to eat, the sheriff shows up and arrests us."

Curly had been so focused on the sumptuous meal that he hadn't thought about this possibility. He told Catwalk, "Nah, this ain't no trap. This lady ain't like that."

"How're you so sure?"

"Well, shit. I ain't sure, but I'm to the point where I'd rather be arrested with a full stomach than goin' down the road on an empty stomach. C'mon, it's O.K."

Although Catwalk had some reservations, he followed his friend. Fried chicken sounded real good.

◆ ◆ ◆

Maxine Puckett watched the boys walk across the road. In her previous profession she'd become an accurate judge of men's character. She didn't think these were the desperadoes Barker had warned her about, but they fit the physical description, and that could be as bad as being guilty. She'd find out what was going on, because according to Chet, the Deputy was ready to shoot the colored boy on sight. She knew of Jones' Klan activities and his reputation as a violent hot head. If anyone needed a warning, it was the two boys and not the local residents.

She met them at the door and said, "Come on in. Dinner will be ready in ten minutes."

The boys shuffled into the kitchen, hats in hand. Maxine noticed the black boy's eyes were the size of saucers. She offered Curly a cigarette, which he accepted. When she offered Catwalk one, he shook his head. She asked him, "Have you ever smoked a cigarette?"

Catwalk shook his head.

She asked Curly, "Who's your friend?"

"This is Luke, but I call him Catwalk 'cause he can run a boxcar catwalk like a rabbit."

Maxine smiled and said, "That so, Catwalk?"

He nodded, his eyes filled with apprehension. Maxine said, "You can talk, I don't mind."

He cleared his throat and managed, "Thank you, ma'am."

Maxine motioned to the table, "Sit down. We need to talk before we eat."

She lit a cigarette and said, "The sheriff and his deputy are spreading the word about a couple of murderers. Seems these guys killed and raped a couple hoboes over by Bailey's Junction. Their description fits you two, but I don't think you're the killer types. You better tell me what this is all about, because there's a misunderstanding circulating, and you could be in a hell of a lot of trouble."

Curly took a drag on his cigarette, and then told his story.

When he finished, Maxine asked Catwalk, "Did you hurt the guy before you threw him off the train?"

Catwalk looked at Curly; he wasn't sure what to say.

Curly answered, "He broke his arm to get the knife away before he threw him out the door."

Maxine again asked, "You sure that's all you did?"

This time Catwalk answered, "Yes ma'am, when I saw they had Curly's pants down. … "

"Ya' didn't have to tell her that." Curly piped up.

Maxine said, "Were they trying to rape you, Curly?"

Sheepishly, "Uh, yes ma'am."

Maxine asked, "So what happened to the second hobo?"

Curly said, "Well, see these guys were some real mean bastards. I didn't know what to do, so I threatened to cut him. He begged me not to, but I felt like hurting this guy really bad."

He took a drag off his cigarette and Maxine asked, "What did you do?"

"I wanted to stick that knife in him, but Catwalk told me not to, or he'd die for sure."

Maxine said, "Good thinking, Catwalk."

Curly continued, "I made the guy jump off the train without his pants."

Maxine talked as she served dinner. "You better listen close because these are the cold, hard facts. You both murdered someone. The circumstances point to self defense, but unless you can find a lawyer to defend you and a jury to acquit you, you're going to do hard time. And Catwalk, in this part of the country, they'll find a way to string you up before you even see a courtroom. Now this deputy that saw you duck into the field, he's as mean as the guys you threw off the train. He hates black people and he uses his badge as an excuse to shoot them. The sheriff ain't got the guts to do anything about it, so he pretends it ain't happening."

Everyone started eating. Maxine said, "I want you guys to stay in the hayloft until it gets dark. I'm going to give you directions to a farm that has hay trucks leaving in the morning for Oklahoma. Hop on one of those trucks and stay out of sight. Don't try to hop a train 'cause the railroad bulls around here are bad. Head north and try to find work on a harvest crew."

Curly said, "Trouble is, Maxine, there ain't no work out there."

Maxine became upset that the boys didn't realize how much hatred they were up against. "Curly, damn it! You can't stay around here. There are too many people looking for someone to take out their anger on. You stay around here, you'll end up behind bars and Catwalk— you're a dead man walking."

This brought about a silence while two boys, who were growing up much quicker than they'd planned, finished their meal.

◆ ◆ ◆

For the search, Deputy Jones had been paired with John Townsend. He'd chosen John because he had an Oldsmobile sedan, and was meek enough not to question the deputy.

The Deputy had planned his strategy. Ever since she'd moved in, Jones had been trying to gain Maxine's favor. Because she was a retired whore from New Orleans, he thought she'd be an easy mark. She'd been more discriminating and had resisted his advances. Now, he had a reason to go by her place, and he was determined to impress her. First, he had to get rid of Townsend.

They drove to an intersection of two farm roads and he told Townsend to get out and watch the roads from all four directions.

The farmer asked, "What should I do if I see them?"

"Just fire a couple of shots into the air; I'll be back right away."

As the deputy drove to Maxine's place, thoughts of the shapely red head brought a lecherous smile to his face.

# Chapter Six

The boys had been in the hayloft for an hour when Maxine saw the car pull into the yard. When Deputy Jones stepped out, she swore out loud. He was the last person she wanted to see.

Jones yelled, "Hello, the house."

Maxine walked out to meet him, while thinking of the quickest way to get rid of him without raising his suspicion. She said, "Hello, Alton. What can I do for you?"

With an air of importance, Jones hitched up his gun belt and said, "I came to tell you about a couple of bad hombres that might be around here."

"Chet already told me about them. I haven't seen them; nobody's been here."

Hoping he'd get the hint that the conversation was over, she turned and walked toward the door.

Jones said, "You ain't bein' very neighborly. Most people would invite me in for a cup of coffee."

"I don't have time, Alton. I have to get a pie out of the oven and then feed my chickens. Thanks for stopping by."

Maxine walked into the house, locking the screen door behind her.

Jones, seething from her rebuff, decided to use his official status to extend his stay. Through the screen, he said, "You sure there ain't been anyone here?

"I'm sure, deputy. Why don't you go look for these guys elsewhere?"

Maxine's uncooperative attitude infuriated Jones. He yelled, "Lady, you ain't bein' very cooperative with the law. Maybe you'd better let me come in and take a look around."

From the kitchen, Maxine said, "There's no one here deputy. Why can't you get that through your thick redneck skull?"

Her last comment pushed Jones over the edge. He jammed his fist through the screen, unlocked the door and walked into the kitchen.

When she heard his boots, Maxine stood up next to the oven and said, "What the hell do you think you're doing? I didn't invite you into my house."

"I though, since you're behaving so strange, that I'd better take a look around. I think you're hiding something."

Maxine yelled, "I could be hiding a bull elephant in here and you wouldn't know it. Get out of my house, now!"

Jones walked closer to her and said, "And if I don't leave, what're you gonna do, baby? You gonna whack me with a spatula?"

Again Maxine said, "I'm warning you, deputy; get the hell out of here."

Jones saw the Colt revolver lying on the counter. He walked over and picked it up, spun the cylinder and looked hard at Maxine. "What are you doing with this? Is there something you're not telling me?"

"No, there's nothing I'm not telling you. Now get the hell out of my house."

With a lecherous leer on his face, Jones walked up until he was very close to Maxine and said, "Take it easy, baby." He then tried to put an arm around her shoulders.

Maxine knew she had to nip this in the bud. Using the only weapon within reach, she threw the hot cherry pie in Jones' face.

"Arrgghh." Jones screamed. "God damn it." He yelled as he frantically tried to wipe the hot pie filling off his face. "You done it now, bitch. You're gonna pay." He went to the sink and began pumping water to wipe his face. Then, he saw the sink full of dirty dishes.

He glared at the redhead and said, "You said no one was here. You got a lot of dirty dishes for no one bein' here."

Maxine backed away, moving toward the forty-five. With her eyes on the enraged deputy, she felt for the pistol. When she came up with the gun, Jones grinned.

"You gonna shoot me, whore lady?"

"I'm not kidding, Jones. You leave now and we can forget this. If you don't, I'll pull the trigger, just as sure as it's daylight."

❖ ❖ ❖

The boys heard the car drive up, and watched the Deputy force his way into the house. When they heard the shouting they became concerned.

Curly said, "I don't like this, Cat. That guy sounds like a mean bastard and he could be forcing Maxine to tell where we are."

Catwalk answered, "That's the same policeman who was looking around the corn field earlier. What're we gonna do?"

"I'm going to see what's going on."

"But, Curly, that man is the po-lice. You want him to see us?"

Curly said, "You stay here. I'm gonna sneak up to the house to see if Maxine's O.K."

"O.K., Curly. But if you don't come back, I'm gonna hightail it outta here tonight."

"Don't worry partner, I'll be right back." Curly slid off the hay bales and out of the barn.

✦ ✦ ✦

Jones said, "You ain't gonna shoot a deputy lawman. They'll hang you for it."

"In this county, they'll pin a medal on me for getting rid of you."

Jones stared at the redhead while he weighed the odds of her shooting. She looked ready to kill, but he knew it took more guts to pull the trigger than most people had in them.

Maxine said, "Get out, Jones. Get out while you can walk out."

Jones held up a calming hand and walked toward her. He said, "Now just wait a second ... ." Jones then slapped her across the face.

She backed up a step and said, "You bastard! You're good at hitting women, aren't you? Well, I've seen your kind before and that's all you're good for. You couldn't please a woman on your best day. Hell, I'll bet you can't even get it up."

Jones turned red and screamed, "You fuckin' whore. I'll show you how a real man treats a woman." He stepped toward her while watching her trigger finger.

Maxine held the pistol at arms length and yelled, "Damn you, Jones. One more step and I'll shoot."

Jones took a small step and laughed at her. "You're bluffing whore lady. You ain't gonna shoot."

Maxine fired. The shot rang out. She waited for Jones to fall to the floor.

He glared at her, then held up his arm, showing her the hole she'd shot through his shirt. The bullet never touched him.

She thumbed back the hammer, intent on firing until he fell.

Jones saw this. Without hesitation, he drew and fired. The bullet went through her heart. Maxine was dead before she hit the floor.

✦ ✦ ✦

Curly approached the back door just as Jones shot Maxine. He blurted out, "Holy shit."

Jones turned toward him.

Curly took off running toward the road.

Jones ran out the door and shouted, "Stop kid, or I'll shoot."

Curly knew the deputy would shoot him in the back. Scared, he stopped and raised both hands.

"Come here, boy."

# Chapter Seven

Hands in the air, with the deputy's gun on him, Curly walked to the house.

Jones motioned him into the kitchen. "What'd you see, boy?"

"N-nothin'."

"Nothin', huh. You must be blind."

"I didn't see nothing. I was outside."

Jones shoved his pistol into Curly's gut and said, "Where's your buddy?"

"What buddy?"

"The nigger boy. Where is he?"

Curly stared back at Jones, but said nothing.

Jones persisted, "I said, where's your buddy?"

"I don't know what you're talking about. There ain't no one with me." His shaking voice gave him away; he cursed his stupidity.

The Deputy laughed and said, "You and that colored boy are wanted by the law for them two hoboes you fucked and murdered. You got one chance. Say the right words and you can walk outta here a free man, without going to jail for killing them hoboes."

Curly didn't know what the deputy wanted. He said, "Wh-what do you mean?"

The Deputy said, "You give me your buddy and you walk outta here as free as a bird. You clam up, you're dead, just like that Louisiana whore lady."

Curly's mind whirled; he couldn't give up Catwalk 'cause the Deputy would kill him for sure. If he didn't talk, he'd die.

✦ ✦ ✦

Catwalk heard the shot that killed Maxine. Then he saw Curly running, and heard the deputy yelling at him. He watched Curly go back in the house, at gunpoint.

He had to help his friend. He climbed down from the loft and headed for the house. He was outside the back door, when he heard the Deputy threaten Curly.

30

Catwalk backed away from the door. He was scared of the police-man, because he was a mean guy who hated blacks and because the man could arrest him and take him to jail. He'd heard about what happened to black men who went to jails in Texas. Then he thought about Curly. The deputy would kill him if he took a mind to, and it didn't make any difference if he was a boy.

Scared to death, he knew what he had to do. He stood on the steps and in a loud voice he said, "I'm right here, Deputy. Let him go."

Jones grinned. He hadn't expected to capture the other murderer so easily. He walked toward the back door and said, "We'll, I'll be damned. Look what we got here. A murdering nigger boy. An' he just turned himself in."

Jones opened the door and immediately snapped his handcuffs on Catwalk's wrists. He then led his prisoner to the sedan wearing a grin of satisfaction.

Curly watched from the kitchen door, feeling as helpless as a new-born child.

After handcuffing Catwalk to the car, the Deputy came back. He grabbed Curly by the front of his shirt and pulled him close, until their faces were inches apart. He said, "Now you listen to me, boy. You hop a train and get as far way from here as you can. You don't tell no one about this an' you don't talk to no police about this. If I find out you told anyone about me taking him, I'll hunt you down and cut your throat. You got that?"

Curly nodded, knowing the mean bastard meant every word of it. The Deputy then pushed him away and headed out the door. As the car drove away, Curly sat down on the kitchen floor and cried. As long as Catwalk was the prisoner of the Deputy, he was in danger of being hung. Now he knew what Catwalk meant when he said he could tell the ones that got the hate in them. That deputy was one of the most hateful people he'd ever seen.

He picked up the Colt Forty-Five and checked the ammunition. Five rounds. He left the house to find some help.

◆ ◆ ◆

Alton Jones drove to a friend's house, avoiding areas where some-one might recognize the car. The anticipation of the next few hours had his pulse racing.

Catwalk knew he had to do something—his life depended on it—but he didn't know what. He'd never been in a situation like this. In his sheltered life he'd had to defend himself in fights with other kids, but they never resulted in injuries, let alone death. Now his life hung in the balance and the odds were stacked against him.

In a raised voice he said, "You're arresting an innocent man, deputy. We threw those guys off the boxcar in self defense. They attacked Curly and I tried to help him."

"Shut up!"

He shouted, "I'm innocent!"

The deputy held up his thirty eight revolver and said, "See this, boy. One more word out of you and I'm putting a bullet right between your eyes."

Catwalk didn't challenge his claim.

The deputy parked in front of a small house and said, "You just wait here, boy."

Jones' voice chilled Catwalk to the bone. If he wasn't handcuffed to the door, he would have run. He doubted he'd survive the night.

A tall bearded man in a dirty white tee shirt appeared in the doorway.

Alton shouted, "Get some rope and your gun, Larry."

The man took a pull off a brown bottle and opened a screen door. "Alton, what're you doin' here? I thought you was going after them murderers. Whose car is that?"

"Larry, look at what I brought you." Alton took the bottle and turned it up in a long swig.

His friend looked into the back seat of the car and said, "Damn Jones, is that the murderer you got there?"

Jones passed back the bottle and said, "What the hell does it look like, Larry?"

"You taking him in to the lockup?"

"Larry, you stupid shit, why would I want to do that? Can't you see, he's guilty? We're gonna round up some of the boys an' string him up. We'll save the county some money."

"I'll get some rope."

# Chapter Eight

Darkness had fallen and Curly was growing tired, but he had to keep going. If Catwalk had any chance to survive, he was it. No one else would take a black man's side. He needed help, but couldn't go to the police. He headed for the nearest tracks, intent on finding a hobo jungle. A locomotive approached with its groaning, hissing and grinding. After the train took on water, Curly saw two men making the practiced trot of experienced hoboes, along side an open box car. One by one they vaulted into the open door. He hopped on right behind them.

Once in the car he asked them, "Where's the nearest jungle up ahead?"

"There's one just before the next grade, kid, under the bridge. About seven miles ahead."

"Good, do you know if there's any black folk hang around there?"

"Hard to tell. People come and go so much; you never know who's going to show up."

◆ ◆ ◆

Curly sensed the train slowing. As soon as they'd cleared the trestle, he jumped off and turned back toward the bridge. He saw two or three small fires that gave away the location of the hobo jungle; a place to rest, maybe get a meal, and talk to other down and out souls. He spotted three black men sitting under a huge oak tree.

He approached them and said, "Can I talk to you guys for a minute?"

One of the men said, "Sure, sit down. Care for some coffee?"

"No thanks. I ain't got nothin' for the pot."

A smile and the man said, "That's OK, that's about what this coffee's worth, nothin'."

Curly sat down and took the steaming tin can. He took a sip and said, "I got a friend, a black man and he's in a bad jam. I need help to spring him before a crooked deputy hangs him."

Another man asked, "Where is your friend?"

"He's back towards Dillard. This mean and hateful deputy took him and he's gonna hang him, 'cause he thinks Catwalk and I murdered a couple of hoboes."

The man said, "Are you an' him the ones we been hearing about?"

Curly looked around him. Satisfied they were alone, he said, "That's us, but we acted in self defense. Those guys attacked me, an' my friend stopped them."

"Did he kill them 'boes?"

Curly cautiously looked over the three men. A reward could have been posted for him and Catwalk. If he admitted their guilt, these guys could jump him and opt for some easy cash. He was ready to run when he said, "They attacked me an' we each threw one of them off the train. They both died. Call it what you want."

The three men looked at each other, then one said, "How are you going to find him?"

"I'm going into town to find someone who should know their whereabouts, and make them talk." Curly pulled the forty-five out of his jeans.

One man whistled and another said, "Boy, you mean business, don't you?"

"We ain't got much time, if anyone wants to help save a life, you can come with me. If you don't wan'na get in the middle of this, I understand."

One man stood up and said, "C'mon kid, I'll go with you. These two, they got families waiting for them. It's better if they stay here."

Curly tipped his hat and said, "Thanks for the coffee."

◆ ◆ ◆

Alton drove into a dark grove of trees

The deputy's threats notwithstanding, Catwalk pled his case again. "You're going to hang an innocent man. We were acting in self defense."

Jones said, "Self defense, my ass. We had a statement from one of them hoboes before he died. He named you just as plain as day, and you're gonna swing for it."

"They attacked Curly, an' I helped him before they hurt him."

Alton stopped the car and turned around. "Listen, boy. You keep your mouth shut because your lies ain't gonna get you out of this."

Catwalk knew deputy wouldn't listen to him. If he got a chance to escape he'd have to take it, no matter how risky. It was that, or death at the end of a rope.

A minute later he saw another car drive up and more men got out carrying bottles, rifles and lanterns. They met Alton under a tree, where they drank, laughed out loud and pointed towards him. They were fueling their blood lust with liquor and camaraderie.

◆ ◆ ◆

Curly and the man called Slim, flagged down the first car. When the driver stopped, Curly pointed the gun at him and said, "Mister, if you drive us to Dillard, I won't hurt you."

With wide eyes, the driver nodded.

Curly asked him, "You from around here?"

"No, I live over in Fort Worth. I'm just visiting someone."

Curly cursed and said to Slim, "We've got to find someone who knows where they'd have a Klan meeting."

Slim said, "We need to find a diner."

They cruised down Dillard's main street, but Curly saw a dark town that had already turned in for the night. He saw a man smoking a cigarette under a street light, and asked, "There any all night diners around here?"

"There's one in back of the blacksmith shop, the next block over."

Curly thanked him and told the driver, "Drive to it."

When they pulled up outside the diner, Curly saw two men sitting at the counter. He stuck the revolver in his pocket, walked into the diner and sat down two stools away from the men. The man closest to him nodded.

Curly said, "Say, I'm not from around here, and I'm looking for a friend. His name is Alton and he's a deputy."

"You're talking about Alton Jones. He's a deputy in the county."

"Well, he asked me to come to a Klan meeting they're having to-night, but I forgot where he said it was. Do you guys know where they hold their meetings?"

The men looked at Curly. In these times people were suspicious of strangers, and he looked too young to be a member of the Klan. One of them said, "Where you from, boy?"

Curly said, "I've been on the road, looking for work."

The guy seemed wary. He said, "Why would you want to go to a Klan meeting?"

Curly lost his patience. He pulled the gun, and said, "Look, if you don't tell me, an innocent man is going to die. I need to know where I can find Alton and his Klan buddies, and I need to know right now. If they were having a Klan meeting, where would they go?"

❖ ❖ ❖

Catwalk smelled liquor on the breath of the man who stuck his head in the window and said, "C'mon out, boy."

The guy held a pistol to his head as they walked toward a tree. Someone said, "Sit down."

As soon as he sat down someone kicked him in the ribs from behind, followed by a rifle butt to his neck. He covered his head and said, "They were going to rape Curly."

One of the men said, "What'd you say, boy? Who was gonna rape who?"

"The two men, they were going to rape Curly. I was just helping him."

"Where you from boy?"

"My family lives on the Moore's farm, near Meridian, Mississippi."

Alton whacked him with his rifle barrel. "You listen to me, nigger. I don't know what they do in Mississippi, but out here ain't no white man gonna rape another white man. It's just you bucks that pull that shit, an' now you're gonna swing, boy."

Catwalk was pulled to his feet and led to a step ladder positioned under a tree branch. He thought about trying to run. Two men had rifles, but they'd been drinking liquor and that made a person crazy, so they might not be able to shoot straight. Before he could run, however, someone put the loop over his head. His hesitation might have cost him his life.

One of the men threw a rope over the branch and Alton said, "Climb that ladder, boy."

Catwalk stepped on the first step. He thought of his Momma and wondered how she'd find out about his death. Sometimes when people on the road died, they were just buried in a hole. If that happened, she'd go her whole life without knowing what happened to him and he didn't want that.

A guy jabbed a rifle in his back. "C'mon, boy. Get on up there."

Catwalk had taken another step up the ladder when he saw the lights of a car approaching. The men turned their attention to the intruders.

❖ ❖ ❖

One of the men asked Curly, "Who's going to die?"

Curly said, "A friend of mine that Jones is going to hang. Jones killed Maxine Puckett and took my friend to hang him."

One of the seated men asked, "Did you say Jones shot the Puckett woman?"

"Yes, she gave us something to eat and the deputy showed up. They got in a fight, an' he shot her and took my friend."

The cook said, "That sounds like Jones. Are you the two the sheriff warned us about?"

"Yes, but we're not guilty. We acted in self defense against a couple of mean hobos. We've got to move if we're going to stop a lynching."

The man closest to Curly said, "Kid, you take that hog-leg outta my face and I'll take you there. It's only a few minutes from here."

# Chapter Nine

Catwalk saw two men get out of the car. In a hopeful moment he thought it might be Curly with help. He soon discovered they weren't here to help him; they were friends of Alton's.

One man walked over and looked at him, "You guilty, boy?"

In desperation Catwalk said, "No. I'm not guilty. I was just helping a friend who was being attacked by a couple of hateful men. I didn't do anything wrong."

The guy looked at him like he was considering his claim. "Where's your friend?"

"I don't know. I gave myself up so the deputy would let him go."

"You gave yourself up, so Alton would let your friend go?"

"Yes."

The guy tried to pull Alton aside. Alton resisted and said. "What is it, Lester?"

Lester said, "Alton, if this boy and his friend are guilty, why'd you let the other one go?"

Alton looked at the man like he was crazy for questioning a deputy sheriff. In a loud voice he said, "Lester, the nigger's the one that raped and murdered 'em. He's the one that should swing. The other guy is just an innocent kid who was in the wrong place."

"Are you sure he's guilty?"

"What do you mean, am I sure he's guilty? I'm gonna tell you guys something. Not only did he murder and rape a couple hobos, he killed Maxine Puckett too. She fed them and he gunned her down in cold blood."

"How do we know it was him, Alton?"

Alton looked aghast. He said, "Lester, I found them out at her place, with her dead body lying on the floor. Are you taking the nigger's side?"

Lester stood his ground. "I think we should make sure he's guilty before we hang him."

38

"Lester, get outta here an' let us take care of a man's job."

The crowd moved toward Catwalk as if they wanted to get this over with before they were overcome by their conscience. One guy prodded him up the ladder with a rifle while the others were hollering support. He was on the third step when he felt the ladder being kicked out from under him—and a shot rang out.

◆ ◆ ◆

Two more shots and a shotgun blast followed. Jones and another man took cover and started firing. All the other men jumped in a car and fled.

Curly ran toward the tree, stood the ladder up and grabbed Catwalk's legs. He heard him cough as he took the rope off him and yelled, "Follow me."

They dashed for cover amid the gunfire. In the cover of a tree, Curly asked, "You O.K.?"

Catwalk rubbed his neck and said, "I'm O.K., but that deputy is going to pay."

"There ain't nothing you can do right now."

Slim crawled to the tree where Catwalk and Curly hid. He said, "C'mon. I told them to keep those guys pinned down so we can circle around behind the deputy." He slipped into the foliage.

They moved silently through the bushes. After ten minutes, Slim stopped and let out a bird call. The gunfire stopped. Slim pointed. In the moonlight Catwalk saw two prone figures holding rifles.

They were within ten feet when Slim raised a rifle and shouted, "Drop your weapons. You're covered."

Alton turned toward the voice. Slim fired a round that slammed into the ground inches from the deputy's face. The two men dropped their rifles.

Curly retrieved the arms as Jones yelled, "You're gonna regret this, kid. You're going to jail along with the nigger."

The two men from the diner approached. Jones recognized one and shouted, "Is that Gene Spencer? Gene, what the hell you doin' helping the nigger? God damn it, I'm gonna throw your ass in jail for aiding and abetting. You're interfering in an official law enforcement function. We were arresting that guy."

Spencer stepped up to Jones and said, "Alton, you weren't going to arrest him; you were going to murder him. I won't stand by and watch it."

While Slim tied them up, Spencer asked Curly, "You got 'em, kid. What're you gonna do with them?"

"Take 'em to the Sheriff so he can put them in jail."

Spencer said, "Come here, I want to talk to you two." When they were out of earshot of the deputy, he said, "That sheriff ain't gonna do anything to Jones. If he does anything, he might put you two in jail on suspicion of murdering the Puckett woman."

Catwalk and Curly stared back, not believing what they heard. Spencer said, "If I was you two, I'd leave them here and get as far away as you can. Get out of the area and stay out. There's nothing for you here but trouble."

Catwalk said, "Will we still be wanted?"

Spencer said, "I'll talk to the sheriff and ask him to recall the wanted notice. I don't know if he'll do it. Either way, you'd better get out of the area."

Catwalk said to Curly, "He's right. We gotta get back on the road, but I want to leave these guys somewhere where they can't chase us."

Amid vicious threats, Deputy Jones and his friend were taken to a nearby farm house and led to the outhouse. Catwalk had dug enough outhouse pits to know that the pit under a two-holer was big enough for two men, and deep enough that they couldn't get out without help.

In the first violent act of his life, Catwalk slugged Deputy Jones, then picked him up and threw him into the stinking pit under the outhouse. His screams and pleas notwithstanding, the other guy was thrown in the slimy mess to join the deputy.

Catwalk and Curly told the men what they'd done to the Klansmen. The men were still laughing when Catwalk and Curly lit out through a field.

◆ ◆ ◆

The boys didn't sleep, but used the cover of darkness to make their way to the farm that Maxine had mentioned. Once there, they bedded down in a field within sight of the house, and slept in shifts. Dawn hadn't yet broken when Catwalk saw the first light in the house.

"They're getting up, Curly. We'd better get in the hay, before they leave without us."

The boys ran to a truck loaded with hay and burrowed their way inside. Fifteen minutes later they heard the engine start. A minute later they were heading toward an unknown destination. They hoped Maxine had given them good information.

◆ ◆ ◆

Gene Spencer drove to the Sheriff's Office. He told Sheriff Tyler the entire story, including the final disposition of his deputy. Tyler laughed and said, "I can't think of a better place for him. Where's the colored boy now?"

"You know, I was going to bring them in so you could question them, but they disappeared."

"Do you think they murdered those hoboes?"

"If they did, it was in self defense. These guys aren't criminals."

"How about the Puckett woman?"

"No. Take my word for it, Wendell. These guys aren't killers. Just a couple scared boys trying to find work. You should think about canceling the wanted notice on them."

"I think you're right, but I can't do that on your word. I'm going out to the Puckett woman's place. Thanks for the information."

♦ ♦ ♦

Alton Jones and his friend were found the next day by a passing hunter who heard their screams for help. When they were freed from the outhouse pit, they found a nearby stream and jumped in trying to wash off the smell and stench.

Seething, Deputy Jones vowed his revenge. "Ain't no nigger alive that throws me into a shithouse an' gets away with it."

"What're you gonna do, Alton?"

"I'm turning in my badge and going after that black bastard. I ain't quitting until he's dead and buried."

"They got a couple hours head start. Where you gonna look for them?"

"I don't know but once the word gets out that they murdered the Puckett lady, I'll have lots of help. They won't be hard to find."

# Chapter Ten

Huddled together under the hay the boys said little as the truck bounced down the road for several hours. At a fuel stop, Catwalk said, "Do you think this is where we get off?"

"No, I heard the driver tell someone to fill it up. They're getting gas."

Catwalk said, "When that deputy gets out of the pit, he's going to be real mad and he'll be looking for us, sure as shootin'."

"I know. We gotta keep moving and get as far away as possible."

"That deputy will make sure no one forgets about us."

Curly said, "You think we should look for work up ahead?"

"We can't. As soon as we get off this truck, we lay low until dark and then catch out on a west bound. My Momma told me about a place out west called New Mexico. We should try to find a red-ball that's headed out there. It might be far enough away where no one knows about us. We'll look for work there."

"Anywhere we can find work and they ain't hunting us would be great."

❖ ❖ ❖

Several hours later, the truck stopped again and Curly peeked out from under the hay. "I think this is as far as we go. The driver's going into a big barn. Let's get out of here."

The boys slid out of the hay and ran into a corn field. They silently walked through the field, each with his own thoughts about their situation. Finally, Curly said, "I wish we could find something to eat before we catch out."

"Do you want to try some of the houses around here?"

Curly said it like it hurt, "No, let's keep moving."

On the other side of the field they heard the distant wail of a train whistle, and instinctively headed toward the sound.

❖ ❖ ❖

Just after dark, Catwalk and Curly hopped onto the ladder of a refrigerated boxcar. Catwalk knew it was dangerous riding in reefer cars

42

because you had to use the top door, where they loaded the ice to get inside. If the door closed they were trapped until someone unloaded the car and might freeze to death. Because of the dangers there wouldn't be any other hoboes riding in the car, and it might be carrying fruit.

Curly opened the top door and Catwalk jammed a stick into it to prop it open. While Catwalk watched for bulls, Curly climbed into the dark car to check out the cargo.

A minute later Curly hollered, "We're in luck, Cat. We got all the peaches and apples we can eat for a year, but it's colder n' hell down here."

"Bring up some peaches." As soon as he said it, Catwalk saw a swinging light in the distance—the lantern of a railroad bull. He stuck his head through the door and yelled, "Hurry up, Curly, there's a bull coming."

A gun shot pierced the darkness. A foot from Catwalk's leg, the wood splintered. He yelled, "He's shootin', Curly. I'm going down to ride the rods. I'll be back to get you."

Catwalk closed the door, ran to the next car and scrambled down the ladder. At the bottom he climbed onto the two thick metal rods under the boxcar that ran the length of the car. This was the most dangerous place to ride a boxcar because he was barely a foot above the ties and gravel that were whizzing by at seventy miles an hour. If he fell off, it was certain death, but he hoped the bull wouldn't look down here.

Catwalk waited for several minutes. He thought about Curly in the freezing boxcar. Did the bull find him? Most likely, if the bull knew he was in there, he'd let him freeze to death.

Then Catwalk saw the glow of the lantern and heard a voice. "You ain't getting away from me by ridin' the rods, boy. I got ways of dealing with you."

Catwalk knew what was coming. The more vicious bulls carried foot-long lead weights and ropes with them. When they found someone riding the rods they tied the weight onto the rope and let the rope out under the boxcar. The five pound weight bounced off the ground until it got to the hobo, then it beat the hell out of them. Once the bull heard the hobo scream, they'd leave it there until the rider fell off, or got beat to death.

Catwalk had heard of a way to avoid getting killed. He watched for the sparks from the weight as it made it's way toward him. When it was within his reach, while balancing precariously on the rods, he caught the weight, and started screaming for the bull to pull the weight in. Catwalk then untied the weight and dropped it. He let out one last agonizing scream and hoped his act was convincing.

He saw the lantern light growing dim. He slid to the end of the car and saw the bull walking away. When the bull was out of sight he crawled out of the death trap.

He climbed to the top of the reefer and opened the door. "Curly, c'mon, the bull's gone, but he'll be back."

Curly handed Catwalk a half a bag of peaches and climbed out the door. "Jesus Christ, you took your time. I'm freezing."

"I had to go down and ride the rods. The bull used a lead weight on me."

"No shit. How'd you survive?"

"I'll tell you later. We got to drop off. I want to get away from that bull."

The boys found a creek not far from the tracks. After eating several peaches each, they took time to bathe. Afterward, lying on the bank, Catwalk said, "Those peaches sure tasted good, but they ain't as good as Maxine's fried chicken."

"Yeah, she was a nice lady. I wonder if they found her body yet."

"I don't know. I hope someone gives her nice burial with a preacher to read over her."

"Hey Cat, do you suppose that deputy is going to tell people that we murdered her?"

"I'm sure he is. It was either him or us, and he ain't going to confess to no murder."

"God damn it. What are we gonna do?"

"Just keep moving. There ain't nothing else we can do."

✦ ✦ ✦

Sheriff Wendell Tyler looked around Maxine Puckett's house after the ambulance had taken her body to the morgue. In the wall he found the slug that had killed her. He dug it out and studied it. Clearly, it was a .38 caliber slug. His deputy, who carried a .38 police special, had told him the boy had shot Maxine with her Colt .45. As he drove back to his office, he thought over the events of the past few days and didn't like what he saw.

✦ ✦ ✦

Deputy Alton Jones returned to the sheriff's office, with the intent of handing in his badge and resigning. Sheriff Tyler had other ideas.

In an unusually aggressive tone the Sheriff said, "Alton, I'm placing you under arrest for the murder of Maxine Puckett and the attempted murder of that colored boy. Hand over your badge and weapon."

Alton, who still smelled like the disgusting pit he'd been in, drew his revolver and challenged the sheriff. "You ain't gonna arrest me, Wendell. You got no proof that I killed the whore lady, and that nigger boy had it coming."

"Jesus Christ, man. Have you gone nuts? You claim that one of the drifters shot Maxine with her forty-five. I've got a thirty eight slug that I took out of her wall. Now hand me your sidearm and don't give me any trouble or I'll add on a charge of resisting arrest."

"Sorry, sheriff, I ain't going to jail."

Gene Spencer, who'd been deputized to take Jones' place, had been listening from another room. When he heard Jones resisting, he crept up behind him and clubbed Alton over the head. They took his limp, stinking body into a cell and locked the door.

The sheriff said, "When he comes to, make him take a bath. I ain't living with that odor."

◆ ◆ ◆

The boys slept in shifts until Catwalk heard an approaching engine. He woke Curly and said, "We're in luck. It's a Big Boy from the Atchison, Topeka and Santa Fe."

Curly stood up and saw the monstrous engine carrying the two white flags with red balls that marked a train carrying two tenders. "This is our lucky day, Cat. This baby can make a couple hundred miles before the next stop. By tonight we'll be far away from here; we might even make it to New Mexico."

At four in the morning, they jumped through an open boxcar door. They hid in two empty crates and rode the entire day and into the night. Catwalk wondered if they'd really get far enough away that the law wasn't looking for them.

◆ ◆ ◆

The next morning Catwalk heard the hiss of air brakes, meaning the train was stopping for water. He saw several groups of men waiting to board the train. He said, "There's a bunch of men getting on, Curly. Let's drop off."

He squinted into the sun and tried to read the name on the water tank. "Vaw-gun?"

Curly said, "Vaughn, New Mexico. It looks like we made it to New Mexico, Cat."

"I see the town in the distance, but I don't think we should go there yet. Let's head down this road and see if there's any working farms that need help."

"O.K. I'm watching for a chicken coop. Those peaches didn't last long."

◆ ◆ ◆

The boys had been walking for an hour when they saw a farmer struggling with a plow behind a mule. They watched from the shade of a tree. Curly said, "No wonder that guy's having trouble; his arm is in a cast. Ain't nobody can handle a plow with just one good arm."

"Do you think we should offer to help him?"

"He needs help, and we might get a meal out of it."

Catwalk hopped over a stand of barbed wire and walked toward the farmer. The man was eyeing him suspiciously when he called out, "I seen you was having trouble 'cause of your broke arm. I'll help you."

With his good arm, the farmer pulled a pistol out of his overalls and shouted, "Just hold it right there. Tell me what you want and remember, I ain't against shooting if I have to."

Catwalk stopped and held up his hands. "We could use a meal, and I'll finish your plowing to earn it. Honest, I'm not going to do anything except plow. We don't mean no harm."

"You want to help me finish this plowing?"

"Yes sir, I spent lots of time behind a plow. I can finish this field by sunset."

"How 'bout your friend, what's he do?"

Curly shouted back, "I can feed your livestock, repair machinery, shoe your horses, butcher a hog or milk your cows."

The farmer took off his straw hat, revealing a head of dark hair going grey. He was a strapping man, well over six feet and in spite of his suspicious greeting, had friendly eyes. He wiped his brow and waved the boys over. "O.K. You can work 'til sundown, and I'll feed you. If you do good work and don't steal anything, I might keep you on."

Catwalk said, "Mister, we just want to work for our dinner."

"OK, finish plowing this section." He then motioned to Curly, "You can repair the door on the chicken coop. Dang wolf almost tore the thing off trying to get at my hens last night."

"Yes sir." Catwalk said as he hung the plow harness over his shoulder. After the events of the past few days, it felt good to be working. He didn't blame the farmer for being cautious and in spite of that, there was something about the guy that he liked. He hoped they'd be able to stay on and work for him. Maybe they'd even be able to write his Momma that letter soon. With a smile on his face, he laid the whip to the mule.

# Chapter Eleven

Catwalk silently ate his third helping of beef stew. It tasted wonderful after a full day's work and he hoped the farmer, whose name was Barney, would keep them around. He'd seen Barney's look of appreciation at their work and in spite of his broken arm, Barney didn't sit down and watch. He worked harder than most men with two arms.

Their fourth day on the farm found Catwalk mending fences and Curly butchering a hog so Barney could take a ham to the soup kitchen for the transients. Over a lunch of soup and ham sandwiches, Catwalk said, "Curly, we've gone to heaven. Steady work, sleeping under a roof and regular meals, this is great."

"It beats walkin' down the road with your stomach growling. We'll probably get fat."

Catwalk laughed and said, "I think this guy's pretty rich. This is a big spread and he don't seem to be wanting for anything."

"I know. He's got two new Ford trucks in that garage and he said he's buying a new tractor. What do you suppose is in that big building out by the field?"

"I don't know; must be more machinery. What's a tractor? I never heard of a tractor."

"It's kind of like a truck, with a motor and all, but it's used to pull your farm machinery. You can even put a plow behind it so you don't have to plow with a mule."

"No kidding. If a guy had one of those you could plow a whole section in a day."

◆ ◆ ◆

Four weeks later Barney invited the boys to join him and his housekeeper on the porch one evening. A cool breeze rustling through the chinaberry bushes and the thrashers constant chirping made for a relaxing setting.

Catwalk took a long sip of lemonade; it tasted so good.

Barney handed both boys three ten dollar bills and said, "This is your first month's wages. I held off paying you until I was sure you earned your pay without stealing anything. I like the way you work and you can stick around if you have a mind to."

This was more money than Catwalk had ever seen. Tears filled his eyes as he said, "Thank you, Mr. Barney. I'm going to send my Momma twenty dollars, first thing." He smiled, thinking of the joy his Mother would feel when she got the money.

Barney said, "She'll be real proud of that, Catwalk."

Curly said, "We like working here. We'll stick around as long as there's work to do."

Barney said, "I was skeptical because the last two guys I hired, stole from me. One took off with a mare, so I didn't figure to hire anyone else, but when I broke my arm things changed."

Curly asked, "How long you had this place?"

"About four years. I used to be in the oil business back in Odessa. Back then, a small producer with a few wells pumping could make a lot of money, and I did. A few years back I thought the economy was going take a plunge, so I got out of that and bought three farms. Then my wife died in the spring of '29. She'd been sickly for a year or so. That's another reason I got out of the oil business, so I could take care of her. Turns out I didn't have to for long."

Barney looked off into the distance. Catwalk knew he was thinking of his late wife and he felt sorry for the man's loss. He liked Barney.

Barney continued, "Oh, there ain't nothin' I like more than working the land and having a good crop year. I paid cash for all my property and put the rest of my money in a foreign bank. When all the American banks had to close, I was still O.K. I sold one of the farms, but I got this one and another up north by Cimarron. A couple of my hands, Sam and Julio stay up there and run the place. I consider myself fortunate because I've seen what happened to the rest of the country and it's about as sad a state of affairs as I can imagine."

Catwalk asked, "Will the President make things better so they can open the schools?"

"I think so. He's talking about forming a Civilian Conservation Corps to create jobs. Do you want to go back to school?"

Catwalk said, "I'd like that better than anything. My Momma would be so proud . Curly said he'd teach me to read letters as soon as we found some books."

"Son, that's good that you want to learn, but you don't have to be in school to learn things. If you keep your eyes open life is the greatest teacher there is. And, I've got a room full of books you boys can read. Say, have you boys ever seen an airplane up close?"

Both boys shook their heads. They'd seen a few planes flying over during their travels, but never dreamed of seeing one up close. They walked to a large building, off by itself, that looked like a barn. When they saw a real airplane parked in the building, they were speechless.

"This is a Curtis Jenny biplane. It was built in nineteen eighteen and used by the Air Service Corps for training pilots during the big war. I bought a couple of them when the Air Service sold some off. It's got a Hisso four cylinder engine and cruises about ninety knots."

The boys were astonished and watched with open mouths while Barney showed them the details of the airplane; how the engine and propeller worked, and how the rudder made the airplane turn. They marveled at the construction as he let them run their hands over the smooth polished curves of the wooden prop and feel the tension in the wing cables. When they'd had a good chance to look it over, Barney asked, "You want to go up flying one day?"

The thought of flying excited Catwalk. For a change he had a good feeling about their future. That night he slept well, with a full stomach, money in his pocket and dreams of flying through the clouds in a real airplane.

◆ ◆ ◆

Two weeks later, Catwalk had finished painting the new shed when Barney asked him, "Are you ready to go flying?"

"Yes sir, but what about Curly?"

"I can only take one of you up at a time. He's got to finish churning the butter, then it's his turn. Here, put this helmet and goggles on."

Barney pulled the airplane out and told Catwalk to get in the front seat, while he started the engine. On the third pull of the prop, the engine started and Barney climbed into the rear seat.

Barney took off and flew around the area, scaring sheep and buzzing windmills.

With the wind in his face and the sound of the engine purring along, Catwalk was mesmerized. He felt free as a bird, sailing through the sky, and the best part would be writing to his Momma to tell her that he rode in an airplane.

After they landed, Barney said, "Would you like to learn how to fly, Catwalk?"

Catwalk shook his head and said, "I don't know if I could do that."

"Sure ya' can. You learned to drive the truck real fast and this is easier than driving. Over the next couple of weeks, I'll teach you guys how the plane works and then I'll teach you how to fly it."

Catwalk broke out in a wide grin, but couldn't find words to express his excitement.

Two days later Catwalk wrote a letter to his Momma, telling her how well Barney was treating them, that he'd learned to drive a truck and about his airplane ride. He didn't mention his experiences with the Klan back in Texas.

◆ ◆ ◆

For the next two months Catwalk and Curly worked like men possessed. Every few days Barney taught them a little about the Jenny and about the theory of flight. They soaked up the information and spent most evenings at the hangar, marveling at the plane and sharing their dreams about learning to fly it.

One Saturday Barney told the boys he'd take them into Vaughn, so they could buy some new clothes and go to the ice cream shop. Looking forward to another treat in their new lives, they climbed in the back of the truck.

At the dry goods store, they bought new Oshkosh B'Gosh overalls, denim work shirts, a cotton dress shirt, new long johns and two pairs of Red Wing work boots. When Catwalk tried on his new work clothes, he told Curly, "These are the first new clothes I've ever worn. My Momma sewed me new shirts on my birthday, but I never had any good work clothes like these."

Curly admitted, "I haven't had any new clothes since my tenth birthday. Cat, we gotta work extra hard, so Barney keeps us around."

After buying their new clothes, they walked to the ice cream shop. The boys devoured chocolate sundaes while Barney talked to a neighbor about his two new farm hands. When it was time to head back to the farm, Catwalk wore a permanent smile. For the first time in a year he was eating regular and for the first time in his life he had new clothes on his back. And, he was going to learn how to fly an airplane. He felt bad because in his limited vocabulary, he couldn't thank Barney enough. He decided to show his appreciation by doing some extra work on Sundays, rather than reading or fishing down at the creek.

◆ ◆ ◆

Three days later Catwalk and Curly were out on the west side of the spread mending fences. Barney was collecting eggs when he saw a police car drive up. Police Chief Zane Thomas stepped out.

The chief sounded sociable, but his face said this was all business. "Morning Barney, how's that arm feeling?"

"It's a nuisance, Zane. Doc Bowman says the cast'll come off in a couple days."

"That's good to hear. Say, I heard you hired a couple new hands recently."

"Yes, I did. A couple drifters come by. I wasn't thinking of hiring anyone, but they had a good look about them. They're young, but they're hard workers."

"Well, I'm glad they're working out for you, but they might be running from the law. Has the colored boy got a burn mark on his left cheek?"

"Yes, he does."

"The other one about five ten with curly hair?"

"Yeah, in fact he calls himself Curly."

"We got a message a while back about two guys that fit their description who murdered two hoboes back in Texas."

Barney kicked at a clod of dirt. He would have bet money that Catwalk and Curly weren't murderers, but their descriptions couldn't be denied. He thought about the desperate times they were living in, and how good people were driven to criminal acts. Because of the way they might be treated, he hated the thought of handing the boys over to the sheriff. He said, "These boys aren't murderers, Zane. They're just a couple young fellows looking to work for three squares a day."

"I need to talk to them, Barney. Are they around?"

"No, they're out by river mending fences right now. Won't be back until the morning. How about I bring them in tomorrow to talk to you."

"That'll be fine Barney. I appreciate it."

Thomas drove off and Barney breathed a sigh of relief. He then drove across his spread to find the boys.

# Chapter Twelve

Barney found the boys cutting new fence posts off an oak tree. He confronted them, "I had a visit from the police chief today. He said you boys are wanted by the law?"

Curly threw his hat on the ground and yelled, "God damn it!"

Catwalk spoke up. "The law might be looking for us, but we only did it in self-defense."

"Why don't you tell me about it?"

Catwalk and Curly told the story.

Barney said nothing until they finished, then said, "I didn't think you were murderers, but if you surrender, they'll send you back to Texas and all you have is your word. There ain't anybody who will stand up for you, so you're in a bad way."

He paused in thought and ran a hand through his thinning hair. Finally, he said, "You're good workers and I'd like to keep you on, but you can't work here. You'll have to go to the farm up north. You'll make the same wages and no one will know you're there."

Curly said, "What about the police?"

Barney said, "I'll take care of him. Curly go back and fill that truck with gas and take an extra can with you. Catwalk, get your things together. I'll have Mattie pack something to eat."

When Curly came back from gassing up, Barney drew a map and explained how to get to his ranch in the northern part of the state. He then told the boys, "Once you get up there tell Julio and Sam not to tell a soul that you're there. I'm going to tell the sheriff that you guys took off during the night. He might not believe it, but he ain't gonna send anyone looking for you."

Catwalk said, "Will we see you again?"

"I'll be flying up there in a week or so. Now get going."

◆ ◆ ◆

With Curly driving, Catwalk thought about the dismal black cloud hanging over their head. He felt so good working for Barney, eating regular, sleeping in a clean bed, sending money home and looking forward to learning to fly the Jenny. So many good things were happening—and now the scourge that might be with him for the rest of his life resurfaces. Would they ever be able to just go to work and not have to worry about the law?

◆ ◆ ◆

Back in Dillard, Texas, Sheriff Wendell Tyler and his deputy Gene Spencer looked at a three foot wide hole in the wall of the jail cell that had been holding Alton Jones. Tyler said, "It must'a been his Klan buddies that broke him out. He knew your routine of making the rounds and they were ready to jerk those bars out of there. Send a telegraph message about Jones' escape. He'll most likely get a gun from his buddies, so he'll be armed and dangerous."

"O.K. I'll include his description. Do you think he'll go looking for that those two boys that threw him in the pit?"

"I wouldn't be surprised if he went after them, because that man's carrying a ton of hate inside him. We don't know which way the boys went, so we don't know where to start looking for Jones. We'll have to wait until someone spots him."

"I hope those boys are watching their backs,."

◆ ◆ ◆

Catwalk and Curly pulled into the farm in Cimarron just before four o'clock the next morning. They slept in the truck until they heard someone rapping on the window.

Catwalk opened the door and saw a tall Mexican man wearing a black cowboy hat that was new twenty years ago. Piercing brown eyes amid a creased, leathery face stared back at him. Catwalk said, "Good morning. Are you Julio?"

The man looked surprised. "Yes, I am. I thought you guys was lost, but then I noticed you're driving one of Barney's trucks. Did he send you?"

"Yes. My name is Catwalk Jackson and this is Curly Levitz. We were working for him down in Vaughn, but he said there's more work to be done up here. We're ready to go to work."

"I imagine you could use some breakfast first."

Catwalk almost laughed. He wasn't yet used to eating every few hours. After going for days without eating, he'd never pass up a meal. "Yes sir, that sounds good."

Julio took them into a spacious kitchen where he told them to sit while he poured coffee for the three of them. He sat down and said,

"Sam will be here in a minute to fix your breakfast. I'm going to tell you what has to be done around here. It'll be nice to have more help because we've got a lot to do before the snow flies."

Curly said, "Ah, Barney said not to tell anyone we're here."

Julio didn't find this unusual. He said, "O.K. Here's some of the jobs we'll be doing … ."

Julio had been talking about their work for ten minutes, when he looked toward a doorway and said, "Hi, Sam. Barney sent us some help."

Catwalk stood to shake hands with the other farm hand. When he turned to face the person, he froze. A strange emotion washed over him. Sam was obviously short for Samantha. Catwalk looked into the most beautiful blue eyes and loveliest smile he'd ever seen. Samantha Jean Wells was a beautiful young black girl about Catwalk's age, with long dark hair that shone in the morning sunlight. Her eyes were full of life and twinkled with mischief. She had her hand extended, but when he didn't move, she said, "Are you O.K.?"

Catwalk felt himself sweating cold. His voice broke when he said, "Ah, yes ma'am. I'm Catwalk Jackson and this is Curly Levitz."

Curly stood, "How do, ma'am."

Sam smiled at Catwalk, "Now, where did you get a name like Catwalk?"

Curly said, "I gave him that name because he can run a boxcar catwalk like a rabbit."

Sam pulled frying pans and a basket of eggs out of the ice box. "Is that so? Is that what you two have been doing? Riding around the country like a couple of hoboes?"

"We was looking for work, ma'am."

She pointed at them with a spatula. "Well, now you found it."

"Ah, yes ma'am, we've been working for Barney for a while now. We'd like to keep working for him because he's a nice man." After he said it, Catwalk though about their situation with the law. He didn't want Sam to know he was running from the law, and decided not to mention it unless it came up.

"Yes, he is. He's one of the nicest men you'll ever meet." Samantha said, then busied herself fixing breakfast. When she served the boys, she asked, "So why did you come up here? Did Barney run out of work down there?"

Catwalk looked at Curly while weighing the question. His Momma's words came back to him, "Son, not many things in life are important enough for you not to tell the truth."

Curly shook his head, but Catwalk said, "The sheriff down there wanted to talk to us."

Sam didn't looked surprised and said, "Why would a sheriff want to talk to you two?"

Catwalk cleared his throat. "It's a long story, but the law thinks that we murdered two hoboes back in Texas. Somehow the sheriff found out about it and wanted to talk to us."

With surprising frankness, Sam asked, "Did you murder anyone?"

Catwalk told the story—again.

Sam said, "I believe you and I think it's a good thing that you came up here. You can work here and stay out of sight. That's what I'm doing."

Catwalk and Curly looked at each other. The idea that this attractive young lady was running from the law, took them by surprise. Curly asked, "Are you on the lam too?"

"No, silly." She looked for Catwalk's reaction, then said, "My Momma ran a boarding house in Vaughn. She had a couple girls working for her who catered to the men. My sister and I used to help with the chores of the boarding house, but we didn't entertain the men. I also used to do laundry and cleaning chores for Barney. Six months ago Momma died and my sister and I didn't want to keep the boarding house. My sister went to live with an aunt in Alabama, but since I didn't like Aunt Eve, I had no where to go until Barney offered me a room at his place in exchange for work and wages, just like you all are doing. While I was working for him, some men that had seen me at the boarding house, came out to the farm looking for me. I told Barney I didn't like them pestering me and he offered to move me up here. So, here we are, in Barney's hide-away."

Curly asked, "Do you know how to fly the Jenny?"

"I sure do." She looked at Catwalk with a smile that made his heart race. "I've logged over two hundred hours. I can't give you lessons though. Julio will have to do that."

Catwalk nodded because words didn't come easy in her presence. In his sheltered life on the farm, he'd never known a female of his own age, and he'd never even seen one who was so breathtakingly beautiful. Now, nothing on earth would make him leave this farm. He stood and said, "We better get to work. Thank you for breakfast; it was real good."

She smiled and said, "Mr. Catwalk, you're welcome. I'll see you come lunch time."

For Catwalk, lunch time couldn't come soon enough.

# Chapter Thirteen

Alton Jones pulled up to a west Texas hobo jungle in a car he'd stolen after his buddies yanked the bars out of the jail. He approached a dozen hoboes and to get more cooperation passed out a few Players cigarettes. He then asked the same question he'd been asking for a thousand miles. "I'm looking for two young guys. One's a tall nigger with a burn mark on his cheek and the other is a white guy, medium height with real curly hair. Have you seen them?"

The guy closest to him thought for a moment, then said, "No. Can't say that I have."

"Where'd you guys come from?"

"We was in Denver working on the strawberry crop. There ain't near as many people up there 'cause everyone is heading south for the winter. We didn't see no one looked like them."

"Thanks."

Jones moved to another group, passed out more cigarettes and posed the same question. Still there was no help, but he was determined to keep looking. Men in hobo jungles and Hoovervilles had nothing else to do but watch people. Sooner or later he'd find someone who crossed paths with the boys. Then he'd pick up their trail and it would only be a matter of time until he got his revenge.

◆ ◆ ◆

Catwalk was working harder than ever on a new horse corral. Julio told him they weren't trying to set any records, but he just kept working like a madman.

When Sam brought lunch, Catwalk proudly showed her how much they'd finished. She smiled, flattered at his attempt to impress her, and said, "Cat, you keep this up and there won't be any more work to do."

That evening at the dinner table, Catwalk asked her, "Down at the other farm, Barney said he had some books I could read. Are there any here?"

"Why yes. Are you a good reader?"

"No, I'm not too good, but Curly was helping me learn."

"Well, I'll help you now, so Curly doesn't have to."

Catwalk liked the idea of Sam teaching him reading, but felt somewhat embarrassed because of his limited education. Recently, he'd come to the realization that he was capable of learning things he'd never thought possible. He'd easily learned to drive the truck and soon he'd be learning to fly the Jenny. A new horizon of achievement was opening up to him, but if he was ever going to make anything of himself, beyond a farm laborer, he had to learn to read and write.

After dinner he and Sam went out on the front porch with The Adventures of Tom Sawyer. As he read, Sam helped him with the difficult words, but he soon discovered when Sam sat close to him, he had a hard time concentrating.

◆ ◆ ◆

A few days later, on a crisp, clear high-country morning the men finished the corral and Julio asked Curly, "You ready for your first flying lesson?"

"Yes!" Curly shouted. He then ran toward the hangar, leaving Catwalk sitting on the porch working his way through a book.

Catwalk watched Julio take off and then returned to the porch. Sam came out and said, "You've got your nose in a book again. Are you going to read every book we've got?"

Catwalk looked up. "I might. I like the stories, but mostly I want to learn to read better."

Sam knew his Momma's pride was his motivation to learn. She took the book from him and looked into his eyes with her beguiling smile. "Catwalk, it's wonderful that you want to learn to read and better yourself, but I have to tell you, your Momma is very proud of you now."

Catwalk said, "How do you know? How do you know what my Momma feels?"

She took his hand and said, "Let's go for a walk. I know a wonderful place down by the creek. C'mon, I'll show you."

As they walked, Sam said, "Catwalk, there are some things you can't learn from books. One of them is, women folk know what another woman feels about her son, even if they've never met her. Your Momma is just as proud of you now, as if you had the best job in the world. She knows that you're doing your best to help her and she's probably telling everyone about her son that sent her all that money. When she saw that, she was probably the happiest and proudest mother in the world.

Catwalk, I think you should keep learning to read and write, and go back to school if you can. But, no matter what happens, your Momma is real proud of you now."

He thought about Sam's words, then said, "I sure hope so. My Momma works real hard, trying to take care of all my brothers and sisters. I wish I could help her get off the farm and go live in a nice house, with curtains on the windows, maybe even a flower garden."

"I don't see why you can't do that. How many brothers and sisters do you have?"

"Eight. My baby brother is Petey, then there's Alice, Martha, Mathew, Cecil, John, Rose Ann, and Georgie. Georgie is older than me, but he caught the fever a few years back and he ain't been right in the head since then. Rose Ann, Cecil and John are the only ones that can help Momma in the fields."

"They'll appreciate the money you sent to them."

Catwalk smiled. "I hope Momma can buy herself a new dress or something nice."

"I'll bet your mother will buy something for your brothers and sisters first. But maybe when Barney pays you again, I can help you buy a new dress and we'll send it to your Momma."

Catwalk broke out in a wide grin. "Sam, that would be the best thing of all."

Sam led him to a clearing by a babbling brook. They sat down and she said, "What about you, Catwalk?"

"What do you mean?"

"I mean, you're so worried about your family that you never stop to think about what Mr. Luke Jackson is going to be doing in his life?"

"I'm going to work for Barney, and learn to fly the Jenny."

"So, that's going to be your whole life? Work for Barney and fly the Jenny?"

Catwalk looked at Sam. She was dead serious, but still very pretty. In his haphazard, nomadic life of trying to survive in a hostile world, he'd never thought about his future; a future that only consisted of the next freight he'd be catching. He said, "I don't know what I'm going to be doing in my life. When someone is trying to hang you, you don't think about the future because you ain't sure you're going to be alive."

Sam looked at him with a hurtful expression. "Someone tried to hang you?"

"Back in Texas. This hateful deputy and his Klan friends were going to hang me because they thought I'd killed those hoboes."

"That's not why they were trying to hang you. You know darn well why they were trying to hang you—because you're black—that's why they were trying to hang you."

"I suppose that's so. I don't like to think of one person doing that to another, because of his color."

"You're so kind hearted, I've never met anyone who was so gentle."

"Being kind hearted don't mean you're stupid."

Sam moved closer to him. Her smile had returned and she ran her hand across his muscular shoulders. She felt him shiver from her touch. "No, it doesn't, and you're not stupid, that's for sure."

She wanted to throw her arms around Catwalk, but she suspected her closeness was making him uncomfortable. She retreated and asked him, "How'd you get that burn mark?"

"A branding iron. We were branding cattle and my brother did this by accident."

"I'll bet he felt as bad as you did."

"Yeah. He cried the whole time they were putting the liniment on me."

"You're lucky to have a big family that cares so much for each other."

"Yes, my family is very special. Do you have family anywhere?"

"I've got a twin sister somewhere. When my Momma died she went to live with an aunt who lived in Alabama, but my aunt died a few months later. I never heard from my sister, so I don't know what happened to her. As far as I know, she was my only family."

Catwalk said, "I'm real sorry you don't have anyone, Sam, but I'll always be there for you, just like you're part of my family."

Sam kissed him on the cheek and said, "Catwalk, you are so sweet." Then she stood up and said, "I have to get back to work. Julio likes apple pie and we have only two pieces left, so I have some baking to do. He might take you flying when he gets back."

Catwalk walked with her wishing they didn't have to go back to work, because he enjoyed talking to her so much. He hadn't had anyone to talk to except Curly, who was his best friend, but talking to Curly was nothing like talking to Sam.

◆ ◆ ◆

Alton Jones was in a hobo jungle north of El Paso. He'd been asking again about the two boys and still hadn't found anyone who'd seen them. He did, however, get some help from a guy who told him, "If you're looking for someone in this part of the country, go on up to

Vaughn. There's a good soup kitchen at the mission there. Anyone who is on the road knows to stop in Vaughn for a good meal. Chances are the guys you're looking for have gone through there."

"Thanks, mister. I think I'll go up there and get a meal myself."

# Chapter Fourteen

When Catwalk and Sam returned to the house, Curly met them, shouting, "Catwalk, I flew the plane! Julio told me what to do and I flew it all over, turning and diving, it was great!"

With a smile, Catwalk said, "Curly, the pilot. Ain't you something."

"It was easy, Catwalk. There ain't nothin' to it. You gotta try it."

Sam said, "I'm hoping Julio can take him up this afternoon."

Julio said, "We're kind of short on gas, Sam. We'd better wait until the Sinclair truck gets here on Thursday."

Sam turned to Catwalk and said, "Sorry, looks like you'll have to work."

Julio said, "That's right, we're going to pick corn. If we get started, we should be able to finish the small field by Thursday."

Catwalk tugged at Curly's arm and said, "Let's go, mister pilot. Picking corn will make you feel like you're back home."

◆ ◆ ◆

The next day the men were in the field and Sam was baking bread when Barney landed in the Jenny.

Sam went out to meet him and he said, "Morning, Sam. Is Catwalk around?"

Concerned that this might have something to do with the police, she said, "He's out picking the small field with Julio and Curly. Is anything wrong?"

"No. I got a letter for him from his Mom."

Sam smiled, "Oh my, is he going to be excited. I'll drive out and give it to him."

"Thanks, Sam."

She made it out to the area they were picking in minutes. She hollered, "Catwalk, can you take a break? I've got something for you."

Catwalk wiped his brow and said, "Did you bring a slice of fresh apple pie?"

"No, silly." She held out the envelope with a wide grin. "A letter from your Momma."

Speechless, Catwalk looked at the envelope. Then, he smiled and tore it open.

As he read it, Sam saw his smile disappear. She asked him, "What does she say?"

"It ain't from Momma; it's from John. He says Momma took sick." With a worried look on his face, Catwalk held the letter out to Sam, "What's that word?"

Sam said, "Leukemia."

"What's that?"

"I don't know." She asked Julio, "What's leukemia?"

The old man looked at Catwalk with sad eyes. "It's a blood disease, son. I'm not sure how serious it is, but a doctor should be able to help her."

Catwalk said, "Trouble is, doctors are for white folk. My Momma ain't got enough money to pay for a doctor. When a black worker takes sick, they just let the sick person lay up until they die and then they find another worker."

He'd reached a point where the unfairness and injustice of the world was about to rear it's ugly head in the worst possible manner. If his Momma died because she couldn't get the medical help that was available, he felt it was just as bad as if he'd been hung back in Texas.

Sam grabbed his arm, "Hey, you don't know she's going to die. This might be a sickness that doesn't kill people. It might just make her sick for a while.'

Catwalk said, "I want to go back there and find out how bad it is."

Sam led him to the truck. "Come on. We'll go talk to Barney."

When they arrived at the house, Sam told Barney about Catwalk's mother. Barney said, "You can take off to go back to see her, Catwalk. I'll loan you enough money for the train trip and medical help she needs."

Catwalk immediately thought about traveling while he was a wanted man. It was a chance he'd have to take.

As if he was reading his mind, Barney said, "I don't think the railroad police will bother you if you're riding in the pullman."

Catwalk said, "Barney, if I'm riding the cushions, there's still a chance that a conductor will recognize me, and turn me over to the law."

Sam asked Barney, "Can I have some time off too?"

"Sure, I don't need you right now, but why do you need time off?"

"I want to go with him. The police are looking for a black man and a white man. They're not looking for a woman. If I'm with him, we'll just look like your average couple."

Barney said, "It might help if you're traveling with him."

Catwalk gave this some thought. He liked the idea of having Sam along, but he worried that if he was arrested, he'd be dragging her into his problems. He said, "Are you sure you want to? Even if we've got tickets, it's not easy for black folk out there. Lots of times it's hard finding something to eat even if you have money in your pocket because so many places don't serve meals to black folk."

Sam said, "I want to go. Don't you want me to?"

"Yes, I want you to go, I'm just worried, that's all."

"Quit worrying and get your things packed."

✦ ✦ ✦

Alton Jones pulled into Vaughn and stopped at the soup kitchen. After his meal, he talked to some of the other patrons, but came up empty. He left the mission and sought out some of the locals to continue his search. He struck gold. The locals were talkative and in twenty minutes he knew about Barney's two new farm hands. He also got directions to both of Barney's farms.

Jones drove to Barney's farm north of town. Except for the chickens the place looked deserted. He knocked on the door. When Mattie answered he asked, "Is Barney around?"

She said, "No, he's gone right now."

"I'm an old friend, is he at the farm up north?"

Mattie didn't like the looks of this guy, but if he knew about Barney's other farm, he must be O.K. "Yes, he is."

"Thank you." It was late, so Jones decided to spent the night in town and leave early for Cimarron. Then, he'd find the Jackson boy and settle the score.

✦ ✦ ✦

The next morning Barney, Catwalk and Sam left before sunrise. Even though it was a two day drive, Barney had decided to drive them to Denver to catch the train. This way they wouldn't be taking the route through Texas where the bulls were looking for him.

Once they reached the train station, Sam kept up a running dialog as she steered Catwalk to a seat. She knew he was nervous and hoped the talk would keep his mind off the law. Once they were seated in the car for "Blacks only," she said, "Cat, have you ever thought of who you're going to marry?"

This caught him unaware, as did many of Sam's questions. He loved Sam's company, but wondered how she came up with some of the things she asked him. He said, "How would I know who I want to marry, when I don't know any girls. There weren't any girls on the farm."

"Did you say, you don't know any girls?"

"Yeah."

"Well, Mr. Jackson, what am I?"

"You're a girl, but … ."

"But what?"

"Well, we're friends."

"Aren't you going to be friends with your wife?"

He wasn't sure what Sam was getting at. As much as he liked her, he'd never thought about marriage. He said, "Of course, but before two people can marry, they have to be in love."

"Are we in love?"

"I don't know. You're the first girl I've known. I don't know how to tell if I'm in love."

"Well, you're the first guy I've ever rode across the country with. Does that mean anything?"

"I don't know, but I don't think riding cross country makes us in love."

Sam said, "Ugh!" She didn't believe what she was hearing. She read her magazine while Catwalk thought about how someone knows when he's in love.

◆ ◆ ◆

Alton Jones looked over Barney's farm outside of Cimarron. This place, like the one in Vaughn, bespoke of money with its new equipment, fresh paint, good crops and livestock. He walked toward the house wearing a grin and thinking his search was finally over.

Curly was in the hay loft when he saw the car drive up. He watched to see if a policeman got out. When he saw Jones, he said, "Holy shit! That son of a bitch means trouble for sure."

Jones got no answer at the door, but the sound of a blacksmith's hammer striking an anvil led him to where Julio was working over a hot fire behind the tool shed.

To Julio's back, he hollered, "Hello."

Julio turned around. One look at Jones, with his disheveled looks and angry scowl, he sensed trouble. He said, "Good morning. What can I do for you?"

With an air of importance, Jones said, "I'm looking or a hand of yours. Colored kid, name of Luke Jackson with a burn mark on his face. Where is he?"

Julio said, "Who are you?"

"Alton Jones, Deputy Sheriff, Dillard County, Texas."

Wary as he was, Julio wasn't buying Jones' façade. "You're way out of your jurisdiction, and I don't see a badge."

Jones pressed. "I lost it. This nigger murdered and raped two hoboes and I'm taking him in. Now where is he?"

"There ain't anyone around here that fits that description."

Jones went to the fire and picked up a red hot poker. He approached Julio and stuck the poker in his face until Julio dropped his hammer and backed away. "I said there is a nigger named Jackson working for you and I want to know where he is."

◆ ◆ ◆

Curly scrambled down from the hay loft and peeked out the barn door. The deputy had to be looking for them. He remembered the thirty caliber rifle Barney kept. He ran for the house. He was twenty feet from the door when he heard Julio scream. Curly ran into the house and grabbed the rifle. He checked the chamber—it wasn't loaded. He frantically dug through dresser drawers until he found a box of bullets. He shoved a shell in as he ran through the house and out the door. Once outside, he saw only the cloud of dust that hid Jones' car. He fired two shots in desperation, but the car didn't slow.

Curly found Julio laying on the ground. He was moaning in pain from a bad burn on his chest. Julio said, "I'll be O.K. Find some of that liniment we use on the cattle to cool this off."

Curly smeared the salve on Julio's chest. As soon as he felt some relief, Julio said, "He was looking for Cat. I told him Cat quit and left. He didn't believed me. I bet he'll be back."

Curly said, "That's O.K. I hope the son of a bitch comes back when I'm here."

# Chapter Fifteen

Sam had fallen asleep with her head on his shoulder. Catwalk nudged her and said, "We're coming into Salina for a meal stop. I'm ready for some of that chicken."

While the white people filed into the diner, Catwalk and Sam sat down under the nearest shade tree. He said, "I don't like the way that conductor looks at me. It's like he knows I shouldn't be on this train."

Sam unwrapped the food and tried to calm his worries. "He doesn't see many black people riding his trains. I've only seen one other black couple on this train. I don't think he recognized you or he would have told the bulls."

"I think next time I go somewhere, I'll just catch out and take my chances."

"If you do that, you won't get to ride with me."

Catwalk smiled, "I'm glad you came along. Having you along is better than traveling alone, even if you sleep a lot."

Sam threw her chicken bone at Catwalk and said, "O.K., no pie for you."

✦ ✦ ✦

Early that evening they changed trains in St. Louis. On the ride south, they saw the same curious stares from the conductors, but no one said anything and the bulls didn't bother them. Catwalk managed a few hours sleep as the train sped through the night.

In Vicksburg, they boarded a bus to Meridian and Catwalk felt his excitement grow about seeing his family. It had been almost a year since he'd left home. He thought about the changes his life had taken and the stark contrast to his life one year ago.

Sam said, "Are you getting excited about seeing your family?"

"Yes, and I can't wait for you to meet them. My Momma's going to like you. I think she's always been partial to girls."

"I just hope we can find someone to help her get better."

Catwalk said, "No matter what I have to do, or who I have to find, I'm going to get some help for her."

Sam took his hand in hers and smiled. He was so glad he had her along. Was this a sign that he was in love?

◆ ◆ ◆

On the outskirts of Meridian, Catwalk and Sam left the bus and had to walk two miles to the farm where his family lived. When they reached the farm he took a familiar shortcut along a creek bed toward the black living area. He pointed out several field hands in the distance that he'd worked beside for many years. Then he said, "There's our shack up ahead."

As they neared the shack, Catwalk saw Georgie playing with little Petey in the shade of the porch. He called out, "Georgie. Look who's home."

Georgie jumped up and ran to his younger brother, screaming, "Luke, Luke. You came home. Look Petey, it's Luke."

Catwalk hugged his brother and picked up Petey, who was twice the size since he'd last seen him. He asked Georgie, "How's Momma?"

"Momma's sick, Luke. She lay down all day now, can't work."

Catwalk turned to Sam, "This is my brother, Georgie, and this is little Petey."

Georgie looked at Sam, not sure of how she fit into his brother's life. He said, "Hello."

"Hi Georgie."

Catwalk opened the door to their shack. He saw his Mother lying on a cot looking up at him. He put Petey down and knelt by her side. "Hi Momma."

Delores Jackson wept and held her arms out to hug her son. "Luke, you came home. Oh lord, how I've missed you." Tears rolled down her cheeks as she held her boy. She'd worried that she'd die without seeing him again. Now, those fears were washed away with tears of joy.

She put her hands on his broad shoulders and looked at him. "My baby. And, new clothes. Don't you look handsome."

"How are you feeling, Momma?"

"Oh, I'm just tired. Can't do too much."

Dee noticed Sam standing behind him. Confused, she said, "Who is that woman?"

Catwalk heard the distress in her voice. He said, "Momma, this is Samantha."

Before Sam could say anything, Dee said, "Luke Jackson, you brought a woman home with you? Are you married? Who is she?"

"Momma, we're not married. She works on the farm where I work. She's a pilot, Momma and I'm going to learn how to fly an airplane."

Dee looked at her son with disbelief. "You, fly an airplane? Are you crazy?"

"No, Momma. I'm serious. They have two of them on the farm where I'm working."

Dee cried out loud. Deep sobbing tears rolled down her cheeks. She moaned, "My baby, oh my baby. He's gone from me and ain't my little boy no more."

Luke was disturbed by his Mother's anguish. He'd dreamt of a joyous homecoming. Now, he was afraid he'd caused her more pain and grief, than joy. He didn't know what to say.

Sam instinctively knew what Dee was feeling. She knelt by the cot and took Dee's hand in hers. Softly, she said, "Mrs. Jackson, your baby isn't gone. He'll always be your baby boy. No matter how old he is, or where he goes, he'll always be your little boy because he loves you so much. He'll always love you more than anyone else in the world."

Through tears, Dee looked at Sam; her fingers caressed her face. She said, "My word, aren't you just the sweetest thing."

With a lump in his throat, Catwalk smiled. He knew when to keep his mouth shut.

◆ ◆ ◆

Barney returned to the farm two days later. When he heard what Jones had done to Julio, he immediately drove into Cimarron and looked up the county sheriff. When he found him, Barney said, "Clem, this guy came here with the intent of taking one of my employees under false pretenses, then he assaulted another employee. I want the bastard found and locked up."

"I'll send out a telegraph message and keep an eye out for the guy, Barney. I doubt if he'll be easy to find though. His type are good at staying out of sight."

Barney knew the sheriff was right. Finding Jones would be easier said than done. Curly and Julio told him they were convinced Jones would return to find Catwalk. His only recourse was to be ready for him when he returned. With that in mind, he drove to the nearest supply store and bought two more rifles. When he arrived at the farm, he told Curly and Julio to keep one with them at all times.

# Chapter Sixteen

The next morning Sam stayed with Dee while Catwalk went to talk to Mr. Moore about finding a doctor. Moore recommended he try Doctor Graves who was not far from the farm.

Catwalk made the one mile trek and knocked on the door. A graying man in glasses answered, took one look at the black man standing there and said, "I'm not giving out any more food; I've already helped two people today."

Catwalk countered, "No sir, I'm not looking for a handout. I need a doctor for my Momma. They think she's got leukemia."

"Doctors cost money, boy?"

"I know that, sir. I've got enough money to pay for her treatment." Catwalk showed the doctor the cash Barney had given him. He hoped money was the only issue.

The doctor hesitated, then said, "I can't help her right now. My schedule is too busy. Try another doctor."

"When would you have time, sir?"

"I'm busy for several weeks. Try someone else."

Catwalk got the message; it wasn't about money or busy schedules. He left feeling disheartened, but no less determined. He wasn't going to let people's attitudes stand in the way of his Momma getting the help she needed. He decided to walk to Mr. Slade's farm and talk to him about finding a doctor. His former boss had brought in a black doctor for his father when he was sick. He'd see if Slade could get the same doctor for his Momma.

The walk took him two hours, but he found his former boss working on an irrigation pump. The farm owner greeted him, "Hello, Luke. I didn't know you were back."

"Yes sir, Mr. Slade. I've been working out in New Mexico, but I came back 'cause my Momma's down sick. They think she's got leukemia."

Slade walked a few steps to the shade of an oak tree. When they were out of the sun, he said, "I'm sorry to hear that. Your Momma's a real nice lady."

"Mr. Slade, I'm looking for a doctor. I tried Doctor Graves, but he said he's too busy. I want to find the black doctor that you had for Daddy."

"Oh, yes. Doc Abernathy. I'm afraid he died, Luke; passed on a few months ago."

"Do you know of any other black doctors around here?"

"I don't, Luke. You might try Doctor Sherman in Meridian. If you can wait while I repair this pump, I'll drive you in to town."

Catwalk knew if his old boss was with him, the doctor might be more inclined to help him. He said, "I would appreciate that. Let me give you a hand with that pump."

◆ ◆ ◆

An hour later, they drove to the doctor's office in Meridian and had to wait about twenty minutes before seeing the doctor. When they got in to see him, the doctor agreed to look at Dee, but said it would be two days before he could fit her in his schedule. Relieved, Catwalk paid him for one visit, then rode back to the farm. On the way, he asked Mr. Slade, "I might be here for a while to help my Momma get better. Do you have any work available?"

"Luke, you were one of the best farm hands I ever had; you could out work any two other men, but I've had a hard time selling my crops, and I might have to let some of my hands go."

Luke thought about his family. If Mr. Moore ever had a problem selling his crops, their employment was in danger. What would they do if Moore laid them off? He said, "I'm sorry you're having problems. I guess nobody has much money."

"That's the hell of it, son. Once people stop working, they stop buying soon after."

◆ ◆ ◆

When Catwalk returned home, Sam said his Mother was sleeping. They sat on the porch and he told Sam about Mr. Slade taking him to see Doctor Sherman.

Sam said, "I hope he tells us something good," then added, "Do you know how long you'll be staying here?"

"No, I don't. I have to see that Momma gets whatever she needs to make her better. Are you going back to New Mexico soon?"

"I promised Barney I wouldn't stay long. They'll be bucking barley soon and he'll need me to cook for the harvest crew."

The thought of Sam leaving troubled Catwalk. Her support had been comforting and reassuring. He didn't want her to go, and said, "It's too bad you can't stay."

"Do you want me to stay?"

"I wish you could stay. You've been a lot of help, but I know you have to go back."

Sam smiled and said, "Catwalk Jackson, that's so nice of you to say that."

"I've been thinking it a lot, but everything I think doesn't come out in words."

"I know; I'm the same way. I've been thinking a lot of things that I haven't said either."

"Is it about us getting married?"

"Well, that and having kids one day."

Catwalk looked at Sam to read her sincerity. Her smile told him, she wasn't kidding. He cleared his throat and said, "I better check on Momma."

◆ ◆ ◆

Alton Jones left the area. Because he'd burned that farm hand and was driving a stolen car, the local police would be looking for him. His best plan would be to lie low in a strange town until things cooled off. He was convinced that the farm hand had lied to him and that the Jackson boy would be returning to that farm Then, he'd go back to that farm and finish the job. He had nothing else to do, but avoid the law and wait for the Jackson boy to show himself.

# Chapter Seventeen

Two days later they took Dee to the doctor's office. After the first examination and blood test, the doctor told Catwalk, "Son, I've confirmed that your Mother has leukemia, but most leukemia can be treated. Have you ever heard of a blood transfusion?"

"No, sir. What's that?"

"Well, this disease is caused by her white blood cells becoming abnormal to the point that they don't make enough normal blood cells in her bone marrow. This causes infections, anemia and bleeding. By giving her a transfusion, I am putting normal blood back into her system. This should help her, but there's no guarantee it will work. Also, we might have to do this several times, and the problem is, we don't have enough clean blood to do that."

Catwalk became defensive, "If she was white, would they have enough clean blood?"

The doctor shook his head and said, "Son, it's not a question of color. There just isn't enough blood. The only way we get blood is when people donate it and no one is doing that right now. Also, there's so much disease and sickness around, it's darn hard to find someone who is healthy enough to donate blood."

"Can I donate blood?"

"Yes, you can; you'll have to."

Catwalk said, "How about my brothers and sisters?"

"I'll take blood from the older children, but not the younger ones."

"How about all the other workers? If they have the right blood, can they donate?"

"Yes, if they're healthy, and if their blood is the right type, they can donate."

"When do we start?"

"I'll have to keep your Mother here for a few days. We'll take your blood now. Sometime in the next few days, we'll take blood from your older brothers and sisters."

♦ ♦ ♦

Catwalk went in to see his Momma. He hugged her, then said, "We're going to get you better, Momma. I'm going to donate some blood now so they can give you a transfusion. The doctor said Georgie, Cecil and Rose Ann can donate too. The clean blood will make you better."

Dee smiled. Having him here to help her was an incredible comfort. She said, "Luke, I'm so glad you're here."

"We're going to get you better, Momma. Why don't you get some rest?"

She asked, "When I'm feeling better, will you have to go back to New Mexico?"

"I have to, Momma. I have to repay Barney the money he loaned me."

"Can't you work here, for Mr. Slade, and send the money back to him?"

"I already talked to him. He's not hiring anybody because he's having trouble selling his crops."

Dee turned her head. Luke tried to sound optimistic, "Momma, when I get Barney paid off, Mr. Slade might be hiring. Maybe I can come back here to work."

She knew things wouldn't work out that way. Still, she said, "That would be nice, Luke."

♦ ♦ ♦

Two days later, Sam and Catwalk were talking on the porch. He knew she had to go, but he hated the thought of her leaving. Also, he was worried about her making the trip back by herself. He knew too well the multitude of dangers that awaited a black person in a world ruled by hostilities.

Sam said, "I'm leaving tomorrow morning. I don't want to go, but I promised Barney."

"I knew you'd have to leave pretty soon."

"Oh, Cat. You don't know how much I hate leaving you. I don't want us to be apart."

"I don't either, Sam, but it can't be helped. Once I get back we'll have lots of time together."

Three kids from a neighboring shack started playing around a shade tree in front of the porch. Feeling the quiet privacy was at an end, Catwalk took Sam's hand and said, "Come on. Let's go down to the pond."

They walked hand in hand silently along the creek, each of them trying to savor the few remaining minutes they had together. When they arrived at the pond, they laid down in the grass under a willow tree.

Catwalk put his arms around Sam and looked into her eyes, feeling the love, devotion and strength that emanated from within. She traced the outline of his face with a finger and said, "You have to write me every day to let me know how your Mom is doing."

"I will. I promise."

Catwalk kissed Sam, lightly at first.

"Um-mm. Now I'm really going to miss you."

He kissed her with more intensity. She responded with the passion that had been too long dormant. Soon the pent up yearning and desire of two young people in love took over. Beside a quiet pond in rural Mississippi, Catwalk and Samantha sealed their love for eternity.

✦ ✦ ✦

Catwalk walked Sam to the bus station the next morning. Little was said because nothing was left unsaid from yesterday. Sam again reminded him to write and Catwalk promised he would. She also pressed him to return as soon as possible, to which he also agreed. In tears, she climbed the bus to Vicksburg and waved good bye from the window. Standing in front of the general store, for the first time in his life, Catwalk felt terribly alone.

✦ ✦ ✦

Over the next week, Dee showed signs of improvement. She returned to the farm so she could be with her family, which the doctor thought would be more therapeutic than his clinic. Catwalk enjoyed the time with his family. Whenever the neighbor lady came over to watch Dee, he and Georgie went fishing down at the creek and he spent the evenings reading to his brother and sisters. As much as he enjoyed his family, there was a void in his life that only one person could fill. He wrote to Sam faithfully every day, knowing the time when they'd again be together was inching closer.

Four weeks after her transfusions, Dee had recovered enough that Catwalk prepared to leave for New Mexico. After another tearful goodbye, he took his bedroll, a sack of vegetables and two molasses sandwiches and headed for the tracks north of town. Barney had left him with enough money to buy a ticket, but he'd rather save it to repay his loan. He realized Barney's loan saved his Momma's life, but he'd discovered that he didn't like owing people money.

At the water tank outside of Meridian, Catwalk lay down in the grass to wait for the next freight. When heard the whistle in the distance, he lay still to see how many other riders approached the train. If there were too many, he'd wait for the next one, rather than dealing with railroad bulls that an army of riders attracted. He saw only a few men, so when the drive wheels started their rotation, he looked for a suitable boxcar.

He saw an open door and trotted toward the car. He threw his bindle in and easily vaulted into the moving freight car. Once inside he saw only two other riders and one was asleep. He picked up his bindle and moved to the far end of the car where he'd be by himself.

Catwalk slept for a few hours, but woke up when the train slowed. He looked out the door and saw the sign for Shreveport, Louisiana. This meant he'd be spending the next day or so crossing Texas. He'd breathe a lot easier when he reached New Mexico.

Just as the train started moving, a man and woman jumped into the boxcar and sat down between him and the door. The woman was carrying a small child who was crying. As she comforted the child, she said, "Honey, we're going to get something to eat at the next stop. It won't be long. I can't believe those people back there wouldn't feed a child."

The man said, "They were out of food, Lorraine. The guy said they'd had so many people come through that they just ran out."

Catwalk took his last half sandwich and approached the couple. When the woman saw him, she looked frightened and said, "Stay away from us. We ain't got any money."

Ignoring her fear, he smiled, held out the sandwich and said, "This is for your daughter. It's molasses and the bread is still fresh."

The woman said nothing, but turned toward her husband, confused. He took the sandwich and said, "Thank you. You're very kind."

"That's O.K., I've been hungry myself."

"We stopped at the mission in Shreveport, but they ran out of food. The guy said they just had too many mouths to feed."

Catwalk said, "Winter's coming. More people are coming down south."

He returned to his spot and lay down. Again, he counted himself lucky because although he might not eat until he reached New Mexico, he didn't have any kids to feed. He'd seen a lot of families on the road with children and he always felt sorry for the little ones who had no idea what kind of inhuman hell they'd been thrust into.

As he rode Catwalk thought of Sam and how well she'd fit in with his family. They'd all, including little Petey, told him how much they liked her and didn't want her to leave. He knew beyond any doubt that he was deeply in love with Sam. He also knew this brought with it some responsibility and this worried him. He could make a living wage working for Barney, but he wanted to give Sam a better life than that of the wife of a farm laborer. This raised the question of how. He fell asleep while wondering how on earth he could give Sam the life he wanted and she deserved.

# Chapter Eighteen

Catwalk dropped off at the Vaughn water tank. He walked the seven miles to Barney's farm and saw Mattie working in the vegetable garden. He called out, "Hello."

Mattie turned toward him and said, "If you're looking for work … . Oh, my gosh. If it isn't Mr. Catwalk."

"Hi Mattie. Is Barney up north?"

"He sure is. Won't be back for a week or so." She gave Catwalk a big hug, then took his arm and led him toward the house. "How is your Momma feeling?"

"She's feeling fine. She went back to work before I left."

"I'm so glad to hear that. I'd like to meet that woman sometime. Have you eaten?"

"I can always sit down to your cooking. I know you've got a fresh pie in there."

"Cherry. Just took it out of the oven this morning."

"Do you know if they're finished bucking barley?"

"They finished last week."

Catwalk and Mattie talked while she fixed his meal. He said, "The farmers back home are having trouble selling their crops. Has Barney had any problem selling his crops?"

"I don't know. Mr. Barney gives away so much to the needy, I don't know if he's selling any produce or not. I think he's fed up with the farming business though. When he came back he was fussin' and frettin' around here for a few days. Then one morning he said he's thinking of getting into another business, where he don't work so hard and make so little."

"What business is that?"

"I don't know, child. He didn't say and I didn't ask." Mattie served Catwalk's dinner and little was said while he ate for the first time in two days.

✦ ✦ ✦

Catwalk left early the next morning walking the same roads he and Curly had driven a few months ago. Late afternoon of the fourth day, he arrived at Barney's farm. He walked in the kitchen and found Julio hefting a block of ice into the ice box. Julio said, "Welcome home, son. It's good to have you back again."

"Thank you, Julio. Is Sam around?"

"She was here earlier, but I haven't seen her for the last couple of hours. I don't think she expected you home for another day or so."

"I left two days earlier than I planned on. I'll see if she's down at the barn."

Sam walked in the door, saw Catwalk and yelled, "Cat!" She ran into his arms. Oblivious of Julio, they hugged and kissed each other with the fervor of two lovers who'd been apart for years, rather than weeks.

Discreetly, Julio left the kitchen.

Sam said, "I can't believe you're back. I've missed you so much."

"I've been thinking about you since you boarded that bus. How was your trip back?"

"It was fine, even though I was lonely."

Catwalk kissed her again, then asked, "Is Barney around?"

"Yes, and he'll want to talk to you. While we were gone that deputy, the one who tried to hang you, he came here looking for you."

"What? Are you sure?'

"C'mon, let's go talk to Barney."

Barney was in the living room talking on his new phone. When he saw Catwalk, he shook his hand and said, "I'm glad to see you back. Your Momma must be doing well."

"She is. She went back to work the day before I left. What's this about the deputy from Texas being here?"

Barney told him the whole story, including the rifles he'd bought for Curly and Julio.

Catwalk collapsed into a chair and buried his head in his hands. He said, "I can't believe he came looking for me."

Barney said, "I called the sheriff in Dillard County. He said this guy had been in jail, but escaped. He also said he's carrying enough hate for ten people."

Curly had come into the room. He laid a hand on Catwalk's shoulder and said, "Good to have you back. I wish you didn't have to come back to this."

Catwalk looked at him and said, "Do you think Jones will come back looking for me?"

With a grim expression, Curly said. "I think he will and I hope I see him first. There's nothing I'd like better than to put a bullet right between his eyes."

Catwalk looked at Sam and said, "I'm so sick and tired of violence."

She walked over to him and cradled his head to her bosom. She whispered, "I'm going to take your mind off all the violence you've seen."

Catwalk smiled, then said to Barney, "I'm ready to get back to work. What needs to be done?"

"Go see Julio. He's got enough work to keep you and Curly busy."

Catwalk got up to leave, then asked Barney, "Mattie said there might be some changes around here. What sort of changes?"

"Well, I don't want to let the cat out of the bag yet, but I've got an idea. I'll let everyone know what's in the wind as soon as I decide whether it's a sound idea or scatterbrained folly."

◆ ◆ ◆

That night at dinner, Curly told Cat about his flying experiences and expertise as a pilot. Clearly, he was proud of his progress and wanted Catwalk to join in his success.

Catwalk smiled at his enthusiasm, then said, "Julio said he's starting my lessons in a week or two."

"That's great, Cat. You'll love it. Hey, I'd better go; I'm meeting a girl at the Bearcat Tavern. She calls me her dreamboat."

"O.K. See you later."

Catwalk returned to the kitchen and read the flying books Curly had accumulated, while he waited for Sam to finish up.

Julio walked in and asked, "Curly gone up to the Bearcat again?"

"Yeah. He said he was meeting a girl."

"There's a lot of them places opened up since the repeal of prohibition. She must be some girl, 'cause he's going up there regular. He's been drinking a lot lately; keeps a pint stashed in the barn. I hope that liquor don't get the best of him."

Catwalk said nothing. He'd noticed the change in Curly as soon as they sat down to dinner. His friend had matured in the time he'd been gone. He'd taken up smoking and his demeanor had become that of someone who was trying to act tough; he swaggered and bragged about his work and his flying. Catwalk wasn't sure if he liked the changes, but realized Curly might be going through a stage in life.

◆ ◆ ◆

When Sam finished cleaning up, she and Catwalk walked out to the hangar so they could be alone for a while. Sitting on a bale of hay,

Catwalk took her hand in his and said, "On the train ride out to Mississippi, you asked me if I thought about who I want to marry."

"Have you thought about that?"

"Yes I did. How old do you think we should be before we get married?"

"Catwalk, are you asking me to marry you?"

"Well, I guess I am, but I'm not sure if this is the right time."

Sam smiled and said, "When would be the right time?"

"I think we should wait until I can find work that's better than a farm laborer."

"Do you know what you want to do?"

"No, I don't, but I'm sure I can learn to do something."

"I don't want to wait too long. You don't want to marry an old woman, do you?"

"No. We won't wait that long."

◆ ◆ ◆

Three days later, Julio started Catwalk's flying lessons. He found out that flying an airplane was easier than he thought and he picked it up quickly. Landings were the hardest part, but as Julio said, they got easier with practice. The fall weather kept them from flying more than once or twice a week, still, he soloed by his sixth hour. After that he flew as often as the weather would allow.

◆ ◆ ◆

On the pretense of the possible theft of some cattle, from his farm in Vaughn, Barney called sheriff Zane Thomas. After talking for a few minutes he casually asked if the law was still looking for the two boys that had once worked for him.

Thomas said, "No, Barney, those boys are in the clear. That wanted notice was cancelled a few weeks back. Are you going to have them move back to Vaughn for the winter?"

Barney smiled. He wasn't surprised Thomas had seen right through his ruse. "Yes, Zane, I probably will. So long."

Over the next two weeks Barney sent everyone except Julio back down to the Vaughn farm. Because the weather was more moderate in Vaughn, the boys flew often. Sam and Catwalk went flying together whenever they had time. Whenever they weren't flying or working, they spent time just being together. Catwalk was happier than he thought was possible and he often wrote his Momma to tell her of his feelings toward Sam.

◆ ◆ ◆

One morning over breakfast, Barney told Catwalk and Curly, "You've both got enough flying hours now. I'm going to take you to Albuquerque to get your pilot's licenses."

Curly jumped up hugged Catwalk. "You hear that, buddy. We're going to be pilots."

Catwalk looked at Sam and said, "Will you go with us."

With a big smile, Sam said, "I wouldn't miss it for the world. You better get to studying the aeronautical regs."

With Sam's help, the boys spent every spare minute studying the regulations from the Department of Commerce's Aeronautical Division. Two weeks before Easter, with Sam and Catwalk in one Jenny, and Barney and Curly in the other, they made the trip to Albuquerque. Even though he'd memorized the book of regulations, and practiced all the maneuvers, Catwalk was more nervous than he could ever remember. Sam stayed close to him and did her best to calm his nerves.

Three hours after their flight test, they were waiting outside the Department of Commerce office when the check pilot walked into the waiting room and handed them their licenses. He said, "Congratulations boys. You passed both parts of the exam with high marks and you're now licensed pilots."

That night they all celebrated over a glass of wine, then he wrote his family. He told them about getting his pilot's license and mentioned the conversation he and Sam had had about getting married. He didn't mention the return of deputy Jones.

# Chapter Nineteen

One week after returning from Albuquerque, Catwalk, Curly and Sam were in the hangar working on the Jenny. Catwalk yelled to Curly, "Throw me a feeler gauge."

Curly looked up from the tool box and said, "Coming up." He then turned toward Cat and froze—Alton Jones was standing just outside the hangar with a rifle pointed at Catwalk.

Catwalk saw Curly's expression and turned to see what had spooked him. He saw Jones, wiped his hands and laid his rag on the wing. Then he slowly walked away from Sam, who had been at his side.

Sam saw Jones and shook her head, softly mumbling, "No, no. It can't be."

Jones said, "I finally got you, you son of a bitch. You ain't getting away from me now."

Jones walked toward Cat, staring down the barrel of the rifle pointed at his chest.

Catwalk said, "If you're going to shoot me here, you better kill me with the first shot. If you miss, I'll shove that rifle down your throat."

"Don't worry, nigger. I never miss from this close."

Curly saw that Jones was focused in on Catwalk. With his eye on Jones, he slowly reached behind him and picked up his rifle. He watched Jones intently, knowing the crazed deputy might pull the trigger any second.

Jones motioned Catwalk out of the hangar. In doing so, he turned slightly and Curly saw his chance. He snapped the rifle to his shoulder and fired, hitting Jones in the left shoulder.

Jones yelled and went down. He then rolled over, raised the rifle with one hand and fired wildly. The bullet hit Sam in the chest. She crumpled to the floor.

Catwalk yelled out, "Sam!!" He rushed over to her.

Curly fired another round, hitting Jones in the thigh. He walked toward Jones, intent on emptying his rifle into the bastard.

Barney came running into the hangar. When the deadly scene registered, he grabbed Jones' rifle and then stepped in front of Curly. He said, "Don't shoot, Curly. He's bleeding bad, he won't last long."

"Get out of my way, Barney. I'm going to finish him off right now."

Barney looked at Catwalk bent over Sam's body. He said, "No, Curly. No more shooting." He then took the rifle from Curly and threw it under the plane.

Barney knelt next to Catwalk and said, "How bad is it?"

Amid tears, Catwalk said, "She's not breathing, Barney."

Barney looked at Sam and knew at once he wouldn't find a pulse. Hoping he was wrong, he placed two fingers behind her ear, praying with all his heart that he'd find a pulse even if it was weak. He didn't. His eyes welled with tears and he said, "Oh God."

He laid a hand on Catwalk's shoulder, but couldn't bring himself to tell his friend that the love of his life lay dead before him. Barney and Catwalk cried openly.

Jones moaned, "I'm hit, God damn it, someone help me."

Curly said, "I'll help you, you rotten bastard." He then kicked Jones in the head as hard as he could. Jones blacked out.

Curly then knelt beside Catwalk and said, "Help me load her in the truck. I'll drive her to the doctor."

Barney looked at Curly and shook his head.

Curly whispered, "Oh, God no. Are you sure?"

Barney nodded his head.

Catwalk stood up and looked at Jones. He walked over to a tool bin and picked up an axe. Knowing what he had in mind Barney rushed toward him. "No, Cat. It won't help. If you do anything to him, you're just as bad as he is."

Curly took the axe from Catwalk and said, "He's right, Cat. Jones ain't worth it."

Catwalk hung his head with tears dripping off his face. He said, "I'm taking her up to the house."

Barney told Curly, "Put Jones in the truck. Take him to Doc Crandall's place, but drive slowly. Then find the sheriff and tell him what happened."

Catwalk bent over Sam, kissed her cheek and smoothed hair. Then he picked up her lifeless body and carried it to the porch. He lay her on the divan where they'd spent so many pleasant hours reading and talking. He knelt beside her and kissed her again, hoping he'd hear a moan escape her lips. He felt again for a pulse, only to feel the stillness of her death. He lay his head on her chest, next to the ugly hole where the single bullet had blown the life out of her. She just couldn't be dead.

When he heard footsteps, Catwalk turned to see Barney. Through his tears he said, "Maybe she's in a coma. My Momma told me about those people in a coma that lie still for many years and then wake up."

Barney hung his head, knowing he had to tell Catwalk what he didn't want to hear. "Cat, I wish to God she was, and I wish we could breath life back into her, or perform some sort of operation to bring her back to life."

Barney turned away for a few seconds, then said, "She's gone, Cat. And I've never been so sorry in all my life. I know how you feel because I felt the same way when I lost Mary. I know the hell of it. I know that there's nothing more final than death."

✦ ✦ ✦

An ambulance from the morgue picked up Sam's body later that day. Catwalk went down to the creek and sat where he and Sam used to have their long talks. Unbeknownst to him, Curly was watching him from a distance. Curly didn't want to intrude upon him during his time of grief, but he felt he should be watching over his closest friend during the darkest time of his life.

Catwalk was still stunned about Sam's death. He was incapable of thinking any clear thoughts; he just sat there and stared into the creek. When it started to rain, he didn't even notice the drops. Nothing could affect him more than the loss of the only woman he'd ever loved. At times he started to question the ways of the Lord; taking someone so precious from him, just as they were starting their lives together, then he decided that was futile. Divinity be damned, there was no reason for this to happen. There couldn't be any explanation for something so cruel.

Catwalk spent a cold, wet and dreary night by the creek. He didn't want to face anyone and he didn't want to talk to anyone. He had to be alone, regardless of the circumstances.

From a distant hill, Curly sat in his vigil, taking a break only to tell Barney about Cat, then walk to the barn to get his pint of rye. When he thought of the anguish his friend was experiencing, he often came to tears.

# Chapter Twenty

They buried Sam beneath a big oak tree, not far from the grave of Barney's late wife. Catwalk visited her grave daily and often told her of his work on the farm, just as if they were sitting in the kitchen.

Life was difficult for Catwalk in the weeks after Sam's death. Tragic events affect everyone differently and the time it takes for tragedy to melt into the blend of a normal life can take years. In Catwalk's case, everything on the farm reminded him of Sam. Whenever he went to read, he found he couldn't concentrate, because his thoughts kept turning to her. Barney made sure he kept busy so he'd keep his mind occupied and everyone on the farm made a point to talk to him whenever he seemed despondent, which was often.

One month after her death, Barney and Curly were changing the wheel on a wagon, when Barney said, "Have you noticed any improvement in Cat?"

"A little, but it's slow. I actually saw him smile the other day."

"I don't know what else we can do. I guess we have to let time heal the wounds."

Curly drove the wheel onto the axle, then stopped to light a cigarette. "They'll never heal completely. He'll carry his grief for her to his grave."

◆ ◆ ◆

Proving that some people are just too ornery to die, Alton Jones survived his injuries. He was remanded to the Colfax County jail until he was healthy enough to stand trial. Barney knew the chances were good that Jones would get a light sentence, because the person he'd murdered was black. With this in mind, he made sure that the prosecuting attorney knew all of Jones' crimes in the past. Barney also made it a point to attend the trial every day. Whether his efforts were the reason will never be known, but Jones was convicted of charges of first degree murder, two counts of auto theft and escaping from jail. He was sentenced to the Collinsville Federal Prison for twenty four years. He would be eligible for parole in eight years.

♦ ♦ ♦

Catwalk found little consolation in the conviction and prison sentence. He was glad Jones was behind bars where he belonged, but no matter what happened, he just wanted Sam back. He had tried, several times, to tell himself that he had to quit thinking about her and go on with his life. Although they didn't come right out and say it, he knew everyone around him felt the same way. He could see the looks in their faces that said, "When are you going to get over her and move on with your life." Unfortunately, everyone else didn't know how much Sam had become a part of him. Still, he knew, somehow, he had to learn to live without her image haunting him every waking minute.

♦ ♦ ♦

Two months later, on a rainy January morning, Barney gathered everyone in the kitchen. He'd been gone for six days, and the news he brought home with him shocked everyone. "Crops aren't selling well. I'm giving most of the produce and some meat to the soup kitchen in Vaughn. I'm going to keep the livestock for us to eat, but all we'll be doing on the farm is tending to the livestock and growing our own produce. The rest of the land will lay fallow, except the field adjacent to the hangar barn. That field is going to be leveled and mowed so we can land larger planes out there. While I was gone, I bought two Boeing Model 80s, and I'm going to start flying an airmail route. Once it starts paying, I'll start flying passengers."

A stunned silence fell over the kitchen. Catwalk and Curly exchanged surprised glances. Julio, who'd known about Barney's plans, just smiled. Barney said, "I've applied for a mail route between Albuquerque and Denver. I expect it to be approved within three months. We'll start with one trip to Denver in the morning and a trip back to Albuquerque in the afternoon. Julio is going to run the maintenance end. You guys will start out doing maintenance and working at the airport to get a feel for the business. Eventually you'll be flying on the line."

Curly spoke first, "Do we have enough experience?."

Barney said, "Not yet, but by the time we're ready to start operating, you will have."

Catwalk said, "But Barney, we're in the middle of a depression. People can hardly afford to eat, much less fly on airliners."

"That's the part that you've seen. I just spend the last few days talking to people in the airline business. Tom Braniff started with one Stinson Detroiter and a route between Tulsa and Oklahoma City. Now he's got routes to Chicago and Dallas. Walter Varney of Varney Speed

Lines started with a route from Elko, Nevada to Pasco, Washington. He's branched out all over the northwest. United Airlines has been flying passengers coast-to-coast since 1927 and last year their passenger revenue was almost four million dollars. This is still a time of haves and have-nots. The people that can afford it are flying and the airline business is going to grow. I can buy and refurbish airplanes cheap, so now is the time to get started. This way we'll be established when the public starts flying again."

Barney looked at Catwalk, "What do you think?"

"Does this mean that Curly and I are going to be airline pilots some day?"

"There's a lot of work to be done, but in the end you should be airline pilots."

Catwalk and Curly looked at each other with wide grins. Barney pulled the cork on a bottle of rye whiskey and poured three fingers for everyone. Catwalk was wary about drinking, but this seemed like an appropriate occasion for his first drink. It isn't every day that a black man from a sharecropper's farm becomes an airline pilot. He just wished Sam was there to share this momentous event with him.

◆ ◆ ◆

Two months later Barney and Julio went to Denver to take delivery of the first Boeing Model 80. While they were gone Catwalk and Curly worked dawn 'til dark. They enlarged the hangar barn to make room for the Boeing, so maintenance could be performed out of the weather. They then installed the wiring for additional lights and electrical outlets. They partitioned off part of the building for a maintenance office, complete with built in desks and file drawers. They mowed, leveled and installed a wind sock on the landing field.

◆ ◆ ◆

After dark Catwalk often listened to the radio. He'd always been impressed with Barney's wealth of knowledge, and he found his own interest in current events growing. He looked forward to the different radio programs, such as Amos n' Andy, The Lone Ranger and Fibber McGee and Molly. One evening, after listening to President Roosevelt's fireside chat, he asked Curly, "What do you think is going to happen in this country?"

"I think the President has good plans for those programs that will put people back to work. I'm betting he gets the country out of this."

Catwalk said, "I guess we have to believe in him. He's the only one who can help us."

Curly tipped up a bottle of beer, then asked, "Hey, Cat. Do you think airline pilots get to meet a lot of girls?"

"I don't know. I guess if there were girls on your plane you could meet them. I thought you already had a girl down at the Bearcat."

"Nah, she ain't nothing serious. Just a handy piece of ass every now and then."

"How many girlfriends do you want?"

"Hell, how do I know. I'd just like to meet some new girls every now and then. You should get out and meet some too."

Catwalk looked at Curly and said, "Where am I supposed to meet girls? I can't go to any of the bars, there's only a few black families around here and there aren't any girls my age."

Curly silently cursed his stupidity for the comment. He hadn't thought of that, but Cat was right; there were no girls for him to meet and there were very few black people, period. Curly tried to imagine how he must feel. He told himself he'd make up for his stupidity by spending more time with his friend.

◆ ◆ ◆

Two days later Barney landed in the Model 80. When he first saw the plane, Catwalk couldn't believe his eyes; it was monstrous. Like the Jenny, it had two wings, but it had three engines with one mounted on the nose and the other two mounted between the wings. The cabin was large enough to carry twelve passengers in seats with cushions, just like a Pullman car, and the cockpit was amazing. It had room for two pilots to sit side-by-side, six levers on a center console for the engine controls, plus a staggering number of switches, dials and gauges.

Upon seeing the cockpit, Curly muttered, "Cat, can we learn to fly this thing?"

"Yes, and I can't wait."

Barney heard his comment and said, "You're going to have to wait a couple weeks, Cat. I'm taking it over to Albuquerque to be painted and have the interior replaced. The color scheme will be tan with orange and brown accents. While I'm gone you guys have a lot to do. Julio will be working with you to finish the hangar. We'll use this field for a maintenance base until we can move onto the airport at Albuquerque. When we get the other plane, I'm putting one aircraft in service and keeping the other here in standby. When I get back, I'll check you out in the airplane and then you're going up to Denver to attend an instrument flying course that's put on by United Airlines. I want you to study the aircraft operating manual and fly the Jenny for an hour or two every day. You've got to build your time, and when you get two hundred hours, you can test for your commercial license. Any questions?"

Catwalk and Curly looked at each other. Things were happening fast in their lives and the rapid advancement of their flying careers was too good to be true. They both shook their heads and Barney said, "By the way, the airline you'll be flying for is Rocky Mountain Airways."

◆ ◆ ◆

Julio proved to be a relentless task master while Barney was gone. Every morning they spent time working on the hangar, installing equipment such as air compressors, welding tanks, engine diagnostic and maintenance equipment, instrument calibration gear and hydraulic jacks.

Amid their busy schedule, Catwalk and Curly also flew as often as they could. When they weren't flying or working, they spent time reading the Commerce Department regulations for commercial pilots and studying up on instrument flying procedures.

Even though he was busier than he'd ever been in his life, Catwalk still found time to visit Sam's grave and tell her how his life was improving. He often talked about how this was the job that would get him off the farm and give him a life beyond that of a laborer. Unfortunately, the life he'd often dreamed of, would also be a lonely life.

# Chapter Twenty-One

In the Albuquerque airport lounge, Barney was sipping coffee while talking to a pilot from Transcontinental and Western Air. Workmen had started painting the Model 80, but it wouldn't be completed until the day after tomorrow. He was staying in town to talk to the airport manager about getting parking ramp space when his flights started. The other pilot told him about two pilots that had to be laid off. "They're good pilots with over five hundred hours each, but they're black. We found out there's a lot of passengers who don't want to fly with a black pilot. Over in Tucson most of the passengers got off a Tri-Motor when they saw a black pilot. The chief pilot tried to stick up for the two guys, but we need to fill every seat we can, just to stay in business. He got orders to lay them off last week."

"That's a shame that someone has to lose a job because of his color."

"It is, but there wasn't anything else we could do."

"No, I guess not. I'd better go, good talking to you." Barney paid for his coffee and left the café. On the way to the airport office he thought about the constant battles Catwalk had been fighting because of racial injustice, and it rankled him that a person should be subjected to such treatment. He decided no matter what happened, he wouldn't lay off Catwalk. If the passengers didn't wan to fly with him, they could take another airline.

At the airport office he heard good news; the airport was trying to attract business, so his first two months of parking ramp fees would be waived. After that his spirits improved slightly, but the conversation with the other pilot lingered in the back of his mind.

◆ ◆ ◆

Catwalk pulled the chain slowly until the Jenny's engine rose out of the cowling. Once it was clear of the aircraft he pulled the plane out of the hangar. He then lowered the engine onto an engine dolly and bolted it down. He yelled to Julio, "It's out, what are we going to do first."

"Drain the oil and coolant, and pull the rocker arms. Then wheel it over to the bench so we can start a valve job. Where's Curly?"

"I don't know, he was here a minute ago."

Julio slammed down a wrench. "I know where he is."

He found Curly behind the barn, smoking a cigarette and sipping off a pint of whiskey. He yelled, "I didn't tell you to take a break."

Curly hollered back, "I finished straightening up the parts bin, just like you said, Julio."

"There's more work to do and I want you to do it with a clear head."

"I ain't drunk. I only had a few sips."

"No, but it's only eleven o'clock. You start drinking earlier every day."

"God damn it, Julio. What do you want me to do?"

"Put the bottle away. We're doing a valve job on the Jenny."

Curly flipped his cigarette into the dirt and followed Julio. He'd been at the tavern until two o'clock last night, then started work at five this morning. On short sleep he found Julio's regimen hard to take. If he wasn't afraid of blowing his chance to be an airline pilot, he would have told the old Mexican to go to hell.

◆ ◆ ◆

Barney returned two days later. The plane shined with its new paint job and the Rocky Mountain logo on the tail. Barney told Cat, "I saw some of the pilots have taken to putting names on their planes. I took the liberty of painting a name on ours."

Catwalk looked just in front of the cabin door and saw "Samantha Jean" painted in large orange script. He smiled and said, "Barney, I think that's very appropriate. Thank you."

Barney asked, "Are you ready to fly it?"

"Yes, sir."

Barney took the right seat and Catwalk the left. Barney then started the engines. Catwalk couldn't believe how quiet and calm it was in an enclosed cockpit, as compared to the Jenny's open cockpit. With three propellers turning he felt a sensation of power, but the noise and prop wash weren't there. He looked over the gauges and saw the familiar turn and bank indicator, fuel gauge, airspeed and altimeter, but the rest of the gauges mystified him.

He noticed, when Barney taxied to the edge of the field, that the plane had a much softer ride and didn't bounce around like the lighter

Jenny. When Barney turned into the wind and applied power, he felt the thrust of the powerful engines pushing him back in the seat.

Once airborne Barney turned to the east and climbed to fifteen hundred feet. He leveled off and told Catwalk, "She's heavier than the Jenny so the controls are more firm. Keep your power at twenty five inches of manifold pressure and your RPM about three thousand. Other than that, she flies just like the Jenny. She's all yours."

Catwalk took the controls and felt the heavier pressure from even the slightest movement. He banked into a turn and the big plane seemed to turn gracefully rather than the quick jerky turn of the Jenny. When he leveled off he looked at the airspeed indicator—he was doing a hundred and forty knots, but it seemed like they were hardly moving. He pushed the throttles forward to climb and felt the surge of power, as the three engines responded. The plane was at twenty five hundred feet in less than a minute.

He smiled at Barney, "She's an amazing aircraft. Powerful, but graceful and easy to fly."

"It won't have nearly as much power with a cabin full of passengers and cargo. Head back to the field and we'll do a couple touch and goes."

When Catwalk lined up on the field, Barney said, "You don't have to flare as much as with the Jenny. She's faster so you can fly her right down to the deck. Also, a cross wind won't throw you around as much so there's less crab."

Catwalk first landing was O.K., but he knew he'd have to get used to the increased landing speed and the feel of the heavier aircraft. When he pushed the throttles forward, again he was amazed at the power he commanded.

After their final landing, they were taxiing to the hangar when Barney asked him, "Have you noticed Curly drinking more lately?"

Catwalk immediately thought, if he answered yes, he might jeopardize Curly's flying career. On the other hand, he had to be honest with Barney. "He goes out to that saloon almost every night, but he's seeing a girl out there. I don't know how much he drinks there, but I've never seen him get stupid from liquor."

"Julio said he's found him drinking on the sly and this worries me. I can't have a pilot working for me who hits the bottle too much. I'll have to talk to him."

◆ ◆ ◆

Catwalk found Curly putting a coat of wing dope on the Jenny. Curly asked him, "How'd ya' like flying the Boeing?"

"It's a dream. The controls are more firm than the Jenny, but she's got a lot more power. It lands faster and you don't have to flare it as much."

"Did Barney tell you what all the gauges mean?"

"He did. They're not hard to learn, but you have to learn to scan them."

"I can't wait until I can fly it."

Catwalk hesitated a few seconds, but knowing he had to get this out in the open, he said, "Curly, Barney asked me about your drinking."

Curly looked up with concern all over his face. "What did you tell him?"

"All I said was you've been going to that tavern every night because you got a girl there."

"Aw shit! I ain't been drinking that much."

"Barney said he doesn't want a pilot flying for him if he's hitting the bottle."

Curly walked away from the flammable wing dope and lit a cigarette. He felt like a drink right now. He said, "It's that damn Julio. He told on me an' got me in trouble with Barney."

Catwalk had always kept his opinions to himself, but now trying to help his friend, he said, "You better quit drinking, if you want to fly."

"Hell, Cat, sometimes I wonder if it's all worth it."

"You can always go back to riding in reefers and dodging the bulls."

Curly slowly nodded his head, then smiled and said, "I ain't never going back to that life. I'll try to take it easy on the booze. Thanks, Cat."

# Chapter Twenty-Two

Rocky Mountain Air Service flew its first mail and cargo flight on April 15, 1934. For the first two months Barney flew two trips daily; one from Albuquerque to Denver in the morning, and back to Albuquerque in the afternoon. He planned to fly this schedule six days a week, but mechanical problems often reduced his schedule to three or four days a week.

Catwalk and Curly were alternating as ground crewmen; loading cargo, refueling, cleaning the plane and handling wheel chocks. Barney had wanted them to learn the business from the ground up, and although he hadn't said anything, he wanted Catwalk to be visible around the aircraft. He hoped people would get used to seeing him and thereby accept him when he started flying.

Passenger service was inaugurated on August 20. Most of the kinks of a new business had been worked out, and in September Curly started flying as co-pilot. Passenger flying was still in its infancy, so many people wouldn't fly because they were concerned about aircraft safety and reliability. Still, there were enough adventurous souls that the loads were better than expected.

Barney did everything possible to keep the passengers at ease, and one of Curly's duties was to greet the passengers when they boarded and check up on them during the flight. A few people made comments such as, "You look awfully young to be flying this plane."

With a smile, Curly replied, "I've got over three hundred hours of flying time and hold a commercial pilot's license. Also, there is a more experienced pilot who is the pilot in command of this flight." This seemed to quiet their concerns.

On a cool Tuesday morning, Catwalk was scheduled to fly his first trip as co-pilot. Steel grey clouds hung over the Albuquerque airport, but the weather report for Denver was clear skies and good visibility. Barney elected to take off, hoping the weather would improve enroute.

In his preflight briefing, he told Catwalk they'd turn east, as soon as they cleared Sandia Peak, to avoid the mountains to the north. Then they'd fly east of Las Vegas and turn toward Raton. If the weather hadn't cleared by the time they reached Raton, they'd return to Albuquerque, rather than chance the pass in bad weather.

Finally, the time arrived to see how the passengers reacted to a black co-pilot. Barney had talked this over with Catwalk, to prepare him for possible adverse reactions from the passengers. Catwalk had been preparing himself for this moment since Barney had first mentioned the formation of the airline. He was excited, but he was also apprehensive about the cruel possibilities afforded by human nature.

For his first trip Catwalk wore a new leather jacket, new chinos with a white shirt and polished boots. Nervous but smiling, he took his place at the foot of the boarding stairs and the first three passengers merely looked at him when they handed him their ticket. The fourth passenger asked, "Are you the co-pilot?"

"Yes, sir, I am. My name is Catwalk Jackson and I hope you enjoy your flight today."

"I ain't flying with no nigger pilot."

As hard as it was, Catwalk smiled and said, "You can get a ticket refund inside the terminal, sir."

The man returned a blank stare. Clearly he didn't know what to do. Catwalk thought they guy probably needed to get to Denver, but his prejudices were preventing that. The passenger said, "You really know how to fly this airplane?"

"Yes, sir, I do. I have almost four hundred hours flying time and I've logged thirty hours in this aircraft. There is a more experienced pilot who is in command of this flight."

The man climbed the stairs and Catwalk kept his smile in place for the remaining passengers. When he and Barney took their seats, Catwalk said, "Only one guy out of seven had a problem. Better than we expected."

"Maybe we'll find some rough weather and we can bounce him around a bit."

Catwalk grinned and said, "Trouble is we'll be bouncing the others too."

The weather broke when they were thirty miles northeast of Las Vegas, and the rest of the trip was in clear skies. Catwalk breathed a sigh of relief that his first trip as an airline pilot had gone better than expected. He loved flying the Boeing and if the passengers accepted him, he hoped he could continue flying airliners for the rest of his life.

In Denver, however, the passengers for the trip back weren't as agreeable to a black pilot. All but one refused to take the flight and Barney, true to his word, stuck by his co-pilot and advised them to take another airline.

On the flight south, he told Catwalk, "The trouble is, there's two other flights available from Denver and the passengers know it. This morning we were the only flight departing for Denver, so the people had no choice."

Catwalk said nothing, but wondered if this was an unusual situation, or a precursor of things to come. That night he said little over dinner as he thought about people's attitudes that threatened to shatter his dreams before they could become a reality. He remembered his Momma's advice to avoid white folk and stick with his own kind. For the first time in his life, he found himself questioning her guidance. He was trying to break into a white man's profession, so avoidance of white folks was out of the question. He knew he was competent enough to fly airliners, but the passengers had to be convinced. Until they accepted him, he would have a harmful effect on Barney's efforts to get the airline off the ground. After all that Barney had done for him, he felt terrible about being such a liability. He decided that his first priority would be to help Barney, even if it meant resigning.

The next day was worse. There were only three paying passengers for the morning flight and two of those cancelled because they didn't want to fly with a black pilot. On the return trip, out of eight passengers, six refunded their tickets and sought another airline.

Once they were airborne, Barney said, "They'll get over this, Cat. I think some people do it because they see someone else who refuses to fly. It's a matter of acceptance, and that takes time. We have to be patient."

Catwalk pulled the throttles back to cruise power as they leveled off at six thousand feet, then stared out the window. He knew Barney was going to stick by him, and he appreciated his support, but he had to stick with his decision made last night. Barney was trying to get an airline off the ground under the worst possible conditions. In the grip of the depression, many people couldn't afford to fly. Of those that could afford a ticket, many were apprehensive about flying; they didn't trust airplanes and were perfectly comfortable taking a train even though their trip took twice as long.

Catwalk decided to fly a few more trips. If there were a significant number of passengers who refused to fly on his flights, he'd hand Barney his resignation and do something else.

He reached for the prop controls and told Barney, "Have you noticed the props are harder to synchronize on this plane, than on the other one?"

"Yeah. I noticed that yesterday. They're always just a touch out of sync."

"What do you think causes that?"

"I don't know. I'm going to have Julio check it out when we take it back to the barn."

◆ ◆ ◆

That night over dinner Catwalk told Curly about the passenger's reaction to a black pilot, and his thoughts about resigning.

"No, Cat! You can't resign. This is the best chance you'll ever get. If you give it up, you'll regret it for the rest of your life. Those passengers will change their minds."

"That's true, but Barney needs the business to get this airline off the ground."

Curly fired back, "You heard what he said that day back on the farm; he's planning on operating at a loss for two years. He knew the loads wouldn't be good at first."

Catwalk thought about this, but still came to the conclusion that he was a liability. He said, "I'm going to make a couple more flights. If the passengers still refuse to fly with me, I'll do something else."

"Damn it. I hate to see you do that." Curly knew Catwalk's mind was made up. He looked at his friend with a devilish grin and said, "Maybe I'll tell the passengers on my flights, if they don't fly with you I'm going to knock their fucking blocks off."

"That would be good for business."

◆ ◆ ◆

By the end of the week, the situation had deteriorated. Catwalk and Barney were walking through the terminal when they saw a sign that read, "Rocky Mountain Airways hires niggers when there's a million white men out of work."

Barney ripped the sign down, and told the ticket clerk to watch for anyone posting another sign, but the damage had been done. There were no passengers for the morning flight. Nothing was said about this until they were halfway to Denver. Then Catwalk said, "After the flight back, I'm resigning. I'll go back to help Julio with the maintenance, or maybe take a Jenny out to do some barnstorming."

Barney turned in his seat to look at Catwalk. He'd known this was coming and he thought about how to handle it, but it was still difficult. He said, "How about if I don't accept your resignation?"

Catwalk grinned and said, "How long can you afford to fly empty planes between Albuquerque and Denver?"

"If you resign, every one of those ignorant bastards who refuse to fly with you, wins. They have proven their point and you have lost."

"Barney, I don't see it as being about winning and losing. I know those people are wrong because I'm a good pilot, and their refusal to fly with me has nothing to do with my ability to fly the plane. But it's not about being right or wrong either. This is about the attitudes that are affecting your efforts to start an airline. Here's what I'd like to do. I'll go back and help Julio for a month or two. Then, if he agrees, I'd like to rent one of the Jennys from you and go out on my own, to do some barnstorming. Maybe later on, if people's attitudes change, I'll come back to work for you."

Barney stared out the passenger window. He didn't like giving in to the people's prejudice, but he also didn't like subjecting Catwalk to the constant, insulting attitudes. He said, "Your mind's made up?"

"It's best for everyone. You'll get your feet on the ground with better passenger loads, Curly will get more flight time, and I'll either learn more about the maintenance end, or I'll be flying every day while entertaining the crowds at county fairs and air shows."

"You know, barnstorming is a hard way to make a living. You have to travel to a different event every day and people might not pay to see you perform acrobatics."

"I've read up on it, and it's not easy, but at least I'm not dodging the railroad bulls."

"O.K., I'll accept your temporary resignation, but in six months, you're coming back to work for Rocky Mountain."

"You've got a deal."

# Chapter Twenty-Three

When Catwalk arrived at the farm, Julio tried to console him, but it didn't heal the wound that had been inflicted by human cruelty. He attempted to keep his mind busy by helping Julio with maintenance on the other Boeing and routine work on the Jenny. Still, he didn't feel like he was in the right place; he wanted to fly airliners.

One morning he said to Julio, "There's not enough work to keep two men busy. What would you think if I took one of the Jennys and hit the barnstorming circuit."

"I think it's a good idea. You need to be flying somewhere. When will you leave?"

"A few days. I've got some work to do to get the Jenny ready."

♦ ♦ ♦

That afternoon Catwalk put the Jenny on jacks and greased the axle bearings. Next he beefed up the king posts and bottom skid in case he worked with a wing walker. Then he adjusted and tuned the rigging, which included four hundred turnbuckles, on the wings. When the rigging was tuned he installed an oil injector on the exhaust that would provide the smoke trail during his routine.

After the aircraft was as fit as he could make it, Catwalk spent a couple days polishing his acrobatic routine. Over dinner, he asked Julio, "Are you sure there's nothing around here I can help you with?"

"Cat, all I'm doing now is grading the new parking area for the Boeing. When that's done, I just have to wait for the other plane to come in. I think you should head on out and find yourself an air show. Show those people what a hell of a pilot you are."

♦ ♦ ♦

The next morning Catwalk packed his bags and headed for an air show at El Paso. After refueling and paying his fifty cent entry fee, he was told he'd be the second event, following a flight of two de Havilland Moths. He waited until the Moths landed and the pilot had a chance to pass the hat through the audience. This was the only method of the pilots getting paid, so he wouldn't be waved off until the preceding act had time to work the audience.

When his time came, he took off and turned back over the crowd. His routine started with a slow roll that was followed by a loop. He then went into a split S that terminated in a high speed pass over the audience, which he followed with an immelman turn and another high speed low pass. A couple Cuban Eights and a hammer head stall rounded out his routine.

After his routine, Catwalk parked in front of the audience to see if anyone wanted a ride for a quarter. He received a moderate applause and surprisingly, heard no racial slurs, but no one stepped up for a ride. When he passed the hat he collected only two dollars and twenty cents from the sparse crowd. As he walked back to the Jenny, he heard the air show organizer calling him, "Hey, fella'. You got a second?"

He walked over and the guy said, "You ain't got a bad routine, but if you really want to make the money you gotta get a stunt man or a wing walker. People have seen all the acrobatics, so it's nothing new any more. You gotta add someone to your act."

Catwalk thought the advice sounded good. He asked, "Where do I find a wing walker?"

"There's a fair going on in Odessa. Ask over there because a stunt pilot was killed out there. He might have had someone working with him that's looking for work."

Catwalk thanked him and took off. Halfway to Midland, the Jenny started overheating so he landed in a field and changed the radiator hose. By the time he filled the radiator from a nearby stream it was almost dark, so he ate two biscuits for dinner and slept under the wing.

The next morning at Odessa he asked the fuel attendant, "I'm looking for a partner to work with me as a wing walker. Do you know of anyone that might be interested?"

"Could be that Billy Sue Jenkins will work with you. She was flying with Dangerous Dan Farrell until he flew into a silo. Luckily, she wasn't with him, but he's dead and she's out of work. She ain't here right now though. You can wait to see if she comes around later on."

"Thanks, I'll wait." Catwalk looked at the diner on the airport, and saw the familiar "Whites Only" sign. He asked the guy, "Is there anywhere I can get a cup of coffee?"

"Well, that diner won't serve you, but they'll serve me. What do you like in it?"

Catwalk handed him a nickel and said, "Just black coffee is fine. I appreciate it"

◆ ◆ ◆

Catwalk moved the Jenny away from the fuel barrels and drank his coffee in the shade of the wing. He had no idea what kind of a routine he could dream up with a partner, but if this woman had been flying with someone else, she must have her own routine.

He'd just finished his coffee when a '27 Ford roadster roared into the auto parking lot and a girl with blonde curly hair jumped out and yelled, "Arnold, I need some gas on the cuff. I'm broke for a while."

The fuel attendant said, "So what the hell else is new."

"I'll pay you Thursday. I'm going to start waiting tables at Millie's."

While the attendant serviced her car, he talked and pointed toward the Jenny. The woman looked toward the plane, then walked across the parking lot. She looked over the aircraft and said, "This old bird's in pretty good shape. You looking for someone to fly stunts with you."

"I'm Catwalk Jackson and I'm looking for a partner. Are you interested."

The woman held out her hand and said, "Catwalk, I'm Billy Sue Jenkins. Does this have the hundred and fifty horse Hisso engine or the OX-5?"

"It's got Hisso power and it's tuned like a brakeman's watch. The engine has less than ten hours since the last overhaul."

She smiled, "When do you want me to start?"

"There's a show here day after tomorrow. Can we work something up by then?"

"Yeah, as long as the bottom skid and the king posts are sturdy, I can start walking tomorrow. What do you pay?"

"We split the audience collection and the expenses, fifty-fifty. Do you have any problem working with a Negro pilot?"

"Not in the least. Do you have a problem working with a woman?"

"Nope. I'm sleeping here tonight. We can practice when you get here in the morning."

◆ ◆ ◆

The next morning Billy Sue showed up an hour after sunrise. She handed Catwalk a plate covered with a napkin and said, "Here. I figured that diner wouldn't serve you, so I brought you something."

Catwalk took the napkin off to find a plate of grits, toast and bacon. "I appreciate this Billy Sue. I hope everyone at your house has enough to eat."

"My Mother works for the Katy Railroad, so she's making enough money to buy groceries."

They sat down and discussed their routine while he ate. Billy Sue said, "I'll have to bolt brackets on your king posts so I can fasten my straps to them. I can walk in any routine you got except snap rolls. If the wind sock is stiff, or if it's raining, I don't walk. Once we get used to working together we can work out a cable snatch routine."

Catwalk listened and then asked her about flying with a woman standing on top of his wing. Billy Sue told him that as long as he stuck to the pre arranged routine, so she knew what to expect, there was little difference.

Catwalk then helped her install the brackets. Once they finished, he took her up and let her go through her routine. He discovered that he had to concentrate more on his flying, because he had a tendency to watch her while she moved around on the wing. After a few practice sessions, she'd flash her signals and he'd go into the maneuver as if she wasn't there. By the time he landed he felt comfortable flying with her on his wing, and Billy Sue complimented him on his smooth maneuvers. They spent that afternoon talking over improvements to their routine.

◆ ◆ ◆

At the air show the next day, Billy Sue seemed to draw energy from the crowd as she waved to them. On his final pass over the audience, he saw the crowd applauding enthusiastically and hoped they'd respond likewise when he passed the hat.

On the ground, Billy Sue said, "Let me work the audience. I can talk them out of their underwear."

Catwalk agreed and she blended into the crowd. He watched as she passed the hat while talking with them. By the time she was through the crowd was laughing like they were at a vaudeville show. From all appearances, she was perfect at working the audience and Catwalk was content to let her handle it.

When they counted up the take, they'd earned eighteen dollars and forty cents; two weeks wages on the farm. With her usual exuberance, Billy Sue said, "This is nothing. At a show in Dallas last year, Dan and I made ninety bucks for two shows."

◆ ◆ ◆

They flew seven shows in the next few weeks and made expenses plus thirty dollars. Billy Sue had made a name for herself with her previous pilot, so the word began to spread and crowds began to grow.

Catwalk was content to let her have all the notoriety, although she sang his praise when working the audiences. His reputation as a skilled but safe acrobatic pilot grew, and being accepted by the public pleased Catwalk immensely. This, plus their increased purses improved his outlook on the barnstorming profession, but deep down inside Catwalk wanted to fly airliners and he wouldn't be truly content until her was back in the cockpit of the Boeing.

◆ ◆ ◆

When they spent the night outside, which was often because there weren't many hotels that would cater to blacks, Billy Sue had a tent and Catwalk slept under the wing of the Jenny. One night after a show in Abilene, Cat was laying under the wing during a rain storm. Billy Sue stuck her head out and yelled, "Cat, why don't you come in here with me? It's drier in here."

"I'm fine, Billy Sue. It's not raining that hard."

"O.K. Suit yourself."

The next morning, Billy Sue asked him, "Cat, do you like me?"

"Sure, I like you and I like working with you."

"Then why wouldn't you come in the tent last night to get out of the rain?"

"Well, I didn't think it was proper, for you and me to be sleeping together."

"We wouldn't have been sleeping together, not like married folk." She hesitated, then asked, "It's because of Sam, isn't it? You still feel like you're tied to her, don't you?"

"Yes, I kind of, do. I know it's silly, with her being dead, but that's the way it is."

"Well, it's not my place to say this, but I think you should accept the fact that she's dead and get on with your life. I'm sorry if that doesn't sit well with you, but that's my opinion."

Catwalk smiled, "Thanks for being honest with me, Billy Sue."

◆ ◆ ◆

They'd just finished a show in Albuquerque, when Catwalk said, "What would you think about taking a few days off?"

"Sure, I'm game. Are you going somewhere?"

"No, but I'll take you over to the farm where I live. It's not far from here and you can rest up."

As Billy Sue climbed into the rear cockpit, she said, "That sounds great. Maybe while we're there we can work on a new routine."

◆ ◆ ◆

Catwalk landed in the familiar field an hour and a half later. Julio waved as he spotted the Jenny and walked over to the plane. Catwalk climbed down and introduced Billy Sue who shook Julio's hand, than walked over to the Boeing that was parked outside the hangar. "Damn, this is beautiful airplane."

She saw the name and said, "It's her plane, Hunh?"

"Yes, it is."

"God damn, if it ain't the barnstormer!" Curly had come down from the house. He shook Catwalk's hand and said, "Who is this, Cat?"

"Curly, this is my partner, Billy Sue Jenkins."

"Pleased to meet you, Curly. Cat told me about his best friend that flies the big airliners."

Curly blushed and said, "Aw, that ain't nothin'. He's a better pilot than I'll ever be. Hey, you guys want a drink? We ought to celebrate your visit."

Catwalk declined, but Billy Sue was all smiles when she said, "Sure, Curly, I'll have a drink. I'd like to hear all about airline flying."

As they walked away he heard Curly telling her, "There was this one time, when I was landing in Denver. It was pouring rain and I had an engine out ... ."

Catwalk thought of their similar demeanors and how well suited they were for each other. He then wondered if he'd have to look for another wing walker soon. He retired to the shack he and Curly shared and lay down with a book. He couldn't concentrate on the book because Billy Sue's words kept coming back to him, "You should let her go and move on with your life."

Yes, he should.

# Chapter Twenty-Four

Curly and Billy Sue had gone out to the Bearcat Tavern after dinner. At two o'clock they came stumbling into the shack—drunk and in love.

Curly bellowed, "Hey, Cat, guess what?"

Still half asleep, he answered, "What, Curly?"

Billy Sue yelled, "We're getting married."

Catwalk wanted to crawl under the covers, but sleepily he said, "Congratulations. When did you decide this?"

"Tonight," Curly said.

"I mean did you decide to get married when you were sober, or after you got drunk?"

Curly and Billy Sue were in a tight embrace, kissing each other with unbridled passion. When they split, Curly said, "Wha'd you say?"

Cat said, "Congratulations. I'll sleep in the barn, so you can have your privacy."

"Thanks, Cat. Hey, will you be my best man?"

"Curly, I'd be honored."

With that, Billy Sue gave him a big hug and said, "Cat, you're wonderful, and you're the best pilot I've ever worked for."

Catwalk went to the barn with the intention of sleeping, but the sounds of their love making came through the thin walls of the shack for a couple of hours. When dawn broke he walked up to the house to get a cup of coffee. He asked Julio, "Have you heard the news?"

"No, but I heard the two drunks come home late last night. Christ, they were noisy."

"They're getting married."

"Oh, really. You know, Cat, I think liquor causes as many marriages as it does divorces. I'm betting they'll wake up this morning and call a truce; make a more sensible arrangement."

"I hope so."

"If she gets married, will she still fly with you?"

"I wouldn't want to work with another man's wife; traveling around and all."

"Good thinking."

✦ ✦ ✦

Catwalk had just finished breakfast when Curly walked into the kitchen. "Morning," was all he said. He poured a cup of coffee, lit a cigarette and sat down.

Catwalk asked, "So, when is the date?"

"What do you mean? What date?"

Catwalk chuckled, "The wedding date. Last night when you two came home, you said you were getting married, but you didn't say when."

Curly looked at Catwalk with disbelief written all over his face. "Oh shit. Now I remember. Damn it, I wonder if Billy Sue remembers."

As if on cue, Billy Sue walked in, gave Curly a peck on the cheek and said, "Hi, Cat. Hi, honey. You don't look too good this morning."

"Yeah, too much whiskey, I think. How do you feel?"

"I feel wonderful. I haven't danced like that in ages." She twirled and danced around the kitchen, reliving her fantastic night.

Curly said, "I don't remember too much of last night. Do you remember everything that we did, Billy Sue?"

"I sure do." She said with a smile.

Curly looked at Catwalk, who raised his eyebrows. Then Curly asked, "Did we, ah, did we talk about getting married?"

"We sure did, honey. You said we could get hitched right after you get your next pay raise. I'm so excited. What do you think, Cat?"

"I think it's wonderful, but I'll have to find another wing walker."

"Why?" She asked with a hurt expression. "I can still work with you after I'm married."

"I don't think it would be right to be traveling around with another man's wife."

Curly said, "I don't mind. If Billy Sue wants to keep working with you, I'm fine with that. If I can't trust you, Cat, who can I trust?"

Billy Sue said, "There. See. He don't mind."

Catwalk smiled, but then shook his head. "Billy Sue, I like working with you, but it's different now that you're spoken for."

Curly, who wasn't as excited about the upcoming nuptials, seized the opportunity. "Well, maybe we should postpone the wedding for a while so you can fly some more."

Billy Sue countered, emphatically, "No way, Jose!" She sat down and looked Curly in the eye. "Are you having second thoughts?"

"No, Billy Sue, but … ." He never got to finish.

"But, what? Do you want to get married or not?"

"Well, I do, Billy Sue. But, maybe we're rushing into this."

"Oh, now I get it. Last night it was I love you, Billy Sue, and Billy Sue, I can't live without you. But, today after you got your piece of ass, it's a different story. Now that you've ridden the horse, you're not so sure you want to buy it, right?"

"No, Billy Sue, that's not it at all. I just think we made a decision last night that should have been made when we were sober."

Billy Sue turned to Catwalk and said, "When is your next show?"

"I'm going up to the Douglas County Fair in Colorado Springs, day after tomorrow."

Emphatically, Billy Sue said, "I'm going with you, and I'm not spoken for."

Catwalk looked at Curly who shrugged his shoulders. He said, "O.K. I've got to help Julio with some maintenance. I'm taking the Boeing up later if you want to go."

"Sure, Catwalk, I'll go anywhere as long as he's not flying."

◆ ◆ ◆

On his way to the hangar, Catwalk thought about the scene he'd just witnessed. He liked Billy Sue, but she and Curly were two of a kind; wild and prone to making irresponsible decisions. He wondered if they'd end up together, even though she hated him now. Then he thought about Sam. Her questions used to catch him off guard, but she was easy to talk to, and he felt if they'd had the chance, they wouldn't have gotten married until the time was right. It was times like this that he realized how right they had been for each other, and how much he still missed her.

At the hangar Julio asked, "When is the date?"

"Curly had second thoughts, then they had a fight and now the wedding is off."

"Was Billy Sue ready to go through with it?"

"She was, but now she's pretty upset."

Julio shook his head and said, "Curly gets into that booze and you never know what's going to happen."

Catwalk didn't want to belabor this, so he asked, "Do you want me change the plugs on the Boeing?"

"Yes, on engines two and three. I did number one yesterday. Then we've got to clean the fuel filters and you can take her up for a test flight."

"Good, I miss flying her."

"Are you ever going back to Rocky Mountain, or are you going to keep barnstorming?"

"I want to go back to flying for the airline, but not if it's going to affect the passenger loads. I don't want to be the cause of Barney going out of business."

Julio put down the hammer and wiped his hands on a rag. He looked at Cat and said, "Listen to me, son. Barney would rather go out of business with you flying for the airline, than stay in business with you doing something else. He wants you to be an airline pilot because he knows how much you want it. Personally, I think you should go back and don't worry about the passengers. If they want to fly with you, fine. If they don't, to hell with them. Over time people will accept colored pilots, but you can't let the ignorant ones ruin your dreams."

"Thanks, Julio. I appreciate your support."

◆ ◆ ◆

Three hours later Catwalk and Billy Sue went up for a test flight in the Boeing. Billy Sue didn't say much, except that she thought it was the most magnificent airplane she'd ever been in. Catwalk kept up a running dialog about the Boeing because he didn't want her to talk about her fight with Curly. Even so, she finally asked, "What do you think I should do, Cat?"

"I don't know, Billy Sue. It was you and him that decided to get married while you were in your cups, so you'll have to work it out with him."

"Do you think he loves me?"

"Well, he's only known you for one day. Maybe Curly can fall in love in one day, I don't know. If you want to work things out with him, you should do it when you're sober."

"You must think I'm pretty daffy, but I had such a good time last night. I can't tell you how long it's been since I had that much fun; we did the Charleston and Black Bottom for hours. I guess that's why Curly and I hit it off so well."

Catwalk didn't comment.

Billy Sue looked out the window until she asked, "Well, can I still fly with you?"

"I think I'm only going to do two more shows, the one in Colorado

Springs and then one in Garden City, Kansas. You can do those if you want to, but then I'm going to see if Barney will let me go back to fly with Rocky Mountain."

"O.K., I'll do those with you and then maybe come back here and talk to Curly. Maybe after he's had some time to think things over, we can work things out."

Catwalk said, "I hope things work out for you, Billy Sue." He was thinking, however, about his return to Rocky Mountain Airways. It was easy for everyone to say he should just ignore the passengers who didn't want to fly with him, but they didn't have to stand there and feel the revulsion, or look into their eyes and see the hatred, knowing their feelings had nothing to do with his flying ability. But, those passengers were standing between him and his dream and he resented it.

So, now it was time to make everyone proud by stepping up and staring the problem in the face. It was time for him to show the world that he had the ability to become an airline pilot and there were no obstacles that he couldn't overcome.

He returned to the field and made a textbook three point landing that brought a, "Nice grease job!" from Billy Sue. He told Julio the plane was ready to go back on the line and then wrote a six page letter to his Momma.

# Chapter Twenty-Five

Catwalk flew the two air shows with Billy Sue. They both paid well, which helped build his savings that had been dwindling due to parts he had to buy for the Jenny. After the last show he flew Billy Sue back to the farm, so she could talk to Curly. Not wanting to get in the middle of their squabble, he took off for Albuquerque, determined to shed the life of a barnstormer and resume the life of an airline pilot.

◆ ◆ ◆

When Barney saw him sitting in the operations office, he didn't mince words. "I hope you're here to work."

Catwalk stood up to shake his hand and said, "I am."

"Good. In two weeks I'm adding two trips daily to our schedule. I'll be putting both birds in service and buying a third. I'm going to need a couple more pilots. I'm breaking in a new pilot for the next two days, but starting on Wednesday you can fly with me through the end of the week to get back in the swing of things?"

"I'd like that, Barney."

"Good. In the mean time, you can help out on the ramp. I've ordered uniforms for all the employees. The ramp personnel will have tan coveralls with Rocky Mountain Airways on the back. The pilots will wear white shirts and a tan jacket with the airline symbol on the pocket. When we get everyone fitted out, I'll hire a photographer to come out and take a group picture."

◆ ◆ ◆

Over dinner that night Barney talked non-stop about the changes President Roosevelt was making, in an attempt to revive the economy. "FDR's got this guy named Harry Hopkins who is going to run the Federal Emergency Relief Administration, and he's the type that will get things done. The plan is to establish over fourteen hundred camps for the Civilian Conservation Corps, where they'll employ two hundred and fifty thousand people. The Civil Works Administration is employing eight hundred thousand people with plans of employing close to four million. Now, most of the jobs in these programs are temporary, but when people start working they start spending, and that will fuel the cycle of economic recovery."

Catwalk asked, "How soon do you think more people will be flying?"

"We've already seen an increase in passengers, but a few things have to happen before the increase is continuous. More businesses have to open, so more business people will be flying. People have to accept that flying is safe and they have to learn how much quicker it is than taking the train. One of the problems we're facing is the railroads serve meals and drinks in their dining car, so hell, the people are traveling in comfort and luxury. They're not about to give that up if they think airplanes are unsafe."

"Why can't we serve meals and drinks on our airplanes?"

Barney said, "I've heard some of the pilots at Transcontinental and Western are taking thermoses of hot coffee for the passengers. I'm going to have to keep that in mind because the day is going to come when planes are going to be flying long distances and passengers have to eat."

◆ ◆ ◆

Back at the farm, Curly and Billy Sue weren't making any progress toward a meeting of the minds. Billy Sue was ready to get married, but Curly was more hesitant than ever.

Billy Sue asked him, "Curly, do you want to get married, or not?"

Curly had been thinking about this. He liked Billy Sue and wanted to continue their relationship, but not on a permanent basis. He said, "I don't want to get married right away."

"O.K., when?"

"I don't know, Billy Sue. Maybe in a few months."

"I don't think you want to get married at all. You don't have the guts to tell me you're against it."

Curly lit a cigarette and said, "I like you, Billy Sue, but I'm not ready to get married to anyone right now. I might feel different in the future, but for now, I'm not getting married."

"Well, I'm heading back home. I guess my uncle was right."

"What do you mean?"

"About a year ago he told me, 'Billy Sue, as you go through life remember one thing; if it's got tires or testicles, it'll give you a lot of problems.'"

Curly laughed and said, "That's good, Billy Sue. Can I give you a ride to the bus depot?"

"Sure. I'll take a ride."

✦ ✦ ✦

On Wednesday morning Catwalk showed up for work an hour early. He stowed his charts in the cockpit, helped the ramp crew clean the plane, then preformed the preflight inspection. When Barney arrived they got the weather briefing and waited for the passengers.

Ten minutes before their departure time, he and Barney took their place at the bottom of the stairs. Nine passengers lined up with tickets. Two said something about having a black pilot, but as soon as they did, Barney advised them to refund their tickets and thanked them for making room for more passengers. Only one person refused to fly. The other one got halfway back to the terminal, then turned around and joined the end of the line. Barney winked at Catwalk and climbed the stairs to the cabin.

Catwalk flew the first hour of the trip in fair skies with scattered clouds, but nothing threatening. When Barney took over he said, "I'm going in back for a few minutes." He then pulled a thermos and a dozen paper cups out of his bag and said, "Our passengers are going to ride in comfort."

Catwalk offered coffee to the man who had been hesitant to fly with him.

The man refused the beverage, but asked, "Are you a porter? I thought you was one of the pilots."

Catwalk looked him in the eye and said, "I am one of the pilots."

He then served several other passengers. While serving he made it a point to talk to the people. He noticed a few who appeared to be nervous about flying, so he explained how safe the airplane was, with multiple engines and two pilots.

✦ ✦ ✦

At Denver, three people opted to refund their tickets. Before doing so Barney told them that Catwalk would be flying on a regular basis and they should plan on using another airline.

Once they were airborne, however, Catwalk went back to serve coffee and found a different attitude. The second man he served said, "I'm glad to see that the other pilot stuck by you when those people said they didn't want to fly with a black pilot. That took some guts. I'll fly with you guys any day."

Another passenger said, "Don't let these people get to you, son. You've learned to fly and I give you credit."

When Catwalk told Barney about the support, Barney said, "It's only a matter of time. They'll come around."

◆ ◆ ◆

One week later Catwalk was at the controls on the same trip with Barney. Some people were still refusing to fly, but in a short time he'd already noticed an improvement in people's attitudes toward him. Being accepted by the customers was the best thing that could have happened to Catwalk and he felt good about himself and his job again. He felt like he could fly airliners every single day for the rest of his life.

He'd just climbed to eight thousand feet to clear Raton Pass, when the number one engine started missing. He retarded, then advanced the throttle, but it still sputtered.

Barney had been in back talking to the passengers when he heard the RPM change on the engine. He returned to the cockpit and Catwalk said, "Number one is acting like it's got a clogged carburetor jet."

Number two started doing the same thing. Both pilots realized that the chances of two carburetors jets clogging at the same time, were astronomical. Catwalk said, "Fuel contamination! Try changing tanks. If that doesn't work, we've got to find a field, fast!"

Barney changed fuel tanks, but this didn't seem to help. Number three engine started coughing and number one died completely.

Catwalk looked ahead of them for a suitable landing field, but they had just cleared the pass so the terrain was still mountainous.

Barney muttered, "Ain't a God damned place to land that I can see."

Catwalk looked at his rate of descent in the glide. His altimeter was unwinding at a steady rate and he knew he'd have to find a place to land soon or they'd be crashing into the side of a mountain. He craned his neck to look out the windows and asked Barney, "How about that open space at one o'clock?"

"It ain't any good. There's a shear drop-off at the end. If we don't get stopped and we're all going down the mountain."

Catwalk looked out his side and saw the ground closing in on them. Then, he saw a level field, which was very small, but it might be the only opportunity to land that they'd have. He said, "Over here at ten o'clock it looks like there's a level area just beyond that farm house."

Barney stretched to look out the window. "It's level, but it's too small to for this plane."

"It's our only chance. I'm setting it down there."

Number two engine died as Catwalk maneuvered the powerless plane toward the tiny field. He noticed, not only was the field small, but there were the hills beyond it and he had to clear the farm house to get to the field. If he didn't make this landing, they'd crash into the hills.

He watched as the farm house grew larger in the windshield, but the field didn't seem to get any larger. He skimmed the top of the farm house and saw a man beside the house who looked up in fright as the airliner passed not more than ten feet above his house. Number three engine died as Catwalk saw the roof pass a few feet beneath the plane.

He pushed the nose down toward the edge of the field and seconds before he plowed in, he hauled back on the stick and flared to a hard landing. He and Barney jumped on the brakes and the Boeing came to a stop with thirty feel to spare.

Barney went back to tell the passengers what happened. After he explained about the contaminated fuel, several of the passengers complimented him on the fine job of making a safe landing with all three engines out. With pride he told them it was Catwalk who made the miracle landing in the only place within miles that was level enough for a landing field.

When Catwalk came out of the cockpit, he walked down the stairs to congratulations from all the passengers. He had arrived.

Now, he had to get the plane out of there.

# Chapter Twenty-Six

The passengers were put on a bus to Albuquerque. Barney used the farmer's phone to call Curly and tell him to fly the other Boeing to Albuquerque so it could resume service in the morning. He also told Julio to fly up in a Jenny with twenty gallons of gas. Then he asked Catwalk, "Well, you got her in here. How do you plan on getting it out of here?"

Catwalk scratched his head and said, "We're less than twenty miles from the farm in Cimarron. We'll load just enough gas to fly it to the farm on one engine. With no passengers and minimum fuel load, it should be light enough to take off in the short confines of the field."

"That's what I was thinking too. First, we've got to get that contaminated fuel out of the fuel tanks and engines."

While they waited for Julio, Catwalk and Barney drained the contaminated fuel and bled it out of the engines. When Julio arrived they put the clean fuel into the Boeing and started all three engines. After idling the engines for a few minutes Catwalk taxied to the edge of the field and turned into the wind. When he had the nose pointing into the wind, he saw a tree right smack in his departure path. He had no choice.

He held the brakes, lowered the flaps, applied full power, then released the brakes. The Boeing began it's take off roll, on what seemed like a snail's pace. Barney called out airspeeds as the plane accelerated. At eighty-five knots Catwalk pulled back on the yoke and the Boeing broke free of the field, but the tree loomed large in his windshield.

With the farm house on his right and the hill on his left, Catwalk climbed on the edge of stall speed. He knew the Boeing was going to brush the tree tops; he prayed it would just be the gear and not the props. He felt the tires passing through the tree top leaves, then breathed a sigh of relief when they were clear of the tree. He climbed to fifteen hundred feet, then cut two engines. Barney, who had been silent except for giving him the airspeeds, said, "I don't think we should put that place on our charts as an emergency field."

Catwalk said, "No, but let's send that farmer a case of whiskey."

✦ ✦ ✦

Catwalk and Barney arrived back in Albuquerque the next afternoon, just as Curly and Lem landed. Curly shouted, "Hey, Cat. Did you know you're famous?"

Catwalk wasn't sure if he heard right. "What?"

"You're famous, man. One of the passengers on that plane you landed in Raton was a reporter for the Denver Gazette. He wrote a story on you and it was in this morning's paper." Curly handed Catwalk a copy of the Denver paper.

Catwalk read the account of his forced landing that said he, "Dropped the airliner into a field not much bigger than a boxing ring, and landed as gently as a butterfly with sore feet."

He showed the article to Barney who smiled and said, "Be sure to send a copy to Dee."

✦ ✦ ✦

Catwalk's notoriety from the forced landing resulted in a renewed relationship with the passengers. Not a week went by that a passenger didn't ask him about it and many of the passengers enjoyed having him at the controls. There were still a few people who refused to fly his trips, but it less frequent. As time went on his love of his career increased. He was convinced he was one of the luckiest men alive.

✦ ✦ ✦

Barney had applied for another route, this one from Denver to Salt Lake City, with a stop in Grand Junction. It was approved in the spring of '36. Since the new route took them over the heart of the Rockies, all Rocky Mountain Airways pilots went to Denver to attend a course of flying in mountainous terrain. It was while he was at this course that Catwalk ran into Kenneth Jackson, one of the few black pilots he knew who flew for a small charter outfit.

Catwalk asked him, "What are you doing up here?"

"I put in a job application at United."

Surprised, Catwalk said, "Aren't you with Air Express anymore?"

"No, they cut back and since I didn't have seniority, I was one of the first to go."

"I'm sorry to hear that. Hopefully, you'll hear something soon from United."

"Well, you know how it is for a black pilot trying to land a flying job; damn near impossible. I might head back to Chicago and see if they're hiring there."

"Ken, we're adding another route. Barney might be hiring more pilots, and he just wants experienced, dependable pilots."

"That sounds great. When I get back down to Albuquerque, I'll put in an application."

"I'll mention to him that I know a good pilot who's looking for work."

◆ ◆ ◆

On the flight back Catwalk though about the possibility of Kenneth going to work for Rocky Mountain. After what he'd been through, he wasn't sure if he was doing him a favor by recommending him.

◆ ◆ ◆

Two days later Catwalk was driving home from the airport and noticed a familiar green truck in front of him, weaving all over the road. He recognized Curly driving and muttered, "Oh, no." He honked.

Curly looked in the mirror, recognized Catwalk and pulled over. He got out, flask in hand and obviously drunk. "Hey, Cat."

"Curly, it's only two o'clock and you're drunk again. You know what Barney thinks about your drinking. Are you trying to get fired?"

Curly opened the passenger door, sat down and lit a cigarette. He took another swig and offered the flask to Catwalk, who declined. He said, "Cat, today I've got a good reason for drinking. I might have to quit flying for Rocky Mountain."

"Are you kidding me? What's wrong?"

"I got a letter from my brother. Things are real bad at home. There's no money coming in and they're going to lose the farm. That bitch Theresa is making life so miserable, Jack says he's about ready to shoot her. And, my old man is sick, they think it's cancer."

"Why don't you take some time off like I did. Barney will give it to you. Go back and see what's wrong with your Dad."

"If I go back, I won't be able to leave. My brother didn't say so, but I think he wants me to come back to run the place while Dad's sick. He probably thinks with me there, we might be able to save the farm and that bitch won't be so mean."

"Does Barney know about this?"

"Not yet. I'm going to tell him tonight."

"You better wait and tell him when you're sober. If he sees you drunk again, he might fire you on the spot."

"Let him fire me. I don't care, Cat."

"In case you don't remember, you told me I was crazy for quitting my flying job. You'll never find another job like this, or a boss like Barney."

Curly said nothing for several seconds, then, "So what do I do?"

"Stay away from Barney until you're sober, then talk to him."

"Yeah, I guess you're right. Thanks, Cat."

✦ ✦ ✦

Curly talked to Barney the next day, who understood his dilemma. Barney told him he'd give him the time off, but he wanted two weeks notice to adjust crew schedules. Curly agreed, although he was apprehensive about leaving the airline. He was also worried about what he'd find when he went back to the farm. In his mind, he had a valid excuse for drinking.

# Chapter Twenty-Seven

Catwalk went back to work on the Albuquerque to Denver leg the next morning. He was glad to get back in the air and away from everyone else's problems. Talking with Curly, however, had reminded him that he hadn't been home in several months. In her letters his Mom had said the family was fine, but still he longed to see them.

In Denver, Catwalk laid over for the night, then paired up with Barney for the leg to Salt Lake City with a stop in Grand Junction. As soon as they reached their cruising altitude, Catwalk asked, "I haven't been back to see my family for a while. Any problem if I request some time off from crew scheduling?"

"No problem, but you'd better hurry. If Curly leaves we might be short of pilots." Barney then showed Catwalk a photograph of a new airliner that was being built by the Douglas Company. "They call it the DC-1. She'll carry eighteen passengers; cruise at a hundred and ninety knots, with a range of fourteen hundred miles."

Catwalk couldn't believe his eyes. The plane was all metal, had a single wing and twice as big as the Boeing Model 80. It only had two engines, but if Barney was right, it would outperform the Boeing in every category. He said, "When will they be available?"

"They're starting test flights in a month and they'll be taking orders in July. I'm ordering two. A couple months after that I'll start sending our mechanics back to St. Louis for training."

"Our loads have been good. Having new equipment should increase them even more."

Barney said, "Flying is getting to be very popular and with the faster planes it'll be much quicker than the train. And, this plane will work out well with my long range plans."

Catwalk said, "What are your future plans for the airline?"

"I'm going to apply for two new routes, one from Salt Lake to San Francisco and another from Albuquerque to Phoenix. We'll open the routes when we get the new planes. I've got an architectural firm designing a maintenance hangar and administrative offices that will be built at Albuquerque. Julio will be moving the maintenance duties out there as soon as it's done. I want to make you the chief pilot of Rocky Mountain Airways. This means you'll be in charge of crew proficiency and training, and speak for all the pilots in matters that concern management."

Catwalk was stunned. He was so happy flying for the airline, he'd never thought beyond that. If Barney expanded the routes like he'd planned that meant the airline would soon have several dozen pilots, and he'd be speaking for all of them, a responsibility not to be taken lightly. His concern was how the pilots would feel about being represented by a black man. He knew all the current pilots and got along well with them. As far as he could tell, race was not an issue. If they hired several more, he figured there would inevitably be someone who didn't want him representing them. Obviously, Barney had taken this into consideration, so he wasn't about to let this stop him. He said, "I'd be honored to be your chief pilot, Barney."

"Curly has more flying time and more seniority than you do, but, he might be leaving us for a while and quite frankly, I'm concerned about his drinking. You have to realize that I'm putting you in a position where there might be some disagreement between us in the future."

"Why is that?"

"I know you've read about the labor unions that are being formed to represent the work force in other jobs."

"Yes, I've read about them representing miners and railroad workers."

"Union representation is getting to be very popular. They'll be representing airline pilots before long. When the pilots unionize, you and I will be on opposite sides of the fence."

Catwalk thought about this as he eased back the throttles to start their descent into Grand Junction. He said, "I'm not worried about that."

"Good. Neither am I."

✦ ✦ ✦

Two days later, when Catwalk returned to Albuquerque, he and Curly were talking over lunch and the future plans for the airline came up in their conversation. When Catwalk told him about the plans, including his possible promotion to chief pilot, Curly didn't take the news well. "Cat, after all the shit you been through, I don't have a problem with you getting the promotion, but I don't see how Barney could do this. I'm the senior pilot."

Catwalk had expected him to be upset, and he'd decided he wasn't going to placate him, or sympathize with him. He said, "Curly, you can't blame him. He's concerned about your drinking, and the fact that you might be leaving the airline for a while."

"Aw bullshit, Cat. That's a crock. He could of at least said something to me."

"We all said something to you. Julio and I told you to watch your drinking."

Curly lit a cigarette, then said, "Well, that does it. I'm giving him my resignation and leaving. I'm going back home."

Catwalk warned him against doing anything he might regret later, but his words fell on deaf ears. In his despondent state Curly didn't give Barney the two weeks notice he wanted. Two days later he resigned and left for New York.

✦ ✦ ✦

Because Curly had left them in a bind with his short notice departure, Catwalk had to wait two months to get his week off. When the time came to go back home, he packed his bags and two new dresses that he bought for his Mom into the Jenny and took off. It had been several months since he'd flown the Jenny and he'd forgotten how different flying in the open cockpit was from the plush, comfortable Boeing. However, he enjoyed the flight without having to worry about schedules or passengers.

He arrived at Meridian late the next day and surprised his family while they were eating dinner. He popped his head in the door and said, "Do you have enough for another mouth?"

"Oh my God, Luke." His Mother cried as she wrapped her arms around him.

He sat down to eat with his family and they all had questions about his job with the airline. While talking about his job, it struck Catwalk just how much his life had changed, and how far removed he'd become from his life as a sharecropper. He hoped he could use his experience to help the rest of his family to get off the farm and find work that came with a future.

With this in mind, he told John, "The airline is growing. We'll be hiring more mechanics soon. Would you be interested in becoming an airframe and power plant mechanic?"

John's face lit up in a broad grin. "Of course I would, Luke. Do you think you could get me into a job like that?"

"I'm pretty sure I can. Of course, you'd have to move to Albuquerque and you'd have to go to school, but you get paid while you do."

John looked at Dee who had a smile on her face. He said, "Yes, I'd go in a minute."

Luke knew his Mother was smiling in support of John's wishes, but below the surface, she'd be distressed about another child leaving home. He also knew she'd never let on how she felt, or do anything to stand in John's way. He said, "I'll look into it and write you."

He then unwrapped the new dresses and gave them to his Mother, who was speechless. Everyone urged her to put on the yellow dress, which she did. Georgie summed up everyone's feelings when he said, "Momma, you look too pretty to work in the fields."

Catwalk said, "Momma, you look so elegant. I want to do something for you. How would you like to spend a night in a hotel where I'm staying."

His Mother looked hurt. "Luke, you're not staying with us?"

"Momma, I thought you and I could stay at a hotel tonight and tomorrow morning you could eat in their restaurant. Wouldn't you like that?"

"They won't serve us in their restaurant. You should know that."

"I've already talked to them. They have a black manager and they'll serve us."

"Luke, I appreciate your thoughtfulness, but I'm not going. This is my home and my family. Unless all of us can go, I don't go. Are you too important to stay with your family?"

"No, Momma. I'll stay here tonight." His Momma smiled and he said, "There's something else I'd like to talk to you about."

"What's that, son?"

"Well, I've been able to save some money. When I've got enough saved up, I'm going to make a down payment on a house for you and the family."

"Oh, Luke, do you mean we might be able to get off this farm?"

"I hope so, Momma. I don't have enough saved up yet, but when I do Barney said he'll help me buy you a house, with curtains on the windows and a flower garden."

Through tears of joy and relief, she said, "Luke, that would be a dream come true."

Later that evening, Luke walked down to the creek with John and Georgie. John said, "Luke, that's the happiest I've ever seen Momma. I hope I can help her out like that one day."

"I hope so too, John. She deserves all the help we can give her."

Before he fell asleep that night, Catwalk thought about his job and wondered what the future held for him. Right now, his life was good, although he still missed Sam terribly. He wondered if he'd ever meet another woman who could light up his life like she did.

# Chapter Twenty-Eight

Catwalk returned to New Mexico and spent the next several months splitting his time between flying and helping Julio prepare for the move into the new hangar. The hangar construction wouldn't start for another month, but Barney wanted everything ready so when the first sections of then new hangar were completed, they could start moving. They were going over the blueprints of the hangar when Billy Sue drove up in her Ford roadster.

She waved and said, "Hi, Cat, is Curly around?"

He noticed she was carrying a baby. "Hi, Billy Sue. He's not here. He went back to New York several months ago. They think his Dad has cancer and they're about to lose the farm."

"Any idea when he'll be back?"

"I don't know. He resigned from Rocky Mountain, so I think he's staying there to help his brothers until things get better."

"Wonderful." She pulled back the blanket so Catwalk could see the baby's face. "This is David. He's Curly's son."

Catwalk concealed his surprise and looked at the tiny sleeping baby. He said, "He's a beautiful baby, Billy Sue. Does Curly know?"

"No, and I don't think he'd care if he did know."

"C'mon up to the house."

They walked to the porch where Catwalk said, "You want a cup of coffee?"

"That would be fabulous, Cat."

As Catwalk poured, he thought about this situation. He didn't want to get involved in Curly and Billy Sue's problems, but he was worried that Billy Sue would tell Curly about the baby, and he wouldn't want anything to do with it. He knew the misery she faced trying to raise a baby as a single Mother in these hard times.

He asked Billy Sue, "Are you working now?"

"I'm waiting tables in Odessa, but I don't know how long that'll last. The restaurant is about ready to close. I had to quit wing walking when I got pregnant. Man, was I surprised."

"When Curly left here he was pretty upset. Before he left he said the farm wasn't doing well, so I don't know if he'll be able to help you out financially."

"That figures. If I didn't have bad luck, I wouldn't have any at all."

Catwalk hesitated as he thought of how he could help her. He said, "I'll write him to find out if he's planning on coming back out here. Do you want me to tell him that he's a father?"

"I don't know. What do you think he'll say?"

"I have no idea, Billy Sue. Either way, I doubt that he'll come back out here for a while."

"Don't tell him yet, Cat."

"O.K., I doubt if he'll answer anyway. He never was much for writing letters."

"I appreciate that, Cat. Have you been flying any air shows lately?"

"No, I haven't. We just opened up a route to Salt Lake City, so I'm flying more hours with the airline and we're getting ready to move into a new hangar at the airport in Albuquerque."

"Well, at least for you a dream came true."

"I can't believe how fortunate I've been, and it's all been due to Barney."

"He sounds like such a nice man. I'd love to meet him sometime. Is he flying now."

"Yeah. He's got the Salt Lake to Denver leg today, and tomorrow morning he returns home and I go back to work."

Little David started making hungry noises. Billy Sue Said, "He's getting hungry, I'd better go in and heat a bottle."

Catwalk thought about Curly being a father. He knew he hadn't planned on it, or even thought about it, but he hated to see Billy Sue face the prospect of raising a baby alone. He suspected Curly was not having an easy time of it back on the farm and raising a son was the last thing on his mind.

◆ ◆ ◆

When Curly had arrived back on the farm, he found an atmosphere of hate and chaos. His Father, bedridden with colon cancer, had been given a month to live. Curly's brothers refused to work for their step-Mother, or even live in the same house with her, so they'd moved into the barn. They were still doing the chores on the farm, but everything they grew and harvested was consumed or given away, since there was no market for the crops. With no crop sales, there was no income and they were several months behind on their mortgage payment. In its present state, the farm faced certain foreclosure within a few months. As Curly would learn, however, all the farms in the area were going through lean times. Everyone was working hard, just to keep the wolf from the door.

Curly's Dad, although overcome with his illness and the problems facing them, appeared grateful to see that his eldest son had returned home to help the family.

Curly said, "Papa, I came home because Phil wrote to me and told me about all the problems around here. The first thing I'm going to do is keep the farm from foreclosure, although I'm not sure how. Besides that, I'm making some changes and the first one is, Charley, Phil and Maury are moving back in the house. This is their home and they shouldn't have to live in the barn. Theresa will treat them with the respect they deserve, or she'll be leaving."

His Father knew questioning his son would be futile. When Curly had first walked into his room, he'd seen a grown man who'd been hardened by life on the road. There was nothing he could do to ease the rift between his wife and son, so he merely asked, "Abraham, all I ask is that your treat my wife with the respect she deserves."

Out of respect for his dying Father, Curly said, "I will, Papa." Then he thought, until you die, then I'm throwing her ass out of here.

His Father asked, "What can you do about the farm, Son? We haven't made a mortgage payment in four months."

"On my way out here I talked to Hiram Levine and Shorty Walker. Tomorrow night we're having a meeting of all the land owners around here. Everyone is in the same situation, so we're trying to come up with a plan to prevent foreclosures."

"They already took Seth Henderson's place."

"I know. Maybe we can save the rest."

His Father looked at him with tired, dying eyes and said, "Good luck, son."

Curly left so his Father could get some rest. Theresa came in and sat down beside her husband. He said nothing and turned his head away so she couldn't see him smiling at the peaceful prospect of dying.

❖ ❖ ❖

The following night Curly attended a meeting where the objective was to save their farms in the face of foreclosures. After he'd talked with other farmers, Curly thought of the plush life he'd given up as an airline pilot. Life in the farm, especially a failing farm was about as far from that life as you can get. He wondered if he'd ever return to the good life of working for Rocky Mountain again.

His thoughts were interrupted as a man stood on a flour barrel and said, "Men, listen up. I've been talking to people from other parts of the country, and I've got news; some good, some not. The CCC camps and WPA projects have put people back to work, but the impact of the new jobs hasn't affected the crop demand yet. The farm bureau estimates several months yet before we see the demand for our crops increase. The estimated number of farms that have been lost to foreclosure is seven hundred thousand. But, out in Iowa they've had some success at dealing with foreclosures. Here's how they did it; every time they held an auction, the local land owners would make low bids, less than a dollar, until the farm was sold for a price that would allow the owner to buy his farm back. If anyone came in and tried to get the place with a higher bid, they found themselves looking down the barrel of a shotgun."

Someone shouted, "What about the police? I heard they were bringing in police to stop this sort of thing."

"If the police show up and try to stop our bidding, we've got to be prepared to disarm them and throw them off the property."

Shouts of agreement filled the room. Although the men knew this plan could turn violent, they were desperate, willing to try anything to save their property. If violence was included in the solution, so be it.

The man continued, "Day after tomorrow they're having an auction at George Pearson's farm. I say we show up and put this plan into action to see what we can do for George." The place erupted in shouts of unity and acceptance of their plan. This was the first glimmer of hope the men had seen for keeping their farms. The meeting was adjourned and the men congregated around a keg of beer that Curly had provided.

◆ ◆ ◆

The next night, Curly showed up at the Pearson auction, as many other men from the area did; armed with a pistol concealed in his overalls. They then took their stations and waited for the auctioneer to begin the auction proceedings. The first item to be auctioned was the mortgage on the farm which was for eight hundred dollars. One man opened the bidding, "I bid five cents."

The auctioneer acknowledged the bid and another man cried out, "Ten cents."

As was bound to happen, an outsider who didn't know what was going on, made a higher bid, trying to steal the farm at a bargain price. "Two hundred dollars!"

He immediately found himself surrounded by several scowling farmers. Two men held him as Curly stuck his pistol in the guy's gut and said, "You bid is a little high. Why don't you withdraw it, so I don't have to pull the trigger?"

Just loud enough for the auctioneer to hear, the man said, "I withdraw my bid."

As this took place, a deputy made the mistake of approaching the men who'd forced the bid withdrawal. The men surrounded and overpowered the officer, then took his gun and badge and threw them in a watering trough. The deputy was told, "You just stay out of this and everything will be peaceful like."

By now the auctioneer knew what the locals had planned; the bids were going to be kept low enough so Pearson could keep his farm. He finished the bidding for the mortgage, which sold back to Pearson for two dollars. The livestock was sold to other men, who gave it back to Pearson, for a nickel a head. Everyone left the auction feeling like a ten ton lead weight had been lifted off their shoulders. It wasn't because Pearson had kept his farm that had them so elated. It was because for the first time in several years, they felt like they had some control, albeit slight, over their destiny. They left the auction feeling like they could stand on their own two feet again without being repeatedly knocked down.

As a show of unity and fellowship, the farmers then took several cans of milk to the nearest towns where they donated it to hungry children. When Curly arrived home and told his brothers about the auctions, they thought he was a miracle worker. His Father admonished, "You better be careful, son. People are getting killed in some of these shenanigans that are taking place."

Curly told him not to worry, then left for the local tavern for a much needed drink.

# Chapter Twenty-Nine

Barney and Lem departed Grand Junction at eleven o'clock bound for Denver. They'd seen the weather report that indicated thunderstorm activity in their route of flight, but Barney thought if the storms became a factor, he had plenty of room to circumnavigate the storm.

As they passed Glenwood Springs darkening skies filled the distant horizon. Barney told Lem, "Plot me a course that'll take us north of Mt. Powell and then toward Boulder."

Lem taped a slip to his yoke with a heading of zero-five-zero degrees.

Barney had been on this heading for ten minutes when he said, "This storm is moving right into our flight path. I'm turning further north."

When he turned, however, the darkening clouds seemed to follow him. He noticed several lightning strikes, which mean thunderstorm activity—an airliner's worst enemy. Storms like this could spawn severe turbulence and down drafts that could easily slam the Boeing into a mountain like she was a toy.

He said, "This is getting bad, Lem. The tops are too high to go over the storm; we might have to turn around and head back to Glenwood Springs."

"I think that's our best bet. Let me get you a heading."

Barney started a slow turn and said, "Before you do, go back and tell the passengers that we're turning around due to the weather. We'll try to land at Glenwood, but we might have set down up in Meeker."

Barney rolled out on a westerly heading and his worst fears were realized; the storm had closed in behind them. He faced a wall of black clouds streaked with lighting and wind-whipped rain. Lem sat down and Barney said, "We're right in the middle of this thing and it's building fast. Plot our position and get a heading to the Colorado River. If I can descend into the river valley, we might be able to get under the clouds." As Barney said this, he knew he was playing Russian Roulette. Making a blind descent in mountainous territory, while in the middle of a violent thunderstorm was risky at best.

In gale force winds Barney fought the control yoke. Lightning flashed and booming thunder filled the airplane, as streaks of St. Elmo's fire danced across the instrument panel.

Lem poured over a chart for a minute, then shouted, "We should be right over the river valley. Descend on this heading and we can follow the river into Glenwood Springs."

Barney started a five hundred foot per minute descent. He tried to weave his way around the clouds to maintain some forward visibility. Despite his best efforts, the turbulence continually threw the plane into the clouds. He saw only the driving rain. His grim realization was, the violence of the storm had transformed he and Lem from pilots— into passengers.

The altimeter unwound through ten thousand feet, as Barney fought to keep the plane on a westerly heading. An incredibly loud crash of thunder reverberated through the plane and Barney felt the rudder go slack under the pedals. He yelled, "Lightning strike, got the rudder!"

A second later, Lem saw an opening in the storm and shouted, "A field, one o'clock!"

Barney caught a glimpse of a beautiful green pasture a couple thousand feet below them, but a violent updraft grabbed the plane and tossed it to a south heading. The field, which might have saved their lives, disappeared. The updraft was followed by an intense down draft that stressed the wings to their limit as Barney fought the controls.

The next thing they saw was the side of a mountain rushing at them. Both men cranked the yoke hard to the right, barely avoiding a head on crash into the mountain. Barney thought they had saved the plane, but then heard the grinding sound of a treetop ripping off the landing gear. The plane plunged nose first into the trees. When he felt the jolt, Barney's last conscious act was to turn off the fuel switch— then, darkness.

✦ ✦ ✦

Catwalk, Julio and Billy Sue were in the middle of dinner when the phone rang. Julio answered and started asking questions. Catwalk overheard enough to know something bad had happened. Julio confirmed his fears, "Barney and Lem's flight is overdue in Denver. They departed Grand Junction at eleven this morning, but there was a bad storm system in their route of flight. They haven't been heard from since."

Catwalk thought about the extensive mountainous terrain on the route of flight. Other than the open ocean, there was no more daunting place to make an emergency landing. "Did they say how many passengers were on board?"

"Six passengers, three hundred pounds of cargo and two hundred pounds of mail."

"Call the weather service and see which way that storm was moving. That might give us an indication where Barney had to deviate. Then call Denver and make sure search and rescue has been sent out."

Billy Sue asked, "What are you going to do?"

"I'm going to get Don Blake to fly my trips for the next few days. Then I'm taking a Jenny to look for them."

Julio said, "I'll go with you."

"O.K. I'll pack our cold weather gear and a couple days food. Billy Sue, you can stay as long as you want to. When you leave just lock the doors."

"Good luck, guys."

◆ ◆ ◆

Barney regained consciousness an hour after the crash. When he saw the way Lem's head was bent, he was sure he'd died from a broken neck. He unbuckled, climbed out of his seat and checked Lem's pulse; there was none. He then noticed plane was laying at an angle with the nose and right side down.

He then looked to the rear and saw four passengers that also appeared to be dead. Two people, however, looked up when they heard him moving. He said, "Are you hurt bad?"

A man said, "My leg is busted, but my wife is OK, just some bruises."

"It looks like everyone else died in the crash." Barney then crawled across the seats, checking the pulse on the remaining passengers. He said, "We're the only survivors."

Barney looked out a window. The mountain sloped sharply downward, but trees were supporting the aircraft and keeping it from tumbling downhill. He said, "We'll have to spend the night in the plane. I'm going to the rear to collect blankets and emergency water, then I'll make a splint for your leg."

The wife said, "I'll find something for the splint."

"Use whatever you need. This plane ain't much good for anything now." Barney then thought about which plane he was flying. He cursed under his breath when he realized—the plane he'd crashed was the Samantha Jean.

♦ ♦ ♦

Catwalk and Julio flew to Albuquerque to talk to weather forecasters. Information on the storm was sketchy, but they learned that it had moved through the mountains on a northerly track. Unfortunately, they had no way of correlating the movement of the storm to Barney's flight. If he departed before the storm, he would have deviated north. Had he departed after the storm, however, he might have flown south around the storm.

Catwalk looked at the chart and said, "I'm betting he went north. Deviating south would have taken him toward the higher peaks, and Barney always preached that mountains and airplanes don't mix well."

Julio said, "I agree, but that still leaves a whole chunk of country to search."

Catwalk said, "Put on your cold weather gear and fill two thermoses with coffee. We'll fly the Jenny to Denver tonight. In the morning we'll back track his flight path."

"Got'cha."

♦ ♦ ♦

Barney carried the dead bodies outside and covered them with a parachute. He looked around the plane to see if there was a chance of it sliding down the mountain. He was relieved to see that it was supported by several large trees. He then looked at the surrounding terrain to determine if they could hike out. They'd have to go straight down the mountain, which would be difficult for him and the woman; it would impossible to carry her husband out.

Back in the plane, he helped the couple, whose names he learned were Art and Helen Gates, get comfortable for the night. Art's leg was in a splint and Helen's cuts had been treated, so now all they had to do was stay warm. Barney went back to the cockpit and made several more Mayday calls, but he suspected there was no one within the range of his radios. He then joined the couple in back and bundled up to wait out the night.

Art said, "Do you think anyone is looking for us?"

"I'm sure someone is, but they probably don't know where to look. We were pretty far off course due to that storm. I might try to start a signal fire in the morning. Trouble is, were in such a wooded area that it's dangerous starting a fire."

Helen said, "Do you know if we're close to a town?"

"I don't think so. I plotted our position, but I doubt it's correct because the storm blew us around so much. Near as I can figure, we're about twenty miles from Kremmling."

A silence fell over them as each person considered their fate.

✦ ✦ ✦

When Catwalk landed at Denver, he couldn't remember being so cold, but he was glad they made the flight. The Rocky Mountain employees were waiting for them with fresh coffee and a hot meal. He and Julio ate, then laid out their plans for the morning. The Denver station manager asked him, "Are you going to wait until you hear from search and rescue?"

Catwalk said, "No. We're going to back track his proposed route of flight and fly a grid pattern in the area where the storm was the worst. Have you checked with the forest service to see if any fires have been reported?"

"We did. There are two fires not far from Aspen that are believed to be from lightning strikes. Forest rangers are enroute to check them out."

"Good. Julio, can you think of anything else we can do?"

"Just get some sleep, and pray."

✦ ✦ ✦

Barney spent most of the night thinking about his next move. His instincts told him to start walking to see if he could find a town or ranch. Taking off blindly, however, could be a mistake. He had no idea of which direction to go and if he became lost, the chances of anyone finding a single person would be worse than spotting an airplane wreckage. Since they had food, water and shelter, he decided to stay put.

At first light he went out to find an area where he could start a signal fire. He'd walked down the mountain a quarter mile when he came to a clearing. He then used his binoculars to search the landscape to see if he could spot any activity, or smoke from a chimney. He saw nothing.

Back at the plane, he told Helen, "I found a clearing where I can start a fire. I'll fix our morning C rations, then drain some fuel and start a fire. While I was down there I looked for signs of civilization. There's nothing out there but trees."

"Well, I'm confident they'll find us. Do you have anything for pain? He hasn't said anything, but I think Art's in quite a bit of pain"

"I'll get some morphine from my first aid kit."

After the meager breakfast, Barney collected enough fuel for a fire. He then walked back to the clearing. His next step was to find some dry wood. He was carrying his second load of wood back to the clearing when he heard what he thought was a car engine in the distance. He dropped the wood, grabbed his binoculars and hurried back to the area.

He stood at the edge of a drop off and scanned the mountain side. He heard and saw nothing. He scanned again hoping to see some sort of human activity, but there was nothing.

As Barney turned to leave the rain soaked ground gave way under his feet. He turned to grab anything that might stop his fall, but only clawed at the dirt, while he slid downward. Gaining speed, Barney slid down the steep incline until he came to a cliff. Unable to stop, he went over the cliff and landed on his upper back thirty feet below.

The fall knocked the wind out of him, but that wasn't the worst of his problems. When he regained his breath, Barney made a horrifying discovery—he could not move his body below his neck. He yelled for help, knowing it was futile. He was too far from the airplane; no one would hear his desperate call.

# Chapter Thirty

Catwalk and Julio took off half an hour before sunrise, to search the area east of Glenwood Springs. Cat started by flying a north to south grid with twenty minute legs. Each time they refueled he'd fly a grid farther east. By noon they had logged five hours air time, but hadn't seen a thing that resembled the remains of the Boeing.

◆ ◆ ◆

After an hour Helen began to worry about Barney. She lived in Grand Junction and knew the hills were full of bear and large cats. Attacks on humans were not uncommon. Art had dozed off and Helen climbed out of the wreckage to look for Barney. She remembered him telling her that he had found a clearing a quarter mile down the mountain side. She started down.

Barney yelled for help every few minutes. He could see enough of the terrain around him to tell he was on a shelf in the side of a mountain. No one was going to run across him by accident. If he was going to be found, he needed to let someone know where he was.

Helen found the clearing and his two cans of fuel. She then saw the logs he'd carried over for the fire. She yelled, "Barneyyy!"

Barney heard her and returned the cry, "Down here, Helen."

She heard his voice but couldn't tell where it was coming from. She walked toward it and heard, "Helen, I've fallen down on a shelf and I can't move. Can you hear me?"

"Yes, Barney, I can hear you."

"Don't try to get to me, because you might fall. Clear out an area and start the signal fire. Once it gets going good, put some moss or wet logs on it to make it smoke."

"O.K., Barney. Is there any way I can get down to you?"

"I don't think so. Get the fire going."

Helen went back to the clearing and built the fire. She then returned to check on Art, who was still asleep. She worried about Barney because he said he couldn't move, which meant he'd have to spend the night with no protection from the elements, or the predatory animals.

✦ ✦ ✦

Catwalk and Julio flew all afternoon, but saw nothing. Every couple hours, they coordinated with Rocky Mountain Rescue to insure that they didn't duplicate their search efforts. They were on their last grid before returning for fuel when Julio yelled, "Cat, I see smoke. Three o'clock, halfway up that hill in the distance."

Catwalk banked right and searched for the smoke. "Where is it, Julio? I don't see it."

"Hold this heading; it's at twelve thirty."

Catwalk spied the thin wisp of smoke and said, "I've got it!. Mark it on a chart. It looks too small to be a forest fire."

"Yeah, but there sure as hell ain't no where around there to land."

"We'll have to land down below the hill and hike up to the fire."

"First, we have to refuel."

Catwalk looked at the fuel gauge. He muttered, "Damn it. By the time we get back, it'll be dark." There was no denying that fuel was their first consideration. He yelled to Julio, "I'm going to make a low pass over the fire. If they see us, they'll know help is on the way." Catwalk maneuvered the Jenny to make his pass as close to the fire as he could.

Helen didn't see him because she was in the Boeing with Art. Barney, however, heard the Jenny when it was several miles away. As the sound grew louder, he craned his neck toward it. When he saw the familiar Jenny, he yelled, "God almighty damn! We're down here; you've found us!"

He then looked at the skies. Twilight was just setting and the Jenny couldn't land anywhere close. That meant the rescuers would have to land elsewhere, then climb up to them and that could take hours. He wondered, would they try tonight, or would he spend the night here, unable to move and exposed to the elements and the creatures. He heard Helen's voice. "Barney, can you hear me?"

"I can hear you, Helen. Did you see the airplane?"

"No, I was in the plane with Art. I came out to put another log on the fire."

"Someone knows where we are, but I don't think they'll get to us tonight. They should be here in the morning."

"I brought some blankets. I'm going to try to climb down to you so I can cover you up."

Barney thought, a couple blankets would help him make it through the night, but he was worried about her trying to get to him. He yelled, "Don't try it, Helen. I don't want you to fall. You have to keep the fire going."

Helen knew he was right, but hated the thought of him spending the night down there with no protection. Finally, she decided she had to get to him. She said, "Barney, I'm coming down there while there's still some daylight."

Barney didn't answer, but said a prayer for the three of them.

✦ ✦ ✦

Catwalk landed at Glenwood Springs and saw a disturbing sight. The fuel office and terminal shack were both dark. Because very few aircraft flew at night, it wasn't unusual for employees at smaller airports to lock up and go home at sunset. He'd mistakenly thought with a search in progress they'd stay open.

He and Julio climbed out and looked for the refueling attendant, but saw no one. Catwalk said, "I don't believe this. Everyone just locked up and left. I'm going to find a way to get the lock off that fuel barrel."

"Are you planning on going back out there tonight, Cat?"

Catwalk thought about the situation. He could find the mountain with no problem because the moon was bright enough. He wouldn't be able to see the smoke, but he might be able to find the fire, and thereby find the wreckage.

"Yes. Time might be critical if someone needs medical attention."

"How are you going to find a place to land in the dark?"

Catwalk found an iron bar and began prying on the fuel pump lock. He hadn't thought about finding a place to land, but the moonlight should be bright enough to spot a suitable field.

"We've got enough moonlight. We can find a field."

Julio clearly had second thoughts about going back in the dark. "Cat, I want to find them too, but if we go stumbling around in the dark, somebody will be looking for us."

Catwalk had pried the lock off, so he started pumping gas into the Jenny. He said, "O.K., you're right, Julio. Here's what we'll do. Let's fly out there tonight and sleep in the plane. Then we'll be close enough, so at first light we can hike up the hill."

"All right. I'm game for that."

✦ ✦ ✦

Helen carefully made her way down the hillside. Because of the rough terrain, she had to descend past Barney's position and then climb back up to him. She found him lying on his back.

To Barney, she looked like an angel. He said, "Thanks for coming down here. I figured it might get kind of cool tonight."

"Can you move at all?"

"Just my head. I must have broke my back, or something."

She covered him with the blankets and said, "Do you think that plane saw the smoke?"

"Yes. It looked just like one of my planes. Make sure you keep the fire going, so they can find us in the morning."

"I will, Barney. Now that I know how to get to you, I'll come back down here during the night to check on you."

"I appreciate it, Helen. How is Art feeling?"

"Thanks to the morphine, he's been sleeping."

"I'm glad he's not in pain. Listen, there's a thirty-eight pistol in my flight bag, Helen. Use it if you need it."

Helen climbed up and put another log on the fire. She was walking back to the wreckage when she heard the first coyote howl. She thought about the dead bodies and wondered if they'd draw animals. She found the thirty-eight and made sure it was loaded. As she waited in the plane, however, Helen knew if a bear came around, the pistol might not be big enough to stop it.

# Chapter Thirty-One

Catwalk found a field with no problem, but upon landing in the darkness, he ran into a fence. The only damage was a few yards of wire wrapped around the prop, which, luckily, was not damaged. While untangling the wire off the prop, he told Julio, "I won't be able to sleep tonight. I'll be awake wondering what we're going to find on that mountainside."

"Think positive, son. Barney always flew well equipped. If they survived the wreck, they'll be O.K."

Catwalk smiled at Julio's optimism. "If you say so." Inside, he worried.

◆ ◆ ◆

At first light they took off and found the smoke from Helen's fire. Catwalk made a turn around the area and Julio said, "There's the Boeing! Farther up the hill, in the trees. I don't see anyone around it, but it looks like the crash was survivable and it didn't burn."

After picking out prominent landmarks to help them find the crash area, they flew back to the field, then set out on a hike that would be at least a mile uphill. The mountain was wooded, but fortunately, not to the point where it impeded their progress. Three hours later they came to Helen's fire.

When Helen saw them coning toward the plane, she broke out in tears of relief, and said, "Oh my God, our prayers have been answered."

Catwalk asked, "Are you two the only survivors?"

"Us and Barney, but he went for firewood and fell. He must have broken something in the fall because he's immobile."

"Immobile?"

"Yes. Come on, I'll take you to him."

"Julio, stay here and see if there's anything you can do for her husband."

Catwalk turned to follow Helen, and in doing so noticed the name on the crumpled plane. He stopped and leaned against the fuselage.

Tears came to his eyes. For a moment he felt like Sam had been killed all over again. Seeing the wreckage of her plane resurrected all the pain and anguish he'd suffered. Then, he decided her death had haunted him long enough. He realized this was an indication that the time had arrived for him to let go of her and get on with his life. She would live in his memories forever, but she would no longer play a part in his destiny.

Helen turned around and asked, "Are you O.K.?"

"I'm O.K. It's just that this plane was named after someone very special to me." He gathered himself and said, "Let's go find Barney."

✦ ✦ ✦

When Catwalk saw Barney lying immobile he felt terrible for his friend, but told himself to be thankful he was alive. He listened as Barney replayed the flight and the eventual crash. Catwalk thought, he would have done the same thing because storms can be so unpredictable, and they have a way of drawing you into predicaments.

After talking with Barney and making sure he was comfortable, Catwalk returned to the plane and discussed further plans with Julio, who then left to get more help. They'd need at least four more men to get Barney and Art down the hill, plus people to carry out the dead bodies.

Catwalk returned to Barney, who said, "Sit down. It'll be a few hours until someone gets back. While I've been lying here, I've had a lot of time to think. I don't know what's going to happen to me. It might be a while before I can move again, if ever. You and Julio will have to take over the airline and you'll have your hands full because a lot of changes will be taking place. Do you think you're ready for that?"

Catwalk thought about the question. He said, "I don't think I have a choice. I've got more experience than anyone else, so it's not a question if I'm ready; it's a question of, is everyone else ready to work for a black man."

"That's what I was thinking too. I don't think you'll have a problem. When I hired the people, I told them we had a black pilot and asked if they had a problem with that. No one said they did, but I think a couple people lied. I know for sure Jennings in Albuquerque has been saying things behind our backs, so I was going to replace him. Find someone who is familiar with aviation and friendly to the passengers, but has the guts to make the hard decisions."

Catwalk thought of Billy Sue and said, "I might know someone who will fit right in."

"Good. They're supposed to start on the new hangar in two weeks. They said it'll take three months to complete and it'll be big enough for two of the new Douglas planes. I want you and Julio to stay on top of that and make sure they don't cut corners. You'll also have to hire a couple pilots. Hire Kenneth if he's available, and check with the universities that have flight schools. See if you can steal one of their instructors."

"Is Julio moving the maintenance operation into the new hangar when it's finished?"

"Yes. As soon as they complete the post construction inspection, he can hire a moving company to move the gear from the farm."

"Should I hire someone to help Mattie run the farm?"

"Yeah, I guess you might as well. Make sure they keep raising enough livestock and produce to give to the soup kitchen in Vaughn."

Catwalk thought of his brother. Although he wanted to go to mechanics school, if he moved out to help on the farm, he'd have a place to live until he was accepted at the school. They talked for another hour and it became apparent to Catwalk just how much responsibility he'd be taking on. There was enough work for four men, but he also knew he'd have help from other airline employees. Thanks to Barney, the people who worked for Rocky Mountain were the type to pull together and help each other. His boss had always been a firm believer in building strong personal relationships with his employees. It appeared he would be the beneficiary of Barney's wisdom. He looked forward to the new challenges, but above all, hoped Barney would recover and be back at the helm of the airline before long.

◆ ◆ ◆

The next morning Barney and Art were carried off the mountain by search and rescue personnel. They were driven to Glenwood Springs and loaded onto a Boeing for the flight to Denver. Julio and Helen went with them and Catwalk flew the Jenny.

When he landed in Denver, he steeled himself for bad news. He'd seen farm workers who had suffered back injuries and they were almost always permanently disabled. A nurse told him they'd taken Barney to the x-ray lab, which was on the third floor. When he walked in, Julio told him, "They're taking x-rays now. The doctor said it'll be a couple hours before they'll know anything."

"How was he feeling?"

"They gave him a bunch of drugs; he doesn't know what country he's in."

"At least he's not in pain."

"No. On the flight over, he said you're running the airline now."

Catwalk nodded his head. "That's what he told me. Did you get a good look at the Boeing?"

"Yeah, it's in pretty bad shape; the trees just tore it up."

"Any chance we could disassemble it and salvage some parts?"

"Oh boy." Julio thought for a few seconds. "The main spar and all the wing spars are bent. We might salvage the instrument panel and engines. It'll take a team of men to get them down the hill."

"It'll be worth the money. Boeing quit making the Model Eighties last year, and we'll be flying them on our short routes for a while. Three spare engines will come in handy."

"I'll send a couple guys from Denver to remove them and crate them up. It shouldn't be a problem finding men who want to make a few bucks hauling them down."

"Give them a weeks pay and some free passes on the airline."

◆ ◆ ◆

The next day Catwalk went to see Barney, who said, "The first x-rays don't look good. My spinal cord is severed at C-5. The damage appears to be permanent, but they're doing more tests. They won't have the final diagnosis for about a week."

"My money says you'll be walking out of here."

"I appreciate your optimism, Cat, but I don't think so. I just have a feeling that this is as mobile as I'm ever going to get."

Catwalk hated the thought of this man, who'd been such a major influence in his life, and had changed it overnight, not being able to move. To change the subject, he said, "We'll be able to salvage the engines and instruments out of the Boeings. Julio's sending some people from the Denver station to do the salvage work."

"I'm glad you can get something out of it."

Catwalk tried to build his spirits. "Considering the terrain, you did an amazing job."

Barney rolled his eyes and said, "I'll dictate an account of the crash. Make sure it's circulated to all our pilots with a strong reminder about avoiding storms that are building."

"I'll do that. I'd better go. I've got to get back to Albuquerque, but I'll be back as soon as I have time in my schedule."

"Thanks, Cat."

◆ ◆ ◆

After a week at the hospital, Barney returned to the farm and hired a full time nurse who also functioned as a personal secretary. He also had a TELEX and multi-line phone system installed so he could stay in contact with his employees and other airline personnel. He wasn't going to second guess Catwalk's decisions, but with him flying on the line and making the management decisions, he could use help, even if it was from someone flat on their back.

He hadn't said anything to Catwalk, but with the expense of the new hangar, the proposed construction of new hangars at other airports, and more route expansion, Rocky Mountain Airways was becoming an organization that was outgrowing private ownership. So far, all of the expansion had been paid for by the revenue generated by the airline. The day was fast approaching when he'd need to borrow money to finance expansion. The banks that were open, weren't loaning money, and he wasn't foolish enough to risk any of his personal fortune. This left only one method of financing growth—by becoming a public corporation and selling shares of common stock.

This worried him, because Catwalk's employment would be at the mercy of a board of directors. He didn't have a problem with this when he was mobile, because he could be enough of a presence that he could influence anyone who wanted to replace him. Now, even though he'd be the majority stock holder, he couldn't exert as much pressure. He had no choice. He had to set the wheels in motion to become a public corporation and hope that he could select directors for whom color was not an issue.

◆ ◆ ◆

The next time they talked, Barney asked Catwalk if he'd have time to come out to the farm. Catwalk agreed and drove out there the next Saturday. Barney came right to the point. "Cat, as soon as I got home from the hospital, I started going over our financial situation, with regard to our growth. There's no getting around it, I have to file the paperwork to become a public corporation."

Catwalk immediately thought of a possible problem with the board of directors accepting a black man as the president of the airline. If there had been other black people in airline management it wouldn't bother him, but he knew of no other black people who held any kind of management position. He decided not to worry about this until it became a problem. He said, "If it'll help finance our expansion then there's no reason not to do it."

"I'm going to select the directors myself and they'll be subject to the approval of whoever underwrites the stock offering."

Catwalk had gotten this far by standing firm in the face of adversity. He wasn't about to start avoiding issues before they became issues. He said, "I'll take my chances with the directors and I've got a solid record to back me up."

"You certainly do. Considering your workload, the airline is doing exceptionally well. I'll keep you advised on the progress."

Catwalk stayed for dinner so he and Barney could discuss other issues with the airline. As he drove back to Albuquerque, he thought of how much he appreciated Barney's support. With the upcoming changes, however, he felt more vulnerable than he had in the past. He knew life was nothing more than a series of cycles and wondered if his idyllic life was about to spiral downward.

# Chapter Thirty-Two

Catwalk's first official duty as the acting president of Rocky Mountain Airways was to hire Billy Sue as an operations clerk at the Albuquerque station. He gave her a month to get used to the job, then promoted her to operations manager. She ran the department like a four-star general and was clearly thrilled to have a steady, well-paying job so she didn't have to approach Curly for financial support. Curly never answered his letter, so Catwalk and Billy Sue were in agreement that he'd be no more interested in raising a child than he'd been in getting married.

Kenneth Jackson and two other pilots were hired as line pilots. For Kenneth, who proved to be a professional and skillful airline pilot, this had been a dream of his since he first learned to fly. Being black, he'd assumed his dream would never come to fruition. Now, he was living his dream and he often told Catwalk, how much he appreciated the job.

John moved out to help Mattie run the farm while he waited for an opening in school. After three months on the farm he started in airframe and power plant school.

The two new routes to San Francisco and Phoenix were approved by the Commerce Department, and service started in late 1935. Their fleet, which now consisted of six planes, kept growing. In the spring of 1936, they took delivery of two Douglas DC-2 airliners. When Catwalk first flew the DC-2 with a Douglas test pilot, he was amazed at the power and performance.

After landing the Douglas pilot said, "Jack Frye and Eddie Rickenbacker flew this baby from San Francisco to Newark in thirteen hours and four minutes. Can you believe it?"

"I don't doubt that, but I'm concerned with passenger comfort more than performance. The passengers keep us in business."

"Mr. Jackson, when you consider the improved heating and ventilation system, along with a smoother ride at higher altitudes, wider seats and toilet facilities with lavatories, your passengers won't even know they're on an airplane."

"Wonderful. As soon as we can train our maintenance and ramp people, we'll put the planes into service." For Catwalk the new planes made him feel like the airline went from a fly-by-night operation, to a first class carrier over night. Now, they had the same equipment to compete with United, Continental, Western and Braniff.

◆ ◆ ◆

With the new planes they hired stewardesses, who were all registered nurses, and began serving hot coffee, pastries and cold beverages on their flights. Passenger feedback and increased loads told him this was greatly appreciated.

Six months later, the airline added two more upgraded DC-3s, the latest in the Douglas line that featured full feathering propellers and deicing boots on the wings for safety.

◆ ◆ ◆

Although time away from his duties was hard to come by, he drove out to see Barney as often as possible. Unfortunately there was no good news about Barney's medical condition. He'd visited several different medical specialists, but their prognosis was always the same: his spinal cord injury was permanent and there was no known medical procedure to restore his mobility. His only hope was that medical research came up with a new procedure in the future.

On Catwalk's last visit he and Barney discussed the future of Rocky Mountain Airways. Barney said, "I know you like flying more than you like the administrative duties, but it's time you became the official President of Rocky Mountain Airways. By some standards, you're pretty young, but you've been here since day one and this is a young industry. You can still fly on the line, but most of your time will be spent at our administrative headquarters."

Catwalk asked, "Is there anything about the airline's operation that concerns you?"

"No, but we're growing up fast. There will be a lot of expansion in the coming years. We're going head to head with TAT, Western and others on many of our routes. If we sit still, we lose passengers to them."

Catwalk had known this was coming and he couldn't say no to Barney even though he'd prefer to fly more. He said, "I agree and there's something I've been thinking about doing for a couple months now. I'm going to adjust our schedules so we always leave half an hour before our competitors. They're scheduling flights at the same time as each other to try and pick up a share of the passengers, but I'm going one better. While they're fighting for passengers we'll already be in the air."

"I like it. While you're at it have our ad agency take out some newspaper advertisements that tells folks if they're flying with us, they'll get there first."

"All right. Anything else?"

"How's your brother doing?"

"He's doing great. He's certified on all our equipment and he loves his job. He's on Jack McMillan's crew and Jack says he takes to aircraft maintenance like a duck to water."

"I'm glad to hear that." Barney paused while his nurse gave him a drink of water. "Have you been reading about the war in Europe?"

"Yes. A couple days ago I read that Hitler said he's going to conquer Europe—then the world. Is he a crackpot, or someone to be concerned about?"

"Well, I think he's a crackpot to be concerned about, and I wouldn't be surprised if we don't end up right in the middle of this thing."

"What will that do to the airline?"

"I don't know, but it sure as hell won't be business as usual. We'll probably be pressed into service to fly troops and you might end up wearing a uniform. Nothing is going to happen soon, but when it does we might lose most of our pilots, and planes to the military."

"That means no revenue, which will mean lots of layoffs, right?"

"I hope not, but at this point I don't know, Cat."

◆ ◆ ◆

On the drive back to Albuquerque, Catwalk thought about his conversation with Barney. He'd adjust his schedule to accommodate Barney's wishes, but would make it a point to fly often, both for proficiency and to stay abreast of the operation.

As far as the war, Barney had always been one to stay well informed. If he thought the country was going to war, chances are it would come to pass and he would end up serving with the armed forces. He wouldn't mind serving his country, but was concerned that his Momma would worry herself sick about it.

◆ ◆ ◆

In March, 1937, Rocky Mountain Airways became a public corporation. The stock opened trading at two dollars a share and quickly went up to four dollars a share. Catwalk had invested half of his savings in the stock, and as president of the company was given five hundred shares, so he doubled his money over night. In turn he bought more stock, which continued to increase in value. His Momma's house was getting bigger all the time.

The board of directors consisted of five men, three of whom were in the airline business. The other two were executives from the Union Pacific railroad and the Fred Harvey hotel chain. Before their selection for the board, Barney talked to all of them at length; none of them seemed to have a problem with the airline having a black president.

Catwalk made it a point to talk to the men at the first board meeting and his instincts told him that none of them had any racial issues that they were hiding. They all seemed pleased with the way he was managing the airline. He and the railroad executive, who had once hopped a freight to get to his first job, shared a few laughs about their mutual experiences with railroads.

◆ ◆ ◆

Between his duty as the full time president and his required flying, Catwalk had time for his passion, reading everything in sight, but little else. To say that the industry and Rocky Mountain Airways were growing was an understatement. He took this as a sign that the country was healing its wounds and pulling itself out of the depression.

Over the next year routes to Cheyenne, Los Angeles and Portland were approved and the fleet was expanded with the delivery of ten DC-3 aircraft. A high-speed reservations system was implemented and sleeper service was introduced on Rocky Mountain's long night flights.

The industry as a whole saw improvements such as high octane gasoline introduced by the Texas Oil Company, and two way radios, which enabled the pilots to call station managers to see if there were any passengers at intermediate stops. Continued research of instrument flying techniques brought equipment such as the radio direction finder, or "homing beacon."

◆ ◆ ◆

Catwalk had proven himself as a shrewd and savvy airline president who gained a reputation for taking care of his employees. He'd been known to reprimand an employee on-the-spot, for infractions such as working out of uniform, but he'd also encouraged bonuses for meritorious performance. He made it known that if you did your job well, you could go far in the airline, but if you were a slacker, your tenure would be short.

Barney had told him that he was only as good as the people around him. To that end, he hired the best airline management personnel he could find, often luring people away from other airlines with attractive pay packages and incentives. He also hired top executives from other non-aviation companies and trained them in the airline business.

One day he told his secretary, "Melba, I'm taking a week off. I'm going to visit Barney, and then I'm going out to see my family in Mississippi. Get me a seat on a flight to Meridian leaving day after tomorrow."

"I'll take care of that and Telex the information to you at Barney's. Tell him we said hi."

✦ ✦ ✦

On his drive to the farm, Catwalk felt like he was on top of the world. With the new planes and new reservation system the airline business was growing at an astonishing rate. Their loads were better than ever and in two months they were going to start competing with the railroad by offering exclusive cargo flights and freight forwarding by the Railway Express Agency. Now, Rocky Mountain Airways offered an exclusive service, which meant businesses could send merchandise by air and have it arrive the same day.

✦ ✦ ✦

Barney greeted him from a wheel chair in the yard with his nurse. "It's a beautiful day out here. You should take up golf so you could enjoy a day like this."

"I don't have time for golf, and you know those golf clubs don't allow black people."

"Well, I'll build a golf course and we'll allow only black people to play it. How's that?"

"Maybe when I retire. I want to ask you for a favor."

"Sure. What is it?"

"I'm going back to visit my family. With my stock and savings, I've got over two thousand dollars saved up and I'd like to buy my Momma a house, so my family can get off the farm. I know they won't give me a loan for property, but they'd give you a loan."

"Yes, they will. Are you going to look at houses while you're back there?"

"If Earl Slade can help me, I will. I don't know a thing about buying a house."

"Well, you might be better off buying some land and then build a house. How many kids are still at home?"

"Seven, but Cecil is going out looking for work, so he might not be there."

"Have Slade call me. We'll find some land and build a house that she'll love."

Barney then said, "Have you heard about the DC-4?"

Catwalk had seen promotional pictures of the newest aircraft in the

Douglas line. "Yes, I have. Douglas sent us a promotional package."

Barney said, "She carries 112 passengers at two hundred and seventy miles an hour, with a range of 1,500 hundred miles."

"It's an impressive airplane, but I don't think this is the time to be buying new planes."

Barney looked at Catwalk with unspoken questions on his face. His philosophy was, in order to stay competitive, it was best for the airline to maintain an inventory of state of the art equipment. Catwalk had always embraced this concept so the statement surprised him. Rather than ask the obvious question, he said, "American Airlines already ordered ten of them."

"Good for them. I don't care if they ordered fifty. It's not a good time for us to buy new equipment. The war in Europe is heating up, and I agree with what you, that we're going to end up in it. When we go to war, our inventory will be taken over by the military, and when the war is over, our planes will be extremely used; worth very little. I'd rather have a bunch of used up DC-3s that we own, rather than hold the loan on a bunch of used up DC-4s. After the war, we can buy as many DC-4s as you want. Then, we'll have new state of the art equipment."

"Well, I don't disagree with you, Cat. I was thinking about this Trippe fellow that started up Pan American Airways. He's got routes to Europe and South America, so he thinks there's a market there. If we had long range aircraft, like the DC-4, we could go head to head with him."

"We still can, but now isn't the time. I say we wait to see what happens in Europe. While that's going on, we can expand some of our hangar space, so we'll be ready for new aircraft. Maybe the war will be over in a year or two. Then we can buy the new equipment. Douglas will have made upgrades by then, so we'll be going after those new routes with the newest planes in the sky."

Barney smiled, "O.K. It goes against my grain to stand still and watch everyone else get the new planes, but I guess you're right."

"The worst that can happen is we own all of our equipment, which gives us the best debt to equity ratio in the business."

Barney smiled and said, "We'll talk more about this. Go home and have a nice relaxing visit with your family. Tell them I said hi."

"I plan on doing a lot of fishing and reading."

# Chapter Thirty-Three

Curly had been home for two years when he decided he'd had enough of the farm. His Dad had passed away two months after he'd returned. As soon as they buried him, Theresa didn't need to be told she wasn't welcome. She left on her own to go live with a sister in Detroit.

Curly landed a job giving flying lessons at the local airport. Even though the money was meager, it was enough to keep the farm from foreclosure until the market for crops picked up. With his brothers running the farm, Curly went to New York City to apply for a job with Colonial Air Transport. Colonial flew the Boeing Two-Forty-Seven, an all metal twin-engine monoplane that was similar to the Boeing Model 80.

The personnel manager at Colonial, said, "Mr. Levitz, I'm impressed with your experience in Model Eighties, but there aren't any openings, right now. I'll keep you in mind if anything opens up. Have you tried American Airlines or Eastern?"

"Not yet, but I probably will. Thanks for your time."

After the interview, Curly hung around the airport to watch the planes. While watching the activity, he realized how much he missed flying. Life on the farm held nothing for him and if he never milked another cow that would be just fine. He thought about returning to Rocky Mountain and wondered if leaving with a short notice would be a move he regretted. Undoubtedly, any airline that considered hiring him would call Rocky Mountain for references. He hoped they talked to Catwalk, or someone at the airline who didn't know him. With this in mind, he decided he'd call Catwalk as soon as he returned to the farm.

He spent another day in the city to take in a Broadway show. When he returned to the farm it was late in the afternoon so he decided to wait for the morning to call Catwalk.

✦ ✦ ✦

On his first day home, Catwalk took Petey and Georgie fishing. That night, over a dinner of fresh catfish, he told his Mom about the recent advances in the airline industry. She didn't understand most of the technical terms, but she was immensely proud of him and pleased that he was so successful and enthusiastic about his job.

After dinner, she asked him, "Do you think we'll be going to war, Luke?"

"Yes, I'm afraid we will."

"That means the military will be looking for pilots doesn't it?"

"Yes, I'm sure they will be." He added, "I don't know if they'll take black pilots though. There's talk of integrating the military services, but no one is doing anything about it. Secretary Simpson is against it, so they won't take me in the military now, and this might not change."

His Momma sounded grimmer than he'd ever heard. "Well, it shouldn't change. Any country that doesn't treat black people as equal citizens, doesn't have any business sending their sons to war. If they want to give us equality, then it's fine, but right now, there's no reason you should go to war."

Catwalk took a deep breath. She wouldn't like what he was about to say, but he had to stand up for his beliefs, even if it meant opposing his Mother. "Momma, if we're in a war, and they'll take me, I'm going to serve."

"Why, Luke? Why on earth should you go get shot at?"

"Regardless of how we've been treated, I'm still an American, and I have to serve my country. I don't want anyone saying that we weaseled out of our responsibility by taking advantage of the military segregation."

"I don't see why we shouldn't take advantage of it. This country hasn't given us much."

Catwalk didn't want to argue with his Momma. To change the subject he said, "I've got some good news, Momma. I'm going to ask Mr. Slade to help me look for a house for you."

His Momma beamed a smile at him and said, "Oh, Luke."

The rest of the kids started buzzing amongst themselves about their new home. Cecil said, "There's only a few areas where they'll let blacks live, Luke. You buy a house anywhere else and the Klan will burn it down."

Determined, Catwalk said, "I know. I'm not going buy anywhere that anyone will have a problem with our presence. I'll look for a home in one of the safe areas." As he said this, Catwalk knew there was no where in the south that was completely safe from the ravages of the Klan. But he wasn't about to let them keep him from buying his Momma's dream house.

◆ ◆ ◆

The next morning Catwalk went to the Slade farm. He found Earl looking over a field of soybeans. "Good morning, Mr. Slade."

"Hello, Luke. You must be home visiting your family. How is the airline business?"

"Oh, it's getting better all the time. We've got a lot of new equipment and we're growing by leaps and bounds."

"Well, you knew this economy had to pick up sooner or later. We've even had some buyers for our soybeans."

"I'm glad to hear that. You always had the best crop of beans around."

Both men looked over the field, then Catwalk said, "Say, Mr. Slade, I'm thinking about buying my Momma a house. Only thing is, I don't know anything about buying real estate property. I was wondering if you could help me."

"Luke, I'd be glad to." They walked toward the house and sat down on a veranda where Slade told a plump, black housekeeper with a wide smile to bring them some lemonade.

The woman said, "Hello, Mr. Luke. I seen your Momma at Sunday meeting last week and she sure is looking fine. Looks just like she never was sick a day in her life."

"Thank you, Florence. She's feeling well, too."

The woman left and Slade said, "Luke, the first thing is, you've got to decide is how you're going to pay for the place. If you can put cash on the table that means you don't have to deal with the banks. They're not loaning much money right now, even to white folks."

"Yes, sir. Barney said he'd get the loan if I needed one, but I'd pay cash if I could."

"Personally, I'd buy a lot and build a place. Most of the houses for sale around here have been vacant for some time so no one has taken care of them and they're in pretty bad shape. I'll take you for a drive and show you what I mean."

◆ ◆ ◆

Slade drove out a muddy Highway Eighty past Key Field where Catwalk saw a Lockheed Vega departing. Earl said, "That's a guy who just started serving this area. He flies to Montgomery and down to Mobile. I guess he's doing pretty well, for only having one plane."

"If he can keep the seats filled, that's all he needs."

"How many airplanes does your airline have?"

"We've got 16 DC-3s and six Boeing Model 80s."

"That's a big outfit. Here's one of the houses that's for sale." Earl pointed to a run down two bedroom house that looked as if it had been vacant for many months. Luke walked around the house, then said, "I see what you mean. I agree we'd be better off building a new house."

Earl scratched his head and said, "Of course, you might consider buying this place because the lot is big enough to build a second house. Then, if you want to you can fix up this one later on and rent it out. Let's go to the bank and see what the asking price is."

Luke thought about the place on the way to the bank. The location was good because the only neighbors were other black folk that lived a quarter mile up the road. There were no white folks in the area that he knew of. He and Cecil could frame a new house in a few days and once the old place was fixed up his Mom could rent it out and possibly get enough income where she wouldn't have to work.

The banker told them the house and lot were selling for two hundred dollars. He added that although the house was run down, the lot had a good well and this was one of the few houses in the area that had electric lines connected to the house.

Catwalk stepped outside so he and Earl could talk this over. He was excited about the house, but didn't want his exuberance to push him into a transaction that he'd regret later.

Earl said, "I think it's a good investment, just for the land, which should increase in value. It'll take some work, but that's the case with any house you're going to buy in that area."

"That's good enough for me. Let's close the deal."

Catwalk went back inside and laid down ten twenty dollar bills. The banker said he'd draw up a bill of sale and deed for the title transfer.

That night his family celebrated and began making plans to move to their new home. Dee told Catwalk, "Son, you've given me the one thing I've wanted for my entire life, and you've made me the proudest Mother on earth."

Catwalk had never felt better. The next morning he and Cecil borrowed a truck from Mr. Slade and brought the first load of lumber to the new house. By the time he had to leave, they had poured the foundation and framed the house. Cecil said by working evenings and weekends, and with help from some of the farm hands, he'd be able to finish it in a couple months.

Catwalk wished he could stay and help, but he knew how much work was piling up at the airline. He left the next morning feeling like he was on top of the world. The trip home had done wonders for him and he felt like he could take on any challenge thrown at him.

# Chapter Thirty-Four

Over the next year, due to deaths and retirement, the board of directors for Rocky Mountain Airways changed. It was expanded to seven directors, with four of them being new members. In spite of Barney's best efforts, they weren't as liberal as the previous board members. They were hardened executives who placed little value in longevity or familiarity. Their method of operation was to install managers whom they could manipulate, and reward people of their choice with the best jobs, regardless of ability or experience.

Their move to replace Catwalk started with a clandestine board meeting that had been scheduled with short notice so Barney wouldn't be able to attend. John Sullivan, an original board member, and the president of Fred Harvey Hotels had seen the writing on the wall. He knew the new members were after Catwalk's job.

In an effort to forego Catwalk's ouster, Sullivan was arguing his point. "The man has done an incredible job while he's been president of this airline. Our passenger revenues have increased every quarter and our cargo revenues have doubled, while maintaining the best safety record in the business. Our stockholders have seen the value of their stock quadruple. You can't ask for much more than that out of your president."

Franklin Davis, an oil company executive and new member, countered, "We're not questioning his ability, John. It's his image that we have a problem with. Here it is, almost 1940 and we're still hung up with Jackson because he was one of the founding pilots of this airline. It's time we moved him aside and brought in a business man who will present a more business like, progressive image to the corporate world."

Sullivan fired back, "You mean you want a white man to be president of Rocky Mountain Airways."

Davis said, "Now, that's not what I said and I resent you putting word in my mouth."

Anthony Fielding, another new member and a cohort of Davis', piped up, "John, you have a problem that has been plaguing this air-

157

line for some time now; you're not thinking in the future. This airline will be going international before long and we'll need working agreements with foreign carriers. We're going to be moving into countries where a black president would be a serious liability. He's the first impression many people will have of this airline and he might send many of them scurrying for the doors."

Joseph Oates, another original board member, had been quiet. He tried to look as if he was considering the points of view, but his mind had been made up prior to the meeting. To Sullivan's surprise, he spoke up, aligned with the newer members. "John, perhaps we can find a place for Jackson where he can continue to exert his management expertise, but where he wouldn't be as visible. Then, a more suitable president can represent the airline in business matters."

Sullivan sat down, knowing if Oates capitulated, the fight was over. Catwalk would be reassigned to another position and a new president would be voted in. He glared at the man and said, "What was it, Joe? Did they buy you a new car, or a couple nights with an expensive whore? What swayed you?"

Oates stared out the window and said nothing. Actually, his price had been both; a new Chrysler convertible and two nights in a Los Angeles hotel with a knockout redhead.

A motion was carried to remove Catwalk as president of Rocky Mountain Airways and assign him the position of Director of Personnel and Training. Sullivan asked, "How are you going to notify Mr. Jackson? Do any of you have the guts to tell him to his face, or were you planning on sending him a memo?"

When he didn't get an answer, Sullivan stood and said, "I'll notify him." And he walked out. The remaining board members voted in the new president, Franklin Davis' son.

John Sullivan drove to the Albuquerque airport and asked the operations clerk, "I need to locate Catwalk. Is he on flight status?"

"Yes, sir. He's R.O.N. in Phoenix and he'll be coming back on an early morning flight; flight eighty-four leaves at six thirty."

"Thank you. Our pilots stay at the Arizona Biltmore, don't they?"

"Uh, he has to stay at the Stratford Arms, sir."

Sullivan knew the word of Catwalk's firing would spread like wildfire and he didn't want him to hear it through idle conversation. He walked into a vacant office, dialed the hotel and asked for Mr. Jackson's room.

"Hello."

"Catwalk, this is John Sullivan. How are you tonight?"

Catwalk immediately knew something was wrong. There was no reason for Sullivan to call him unless he had bad news. He worried that something had happened to Barney.

"I'm fine, John. Is there a problem?"

"Catwalk, there was a board meeting tonight. It was scheduled at the last minute so Barney couldn't attend. A vote was taken and you are no longer the president of Rocky Mountain Airways. You have been reassigned as the Director of Personnel and Training."

The news infuriated, upset and insulted Catwalk, but it didn't surprise him. When your position requires that you make the difficult management decisions, you have to focus on the future, and in which direction trends are moving the company. You can't afford to be surprised. He'd seen the changes in the board and with each new member, he knew the board was moving toward a more conservative, and socially acceptable management style. He asked, "Who is the new president?"

"Theodore Davis, Franklin's son."

"And they asked you to tell me so they didn't have to face me, right?"

"I called so you'd find out about it first hand rather than through gossip."

"John, I appreciate the call. Does Barney know about this?"

"No, he doesn't."

"I'll call him. Good night."

Catwalk hung up the phone and walked over to the window. Looking out over Central Avenue, he thought about the obstacles he'd overcome and the monumental progress he'd made at the airline. Nobody could take that away from him. Those achievements were his no matter what happened and this brought a measure of comfort. Then he thought about his future. He had a feeling that he wouldn't stay with Rocky Mountain Airways. Regardless, he should call Barney before it got any later.

When Barney answered he said, "Barney, this is Cat. I just got a call from John Sullivan. A board meeting was held tonight and I'm no longer president of Rocky Mountain."

"Those God damned sons a' bitches! It's Davis and his bunch. I knew they were going to pull something like this. It's a good damned thing I can't move or I'd kick some ass."

"Take it easy, Barney. You're taking this worse than I did."

"Those gutless bastards make me sick. What are you going to do?"

"Well, I was just thinking about that. They want to reassign me as Director of Personnel and Training, but I don't want that job if we have an inexperienced man at the top. I wouldn't get any support with the tough battles, such as with the unions or the politicians at the Civil Aeronautics Board. This will soon be an airline that I'd not like to work for anymore."

"I know what you mean, son. Every change lately takes the company in a direction I don't want it to go. Well, don't do anything rash. Give this a lot of thought before you make a decision. I'm coming out to Albuquerque in the next few days because I want to tell some people just what I think of them."

"Good night."

◆ ◆ ◆

Catwalk then sat down and wrote his Momma. Without going into particulars, he mentioned that he was caught up in a racially motivated struggle; a struggle in which they both knew the odds were stacked against him. He mentioned that he might not be working for this airline much longer.

Then, for the first time in his life, he walked down stairs and went to the bar. The bartender, a tall handsome black man about fifty took his order. "Bourbon on the rocks please."

When the bartender brought his drink, he said, "You're the guy that runs Rocky Mountain Airlines, ain't you?"

"Yeah, that's me." Catwalk reached across the bar and shook his hand. "Catwalk Jackson. How are you tonight?"

"Harry Porter, and I'm fine. Say, I've seen your picture in the paper and read stories about you, and I have to ask, how'd a young black man ever get to be president of an airline?"

Catwalk took a sip of the bourbon. It felt good, burning off the misery as it went down. He said, "Well, Harry. I met an exceptionally good man, and I was in the right place at the right time. That's all there is to it."

"Dang. That's got to be a cushy job, flying all over the place and seeing different cities. I'll bet you wouldn't give that up for the world."

Catwalk grinned and said, "You never know, Harry. Sometimes things just aren't what they seem to be."

◆ ◆ ◆

Catwalk flew back to Albuquerque the next morning. Without coming to a conclusion, he thought about his future for the entire flight. He knew, compared to the rest of the country, how good he had it, and he was apprehensive about throwing in the towel on his career. His job was a one in a million and he'd never get another like it. In fact, if he resigned from the airline, even though he had over five thousand hours flying time, he didn't think he could get hired as a line pilot for another carrier, much less as a senior executive. One man's desire to move his son into a position, for which he wasn't qualified, had completely upset his life, and there wasn't a thing he could do about it.

After landing, he checked his schedule to make sure he still had two days off. He saw a message that said to call Curly at a long distance number. He dialed and waited, then recognized Curly's voice. After last night it felt good to hear his old friend.

Catwalk said, "I suppose you're looking for a flying job."

"Hey Cat, how you doin', man?"

"I'm O.K., how about you?"

"I'm ready to get off this farm, Cat. How are things at the airline?"

Catwalk told him the entire story of Barney's accident, becoming president of the airline and his downfall at the hands of the board of directors. He admitted he wasn't sure what the future held for him.

"Those fuckin' bastards. Good thing I ain't there. I'd wipe the floor with their face. Are you serious about quitting?"

"Dead serious, but I want to talk to Barney first. I owe him that much."

"So here we are, two out of work pilots. Why don't we buy one of the Jennys off Barney and go out barnstorming?"

"Because people aren't paying to see that anymore. Speaking of barnstorming, Billy Sue is working for the airline. She's the Vice President of Market Planning."

"No kidding. Tell her I said hi."

"I will. I'll tell her to tell your son hi too."

A prolonged silence. Then Curly said, "Are you shitting me?"

"No. She brought him to the farm a couple months after you left. His name is David."

"Why didn't she tell me?"

"She thought you'd be no more interested in raising a child than you were about getting married, and trying to get some help from you would be futile. She's doing fine by herself."

"Oh Jesus! I feel terrible that she thought that of me, Cat. I guess she had me pegged right though. I feel like the world's biggest jerk."

Catwalk didn't agree with him because when Curly had pulled him out of a hangman's noose, he'd earned a lifetime of tolerance for his human imperfections. He said, "Curly, you're not the world's biggest jerk, but you have your moments. Why don't you give her a call. Here's her work number … ."

"I can't give her any money, we're just scraping by out here."

"She knows that, but I still think you should call her."

"I will. Listen, you let me know as soon as you decide what you're going to do, O.K.."

"Sure thing, Curly." The call to his old friend had definitely helped Catwalk's disposition. It hadn't, however, pushed him any closer to an answer to the question: What was he going to do with his life?

# Chapter Thirty-Five

Barney, as Catwalk knew he would, tried to talk him out of resigning. "What are you going to do? You know how hard jobs are to come by. Are you going to go back on the barnstorming circuit?"

"I've been thinking about going up to Alaska."

Barney looked at him like he'd lost his mind. "Alaska? What are you going to do up there, besides freeze your tail off?"

"I might put in an application with Wein-Alaska Airlines, or look for a job flying the bush. From the articles I've read, the depression hasn't had as much impact up there, and their racial attitudes are very liberal."

Barney said nothing; he couldn't blame Cat for wanting to get far away. The recent events had turned his stomach and he wasn't sure he wanted to be associated with the airline anymore, even though he was the founder.

"Well, you've got a good head on your shoulders, so you'll make the right decision. Have you told you Mom yet?"

"I wrote her last night and I'm going out there for a few days. I haven't seen the house since Cecil finished it."

"I know how she'll feel, but she'll still be immensely proud of you, Cat, because of everything you've done, right square in the face of adversity. The undoing was not your fault and she knows that better than anyone. Did you tell her you're going to Alaska?"

"Not yet because I'm not sure myself. There's another pilot from upstate New York that might go up there with me."

Barney smiled, "How's Curly doing?"

"He's ready to leave the farm. His brothers are running the place again, and they're beginning to show a profit. Curly's ready to return to flying."

"I just hope he doesn't drink like he used to. That liquor will do a man in faster than anything. Listen, take one of the Jennys. Nobody flies them anymore. If you decide to fly the bush, you might be able to trade it in on a Norseman, or something suitable for that weather."

"Can I buy it off you?"

"No. You've paid for it ten times over, Cat. Just take it and fly safe."

❖ ❖ ❖

Catwalk tendered his resignation, then worked at Rocky Mountain Airways for another two weeks. Prior to his reassignment, he'd been busy making sure the airline conformed to the new Civil Air Regulations that would soon be effective. They'd been given a six month grace period, but he wanted to get it done as soon as possible, and didn't want to leave it for the incoming president regardless of the circumstances. Among his decisions about his future, he'd also decided he wasn't burning any bridges and he was leaving his job with as much professional dignity as possible. He was going out, but it would be with his head held high.

Theodore Davis, his replacement, showed up at ten in the morning on his last day. From the moment he walked in the office, Davis made it plain to Catwalk that he didn't need any help in assuming the position of president of the company. Catwalk saw it for what it was, a white man that was too good to get help from a black man. He didn't let this bother him, but he felt sorry for the employees of the airline because he knew this was a guy who didn't give a damn about them. Their working environment would slide steadily downhill.

During their brief conversation, Davis saw the Jenny sitting on the ramp and asked, "Who flies that old relic?"

"I do. Have you ever flown in a Curtis Jenny?"

"No, actually, I don't fly that much. I guess I'll have to now."

"Care to take a spin around the pattern? It's just like riding in a sports roadster."

"Sure, why not."

On the ramp Catwalk said, "Sit in the rear so you don't get as much wind in your face."

Catwalk took off and flew to an area ten miles south of the airport. Then with a wide grin on his face, he went into his acrobatic routine, wrenching the Jenny through the maneuvers with as much ferocity as he could coax out of the plane. By the time he finished the second loop Davis was puking his guts out and screaming for him to stop. Catwalk was laughing so hard that tears filled his eyes.

Oblivious to Davis' misery he continued his routine for another five minutes, then landed. When he parked, he turned to Davis and said, "It's hard to hear anything from the front cockpit, did you say something?"

Davis, covered with his breakfast and red with rage, was visibly shaking as he said, "You … ."

Catwalk smiled and yelled, "You better fly some more so you get used to it."

He walked into the office to get his personal effects, and said goodbye to the people on duty. Billy Sue was in tears as he hugged her and promised to stay in touch. The rest of the employees wished him well and he left the airport feeling better, except he'd have to clean out the Jenny first chance he had.

◆ ◆ ◆

Catwalk flew back to Meridian, thinking about his future the entire trip. On one hand his wanderlust was steering him toward Alaska because he yearned to see this unspoiled land where bears outnumbered humans and the humans treated each other equally. Another part of him said he should settle back in Meridian with his Mother and the family, so he could spend some time with his brothers and sisters while they were growing up. The problem was, there was only job for him back in Mississippi and that was working on a farm, which he wasn't about to do.

Another possibility was to use one of his contacts in the airline business to find a job with another carrier. The problem he faced here was he knew the job would be menial at best. This just wasn't a time when anyone, unless you found another saint like Barney, was going to hire a black man for a management position, regardless of his experience. He landed with his mind still tugging him in different directions.

His Mother was overjoyed to see him and the happiest woman on earth in her new house. Cecil had finished enough of the house that the family could move in about two weeks ago. Now, he was working on a third bedroom in his spare time. The first thing he asked Catwalk was if he was going to be there long enough to finish the room.

"I'll be here a week or so. We should be able to get it done. I'll go into town tomorrow to get the paint and shingles we need."

"Good. When I finish this I'm going to start on the other house so Mom can rent it out."

His Mother asked, "Where are you going, Luke?"

"I don't know, Momma. I'm thinking about heading up to Alaska to find a flying job."

"Alaska? Why so far away. Can't you get work around here?"

"Momma, the only job I can get around here is on a farm. I've done enough farm work."

Cecil said, "He's right, Momma. If he's got a chance to find decent work, he should go after it. There's no future working on a farm."

His Mother said nothing, even though she was beset with conflicting thoughts. She wanted her son close to her so badly, that she wouldn't mind if working on a farm accomplished this. On the other hand, she was immensely proud of him and knew his success would not allow him to work in the fields any longer. She hugged him and said, "Do what you have to, Luke. Just come back to see us every now and then."

◆ ◆ ◆

Catwalk had been home eight days when, during his sleep one night, he heard Sam's voice. "Go to Alaska, Cat. Find your destiny in the land of the midnight sun."

He awoke, sat straight up and looked around him; all his brothers were sound asleep. He pulled on his jeans and went out on the porch. Had he imagined that he heard her voice? No, there was no mistaking it; he knew where he was going.

He was still sitting there when Dee got up. He told her about hearing Sam's voice.

She said, "Go then, Luke. Go to Alaska, but be safe, honey."

Catwalk called Curly from a pay phone at the drug store. He told him he'd pick him up at the airport in Norwich day after tomorrow. Curly was ecstatic and sounded like he'd been released from Purgatory. He asked Catwalk, "Do you think there's many women in Alaska?"

# Chapter Thirty-Six

Catwalk and Curly were standing on a pier in Valdez, Alaska, next to a bobbing Stinson Detroiter seaplane that was tugging at its mooring lines.

Staring at the Chugach Mountain range, Curly said, "Do you think they're higher than the Rockies?"

"I don't know, but they sure got a lot more snow, and they got those glaciers too. Do you know what those are?"

"Bunch a' ice, as far as I know."

A voice boomed out behind them. "I'm Hank Conroy. I s'pose you're the two hot-shit pud-knockers lookin' for a job flyin' the bush."

They turned and saw a sawed-off fireplug of a man, with blazing eyes dressed in wool cap, flannel shirt, corduroy britches and knee-high lace-up boots. A plug of tobacco the size of a baseball filled his cheek. Catwalk said, "That's right. I'm Catwalk Jackson, this is Curly Levitz."

The guy flung words at them, then spit a wad of sewage onto the pier for exclamation. "How much seaplane time you got?" Patooey!

Curly said, "We don't have any seaplane time. We flew Jennys and airliners like the Boeing Model 80. He flew DC-3s."

"What?" Patooey! "No seaplane time?" He barked what was supposed to be a laugh. "A couple of crappin'-pee-shit greenhorns." Patooey! He looked over the two pilots like someone assessing a steer. "Well, I'm up agin' it, an' need someone to fly. I'll see what you're made of."

He knelt on the dock and pointed to the floats that kept the seaplane on top of the water. "See that step on bottom of the float? You gotta' remember that. If you got a heavy load and you can't get up on that step, you can go 'til your tank runs dry and you won't get off the water."

He walked up close to Catwalk, spit and said, "Here's how it is. I don't care what color a man is; he can be green, yellow, red or blue, I

don't care. I judge him on two things: courage and good judgment."
Patooey! "You have those, you can fly the bush for years. You don't, you
kill yourself and whoever's with you. You ever fly a Detroiter?"

"No, but I can fly it."

"Unh-huh. Get in the left seat." He turned to Curly and spat,
"You, get in back."

Catwalk sat down and looked over the instrument panel. It was
bare compared to the DC-3 and he knew why. In Alaska, the bush
pilots didn't fly on instruments and very few had radios. Seat of the
pants flying by needle, ball, airspeed and altimeter was the only way
here.

"Here's what you need to know about flyin' a floatplane." He turned
to Curly, "You listen to this good." He spit into a beer can. "Don't try
to turn downwind with power; it'll tip you over. Just let the plane
weathervane into the wind. Don't try to turn a seaplane at all in a high
wind. You tack it like a sailing ship, back and forth. Don't try taxiing at
half throttle; you'll ruin your engine. Either taxi slow, or put the plane
up on the step an' your engine will run cool."

Again he turned to Curly, "You got all that?"

"I got it."

Catwalk smiled because he knew Curly didn't like Hank's demeanor.
He hoped Curly didn't say anything that would cost them a job.

"Good, you guys might not be so worthless after all." He shook a
finger at Catwalk. "Now, you gotta keep the nose up, or your prop will
pick up spray, or it might hit the waves. That'll ruin your prop. Ya'
wanna' be real careful landing on glassy water. Sometimes you get a
reflection off the bottom of a clear lake and it fools you. Last, don't drift
a ship backwards in high wind without power on. You do, an' the floats
and tail will dig in and you'll sink tail first. You don't want to do that,
do you?"

Catwalk looked at Hank and said, "Sinking doesn't interest me in
the least."

"Good." Spit. "Your wind is northwest about eight knots. You got
a light chop, but that's the best kind of water for a seaplane, just a little
chop to let you know there's water under your plane. O.K., full back
pressure on that wheel and let the speed lift you out of the water. Take
off northwest and turn up that valley at two o'clock."

Curly looked at the valley and swore he saw a fog bank lying in the
valley. He thought, nah, this guy ain't crazy enough to fly into the fog.
It must look different up here.

Catwalk taxied away from the dock and remembered the warning about turning into the wind. When he was a safe distance from the dock he let the plane weathervane and applied take-off power. He held the wheel full back and waited for the plane to rise onto the step. When his speed built, the plane broke the bond with the water and they were airborne.

Hank liked it. "By damn, you remembered what I tole' you. You're gonna' be a bush pilot, son."

When they turned into the valley, Curly found his assessment of the fog was right on.

Catwalk asked, "You want me to climb above that fog?"

"Not on your life, boy. You get right down on that river bed and fly the river." He turned to Curly, "There's a hell of a lot of bad weather up here, an' storms build before you can blink an eye. That's why you gotta learn to fly in the weather instead of going around it. You get above the fog and run into a storm, you can't get back down through the soup. This-a-way, you're down here where it's safe."

Catwalk flew into the fog, keeping the river in sight below him.

Hank went on, "One thing you got to remember boys, there ain't no mountains in the middle of a river. You stay down on the river bed and you'll never hit nothin', just keep your eye out for the moose. I been so low I almost hit a few. Then, when you're ready to land, you jes' set her down. But, watch out for sand bars. You'll learn where they are."

Catwalk flew for thirty minutes and came to Blueberry Lake. The weather had cleared so he felt more comfortable, but he was apprehensive about his first landing on water. He turned into the wind.

Hank started again. "Now, boys, one thing you gotta learn is, you gotta learn how to read the water. This is the most important thing about flying a float plane. You don't learn to read the water and you'll be back flying your Boeings, if you don't die first. This lake ain't bad 'cause there's no current like there is on a river, but it's kinda' rough today. Use a full stall so you got the least forward speed. The closer you can land to the upwind shore, the calmer the water will be."

Catwalk set up a final approach and about ten feet above the water, killed his forward speed and stalled just before the floats entered the water. The landing felt rough to him, but Hank nodded his head. He took that as a passing grade.

They pulled the plane onto the shore where they changed pilots. While Hank went to take a leak, Catwalk told Curly, "Just do as he says. Don't say anything that'll blow this job."

"Oh, I won't, but that guy's a real turd."

◆ ◆ ◆

Curly had some trouble taxiing upwind, but finally got the hang of it. They flew back to Valdez through a pass that took them to the shoreline of Prince William Sound and over the fishing village of Tatitlek. Catwalk knew this type of flying was going to take getting used to because throughout his whole flying career he'd been avoiding weather, and now he had to learn to operate in the weather.

Once they landed at Valdez, Hank said, "You boys done pretty good. I want you to make some touch and goes and practice taxiing. Tonight we take your first night flight over to Lake Hood, then day after tomorrow you go to work. I got a gov'ment contract to fly some fellows from the fish and game department 'tween here and Fairbanks and Bettles. Be ready to see the country by then. If you get forced down by a storm, you might have to camp in the plane for a couple days, so here's what you gotta take with you: a Coleman heater and stove, four days of food and water, plenty of warm clothes, and something to read. That's for you, for your plane you take blankets to wrap your engine in and gear to drain the oil so it don't freeze. You wanna' be prepared, 'cause it might be forty below outside."

After Hank left Catwalk looked at Curly and smiled. Curly said, "Camping in a plane for four days. Shit, I'll go crazy sitting in a plane for four days."

"That's why you bring something to read."

Curly lit a cigarette and said, "Cat, what the hell have we got ourselves into?"

◆ ◆ ◆

Their night flight wasn't much different than flying the daytime, as long as they kept the instrument lights turned down, so they didn't ruin their night vision. This time of year there wasn't much nighttime in Alaska, but in six months there would be very little day time. After the flight they went back to the room they'd rented. Curly walked across the street to a bar and Catwalk tore into a Jack London novel. Curly came back in fifteen minutes and said, "Cat, you can come over and have a drink if you want to, There's a couple other black guys in there."

Catwalk went with Curly, and felt good that he could walk into a bar and get served. He was halfway through his first beer when he struck up a conversation with a burly guy next to him. The guy seemed interested that he and Curly were learning to be bush pilots.

"Where'd you guys fly in the states?"

Catwalk said, "We flew out of Albuquerque for Rocky Mountain Airways."

By now a few other onlookers had gathered to hear about the two new pilots. One man asked, "Bullshit! You guys look too young to be airline pilots."

Curly challenged the guy, "Listen, Buster, not only did we fly for Rocky Mountain, he was president of the airline."

Catwalk wished he would have kept his mouth shut. The guy said, "Who are you kidding, ain't no way he was president of an airline. If he was, what's he doin' up here flying the bush?"

Curly stood up and Catwalk pleaded, "Curly, let it go. It doesn't matter."

Curly persisted, "Listen you fat tub of lard, this guy was president of the airline until the board of directors railroaded him, 'cause he's black."

With that the guy took a swing at Curly and Curly tore into him, pummeling his face even though the guy outweighed him by fifty pounds.

Catwalk grabbed Curly and pulled him away from the guy, then stepped in between them. "Curly, if you get thrown in jail, we might lose this job. Take it easy. It doesn't matter."

He turned to the other guy and said, "He ain't gonna bother you anymore. We'll just finish our beers and we're out of here."

He steered Curly to an empty bar stool and they sat down. A few minutes later another black man approached Catwalk with his hand extended and said, "I'm Jack Winters and I used to work for Northwest. I've heard a lot about you. I'm sorry you got shafted so bad. You handled that pretty well."

Catwalk shook his hand. "Thanks. Curly gets a little excited sometimes."

"Listen, you should know, that color doesn't mean anything up here, but the people are a different breed. They're leery of people from the states because so many are running from something. They respect honesty, courage and strength of character. And, if you see someone else who's in a fix, you always help them. Next time it might be you that needs the help."

"Thanks, we'll remember that."

Jack left and Catwalk said, "C'mon, Curly. We've got our first money making flight tomorrow and I want to be well rested because we're flying over the roughest terrain on earth."

# Chapter Thirty-Seven

Catwalk departed Valdez, flying the Detroiter, in beautiful clear skies,. Curly trailed him in a Gull Wing Stinson. They each had four men from the fish and game department and boxes of supplies they were taking to Fairbanks where they'd drop the men off, then pick up five hundred pounds of frozen fish and a couple hundred pounds of animal pelts for the return trip.

The flight up proved to be uneventful and Catwalk was grateful for the fair weather, not only for easier flying, but for a chance to take in the incredible beauty of the land. He never imagined such an expansive and breathtaking wilderness.

When they landed on the Chena River, next to the ballpark that was used for land planes, the temperature was a balmy fifty degrees. Over lunch in a diner, Catwalk told Curly, "On a nice day like this it's hard to imagine all the stories about the terrible weather are true."

"Everyone says it can get a lot worse than those storms in the Rockies. Sooner or later, we'll find out. I'd like to get a few flights under our belts before we run into a real bad storm."

Catwalk smiled, "Well, partner, we got one flight under our belts." He then finished his meal. He'd been surprised to hear Curly express some apprehension about the weather. He would have expected Curly to say something like, "Bring it on, I ain't worried about their piss ant storms." He was pleased that his partner showed some respect for the weather.

◆ ◆ ◆

They loaded the fish and pelts, and departed for Valdez. Following the Chilitna River through the valley between Mt. McKinley and Mt. Hayes, Catwalk saw the skies growing dark in the west. He resisted the urge to turn away from the weather, even though it would be at its worst close to Mt. McKinley. He had to stay over the river in case they were forced to land.

The storm was on them in minutes and they both descended to-

172

ward the river to avoid getting caught above the weather. The wind began howling and changing directions every few seconds. In the space of a few miles he flew through rain, hail and snow. Now he worried about icing which could coat his wings and force him down whether he wanted to land or not.

Catwalk looked down at the river and saw no sandbars, but he also didn't see a bank where he could beach the plane. He checked his wings and saw the build up of ice that he'd feared. He'd have to land soon and if there was no shoreline to beach the plane, he'd be forced to somehow navigate down the river until he found a suitable mooring area.

With the ice building, he touched down on the river with no problem, but immediately found that the current was incredibly swift. He felt like he was making close to ten knots just floating down the river. He wondered, if a shoreline came along, would he be able to maneuver the floatplane to a landing area?

He watched in awe as the plane floated down the river, with the gale force wind trying to turn his airplane in every direction on the compass. Using his power and limited steering he was able to keep it in the middle of the river, but didn't know how long he'd be able to do that.

Then, he saw a bend in the river ahead. On the right side of the curve was a sloping shoreline. He steered for the sand and just before he came abeam it, applied power.

The plane hit the beach with a scrape and crunch, but the floats held fast. He grabbed his mooring ropes and stakes, and hurried out to tie the ship down before it floated away. Once it was tied down he returned to the cockpit, put on his parky and thought about Curly.

✦ ✦ ✦

Curly was three miles in trail of Catwalk when he hit the weather. He'd also flown down the river and like his partner had seen the ice build up on his wings. He'd found a suitable mooring area, landed and tied the plane down. His problems started after he was tied down.

He was sitting in the plane with his heater going, eating a candy bar, when he saw a dark shadow moving through the sleet. The visibility was so poor that he couldn't tell what the shape was, but it wasn't human—it was too big. He watched the form move toward the plane, and when it was less than teen feet from him, Curly recognized it as a huge grizzly bear. Astonished, he started to say something, but caught himself in time. If the bear didn't know he was there, he didn't want to get its attention. He then remembered hearing about a bear's remarkable sense of smell. He put his candy bar in his pocket, but there was nothing he could do about four tubs of fish. Sooner or later, the bear would discover them.

✦ ✦ ✦

Catwalk worried about Curly. He hadn't seen the plane go by on the river, so that meant Curly had landed somewhere, but was he O.K? In these volatile weather conditions and with their limited experience in floatplanes, the chances for an accident were high. He decided to walk the shoreline in search of his partner.

✦ ✦ ✦

Curly watched the grizzly coming closer to the plane. Every now and then it would stand up to sniff the air, and he was amazed at the size of the creature—it looked like it was eight feet tall! He took his pistol out of his flight bag and checked the cylinder. He had six rounds, but was six rounds from a measly thirty-eight was enough to stop this monster?

The bear sat down on the shore line and looked over a dead fish. It started to eat it's find, and Curly hoped this would curb it's appetite.

✦ ✦ ✦

Catwalk walked along the shoreline, knowing there was a stretch of shoreline where he hadn't seen any suitable mooring spots. He'd checked his watch when he left the plane and decided he'd walk for thirty minutes. If he didn't find Curly in that time, he'd return to his plane because he didn't want to be roaming around in this wilderness after dark.

✦ ✦ ✦

The bear had finished the fish and decided to explore the plane. Curly got ready to explode out the door if the bear tried to get at the fish. With his heart pounding, he watched as it came to the right side of the plane to check out the float. The bear pawed at the float and toyed with the struts, less than five feet from him. He felt the plane rock every time the bear tugged at the strut. His mind was racing; Could the bear get into the plane? Did they eat humans? Could he outrun a bear if his gun didn't stop it? Was there any way he could make it go away?

✦ ✦ ✦

Catwalk rounded a bend and saw the Stinson moored onto the shoreline. Upon seeing that the plane was in one piece and in good conditions, he smiled. He was going to yell at Curly, but then saw him in the seat with his back to him. Thinking he was asleep, he decided to sneak up on him and scare the daylights out of him.

✦ ✦ ✦

Curly turned to open the door in case the bear came after him. Then he saw Catwalk coming up the shoreline. He couldn't yell, but he had to warn him somehow. He quietly opened the door and began waving him back. When Catwalk didn't respond and kept coming toward the plane, he yelled, "A bear!"

The bear turned toward the voice an let out a snort. Catwalk stopped in his tracks. He barely saw the creature on the other side of the plane. Curly jumped out of the plane and moved toward Catwalk with his pistol pointed at the bear. The bear ambled around the nose of the plane and looked at the two men. Then it got a whiff of the frozen fish.

From fifty feet away, Catwalk and Curly watched the bear move slowly toward the door. Even though it could be deadly, the large grizzly was a magnificent animal. The bear stuck its nose in the door, then crawled into the plane and dug through the tub of ice for the fish.

As they watched from behind a fallen log, Curly whispered, "The son of a bitch is eating my fish."

Catwalk, who also had his gun out, asked, "You think we should shoot it?"

"Our thirty-eights might not stop it. What if we just piss him off?"

"Let's just leave it alone. Maybe it'll just eat a few fish and then run along. It can't eat two hundred pounds of fish, can it?"

"Damned if I know. If it comes after us, then we start shooting."

The bear sat in the plane for half an hour. It grew dark and Catwalk didn't relish the thought of walking back to his plane in the dark of night, with grizzlies in the area. Finally, the bear crawled out of the plane, looked the two men for a minute and then ambled up the shoreline. When it was out of sight, Catwalk and Curly returned to the plane.

Curly reached the door first and shouted, "Oh, God damn it!"

"What's wrong?"

"That fucking bear spread fish heads and guts all over the inside of my plane."

Catwalk took a look at the bear's mess and couldn't help but giggle. Then he started laughing out loud. Curly said, "It ain't funny."

"Yes, it is, Curly. It's hilarious—bear comes along and eats your fish, then leaves his mess in your plane. I think it's funny as hell."

Curly looked at his friend and started laughing himself. Before long both pilots were standing on the shoreline of the Chilitna River, in the middle of the Alaskan darkness laughing until they had tears in their eyes.

Once the hilarity of the situation passed, they cleaned out as much of the mess as they could, the smell of rotting fish parts was already becoming strong. They decided to walk back to Catwalk's plane and spend the night. Curly said, "It only ate a few of the fish. You think they'll dock our pay?"

"I don't know. We're about to find out how they deal with something like this."

◆ ◆ ◆

The next morning they couldn't takeoff because the freezing rain continued. The heater kept them warm in the plane while Catwalk read, but Curly was growing restless; he clearly wanted to get back in the air. It was early afternoon before the storm abated and they saw sunlight peeking through the clouds.

"It's breaking up, Cat. I'm going back to my plane."

"O.K., I'm going to wait until I see you go by, then I'll take off."

◆ ◆ ◆

Catwalk and Curly landed on Lake Hood two hours later. When they told Hank about the missing fish, he asked what happened. When they told him what the bear did in the Stinson, and how the plane smelled, he roared with laughter, then said, "Funny thing is, it ain't my plane. I just borrowed it from Dave Reynolds. Wait'll he hears that his plane smells of fish guts."

Catwalk and Curly then headed for the bar to get a beer.

They'd been in the bar for ten minutes, when Hank walked in and spread the story about the bear around. The men in the bar thought the tale was hilarious and ribbed Curly unmercifully. A story like this, however, had it's merits. Their adventure had cemented their relations with the local gentry and other pilots. They left the bar, not as newcomers, but as accepted members of the working community.

By the time they left for dinner, Catwalk was higher than he'd ever been in his life, but he felt wonderful. While they waited for dinner, he explained to Curly, "Do you know this is the first time in my life, I've been able to be one of the boys; drink beer, laugh and let my hair down, without worrying about someone making as issue of my presence. Curly, it fells great."

"I'm glad for you, old buddy. You deserve to enjoy yourself after all the crap you've been through. Maybe we'll stay up here for a while."

# Chapter Thirty-Eight

Catwalk and Curly quickly learned the hazards of flying the bush. They avoided major accidents, although they had their share of minor incidents such as, broken oil lines, frozen crankcase breathers, hard landings, broken skis, all of which were part of bush flying. They constantly had to change their planes from floats to wheels to skis, depending on the time of year and their destination. When their planes were on skis, they spent a lot of time thawing out frozen skis with boiling water. When they were on floats, they concentrated on avoiding sandbars. On wheels, they just had to find level places to land because in so many remote locations graded runways didn't exist.

◆ ◆ ◆

One clear, frigid morning they were flying a Stinson L-5, carrying a Caterpillar track to a construction site just north of the Arctic Circle. Trying to stay under a building storm, Catwalk was flying through a river valley, searching for the site in the fading visibility.

"Over there at one o'clock." Curly shouted. "I see a bunch of construction equipment."

"Is there a level place to land?"

"I think so. Circle around that derrick and I think you can set it down just beyond it."

"Is it ice or snow?"

"I can't tell; it's probably permafrost. You'll have to set her down quick because we won't have much braking."

Barely twenty feet off the ground, Catwalk flew a pivot around the drilling derrick. He began to flare for touchdown just as a gust of wind picked up the right wing. He corrected, then touched down, harder than he wanted to.

CRUNCH. THUD.

Curly turned around and looked at the hole where the hard landing had caused the thousand pound Caterpillar track to break through the floor of the airplane.

"Jesus Christ, Cat. Do you believe that?"

"I knew the thing was heavy, but I never thought it'd bust through the floor."

Curly started laughing, and said, "Well, at least we don't have to unload it."

Catwalk was in no mood for laughter. Thinking of their return trip, he said, "True, but we've got to fly back with a hole in the floor. It's going to be a cold trip."

Bundled against the cold, they flew back to Tanana, with the bitter Arctic wind swirling through the cockpit. Huddled around a pot bellied stove, while mechanics affected a makeshift patch for the plane, they talked about the warmer climate of the southwest.

❖ ❖ ❖

One of their scariest moments came on a flight to Kotzebue in a single engine Fokker on skis. Caught in a whiteout, they were searching for a place to land on the polar ice pack. Catwalk said, "It looks flat past the next pressure ridge. Set it down there."

Curly landed and they'd just staked the plane down when they heard a loud crack. "Fuckin' ice is breaking up, Cat!"

"I know." Catwalk looked around them. The ice had broken up and they were sitting on a piece of ice not much bigger than the plane.

Curly yelled, "How the hell are we gonna takeoff now?"

"We have to wait for the ice to pack, and hope we end up with a couple hundred feet of flat ice."

"Great! How long before the ice packs up?"

"Who knows? We might be floating around out here for days."

"You know, Cat, I sure like flying with you, but at times like this there would be a definite advantage to having a female co-pilot."

"There would be a definite advantage to having a boat!"

❖ ❖ ❖

They waited for two days, not know where they were floating. Catwalk thought the ice would eventually 'pack up'. The only problem was, it often formed pressure ridges and they might not have a smooth surface on which to depart.

On the third morning, with only one day of food and water left, the ice started to pack up. Catwalk said, "Start the engine. I'll untie the plane."

Curly didn't share his partner's confidence. "We're gonna end up in the drink for sure."

Catwalk ignored Curly's comment and watched the movement of the ice. The ice chunk on which they were sitting slowly drifted toward two other larger chunks. Once they joined, they should have enough room to depart, but they'd have to move at just the right time.

Curly said nothing as they sat in the cockpit with the engine idling, watching the ice float through the Artic Ocean in a slow ballet.

When the chunks joined Cat gunned the throttle, hoping that they didn't separate or raise any pressure ridges until he was airborne.

"Cat, if you've ever made a short field takeoff, now is the time."

The plane sped down the ice and approached the first joint where the ice pieces met. Cat saw a foot of water between the ice pieces, but his skis flew over it and he looked at his airspeed—fifteen knots shy of his liftoff speed. Then he saw the piece of ice they were on now was shorter than he'd thought. He was running out of ice—fast.

Curly yelled, "Son of a bitch, Cat! We ain't got enough ice."

The edge of the ice passed under his skis. He felt them sink and touch the water, but before they sunk into the freezing ocean, the wings took the load and he slowly gained altitude.

They both held their breath until Curly said, "That was too fuckin' close, partner."

Catwalk turned to him with a wide grin. "We're high and dry, buddy. Never a doubt."

Thirty minutes later, they landed in Kotzebue. As they were unloading the mail and supplies, one of the locals asked Catwalk, "Have a good flight up?"

He thought, well, we made it off the ice without ending up in the frigid ocean. He said, "Yep. It was a great flight."

◆ ◆ ◆

On a rare day off together Catwalk and Curly had gone fishing on the Chitina River.

Curly said, "Did you see the paper this morning? Germany invaded Poland and Hitler ain't showing any signs of slowing his conquest of Europe."

"I read that. The Soviets and Japanese are fighting in Manchuria too. The war is growing on several fronts."

"We're going to end up in this thing before it's all over."

Catwalk said, "You will, but I don't know if I'll see service. There's been talk about integrating the military, it hasn't gone beyond talk. FDR called up the black reserve medical officers and chaplains, but that's the only thing he's done."

"They're starting a civilian pilot training program, so someone knows they're going to need pilots. With all your flying time, I can't see them not taking you."

"It's not a question of flying time, Curly. It's all about color."

"I know, but that's ridiculous. Maybe we don't want to serve in the military if they're that stupid."

◆ ◆ ◆

The next morning Catwalk was reading the paper over breakfast when Hank walked into the restaurant and said, "You and Curly won't be taking that load of mining machinery over to King Salmon."

"Why not?"

"Guy just landed and said there's one hell of a storm, with wind up to eighty knots coming this way. You guys can sit it out."

"It must be bad if you're grounding us."

"The guy said it was the worst he'd ever seen. Find your friend and go tie down the planes. Double the ropes and drain the fuel tanks so they won't sink if they break loose."

Catwalk found Curly at the drug store flirting with a girl who worked the soda fountain.

Curly saw him and said, "Hey, Cat. This is Joanne. I'm going to take her up for a plane ride as soon as we get back from King Salmon."

"We're not going to King Salmon, Romeo. There's a big blow coming from that way and we've got to tie the planes down and drain the tanks."

◆ ◆ ◆

They'd just gotten the planes tied down as the wind picked up to about forty knots. They drove over to the wharf to see if the fishing boats were coming in. The boats, which normally rode out the rough weather, returned to the safety of the docks in droves. When the rain started coming in sheets, they sought shelter in a waterfront bar and listened to the seamen talking.

"Them rollers was forty feet if they was a foot. Roughest seas I've ever seen."

"I had waves breaking over the wheelhouse. Damn near tore off my rigging."

Ten minutes later a man walked in, soaking wet and saying, "Big Jim and the *Oracle* went down off Montague Island. We picked up two survivors, but ain't no one going to survive in these seas."

Catwalk ate a sandwich as he listened to the men talking about fighting the rough seas. He was thankful he and Curly hadn't departed and told him they'd better check on the planes soon. If the storm wrecked the planes, they were out of a job.

They were paying the waitress when a man came in and shouted, "Are there any pilots in here?"

Someone pointed at them and the guy sat down at their table. He didn't waste time, "Can you guys fly in this stuff?"

Curly laughed and said, "Would you want to fly in this weather?"

Dead serious, the man said, "It ain't for me. I just came in from Kodiak. There's two kids got bit by a rabid fox. They don't have any rabies serum on the island. Those kids will die if someone doesn't get some serum to them fast."

Catwalk looked at Curly and instinctively knew what he was think-ing—they had to make the trip. He asked the guy, "Where on the island are the kids?"

"In the town of Kodiak. They was took to the clinic there, but they're out of serum."

Several men holding beer bottles had gathered around the table. One of them said what all of them were thinking, "You guys can't fly in this."

Another said, "This is the worst storm in twenty years. You'll never make it."

A third man piped up, "Trip like that would be suicide."

Catwalk told the guy, "We'll see how it looks out there." He and Curly left and walked toward the planes. Curly said, "The Vega is the best plane for this weather and it's on wheels. But if we fly into eighty knot winds, we'd be making only sixty knots across the ground."

"Yeah, and we can't get down on the water because if the rollers are forty feet high, they'd knock us out of the sky."

"We'd probably ice up before we reached open water."

"We'd have to refuel in Homer and I doubt if we could find the field in this stuff."

"Fighting those winds, we might run out of fuel before we get there."

To get out of the rain that was vertical now, they stepped behind a shed near the dock where the planes were bobbing in the storm. Cat-walk said, "So, what do you think?"

"We can't tell Hank, he'd never let us go."

"Where can we get the serum?"

"Doc Fellars."

◆ ◆ ◆

They walked a block to a clinic and found the doctor eating lunch in his office. They told him about the kids that had been bitten. His reply was, "You guys can't fly in this. The fleet came in early and that means it's bad out there."

Catwalk said, "I'll pay you for the serum."

The doctor shook his head and said, "If you're going to make an attempt to get it there in this storm, I'll give it to you." He went to a refrigerator and brought out two bottles. As he packed it in ice, he said, "This is one hundred percent equine serum. There's plenty here for both kids. Good luck and Godspeed."

# Chapter Thirty-Nine

Curly flew the left seat for the first leg from Valdez to Homer. As soon as they were airborne, Catwalk said, "The wind is worse than I thought it'd be, but it's a warm storm. That might keep us from icing up."

"Hell, Cat, it might clear up too, but I wouldn't count on it."

Curly hugged the shoreline to stay away from the rough seas farther off shore. Normally, he'd head out over open water; because the weather never gets right down to the water, there's always a twenty or thirty foot gap between the clouds and the water. With the rough seas however, he didn't have that option because the swells were too high. He had a quarter mile of water at the shoreline he could fly over, and still some of the breaking waves we're closer than he liked.

"You gonna cut through Moose Pass and fly the west side of the Kenai Mountains, or stay on the leeward side?"

Fighting the controls, and struggling to see through a rain soaked windshield, Curly said, "We'll see how it looks when we get to the pass. I think we'd be better off to stay on this side of the mountains."

"Yeah, I'd rather die in the ocean than slam into a mountain."

Curly looked at Catwalk to see how serious he was and said, "Would you really?"

"Sure. Drowning is supposed to be peaceful."

Curly jammed the throttle forward as a downdraft threatened to drive the plane into the surf. The engine revved and after precious seconds they climbed back to a safe altitude, where he retarded the throttle before they climbed into the overcast. He then watched as a spit of land passed by and the wind increased. They were over open water at the south end of Prince William Sound, and he steered into a thirty degree crab just to hold their course. Without his protection of the shallow water close to shore, the rolling swells were getting dangerously close.

Several minutes later, fighting to keep the plane above the spray of the swells and below the storm clouds, he said, "Who says drowning is peaceful? If someone drowns, how the hell are they going to tell you it's peaceful? Can you answer that?"

Ignoring his question, Catwalk said, "There's some islands up ahead and one of them's got some pretty good hills on it."

"I know, but there ain't no way we'll see them until we see the surf starting to break."

Several minutes later, Catwalk said, "There, at eleven o'clock. Shallow water."

Curly saw the water beginning to break over the reefs and steered to the west to avoid the hills on the island. A bolt of lightning crashed in front of them, hitting the island, and both men instinctively turned away from the flash.

Curly shouted, "Shit, that was close!"

"I don't think it hit us. All the instruments look O.K."

"I ain't so sure this was a good idea, Cat."

"We're doing all right—except for the ice."

Curly turned to look at the leading edge of the wing. He saw the shiny glow of a thin coat of clear ice. It wasn't bad now, but it could accumulate enough to spoil the lift of their wings—before they could find a place to land.

Reading his mind, Catwalk said, "If we need to land, we're coming up on Seward, but I don't think we can find the field in this stuff. Probably have to set it down on the beach."

"I'm climbing into the weather to see if it helps." Curly advanced the throttle and the water below disappeared as they ascended into the clouds.

Watching the compass, Catwalk told him, "Thirty degrees left." Flying in the weather, their one objective was to stay away from the mountains—they had to stay over water. He had to make sure Curly didn't drift toward land.

Curly looked at the wing. The ice had disappeared. That was in their favor. If the ice became a problem he knew how he could get rid of it. He slowly descended out of the weather, but found himself over the angry, turbulent water of the open sea. Again, he let the plane slowly drift toward land until he saw the breaking surf.

At the end of the Kenai Peninsula, Curly turned west-northwest, toward Homer and into the teeth of the wind. They had a quarter of a tank of fuel left and Catwalk summed up their situation. "We're not going to land with a lot of fuel left."

"If we land with a pint left, that's just fine by me."

Forty five minutes later, they saw the field a half a mile inland. With his fuel gauge on empty, Curly slammed onto the dirt runway and chopped power. They breathed easier, but still, the storm threatened to flip them over. Taxiing in, he said, "We're halfway, partner."

"Yeah, but if we refuel in this rain, we risk getting water in the fuel tank."

"I'll see if they got a tarp we can throw over us while we fill the tank."

Catwalk stayed in the plane to study the chart for his leg of the flight. Once they got to Kodiak, he wanted to be able to find the town with no delay. Curly walked into the line shack and a tall, young man in white overalls said, "You must be Curly Levitz."

"That's right."

"Hank called and said, 'If you guys end up drowned in the ocean or dead on the side of a mountain, you're both fired.'"

"I figured as much. You got a tarp we can use to cover us while we refuel?"

"I can't believe you guys flew over in this stuff. You must be nuts."

"We ain't got a lot of time, friend."

The man took him outside where he handed Curly a folded canvas tarp. He then gave them a hand holding it in place while they refueled under the cover of the tarp.

From inside the plane, Catwalk noticed the storm was not letting up and most of his leg would be over open water.

✦ ✦ ✦

Catwalk departed into the same weather they'd fought on the first leg; fifty to sixty knot winds, driving rain, and now sleet, which meant the rain was freezing, and their chances of icing up were increasing. After he passed the fishing settlement of Port Graham, they were over open water and the swells seemed to leap up at the plane, trying to smack it, as if to say, "You'll pay for this foolishness."

Once he found a comfortable altitude, just above the swell and just below the overcast, he felt better for a while. It was always in the back of his mind, however, that the condition of the seas or the level of the cloud bases could change in an instant, and there was always the chance that they could encounter a rouge wave that could knock them out of the sky. They were completely at the mercy of the storm.

He looked over at Curly and remembered that day in the box car several years ago. During their run from the law that followed, he was thankful to have Curly by his side and he felt the same comfort at his presence now. He said, "You think this is better or worse than running from Jones and the railroad bulls?"

"This is much better. Ain't anyone shooting at us and we got plenty to eat."

In spite of having to wrestle with the controls to hold his course and altitude, Catwalk smiled. They'd come a long way since those days and he wondered, where were they going?

He returned his thoughts to the storm because the wind seemed to increase and the plane was being thrown around like a kite. Then, he and Curly heard it at the same time; in unison they said, "A miss!" Curly reiterated, "God damned engine's missing. What do you think it is? You think some water got in the fuel?"

Catwalk listened and watched the tachometer. He said, "It doesn't sound like fuel contamination. I'd say a plug wired got shorted by the rain."

"One ain't bad. We could fly to Hawaii with one bad cylinder, but if it gets worse, we'd better prepare to ditch."

"How far from land are we?"

"Twenty miles." As soon as he said it two lightning strikes lit up the sky in the windshield. Crack!—Ka-boom! Two loud crashes reverberated through the cockpit. The engine was still missing but it seemed like there were longer intervals between the misses; or was this just wishful thinking. He'd learned from experience that when you're flying in a high pressure situation, you often hear things that aren't there and don't hear things, you'd prefer didn't exist.

Ten minutes later they saw the surf crashing on the shore of Shuyak Island. Catwalk headed for the shoreline and felt relieved that the worst part of the flight was over. He and Curly looked at each other. Both of them felt like the worst was behind them, but neither of them wanted to jinx the flight by saying anything.

Catwalk felt the wind let up. He thought it was due to the high terrain to their right and knew, even though he had less wind, he'd have to be careful of downdrafts.

They'd just crossed the inlet between the islands when Curly said, "The town is right up ahead, we got it made partner."

"Not so fast." And just as he said it, the engine started running rougher, then it quit. In the deadening silence, Catwalk looked for a level spot on the beach, but the rain still limited visibility to a hundred feet or so.

Curly shouted, "There after those boulders, the beach is as flat as a pool table."

Catwalk saw the spot and began to flare the plane to land. The wheels had just touched down when he saw the unbelievable.

"Son of a bitch!" Curly yelled.

Catwalk stood on the brakes but the fallen tree, no bigger around than his waist, was coming up too fast. His wheels hit the tree trunk and the nose went over. In a grinding crunch, the propeller dug into the sand.

◆ ◆ ◆

Catwalk felt blood on his face. Then he felt the gash on his forehead from the dash board. He thought, if that's all that's wrong, I'm O.K.

He looked at Curly, who also had some small cuts on his face where his head had slammed into the instruments. He said, "You O.K.?"

Curly looked at him and actually had a smile on his face. "Wait 'til I find the dumb bastard that put that tree there."

"I guess you're O.K.?"

"I'm fine. And we made it, Cat! God damn it, we did it. Now all we gotta do it take the serum into town."

"I wonder what Hank's going to say when he finds out we wrecked his plane that we stole?"

"I wonder where we're going to work next?"

# Chapter Forty

Catwalk and Curly hastily cleaned and bandaged their cuts. This done they walked toward town. Curly said, "Do you think we're gonna have to look for another job?"

"We don't know that Hank's going to fire us, but he probably will. I don't know if I want to stay up here or not. I'm kind of tired of the weather, but there's more flying jobs here than back in the states."

"I know what you mean. I've kind of been thinking about going into the service. With this war coming, I'd have to sooner or later. I think I'd like to fly bombers."

Catwalk looked at his friend. This was the first he'd heard him talk about enlisting. He hated to see Curly leave, but didn't want to dissuade him. He said, "Why bombers?"

"They're like the Boeings, except bigger. I'll bet bomber pilots get a lot of girls."

Go for it, man. There's no reason why you can't."

Thinking of Catwalk's situation, Curly felt bad for his friend. Knowing Cat as he did, he knew he'd want to join the service in the event of a war. But, there were many reasons why he couldn't pursue a hitch in the service. He said, "Some day they've got to change things in the military, so black men can join up. It's ridiculous that they keep you out."

"I think it'll change, but I'm sure they won't make it easy."

◆ ◆ ◆

Seeing docks packed with fishing boats in the distance, they knew they'd reached the town. They walked into the first open business, which was a restaurant. Curly asked a waitress, "Where can we find the clinic? We've got the serum for the two rabies victims."

Seeing their bandages, the waitress said, "Oh, my gosh! You guys look like you could use some patching up yourselves. It's down the street, same side, white sign, you can't miss it."

"Thanks."

They turned and she said, "You guys get done there, come on back. Dinner is on us."

◆ ◆ ◆

Once at the clinic, the doctor thanked them profusely and told them that his staff would clean them up at no charge. He then left to help the kids who'd been bitten. True to their boss's word, the staff treated the two pilots like royalty. They were given hot coffee and donuts while their cuts and abrasions were treated.

While she tended to Curly an attractive young nurse said, "I can't believe you guys flew over in this storm. That must have been scary."

Curly jumped at a chance to impress her. "Aw, it wasn't nothing. Heck, me an' my partner, we do this all the time. If we can help someone, we don't mind risking our necks."

After they'd been treated, Catwalk said, "We'd better go, Curly. We've got to find someone to repair the Vega. If we can't, we've got to find a way back to Valdez. We might have to wait for a fishing boat."

Curly's mind was still on the nurse. With a smile, he said, "I wouldn't mind sticking around here a few days."

Catwalk dragged him out of the clinic and they returned to the restaurant where they were served elk steaks and gravy, fresh fish and greens. As they ate they were beset with questions about he flight over.

Upon hearing about the wreck, one of the locals said, "Denny, down at the airport might be able to make that plane flyable if he can get the parts. Problem is, the high tide might carry it off before you can get it out of there."

Catwalk and Curly looked at each other. Curly shouted, "Damn it! The tide."

Catwalk asked, "How high is your tide and when does it comes in?"

"It's a fifteen foot tide and it'll be coming in about now."

They thanked everyone and dashed back into the storm, which had quieted to a rain shower. When they reached the shoreline, Curly said, "The tide is in three or four feet already; the plane might have floated out to sea. Lucky, the fuel tanks were almost empty so it might float for a while."

When they got to the crash site, they both stopped in their tracks—the Vega was gone. They looked off shore and saw it, a half mile out with a wing up—going under. Curly screamed, "Son of a bitch, Cat! We sunk a plane."

Catwalk added, "Now, we're fired for sure."

✦ ✦ ✦

The next day, Catwalk and Curly returned to Valdez compliments of Wien Airlines. They were met with cheers and congratulations for their feat, which made the papers from Anchorage to New York.

Because it was his plane that had been lost, Hank wasn't as impressed as everyone else. Several of the local pilots took up a collection to have the Vega salvaged and repaired, but still, their notoriety notwithstanding, Hank fired Catwalk and Curly.

When they inquired about jobs with other outfits, everyone said they didn't need anyone right now. Catwalk and Curly knew this wasn't true, but couldn't press the issue.

They were in a bar when another pilot explained it to them. "What you guys did was remarkable, even heroic, but you took a plane without the owner's permission. It turned out good this time, but you didn't show good judgment. People don't want you working for them.

Catwalk and Curly decided to go fishing and consider their future, which would probably not be in Alaska. Even though Catwalk liked the people here and the way he was treated, he wouldn't mind returning to the states. He'd never gotten used to the weather in Alaska. Being from Mississippi, and having spent the last few years in the southwest, he was tired of the cold. He'd also been thinking about Curly's comments on joining the military.

He wanted to enlist in the military for several reasons: As an American, he wanted to serve his country, and he'd like to do it as a pilot. Also, he'd like to show the bigoted military men he could fly as well as anyone, better than most. And, there was no where else to go.

There was one person who could give him counsel on his dilemma, so he dialed the farm in Vaughn. Barney's voice sounded good when he asked, "You froze your tail off yet?"

"No, but I called because I'm thinking about going into the military. What have you heard about them allowing blacks to become pilots?"

"I just finished reading about General Hap Arnold. He assured Congress that the Air Corps could enroll black trainees in basic and advanced courses. I don't know how much stock to put in that because Arnold has been critical of blacks since World War I."

Barney paused, then said, "I tell you, son, it doesn't sounds like anyone is making any progress against the bull-headed military, but next year is an election year. Roosevelt wants to get re-elected and he needs the black vote. Also, the first lady is supportive of blacks in the military. I think you'll see black pilots in the Air Corps, but not right away."

"That's good to hear and I agree with you, it's got to happen, but the question is when."

"Are you serious about leaving Alaska?"

"Probably. All the people up here have been real nice, but we wrecked a Vega on that flight to Kodiak. The guy fired us and now no one else will hire us. Curly is thinking about going into the military, and I've had my fill of this weather."

"If you decide to leave Alaska, you've always got a home here. Why don't you spend some time down here while you make up your mind, what you're going to do."

This suggestion sounded good to Catwalk. He had fond memories of the farm and couldn't think of a place he'd rather be right now. He said, "I think I'll do that."

"Come anytime, the door is always open."

◆ ◆ ◆

Catwalk and Curly spent four days fishing and exploring parts of Alaska they'd never seen. As much as they enjoyed their leisure time, the two out of work pilots knew it was time to move on; they loaded up the Jenny and flew south. Curly thought it was time for him to finally see his son, and Catwalk was glad to get out of the cold weather.

Three days later, they bid each other goodbye. Catwalk shook Curly's hand and said, "Good luck, man. Maybe I'll see you at thirty thousand feet one day."

"I hope so, Cat. I hope you get to join up because I know you're a better pilot than most of the guys flying now."

"Go get 'em, tiger."

◆ ◆ ◆

Catwalk then flew to Vaughn, determined to find a way to enter military service. When he landed at the farm, he found out Barney had been busy. In an effort to find out as much as they could about the integration of the military services, his secretaries had been making phone calls to local congressmen and politicians in Washington, D.C.

After they talked over the airline, which was losing passengers and money at an alarming rate, Barney told him he'd uncovered something that Catwalk might be interested in.

"Son, I don't know if I'm doing you a favor or not, by telling you about this military outfit for black fliers. From everything I've learned, this outfit is set-up to fail, and expected to fail. If by God's will and a little luck, it does succeed, you want to be a part of it.

"It doesn't hurt to talk about it."

"Last year Congress passed a law that authorized private training of military pilots by civilian flight schools, but the law doesn't apply to blacks or black schools. The Army Air Corps, however, submitted a plan for an experiment. They're going to form an all black fighter squadron. The black cadets will be trained at Tuskegee Army Air Field."

"Why do you say it's expected to fail?"

"This is a typical government program conceived for all the wrong reasons. Some people say Roosevelt backed it because it'll help him get re-elected. Others claim that the high and mighty white generals want to see it fail so it'll put to rest the question of segregation in the armed forces. See, no one has the guts to come out and say that this is the beginning of integration in the military. Everyone is conveniently avoiding the tough issue, and this program will get the same kind of support; half-hearted tokenism by officers that don't have the guts to stand up for their principles."

"Are you against the program?"

"Not at all. I think the concept is outstanding, but I know how badly it will be administered and that makes me sick."

"Maybe this program needs some people who aren't afraid to stand up and be counted. People who don't run from the hard issues."

"Oh, I agree. That's exactly what it needs."

"Any idea what kind of equipment they're flying?"

"P-40s. Twelve hundred horsepower, three hundred knots and a ceiling of thirty-two thousand feet. Carries a five hundred pound bomb and six, fifty caliber machine guns. They're a little underpowered and have poor armor plating, but there's a bunch of them available."

"Well, I'd like to get my hands on one and I don't have anything else lined up."

"Are you saying you've already decided to join this group?"

"As soon as I can find out where to sign up. I'm going to stop and see my family on the way to Tuskegee."

"It ain't gonna be any bed of roses."

"War never is."

◆ ◆ ◆

Catwalk wrote his Mother about his decision to join the military. She wouldn't be happy about it, but he thought she'd support him, even if it was begrudgingly. When he arrived at home, he found out this was the case.

"Luke, I'm so proud of what you've done, and I love this house so much that I can't find it within me to question your decision. I'd smile a lot more though, if you'd let someone else fight this war."

"Save that smile for when I get back."

"I will, son."

Catwalk spent three days at home, working on the new house and fishing with his brothers. When the time came to board the bus for Tuskegee, he was as nervous as he'd been when he took his private pilot check ride. This, however, was a four year check ride and unlike flying with a check pilot, those four years will be filled with racially motivated problems and attacks on his character. Still, nothing could have kept him from getting on that bus.

# Chapter Forty-One

When Catwalk arrived at Tuskegee, the Army airfield and barracks were not completed. Their first barracks were overcrowded tents. Water was trucked in and the mess hall was outside, regardless of the weather.

The commanding officer at the Institute was Major James "Straight Arrow" Elliot. A veteran of World War I, Elliot had been in pursuit aviation for years. The word among the troops was, although Elliot was white, he was a supporter of black aviation training. Catwalk found this to be true. Elliot was just there to do a job and color was not an issue. Unfortunately, Elliot didn't stay long. His replacement was Lieutenant Colonel Frederick Kendall, who was not a supporter of black aviation training. For him, color was an issue.

One night Catwalk and several other men talked outside their tent with a cadet who was about to graduate. The cadet said, "The instructors are strict, but they're fair. Before you go up, they'll tell you what you're going to do on that flight and that's all he'll grade you on. As soon as you land, he'll give you a slip with your grade. If you get so many errors, you get a pink slip. Three pink slips and you're out."

A cadet asked, "What if we make a bad landing, or other mistake that's not in our routine?"

"The instructors know you're going to make mistakes, so they'll overlook some. They're not there to wash you out. They're there to make good aviation cadets out of you."

After a four week classroom and indoctrination period, Catwalk marched out to the flight line one morning with his class. His instructor, a tall white Captain called out, "Aviation Cadet Jackson, follow me to the plane."

They walked to a row of PT-17 biplanes, a plane not much different than the Jenny. The instructor said, "Cadet Jackson, we're climbing to ten thousand feet today. Then we're going to do loops, slow rolls and immelmen turns. Do you understand?"

"Yes, sir!"

Once they were taxiing, the instructor came on the intercom and said, "Cadet Jackson, I understand you were president of Rocky Mountain Airways."

"That's correct, sir."

"Have you given any thought to being an instructor at the Institute?"

"No, sir. I'd prefer to go to Europe to fight the Germans."

The instructor laughed. "Cadet Jackson, the Army Air Corps wasn't formed to satisfy your desires. Every man here want to go fight the Germans, but if we let them, who is going to teach the new men?"

"That's a good point, sir."

"We'll talk more, Jackson."

Catwalk's barnstorming experience came back to him quickly and he went though his routine with no errors and no problems. On the flight back to the base, the instructor said, "That wasn't bad, Jackson. I think you'd make a good instructor."

On the ground he was given his grading slip, which read no errors. While he waited for the rest of his class to finish, he thought about being stuck at Tuskegee as an instructor. He was flattered that a white instructor thought him good enough, because most of the instructors had forty or fifty combat missions under their belt. To be considered for this job without any actual combat experience was a compliment, but he couldn't envision spending a whole tour of duty at Tuskegee.

Catwalk found the flying enjoyable, but not challenging. After each day's flight was over, however, the military routine was as ridiculous as he'd expected. Cadets were grouped into advanced or lower preflight groups, with the lower cadets being addressed as "dummies." The advanced cadet slept on the bottom bunk and if he wanted a glass of water during the night, he kicked the upper bunk and the lower cadet jumped out of bed and fetched his water.

On the second morning, a light came on at two thirty in the morning. An advanced cadet entered the tent in his flight gear and said, "What are you guys doing in here sleeping? I'm up there lost and I can't find my way home, and you guys are down here sleeping. Every dummy hit the floor!"

If someone didn't get up, the cadet and their mattress were pulled onto the floor and told. "Go sit on that red stool, Dummy." But, there was no stool, only a pole. The dummy had to prop himself against the pole in a sitting position. The advanced cadet said, "Mister, what are you doing, sitting in that position? Are you comfortable?"

Of course if the cadet answered, yes, they were left there until they collapsed. If they answered, no, they were ridiculed for sitting in an uncomfortable position. Catwalk suffered the hazing and bracing with the other cadets, but he noticed, it wasn't racially motivated and it was done to everyone, equally. This, and the understanding that it was part of the military, made the treatment bearable, although some cadets found it to be too much, and dropped out of training.

Catwalk focused on his flight training so he wouldn't dwell on the events surrounding him. Tuskegee was often described as "A hell hole of racism." The people in town didn't want the black cadets there and often held town meetings trying to find ways to get rid of the base. Although, the microcosm of cadets and instructors were intent on making fighter pilots out of the cadets, very few other people, including most of the military brass, supported the program.

On Kendall's orders, no blacks were allowed to visit or join the officer's club. Promotions to blacks were non-existent and when black officers protested the "colored" and "White" signs on the toilets, they were told, "They were going to take these signs and like them."

Fortunately, help was on the horizon. In 1941 Colonel Noel F. Parrish joined the squadron as director of flight training. Parrish, a keen student of the human mind, eventually replaced Kendall as the base commander and had all "colored" and "white" signs removed. He also arranged for black entertainers such as Ella Fitzgerald, Cab Calloway and Lena Horne to be brought in for dances and celebrity visits.

◆ ◆ ◆

On December 7, 1941, Catwalk was out running when he heard the news from another cadet. "Hey, Jackson, the Japs just bombed Pearl Harbor!" Stunned, Catwalk ran to the mess tent where they had a radio. He found it jammed with cadets eager to hear the news.

"At seven fifty-five this morning the peaceful calm of a Hawaiian Sunday morning was riddled with the sound of Japanese Zeros and bombs exploding in Pearl Harbor. The toll from the raid cannot be determined, but several battle ships in the harbor have been sunk and most aircraft on the island are in flames or shot up beyond repair."

Catwalk left the mess tent with another cadet. He said, "Now, for the first time since I got here, I feel like I'm in a war."

"It's more than just a war. We got the Germans in Europe and the Japs in the Pacific. We're going to be fighting this one for a while."

◆ ◆ ◆

Catwalk's class graduated on April 18, 1942. He then went to Mabry Field in Tallahassee for advanced gunnery training, and back to Tuskegee to await orders. His orders came two weeks later, although their destination was not revealed. They boarded a bus for a ride to the Norfolk Navy Base, where they'd board the USS Mariposa for destinations unknown.

It was on the bus that Catwalk got the surprise of his life. As it was pulling out of Tuskegee, the bus stopped at a red light. Most of the men on board were nervously jabbering, trying to guess their destination. Catwalk was looking out the window, thinking about his family; he didn't know how long it would be before he saw them again.

His thoughts were interrupted by a young lady walking down the street—she looked exactly like Sam. He watched her; she had the same proud posture that Sam had, head held high, walking with confidence. Then, he remembered that Sam had told him that she had a twin sister who'd moved to Alabama. Could it be?

By now the rest of the GIs noticed Catwalk's interest and the taunting began. "Take a good look, Jackson. You won't see any of them for a long time."

"She'll be old by the time you get back."

"Don't ya' wish you could take her with?"

Ignoring their catcalls, he watched the woman. When the bus pulled away and she turned and looked directly at him, as if she knew she was being watched. He saw a smile, and her eyes, her nose, all her facial features were identical to Sam's; he felt like he was seeing a ghost. He almost yelled at the driver to stop, but realized the futility.

When she was out of sight, he tried to remember if Sam had mentioned where her sister lived, but couldn't recall a specific town. The guy next to him said, "Jackson, are you O.K.? You look like you've seen a ghost."

"Yeah, I'm O.K. She reminded me of someone, that's all."

◆ ◆ ◆

For the entire voyage across the Atlantic, Catwalk thought about that woman. He didn't know how long he'd be overseas, or if he'd ever return, but when he did, he was coming back to Tuskegee to find that woman. He had to know.

# Chapter Forty-Two

When Catwalk and the rest of the 99th arrived at Oued N'ja, Morocco, they found their living conditions hadn't improved. They lived in tents with an outside mess and the airstrip, which hadn't been well maintained, was dirt. In dry weather the dust flew so much that visibility was measured in feet. In wet weather, the strip was mud.

Luckily, they brought with them 27 brand new Curtiss P-40 Warhawks and the new aircraft raised everyone's spirits. Shortly after their arrival, two instructors with recent combat experience joined the group and proved to be helpful in preparing the pilots for actual combat. To test heir skills, they often engaged in practice dog fights with a nearby fighter bomber group.

After a month of shaking down the new aircraft and honing their aerial skills, the group moved to Fardjouna, near Tunis. Catwalk's first mission was to bomb gun positions on Pantelleria Island, which proved to be uneventful because the only opposition was light flak. Still, it felt good to be flying in defense of his country.

Five weeks later they were assigned their first mission to escort B-17 and B-24 bombers. It was during his second mission that Catwalk first came face-to-face with German fighters. He was at 10,000 feet in escort formation, when he saw four Messerschmitts coming out of the sun. He radioed his wingman, "Flight of four, ten o'clock, high."

Catwalk then increased power and banked his P-40 to engage the attacking Germans. Screaming toward them at three hundred knots he fired his first rounds of actual combat. His tracers seemed to fill the sky, but the German's flew through his rounds unscathed and kept on coming. He pulled the P-40 through a six-G turn to re-engage the enemy. Before he could sight in on the German, four British Spitfires had jumped the Germans who dove for the deck and fled. Catwalk had just seen that their job as bomber escorts often entailed scaring the enemy away. If they shot them down, however, they'd never again have to deal with them.

The next three days were spent escorting bombers to Sicily, Sciacca and Trapani. Several German aircraft were spotted but they choose not to engage the formation. Catwalk talked to his wingmen on the way back to the base. "The Germans must have heard about us, they didn't even take a look see at the bombers."

"They're smart. They want to survive the war."

Another pilot said, "Maybe they got a sign in the briefing room that reads: "Attack whites only." This brought laughter from the men who'd spent their lives sidestepping the signs that prohibited them from so many activities that were only available to white servicemen.

On the fourth day twelve P40s from the 99th were escorting bombers over the Egadi Islands when eighteen Messerschmitts and Focke-Wulfe 190s appeared above them at eighteen thousand feet. The radio call had just gone out alerting the P-40s to the enemy aircraft, when the Germans attacked.

Catwalk shoved his throttle forward to engage a German, when he saw a P-40 take several hits in the wing and tail. The aircraft went into a dive and Catwalk turned his attention to the German who'd shot his wingman. They wove a switchback trail through the skies until the Messerschmitt filled his sights. Catwalk fired a thirty degree deflection shot and the German aircraft exploded.

He then saw another P-40 with a German with guns blazing on its tail. Catwalk dove on the German and fired. He didn't score, but the enemy aircraft broke off and departed the area. He looked around for other enemy aircraft. Seeing none, they continued on their escort mission, which continued with no further sightings of Germans. Once he landed congratulations were in order for Catwalk's first kill. Over cold beer his fellow pilots gave him the customary ribbing for "breaking his cherry."

Catwalk was feeling pretty good as he and his crew chief painted the first swastika, signifying a downed German aircraft, on the side of his plane. Then came a major assault in the other battle the 99th had to fight—the Momyer report.

A captain held a copy of the report and told the men about its contents. "Colonel Momyer is the white commander of the 33rd Fighter Group, and he doesn't support the black fighter squadron. His report all but called us, the pilots in the 99th, cowards. He said our air discipline is not satisfactory, that we lack aggressiveness, and that the expectations for future performance are low. The report has already gone up the chain of command."

A week later, after they'd extended their perfect record of never having lost a bomber they were escorting, the men of the 99th learned that Time magazine had picked up on the report and published an article that basically asked, "Is the negro as good a soldier as the white man?"

Again a senior officer addressed the troops, "I know you men are as furious about the negative press as I am, but there's little we can do, even though we've actually performed in an exceptional manner. I do, however, have some good news. Colonel Davis has heard about his and he's assured me that he will take some action. Until then, keep up the good work."

Colonel Benjamin O. Davis had been a former CO of the 99th. He knew what an excellent job the men were doing and he knew there were many members of the white military, Momyer being one of them, who sought to discredit them. Davis testified before several committees on the performance of the 99TH. As a result of his actions General Eisenhower went on record as saying Momyer's report was inaccurate, but the damage had already been done.

It was this lack of support that eventually caused the black military men to adopt a double 'V'. Many Americans had taken to flashing a 'V' for victory sign, to signify a victory over axis forces. The black men however used a double 'V' because they had to score a victory over the enemy troops, and score a victory over the racism they faced on both the battle field and at home.

◆ ◆ ◆

Two months later the 99th moved to Capodichino, Italy where they supported the battle of Anzio and escorted allied ship convoys. In the first week at the new field, the 99th downed twenty German aircraft while racking up an incredible eight kills in a single day. By the time they'd been at the field two weeks, Catwalk had scored three more kills, but had also come close to losing his aircraft to enemy gunfire.

They'd engaged a flight of Germans who were firing on allied ships. Catwalk had just fired a short burst at a Focke Wolfe and had gone in for the kill, when he saw tracers whizzing past his own cockpit—someone was firing on him. He stayed on the 190 and fired another burst, then saw the enemy flip over on his back and crash into the sea. It was then that he felt more rounds hitting his plane. A voice on the radio said, "I'm on him, Cat, break left."

Catwalk banked left and saw another P-40 hammer the German that had fired on him. Then he saw the smoke coming from his cowling. A voice said, "You've been hit, Cat, bail out."

He looked at his gauges and saw low oil pressure, but everything else looked good. He decided as long as his engine had power, he'd try to fly it back to the base. He radioed, "I've got power, I'm going to try to make it back to the base."

Then he took a long look around him, because being in a wounded ship meant he was a sitting duck for any Germans. Seeing only friendlys, he turned for the base. A wingman pulled up alongside him and said, "Cat, you're leaking fuel out of your starboard tank."

"I'm not surprised. I should have enough to get back to the base."

He landed with his fuel gauge on empty thirty minutes later. When he looked the plane over, he counted fourteen bullet holes including three in the engine cowling. After seeing the damage the plane could take, and still get him home, he vowed never to utter a bad word about the P-40.

◆ ◆ ◆

Two weeks later, Catwalk took off on a mission to escort bombers of the 55th Bomb Wing to the Ober-Raderach Chemical Works in Germany. This was another flight where they'd be going deeper into enemy territory. Consequently, the fighting had becoming increasingly intense. About the time that the bombers were releasing their bombs, the formation was attacked by a flight of eighteen Germans. For twenty minutes the fighting was constant as Catwalk and his wingmen wrestled their P-40s through the skies to protect the bombers. Possibly it was because they were over the Motherland, but on this day the Germans seemed exceptionally intent on pressing the attack.

Catwalk fired on one aircraft and thought he'd hit it, but the German dived for the deck and left the area. He then picked out another target who was lining up a P-40. He fired a fifty degree deflection shot and saw the Messerschmitt explode in his sights. Then came a call, "Catwalk, a Jerry on your six!"

Catwalk broke hard right and dove for the deck. When he pulled the nose around he saw a P-40 firing on the last German, then he saw the telltale smoke and the pilot bailing out of his injured aircraft.

When the skies cleared of enemy aircraft, the P-40s resumed their escort formation. Catwalk then heard a familiar voice on the radio, "Did I hear someone calling Catwalk?"

Catwalk smiled when he heard Curly's voice, and said, "This is Lieutenant Jackson, which plane are you in?"

"I'm in three oh two. Come on over here."

Catwalk looked through the flight of B-24s and saw the aircraft in the lead flight. He pulled up next to it and saw his old friend smiling at him from the left seat. He said, "Hey old buddy, how long you been with this outfit?"

"About seven months now. We just got transferred to Ramitelli."

"We're moving over there next month when we get the P-51s."

"Good. Look me up and you can buy me a beer."

"What do you mean, I buy, Curly? I just saved your ass from getting shot up by Germans. You're buying."

"O.K., O.K., I'll buy. You hot-shit fighter pilots are all alike."

Catwalk wore a smile all the way back to the base. He couldn't wait to see his old friend again.

# Chapter Forty-Three

Two weeks later, the 99th transferred to Ramitelli Air Base where they upgraded to the P-51 Mustang, the new fighter easily recognized by its huge four bladed propeller, and considered to be the finest fighter ever produced. When Catwalk first flew it he was amazed at the improvement in power and handling over the P-40. Capable of over four hundred knots and equipped with external long range fuel tanks, which were jettisoned for combat, the men of the 99th were now able to provide cover for the bombers on their entire flight.

In an attempt to paint the planes in a common squadron paint scheme, the maintenance men of the 99th had to find enough paint for all the planes. The only color they found in sufficient quantities for the entire squadron was a bright red called insignia red. So it was, the tails of the P-51s were painted bright red. This became one of the most famous paint schemes of World War II, and a paint scheme that the Germans grew to hate.

Catwalk had just finished a test flight of his new plane and was relaxing in the barracks when he heard a familiar voice yell, "Where's Jackson?"

He walked outside to find Lieutenant Curly Levitz smiling at him from the street. "Hey, Cat. How you doing man?"

Catwalk smiled at his old friend who, with his fur lined leather jacket and Air Corps cap tilted jauntily on his curly head, looked like a poster boy for bomber pilots. He noticed Curly had also grown a mustache.

Catwalk shook his hand and said, "Good to see you again, Curly. Why haven't you finished this war off yet."

"They won't give me enough bombs. If I could get enough bombs, I'd blow the whole fuckin' country away, and we could go home."

"How do you like the B-24s?"

"Well, it can carry the biggest bomb load farther and faster than anything else, but it's a bitch to fly. Every position in the plane is cramped and uncomfortable, and most of our flights are six to eight hours; I don't see how the turret gunners do it. There ain't any heat and it's not pressurized so you gotta wear an oxygen mask that usually freezes to your face. If you gotta pee, you use a tube in the back that always freezes up. Compared to those little sports roadsters you guys are flying, this thing is the pits. They call it; The Agony Wagon, but we can sure do some damage. We made a run on Ploesti last week; we came in at three hundred feet and the blast from our bombs almost flipped us over."

"Well, you wanted to be a bomber pilot."

"Yeah, but I thought the damn things at least had heaters in them. How do you like the P-51? I heard those things can do four hundred knots at sea level."

"That's right. It's a screamer; the greatest plane I ever flew. The Germans aren't going to get anywhere near you guys now."

"You guys are getting such a reputation that our pilots are requesting you for our escort. I heard the Germans call you guys Schwartze Vogelmensschen—The Black Birdmen."

"Curly, this is the most courageous group of men I've ever seen, and most of the military brass is too ignorant to realize it."

"I know what you mean. Just hang in there, man. This war ain't gonna last forever."

"Did you get to see Billy Sue before you shipped out?"

"Yeah. That kid is really cute, she gave me a picture to take with me."

Curly showed him the picture, with a measure of pride that Catwalk had never expected.

Catwalk said, "He's a beautiful boy. Good thing he got Billy Sue's looks."

Curly ignored the jab. "I'm gonna marry her right after the war, Cat."

"Were you sober when you decided this?"

"Sober as a preacher."

"Good for you. You won't find a better wife anywhere."

"Hey, Cat, I gotta run. I'm briefing an hour. I'll see you at twenty thousand feet."

"You be careful now, Curly."

"I will. I'll bring you that cold beer when I get back."

◆ ◆ ◆

Three days later the bombers again made a raid on the Ploesti oil refineries, with the 99th flying escort in the new P-51s. The Germans were prepared for this raid however, and the allied aircraft faced numerous dangers, any one of which could send them to a fiery death.

Large smudge pots had been lit throughout the refinery so the smoke obscured the critical targets. This meant the bombers had to go in low and blind. Flying in close formation, through the thick smoke they ran the risk of colliding with each other, or getting knocked out of the sky from the blast of their own bombs. They also faced the gauntlet of heavy ack-ack fire from anti-aircraft guns and more German fighters than they'd ever encountered.

Fifty-three P-51s flew escort that day for seventy-two B-24s. As soon as he saw the heavy opposition, Catwalk had a bad feeling about this raid. He knew the bombers, and the P-51s would suffer heavy losses.

When the German fighters came at them in force, he jettisoned his external tanks and tightened his belts in preparation to engage the enemy. Heavy smoke from ack-ack shells and bombs covered the entire area. Towers of fiery bomb blasts leaped up at the fighters who were often down on the deck trying to protect the bombers. Weaving through the smoke were more planes than Catwalk had ever seen; a midair collision was almost certain.

He engaged his first German and fired a burst at three hundred yards. He thought he'd scored a hit, but the German tried to run. Catwalk used the awesome power of the P-51 to close the distance and fired again. This time the enemy aircraft started smoking, then crashed into the refinery. He turned to engage another Messerschmitt, then saw a B-24 explode in mid air, a victim of anti-aircraft fire.

Tracers flew by his canopy—a German was on his tail. He added power and pulled back on the stick to fly a tight loop and position himself on the tail of his aggressor. Two bursts didn't score, but the aircraft dove for the deck and Catwalk lost him in the smoke.

He turned his attention to the gun emplacements that were throwing a large hail of fire at the B-24s. He raked one with a short burst and saw the gun cease firing. Trying to spot another gun emplacement amid the heavy smoke and bomb blasts, he saw instead two German aircraft that'd drawn a bead on him; with guns blazing.

Again Catwalk applied power and pulled a hard right turn to evade the Germans. Another P-51 appeared behind the Germans and fired a long burst that blew one aircraft to pieces. Catwalk chased the second aircraft until he was within range and knocked him out of the sky with a thirty degree deflection shot.

Searching for another German, Catwalk felt his plane rocked by an ack-ack shell that must have been close. He wondered if he had any damage. Thoughts of his own condition were abandoned as he saw a Focke-Wulf going after a bomber. He gave chase hoping he could get to the German before he fired at the lumbering bomber.

The B-24 dropped his load as the German fired from a long distance, but missed the lumbering bomber. Catwalk came around until he had him broad side in his sights, then fired. The enemy never knew what hit him. As the fiery remains of the aircraft fell to the ground, Catwalk saw another B-24 enveloped by his own fiery bomb blast and crash into the refinery. He briefly wondered if Curly had made it through the raid?

Catwalk chased off two more Germans as the last of the bombers dropped their lethal loads into the blazing inferno that was once an oil refinery. Seeing the damage had been done, and that they were outnumbered by superior aircraft, the remaining German aircraft fled the area.

The surviving B-24s flew out of the range of ack-ack fire. The worst was over. The P-51s formed around the bombers and Catwalk noticed how much smaller the bomber formation had become. At his count, thirty two B-24s had been lost in the raid and several were wounded, not expected to make the flight back to the base. He saw three bombers with props feathered drop out of the formation enroute to the base.

◆ ◆ ◆

As soon as he landed, the men wanted to toast his three confirmed kills in one day, but Catwalk begged off. He explained about Curly, then took a jeep over to the bomber side of the base. He asked a crew that had just deplaned, "Do you know if three-oh-two made it.?"

The ten man crew looked beat and bedraggled, worn out and wasted. A sergeant said, "Sir, I don't know who made it and who didn't, but if you were flying our cover, thanks."

"Don't mention it. I'm glad we could help."

The sergeant then looked down the flight line. "I don't see three-oh-two. He might have crash landed on the way home."

Catwalk drove the length of the flight line and didn't see the aircraft. He then went into the flight operations tent and asked a clerk, "Was Lieutenant Levitz flying three-oh-two today?"

"He sure was, but they didn't return."

A captain looking over a wall chart said, "He had two engines shot up and landed in a field, deep inside enemy lines, about five miles from the refinery."

Catwalk knew there was no chance they could make it back from deep inside enemy territory. Curly was undoubtedly a prisoner of war— if he hadn't died in the crash or been shot already.

He returned to his barracks and thought about whether to write Billy Sue. She'd want to know and he didn't want her reading an ambiguous account in the newspapers. He wrote her, trying to sound upbeat, telling her that Curly might be able to make it to allied territory before being captured. Although he knew it was a reality, he didn't mention that Curly might not have survived the crash landing.

After writing Billy Sue, Catwalk wrote a long letter to his Mom, then got drunker than he'd even been in his life.

# Chapter Forty-Four

Weeks passed and Catwalk heard nothing about Curly, but he wasn't surprised. Information on POWs was hard to get and often misleading. His only recourse was to pray for his friend, and hope, if he was alive, that he was treated humanely.

In spite of the cost in allied lives, the Ploesti raid had been a huge success. Since the raid, there had been fewer German aircraft sighted on their missions and a lack of fuel was given as the reason. This was the first clear indication that the allies were winning the war in Europe and it made a noticeable difference in moral.

With the decline of German aircraft, the pilots of the 99th had turned their attention to the railroads. Germany was trying to move its freight by rail, but the red-tailed P-51s proved to be just as effective at stopping rail traffic as they'd been at defeating the Luftwaffe.

Catwalk had just returned from destroying two freight trains and blowing up a strategic trestle when the squadron orderly called out to him, "Lieutenant Jackson, you've got mail."

The first of two letters was from his brother Cecil with routine news of the family. Everyone was well and they'd finally finished the second house. Catwalk smiled as he read that his Momma had finally planted her first flower garden. This had been a life long dream of hers and he felt good that he'd helped her achieve it.

The second letter was from Julio. Although there was no return address, he recognized the scrawl that he'd seen on so many maintenance reports at the airline. He opened the letter and read, in shock— Barney had died.

His hands trembling, Catwalk stared at the words; it couldn't be! He went into the barracks and sat down on his bunk. Tears welled in his eyes as he read over and over how the nurse had found him dead one morning. Then he cried out loud.

He had never thought about losing Barney because even after the accident, he'd been a strong and vibrant person. Even though he'd been flat on his back he'd still radiated a strength that few people could equal. It just didn't seem possible that he was gone. Next to his Momma, Barney had been the most steadying influence in his life, and he'd often thought of where he'd be, had it not been for Barney's help. Now, his life's mentor was gone. Within weeks he'd lost both of his best friends. He had to question: What kind of God was it that kept taking the people who meant so much to him?

What could possibly happen next? Even if he was shot down and captured by the Germans, he wouldn't feel as bad as he felt right now. He felt incredibly alone, much the same as after Sam had been killed.

He thought of his Momma's words: "In any tragedy, always try to look at the bright side." Sometimes, however, it was very hard to find bright side. He thought about his family. He still had them and he was thankful for that. There was somewhat of a bright side, but it didn't make the hurt of losing someone like Barney, any less.

John Casey, a fellow pilot with whom he'd become close, approached his bunk. "Hey, Cat. You wanna go out and run a few miles?" Then Casey saw him up close and asked, "Good God, man. You look terrible. What happened?"

"Come on. I'll tell you while we run."

Catwalk relayed the bad news. Casey had heard about Curly, but Catwalk's latest loss was news. His friend sensed the magnitude of his loss and asked, "You gonna be O.K. to fly?"

"I think flying is the one thing that'll help me keep my mind off this."

"You're right, Cat. Get as much seat time as you can."

✦ ✦ ✦

Catwalk flew every mission assigned to him and filled in on several others when pilots were unable to make their flight. Germany had come out with the ME-262, the first operational jet fighter, but the P-51 pilots weren't daunted. In air combat the jet had more speed, but wasn't as maneuverable. For all the hoopla, the German jets soon learned if they engaged an aircraft with a red tail, their future would be shortened. The Mustangs still ruled the skies over Europe.

In three months, Catwalk racked up twelve more kills, bringing his total to eighteen, second highest in the air group. One day he was summoned to the squadron commander's office. The C.O. said, "Lieutenant Jackson, you've shot down your share of the Germans. Why don't you leave a few for the other guys. You're going back to Tuskegee to serve as an instructor until your hitch, or the war is over."

"Yes sir. When do I leave sir?"

"Next week. We've got some fresh blood coming in. You break in your replacement, then take your medals and go home."

"Will do, sir."

◆ ◆ ◆

Eight days later, Catwalk packed his duffel bag with his worldly belongings, which included the Distinguished Service Cross with eight Oak Leaf clusters, flew to Rabat, Morocco and boarded a ship for the United States.

When he'd been flying every day, Catwalk had been able to overlook the racial inequities that he men in the 99th were subjected to on a constant basis. Now, however, he found himself thrust back into the world that was distinctly split into two classes—black and white.

The first such reminder was after his ship docked. A sign at the bottom of the gangplank separated the black servicemen from the white. On the train trip back to Tuskegee, while the white servicemen were given cold beer and meals, he rode in the segregated coaches of the train. They were given water.

◆ ◆ ◆

On his first weekend off, Catwalk and another instructor caught the bus to town to the black movie theater to see Casablanca. After the movie, they were walking toward a soda fountain when Catwalk saw the same young woman, who looked identical to Sam, that he'd seen on the bus the bus ride out of town so long ago. He thought of how incredibly lucky it was to see her again. He had to talk to her.

"Wait here, Hal, I've got to talk to someone."

Catwalk approached the woman. Up close, he saw the resemblance to Sam was uncanny. He said, "Excuse me, Ma'am. I apologize for this, but you look like someone I used to know back in New Mexico. Is your name Wells?"

The woman looked at him and started to say something, but stopped when a man joined them. The man said, "Rosemary, is this guy bothering you?"

She said, "No, he thought I was someone else." She turned to Catwalk and said, "You must be mistaken. My name is not Wells."

They turned and walked away.

As he walked to the bus stop, the woman's face haunted him. There was no way she could look that much like Sam and not be related.

◆ ◆ ◆

Two weeks later he was at the theater by himself. The same woman came and sat down next to him. She whispered, "Listen to me. I'm married to the man you saw and he's insanely jealous. If he sees me talking to you, he'll beat me. My maiden name was Wells. Did you know my sister, Samantha?"

Catwalk nodded his head and ate his popcorn.

"Where is she now?"

"She was killed several years ago. Shot by a hateful deputy."

When the woman didn't say anything, Catwalk turned to look at her. Tears streamed down her face. She wiped her eyes and said, "How well did you know her?"

"She was the only woman I've ever loved."

"Can you meet me at the park on the edge of town tomorrow so we can talk?"

"I can, but I don't want you to get in trouble."

"Two o'clock." And she left.

◆ ◆ ◆

Catwalk arrived at the park at one forty five. He was apprehensive about seeing the woman if her husband was the jealous and violent type, but he desperately wanted to talk to her.

She arrived ten minutes later and sat down across the picnic table from him. Seeing her in the daylight revealed lines of fear around her eyes. He cursed the man that could do this to such a beautiful woman.

She said, "My name is Rosemary Trent now. How did you come to know my sister?"

Catwalk told the entire story, from the bogus murder charges in Texas, to the shooting that took Samantha's life. When he finished, she said, "You really did love her. I can tell by the way you talk about her."

"I'm not sure there will ever be anyone else for me. I don't think I'll ever find a woman to measure up to her."

She smiled. It was the same smile that had brought him so much joy and lit up his life for the brief time Sam was with him. The smile he never thought he'd see again. He felt an incredible sense of going back to the happiest times of his life.

She said, "Are you going back to New Mexico after the war?"

"Probably. My family is in Mississippi, but there's nothing there for me. I'll go back to Vaughn and see what kind of work I can find."

"I hope you find what you're looking for, Catwalk. I hope you find happiness and goodness."

"Thank you, Rosemary. And I hope the same for you."

They stood and Rosemary came around the table to hug him. Catwalk put his arms around her and felt the woman he'd been missing for ten years. He held her tighter and longer than he should have, but he didn't know if he'd ever again enjoy the pleasure of holding a woman this much.

He stepped back and said, "Sorry. I, ah … ."

"Don't apologize, Catwalk. I understand."

◆ ◆ ◆

Catwalk returned to the base with a broad range of mixed emotions. On one hand, the woman he'd been missing for so long, existed in her twin sister. But, she was married to another man; a man who didn't treat her well and made her live in fear. He'd be doing himself, and her, a favor if he took her away from him, but he knew it was wrong to interfere in their marriage. He thought about this several times every day. Had Barney been alive, he might have called him. Now, it appeared this was decision he'd have to make on his own, and he knew which way he was leaning.

# Chapter Forty-Five

In recognition of the incredible job they'd done in Europe, Colonel Parrish had put up a sign in front of the barracks. It read: Home of The 332nd Air Group. 200 escort missions without losing a single bomber to enemy aircraft.

This was a small gesture, but for the men of the 99th and other squadrons in the Air Group, it was greatly appreciated. The pilots walked with their chests stuck out just a little further. The confident smiles of proud men were seen more often.

Unfortunately, these were times when a good deed could be neutralized in the blink of an eye. A newspaper article from the Pittsburg Defender, a prominent black newspaper told of the unkindest cut of all; German and Italian POWs were being treated better than the black servicemen in the U.S.A.

Catwalk read the story to several other black instructors. "Due to a lack of stockade space in Europe, many German and Italian prisoners of war have been shipped to the United States. While they are here, the prisoners are often escorted to USO shows, movies and dances; all activities that are off limits to black American service personnel. Restaurants in the communities where they're held are glad to serve them meals, but those same restaurants won't serve black American servicemen. Local laundries will launder the POW's uniforms, but they won't give the same service to the black GIs."

He then said, "Men, I'll be discharged in a few months, and I'll go on with my life. I'll take with me one memory: That I was a member of the finest group of fighter pilots that has ever defended America. We did it with very little support from our own commanders, but regardless of the circumstances, no one can ever take away from us the fact that we were the best of the best. Quite possibly there will never be another group of fighter pilots to equal our record."

The group responded, "Amen."

✦ ✦ ✦

In November, 1945, Catwalk reported to the Godman Field Separation Center for discharge. He then headed for Meridian and arrived at his Momma's home in good spirits.

"Luke, I can't believe it, you're home." She hugged him and planted kisses on both cheeks. "Oh Lord, I'm so glad you made it home. Luke, you don't know how much I worried."

"I'm just fine, Momma. I came through without a scratch."

"My don't you look handsome in your uniform." She yelled out the window, "Roseann, honey, come in here. Luke's home."

His little sister came running and wrapped her arms around him. He said, "My goodness, aren't you getting to be a beautiful young lady."

"I'm gonna be twelve next month."

"I know, look what I brought you." Luke unpacked his duffle bag until he found the music box he'd bought in Morocco.

Roseann unwrapped it and her face glowed with joy. "Oh, Luke. It's so beautiful. This is the prettiest present I've ever had. Thank you." She ran off to play with her present.

After dinner his Momma asked, "What are your plans now, Luke?"

He said, "I'm going back out to New Mexico in a few days. Momma."

His Mother looked forlorn and said, "I thought with Barney gone you might stay here."

"There's nothing for me here. I might be able to find a flying job out there."

"I hope you find happiness, son."

Catwalk didn't say anything, but thought about Rosemary. He hadn't told his Momma about her because he knew what she'd say if he even talked to another man's wife behind his back. Nevertheless, he thought about Rosemary often—and they were pleasant, comforting thoughts.

◆ ◆ ◆

Catwalk arrived at the farm in New Mexico one week later. As expected, the place seemed empty without Barney's presence.

Over coffee Julio told him about Barney's last days. "About six months before he died, he started getting sick more often. The nurse told me the end was near because his body wasn't strong enough to fight off the sickness. She was right."

"At least he didn't suffer."

"No, he didn't; that's one good thing." Julio lit a cigar, then said,

"He left me the farm in his will, with the provision that you and Curly have a home here anytime you want to come back. I'll certainly honor this, but I'd rather have you here than Curly. He's a little on the wild side."

Julio retrieved a large envelope from his desk and handed it to Catwalk.

Before opening the envelope, Catwalk said, "You might not have to worry about him. He got shot down over enemy territory. I don't know if he survived. He was coming back to marry Billy Sue, but now, who knows?"

"Do you think that would have been good for her? Last time I talked to her, she said she was doing real well. I don't know if she needs him or not."

"I think it would be good for the child to have a father."

"Yes, I can't argue with that." Julio paused for a sip of coffee. "In that envelope is five thousand shares of common stock that Barney left for you. If he pulls through, Curly got some as well. At least you might not have to work for awhile if you don't want to."

Catwalk thought about Barney's generosity. It was so typical of him to think of other people even though he might have known the end was near. He did the math in his mind. Although the airline's stock had been falling, it was still worth ten dollars a share. His stock was enough to support him and his family for several years, but he still wanted to find a flying job. He wanted to carry on Barney's legacy and hoped he could influence someone as much as Barney had.

He said, "The farm looks like it's doing well. How long ago did you leave Rocky Mountain?"

"I resigned shortly after Barney died. The airline management expected the maintenance men to save money by cutting corners. I told them I wouldn't do it and they threatened to fire me. I resigned and came back to run the farm full time."

"The airline is in trouble, isn't it?"

"They're hanging on, but only because Davis' group keeps getting bank loans to bail them out."

"Are there a lot of disgruntled employees?"

"Yes. After Davis took over, discontent spread through the airline like a wildfire. The people became indifferent in their work; turn around times and passenger complaints increased. No one in management could figure it out."

✦ ✦ ✦

When Julio went to finish his chores, Catwalk walked down to the oak tree to visit Barney's and Sam's grave. He told Sam that he'd met her sister, and he poured out the conflict he was feeling after seeing Rosemary. He then told Barney how much he appreciated all he'd done for him and Curly. When he left, he felt cleansed after talking to the people who'd meant so much to him, but he also felt an incredible sense of loneliness.

Catwalk then called the Levitz farm. With relief, he listened to Curly's brother, "Curly's fine. He survived in a POW camp, then after being discharged he came home for a few weeks. He left for Albuquerque about a week ago. He said he was going out there to get married."

Catwalk said, "Thanks for the good news. If you should talk to him, tell him to call me at the farm. He'll know where that is."

◆ ◆ ◆

Over the next few days Catwalk stayed busy helping Julio. It felt good to be working in the old familiar surroundings, but he hoped he'd find a flying job. A week after he'd talked to Curly's brother, he got a phone call and heard his old friend's familiar voice. "Cat, I got your message. What are you up to?"

"Right now, I'm helping Julio. How about you? How did the Germans treat you?"

"We weren't treated too badly, but the food was lousy. It's good to be back in the USA."

"Curly, I've got some bad news; Barney died a few months ago."

"Oh, God no. Cat, we owe everything good in our lives to him." As Curly said this he thought about the time he'd resigned in a fit of emotion. He regretted that this was probably how Barney had remembered him.

"Yes, we do. They got a nice marker for him and buried him near Sam and Mary under the big oak tree down by the creek. I went down to his grave this morning and thanked him for giving us the lives we have. He left you some airline stock in his will."

"Well, I'm not sure I deserve it, but that's Barney for you. Is Julio running the farm now?"

"Yes. He resigned from Rocky Mountain shortly after Barney died. He said they wanted the maintenance section to cut corners and he wouldn't do it."

"I don't blame him. Billy Sue said she's thinking about moving to another carrier because of the way they're running Rocky Mountain. Are you out here looking for work?"

"I haven't started looking for work yet, but I'm going to soon. How about you?"

Curly said, "I'm in Albuquerque. I drove out to ask Billy Sue to marry me."

"When is the wedding?"

"Well, we had a long talk and she said she thought we should wait a while, until I find out what I'm going to be doing. I think what she meant was, until I settle down some."

"I'd say that's a wise decision."

"Yeah, I know where she's coming from. How long you gonna be at the farm?"

"I'm not sure. I'm helping Julio and working on one of the Jennys to get it back in shape. They've been neglected for the past couple of years."

"I'll drive out there. I should be there by late afternoon."

# Chapter Forty-Six

Later that day, Catwalk talked while he changed the tail wheel on the Jenny. "Flying is the only thing we know, Curly, except farming and neither of us wants to go back on the farm."

"You got that right, but where do we start? I don't want to go back to Alaska. Should we pick up a used Connie, or DC-3 to start our own outfit?"

Julio said, "The cost of maintaining a Constellation would bankrupt you in six months. Why don't you pick up a surplus B-25 and start by hauling cargo?"

Curly looked around the nose from where he'd been installing the propeller he'd just balanced. "Can we make any money doing that?"

Catwalk said, "There's only one way to find out. Julio, you want to throw in with us?"

"Nah. I like it being retired here on the farm. I don't need that pressure anymore."

◆ ◆ ◆

One month later, at March Air Force Base, Catwalk and Curly signed the paperwork making them the owner of a twin-engine B-25. On the flight back to Albuquerque, Catwalk said, "We need to find a business that's growing fast and needs reliable air freight service."

Curly didn't hesitate. "I found one; the oil business in west Texas."

"Curly, you could've said anywhere but Texas."

◆ ◆ ◆

Ten days later, flying under the name of Aztec Air Freight, they hauled a load of drill bit assemblies from Midland, Texas to the new oil fields in Santa Barbara, California. The choice to feed off the oil industry had been a good one. Due to the fuel demands from increased automobile and aircraft usage, the oil business was booming and spreading out. Over the next few months, they routinely flew supplies to places like Puerto Barrio, Guatemala; Managua,

Nicaragua; and Colon, Panama, as well as several stateside destinations. Their success, however, resulted in long hours in the air, which was taking a toll.

They'd just taken off from a refueling stop in Monterrey, Mexico, when Catwalk said, "Flying twelve and fourteen hour days is killing me. We've got to buy a couple more aircraft and hire some pilots."

"I think you're right, pard. You think we should stick with the B-25?"

"They sure are cheap and easy to get. Why don't we buy two more and then find a couple DC-3s. We've got enough cargo contracts to keep several planes busy and the DC-3s will be better for the long term."

Curly said, "I just hope we can find some reliable pilots."

Catwalk said, "That shouldn't be a problem. There are thousands of ex-military pilots looking for work." Nothing was said for a few minutes while Curly went back to check on the load of refinery pipe that sounded like it had shifted.

When he returned, Catwalk said, "You know, the airlines are hiring many of the ex-military pilots, but they're not hiring any black pilots. I'd rather hire combat tested pilots than take a chance on pilots fresh out of flying school. We can hire the black pilots, many of whom I flew with in the 99th."

"If they fly cargo anything like they flew our escorts, I'm all for it. But, just because they're black doesn't mean they get a free pass. They've got to meet our standards."

"That goes without saying. I'll take out an ad in a few newspapers and we'll see what kind of response we get."

◆ ◆ ◆

Word spread among the community of black pilots and hundreds of applications poured in. For the next several weeks, when ever he wasn't flying, Catwalk interviewed pilots. He enjoyed the luxury of having so many pilots to choose from, but he could only hire so many at a time. He had to send out a lot of rejections and each one broke his heart.

His efforts to help out the black pilots didn't go unnoticed. Four months after they hired their first pilot, a reporter for Life magazine showed up to interview him. The June issue featured Catwalk on the cover.

The article explained how he was building a successful freight airline with the black pilots who couldn't find work elsewhere. The article, which called this a win-win situation, also focused on Catwalk's history, from almost being hung by the Klan, being removed as President of Rocky Mountain Airways, the serum run in Alaska and his success as a fighter pilot with the 99th. It was a flattering article, but in a racially insecure country, it met with varied reactions. Many hard-line traditional southerners still had a problem with a black man achieving success.

◆ ◆ ◆

In a darkened lounge in Austin, Texas a bespectacled man in a dark suit addressed four other men at the table. "Did you see the cover of Life magazine? I can't believe they put a colored boy on their cover and then told the whole country that he was running his business out of Midland. That article made it sound like we welcome blacks with open arms. We're gonna have a migration of uppity coloreds who think they can move here and do as they please."

Claude Givens, Texas Secretary of Commerce, said, "They won't last. Give 'em a year and they'll all be working as Pullman porters or bell hops."

"Bullshit, Claude. This Jackson fella' is expanding and buying more aircraft. Their damn airline is going to be bigger than Lone Star if they keep growing. Ever since Truman signed the executive order to integrate the military, they think they got the same rights as whites."

A tanned man in a grey suit signaled the waitress for another round, then said, "Unfortunately, they have the right to go into business like anyone else, and there ain't a thing we can do about it."

Another man said, "I'm not so sure about that."

Silence fell over the table, then he continued, "They're flying old World War Two aircraft, that are probably unsafe. The guy heading the Dallas office of the Civil Aviation Authority owes me a favor. I'll arrange for the feds to hold some spot inspections on their airplanes—some real tough inspections. We'll send these boys a message that they'd be better off doing business somewhere other than Texas."

◆ ◆ ◆

In the Collinsville Federal Prison, Alton Jones hadn't ever visited the prison library. The one time he walked in there, it was to bum a cigarette from another inmate. He saw the issue of Life magazine with Catwalk on the cover and snatched it off the shelf. "That son of a bitch!"

He read the article then showed the magazine to a fellow inmate and said, "See that nigger, Clem. In a couple years, I'm getting out of here. When I do, that black bastard is dead."

"What the hell did he do to you, Alton?"

"Something no colored boy does to a white man if they expect to live."

✦ ✦ ✦

Three weeks after the conversation in Austin, Catwalk had flown a load of well heads to a natural gas field in Wyoming. He was filing his flight plan to depart when he received a call from his maintenance chief saying one of their planes was grounded because it failed a CAA inspection.

He asked, "What did they ground us for?"

"The bolts on the exhaust headers aren't safety wired."

Catwalk thought, there's no requirement for those bolt to be safety wired; they're just torqued down. He said, "Tell Lenny to make whatever repairs the inspector asked for and not to question him."

"Sure thing, boss."

"Say Dale, did they inspect anyone else's planes?"

"No, I asked around the airport. We're the only ones they hit."

Catwalk smelled the familiar and ugly stench of racism.

✦ ✦ ✦

On the flight back to Midland, he thought about this. His problem was, there was no one in power throughout the government who'd take his side. A white man had the option of complaining to his congressman or state representative about the actions of a federal agency. His complaint would never be acted on. When Curly found out, he might take some action, but not the kind they needed; diplomacy was not his long suit. Still, he wasn't going to sit idly by and get pushed around. He had a feeling that this had to be nipped in the bud, or it could cost them a lot of money in lost revenue.

When he landed, he called the CAA inspector. His maintenance chief was on the extension when he said, "You grounded one of our planes because the exhaust manifold bolts were not safety wired. There is no requirement for those bolts to be safety wired. The requirement is to torque those bolts to sixty foot pounds. My mechanics had done that."

"Mr. Jackson, this is an old airplane that has seen a lot of use. We have the authority to ground the aircraft if we see something that is not required by the regulations, but in our opinion should be changed to meet our standards."

"Are you saying you can impose regulations on the spot?"

"That's exactly what I'm saying."

"Why was our aircraft inspected and not others?"

"I told you. You're flying old aircraft that have a lot of hours on the airframes and power plants. These planes warrant closer scrutiny than newer aircraft."

"Who told you to inspect our aircraft?"

"The directive to spot check older aircraft came from the Flight Standards division in our Dallas office."

"Thank you."

After the call, Catwalk told his mechanic, "This might not be the last episode of this drama. Make sure all the bolts in question are safety wired as instructed. Keep a log of how much time we spend on these mods and leave a carbon copy on my desk."

Catwalk decided to keep a close eye on this situation. He spread the word with his maintenance staff to contact him if there were any more inspections. He was on the phone with a freight forwarding company when Curly walked into the office. He'd just returned from Morgan City, Louisiana. His look told Catwalk he'd heard about the inspection.

When Catwalk hung up, Curly said, "It sure looks like someone is out to get us. Who do you think is behind it?"

"This had to come from a politician, because the CAA would have no reason to increase their work load just to cause us problems. Most of the politicians in Texas are racist and many of them have been in the Klan, in fact, some still are. The list of possible enemies is not short."

Curly lit a cigarette and took a bottle of blended bourbon out of a cabinet. He asked Catwalk, "You flying anymore today?"

"No, I'm done until Wednesday."

Curly poured two glasses half full and handed one to Catwalk. He said, "Do you think it would be worth our time to bitch to the head of the CAA? Or better yet, how about I go to Austin and start raising hell."

"You'd probably end up in jail."

"I'll bet I could find out who's pulling this crap."

Catwalk smiled. This was one of those times when he was tempted to let Curly go and follow up on his threat. He had no doubts, if he encouraged him, Curly would find out who'd arranged the inspections. Unfortunately, as he'd learned from Barney, he was in a business where your mistakes and bad judgment can resurface in the future and cost you dearly.

He took a healthy drink and felt it burn as he thought of the possible consequences. He and Curly had talked about starting a passenger airline once the freight operation was showing a steady profit. To do this they'd need to have routes approved. Making waves with the CAA now could haunt them in the future. He said, "It's hasn't cost us too much so far, and it won't put us out of business. I say we document everything that we have to do, and keep quiet about it for now."

"I hate the thought of some asshole politician getting away with something like this."

"I do too, but we don't know who it is, and there's the possibility it didn't come from a politician. Maybe it is someone in the CAA who wants to hassle us."

"O.K., so I find the inspector and throw him in the shit house like we did with Jones."

"He's just doing his job. His orders are coming from higher up."

Curly finished his drink and poured another. He walked over to the window and watched a C-46 park in front of the hangar. He said, "They're fucking with the wrong guys."

Catwalk swore under his breath. If Curly decided to go off half cocked and drunk, he might do damage that couldn't be repaired. He stood up, looked his partner in the eye and said, "Curly, it's not a big deal right now; it's just an inconvenience. Let it go. Don't do anything we'll regret later."

"Let's go over to Diamond Lil's and get some dinner."

"Good idea, I'm starved."

As they drove to the restaurant, Catwalk worried. He suspected Curly was planning on retaliating, and might do something they'd regret later. He wished he cold keep a close eye on his partner, but with their flying schedules they sometimes went days without seeing each other.

When they were seated he said, "I'd hate to see you do anything we'll regret, because this really isn't your fight, Curly."

Curly smiled and said, "Cat, it wasn't your fight back in that box car when we threw those two hoboes off the train, but you stepped in, and I'm glad you did."

Curly had that gleam in his eye.

Catwalk didn't enjoy his meal.

# Chapter Forty-Seven

In the next two weeks there were three more inspections. They all resulted in trumped up but minor violations. Curly was at the airport in Midland when the last inspection took place. He waited until the inspector had written up his report, then with a smile, asked him if he could talk to him in the office. The inspector agreed.

Curly closed the door behind him and faced the inspector. "You report says our aircraft is grounded until we replace all the fuel strainers with new units."

"That's correct, sir."

"I've got a problem with this. See, the fuel is filtered when it's put on the trucks to be delivered. Then, it's filtered when it's pumped into our tanks. When we pump it into an aircraft, it's filtered again, and then it goes through the fuel strainers. I'm worried that if we filter the fuel any more, there won't be anything left."

Curly walked toward the inspector, his ire apparent. "I would like you to tell me why we need to replace our fuel strainers with new units. Just give me one good reason!"

The inspector tried to speak, but Curly pressed. "Hell, I flew over a thousand hours in the Boeing Model 80 and they didn't even have fuel strainers. Flew two thousand hours in a Jenny and never replaced a fuel filter, just cleaned them."

"But, sir … ."

Curly grabbed a handful of the inspector's shirt collar and drew him close. "Who's giving the orders to fuck with our airplanes?"

"I don't … ."

Curly drove a fist into the guy's gut. "Who?"

The inspector doubled over, let out a moan and looked up at Curly, "I'm not sure … ."

Curly punched him hard in the nose and the guy went down, screaming in pain, with blood pouring from both nostrils. "Wrong answer. You get one more try, then I break your arm."

A mechanic stuck his face in the door and said, "Mr. Levitz, have you … ?" The scene registered and the mechanic said, "What's wrong with that guy?"

"I'm teaching him the finer points of inspecting our aircraft. Get out of here, Stan."

The mechanic disappeared and Curly returned to the bloody inspector. "Now, you have one more chance."

"The orders came from the section chief in the Dallas office. He said to look at Aztec's aircraft real close. Then he said if we value our jobs, we better ground them for something."

Curly lifted the guy off the floor and said, "If you tell anyone about this, I'll break both your arms. You understand?"

The inspector nodded his head.

◆ ◆ ◆

Catwalk landed later that day. He was writing up his trip report when the mechanic who'd witnessed Curly's actions approached him.

"Mr. Jackson, do you have a minute? There's something you should know about." The mechanic told him what he'd seen.

Catwalk asked, "Where's Curly now?"

"He signed out an airplane and took off."

"Where was he going?"

"I don't know, I didn't see the flight plan."

Catwalk ran into the flight briefing office where the pilots filed their flight plans. The board used to track aircraft, merely listed the plane Curly had taken as, "Out of service."

Catwalk looked in the trash under the table and found the copy of Curly's flight plan. He yelled, "Damn it!"

The mechanic asked, "Where's he going?"

"Dallas. He's going to pay a visit to the CAA."

Catwalk looked at the aircraft status board. There was only one aircraft on the ground and it was being loaded with drilling mud and generators to be flown to Houston. He said to the pilot, "Dave, I need you to take a detour on your trip to Houston. Can you drop me off in Dallas?"

"Sure, Cat. We'll be loaded in half an hour."

◆ ◆ ◆

In Dallas, at the CAA receptionist's desk he described Curly and asked if she'd seen him. She said no and he felt relieved for a second, but his instinct told him Curly was there. He asked, "Is there another entrance to the building?"

"There's the employee entrance in back."

"What floor is the Air Carrier Standards office on?"

"Fourth floor."

Catwalk hurried to the nearest elevator and took it up to four. He searched the hallway and found the office three doors down. He approached the door, afraid of what he'd find. When he reached for the doorknob, the door opened and Curly walked out with a smile on his face.

Curly said, "Hey, pard. I kind of figured you might come after me."

Catwalk didn't like the smug look on Curly's face. It was the satisfied look of someone who'd accomplished exactly what they set out to do. He pushed his partner up against the wall and said, "Curly, what the hell did you do?"

"It was Senator Bob Connelly who leaned on them to hassle us."

"How did you find that out? Did you beat on this guy until he confessed."

"I never touched him. Ease up and I'll tell you about it."

They walked to elevator and got in an empty car. On the way down Curly said, "Cat, do you know how you can tell someone who's got the hate against black people in them?" Before he answered, Curly said, "I can look people in the eye and tell the ones who ain't got any fight in them. This guy was afraid of his own shadow. When I took him over to the window and showed him how far he'd fall after I threw him out, he started singing like a robin in springtime."

Catwalk asked, "So what happens when we apply for a passenger route? Are they going to remember us as an airline made up of thugs who resort to violence?"

Curly smiled, "I told this guy, he'd have to deal with Connelly himself and if we have any problems in the future, it's still a long drop from that fourth floor window."

On the cab ride to the airport, Catwalk didn't say much. He didn't like to resort to violence to get things done, but he couldn't argue that Curly had gotten results, where he never could have. Whether his actions would come back to haunt them remained to be seen. Maybe he worried to much. Maybe Curly didn't worry enough. Maybe their differences made them a good team. He decided not to dwell on this. He still wished he had someone with whom he could talk about business problems who was more level headed than Curly.

This prompted more thoughts of Rosemary. He'd been thinking about her a lot lately. Now, he had a strong urge to see her, even if she was married to another man. He wondered if he could possibly find her. There was only one way to find out.

◆ ◆ ◆

On the flight back to Midland, Catwalk said, "I think I'm going to take some time off to see my family. In a week Steve Drake will be ready to step into my slot on the schedule board."

"That's fine. In fact, one day I should go back with you so I can meet your family."

"They know all about you."

"I can imagine what you told them."

Catwalk smiled, "I told them the truth—you're a lousy pilot who can't hold a heading to save your life, but a good guy to be in business with because you always come out on top."

Curly laughed, a hearty belly laugh.

◆ ◆ ◆

Catwalk spent a few days with his family, then told his Mom he was going to Tuskegee to see some of his old squadron mates. The first day he sat through four movies—but didn't see Rosemary. He checked the drug store pay phone, but there was no phone directory. Didn't matter, he wasn't sure if he had the guts to call her. The next day he walked up and down main street for a few hours, spent some time in the park, then asked at a hardware store if anyone knew her. They didn't. He went to the soda fountain to get a cold drink. He'd just paid for it when he saw her walking toward the movie theater. He didn't see anyone with her.

He ran out the door and dashed into the street. Horns blared as he narrowly missed being hit by a green sedan and taxi cab. She looked and he waved, then shouted, "Rosemary!"

She stopped and looked at him like he was crazy. Then she smiled, a warm, sincere smile that said she was glad to see him. She called out, "Hi. What are you doing here?"

Catwalk looked into those blue eyes that looked so familiar and beautiful after all these years. "I came looking for you. I had to see you."

"Oh?" Clearly, she was taken aback by his straightforward reply. She said, "It's been so long since I've seen you ... but I've thought about you every single day. I was always hoping you'd come back."

He pulled her close and kissed her. She kissed him back with all the passion that had been dormant for so long. He held her and buried his face in her long dark hair. "Oh, Rosemary, I wanted to see you so much."

She looked around, then said, "We can't stay here. Go to the theater. I'll be right there."

As he walked, Catwalk made up his mind—he'd do whatever was necessary to persuade Rosemary to come to New Mexico.

When she sat down beside him, he took her hand and said, "How have you been?"

She squeezed his hand and said, "Not good. Living there is so miserable; his drinking is getting to be terrible. I want to leave so bad, but I have no where to go."

He said, "You can leave, and get away from him forever. I want you to come to New Mexico to live with me. I'll come by to get your things and we'll drive west and start a new life, a life that will be full of happiness."

"Catwalk, I'm scared."

"If you don't get out now, you never will."

Rosemary said nothing while she thought about leaving, as she had many times. Now she had the opportunity and she decided to seize the moment. "He works tonight. Can you come by and get me about ten?"

"Just give me your address."

# Chapter Forty-Eight

At ten o'clock that night, Catwalk pulled up in front of Rosemary's house. He walked up the driveway feeling nervous and eager to get her out of this place. She met him at the door and handed him two suitcases. He took them to the car and returned to the house. Rosemary asked him to get some boxes out of the bedroom.

From the bedroom he saw lights of a car wash through the room. Someone had pulled in the driveway behind his car.

Catwalk took the boxes to the front room and met Rosemary who was frantic. "It's Joe! He must have forgot something. Quick, hide in the bathroom."

Catwalk set the boxes near the front door, then ducked into the bathroom and closed the door. He heard the husband's voice. "Rose, I forgot my lunch box. Whose car is that?"

"A man had car trouble. He asked if it was O.K. to park there and I let him."

Catwalk heard the fright in Rosemary's voice; he was sure the husband did too. Then he heard, "What are those boxes doing out here? What the hell is going on here?"

Rosemary screamed, "No!"

The sound of breaking glass followed and Catwalk dashed into the front room. He saw a shattered front window and Rosemary hiding behind a chair. Her husband was going after her.

Catwalk yelled, "Don't you dare hit her!"

The man turned and said, "Who the hell are you?"

Catwalk didn't answer. He'd forgotten how big the guy was.

Rosemary said, "I'm leaving you, Joe. He's taking me away from this hellish place. You've hit me for the last time."

Radiating hatred Joe walked toward Catwalk and said, "You're not taking her anywhere, you son of a bitch. In fact, you ain't leaving this house alive."

Catwalk backed off, saying nothing. There were no words that would stop the man. He needed a weapon. While watching the irate husband, he backed into the kitchen.

He grabbed an umbrella and tried to keep him at bay until he found a way to subdue him.

His attacker kept coming and yelled, "Com'ere you bastard."

Catwalk grabbed a sack of flour off the counter and threw it. The bag hit Joe in the face and burst open. The big man stopped and wiped his eyes. Catwalk clubbed him with a rolling pin, knocking him unconscious.

He said, "I need something to tie him up with."

She found a length of clothes line and helped tie him up. Catwalk quickly loaded the car and drove off.

◆ ◆ ◆

On the drive to Meridian, Catwalk and Rosemary talked about their future together. They couldn't get married until she got a divorce, but at least they were together. Regardless of all things wrong with this scenario, Catwalk felt like he'd done the right thing by getting her out of an environment that had tormented her. And, he felt strongly that she belonged by his side. He said, "It feels good to have you with me. It's like you should have been here all along."

Rosemary said, "First, Mr. Jackson. You've got to accept something right now. I know you loved my sister, and I know that your love for her is what brought you to me, but I'm not her. If you fall in love, just make sure you're falling for the right person."

"I don't think that will be a problem."

◆ ◆ ◆

It was four A.M. when Catwalk turned the lights off and pulled in the drive to his Momma's house. They slept in the car for two hours until his brother woke them.

"Hi Cecil. Is Momma up yet?"

"She's out back, canning tomatoes."

Catwalk took Rosemary's hand and walked to the back of the house. When his Momma saw her she covered her mouth with both hands, "Oh, my God in heaven."

"Momma, this is Sam's twin sister, Rosemary."

"I declare, if I didn't know better … ."

Rosemary smiled. "We were identical twins. How do you do, Mrs. Jackson."

She raised an eyebrow. "Luke, you said you were going to see your friends in your old squadron."

"We met while I was stationed there." Catwalk didn't know what else to say. He couldn't admit that she was going back to New Mexico because his Momma wouldn't tolerate him living in sin, and if she found out Rosemary was still married, she might disown him.

He tried, "I wanted to bring her over here to meet you."

Dee said, "Well, I'm glad you did. How long are you staying?"

"Just today. We've got to leave tomorrow morning."

"Oh, well, have you had breakfast?"

"No, we're both starved."

While they ate, Catwalk thought about his dilemma of keeping their plans from his Momma. They were talking over coffee when his nosy little brother brought his dilemma out in the open. "Hey, Luke, what's all that stuff in your car?"

Without looking at his Momma, Catwalk said, "Just some boxes and stuff from work."

"You sure got a lot of suitcases."

"I've got a lot of clothes."

He should have known better than to try and fool his Momma. She crossed her arms and gave him a knowing look, then said, "Luke, why don't you tell me what's going on?"

He said, "Rosemary is moving out to New Mexico to live with me."

"When are you planning on getting married?"

"Just as soon as her divorce is final."

His Momma didn't say anything, so Catwalk said, "I know you don't approve of me running off with a married woman to live in sin, but she's the only woman who will make me happy. We're going through with this and if you don't approve, I'm sorry."

With tears in her eyes, Dee said, "Luke, you've made me very proud. I love you both and hope you're both very happy. And, I want some grandchildren."

He looked at Rosemary who also had tears in her eyes. At that moment all the injustice, prejudice and unfairness had been forgotten. He was a happy man.

# Chapter Forty-Nine

When Catwalk and Rosemary arrived in Albuquerque, Curly congratulated them with all the gusto of a man who was truly happy for his long time friend. That night over dinner Billy Sue and Rosemary became instant friends.

After dinner Curly brought him up to date on the airline. "There haven't been any more inspections, so I think that's behind us. I made plans for some new freight forwarding facilities at Denver and Phoenix, and I ordered two more DC-3s."

Catwalk said, "I'm glad you ordered the threes, but I think it's time for us to start looking for a DC-4."

Curly realized there was only one reason why Catwalk would want to purchase the big four engine Douglas plane. He said, "Do you think we should apply to the CAA for a passenger route."

"I think the time is right, if we can get a route approved."

"Where'd you have in mind?"

"Albuquerque to Denver."

"Damn, wouldn't that bring back memories." Curly lit a cigarette, then looked at his partner and said, "Cat, you aim to put Rocky Mountain out of business, don't you?"

"Passengers know when an airline is having reliability problems. We can open that route at six cents a seat mile for the first few months. By then the passengers will know we provide more reliable service than Rocky Mountain. Picking up their passengers will be the easiest thing we've ever done."

"Well, it'll take at least four months for the route to be approved. That'll give us enough time to find someone to run the cargo operation."

◆ ◆ ◆

While the men talked, Billy Sue took Rosemary to the ladies room, where she told her, "Rosemary, there's something that might be difficult for you to understand. I'm sure Cat loves you as much as one man can love a woman, but at times it'll seem like he loves his airline more.

He and Curly have worked very hard at building the airline from the ground up and they live and breath their business. Try to keep in mind that it's more like an obsession with the airline, but with you it's true love."

"Thanks, Billy Sue, I'll remember that."

✦ ✦ ✦

Rosemary adjusted well to the life in New Mexico. She spent the first month buying furniture and redecorating the apartment. Although Catwalk still flew a lot, when he was home, he enjoyed the happiest times of his life, when he and Rosemary went walking in the park, to ball games, or picnicking in the mountains. The activities didn't matter as much as the fact that they were together. One day while they were enjoying a rosy New Mexico sunset, Rosemary said, "I want to go back to work until we have kids."

"O.K. How many children are we going to have?"

"How many do you want?"

"Two is a good round number."

She giggled and said, "So is six."

"It might be difficult to find someone who'll hire a black woman. I'll find you something at the airline."

"I've got secretarial training, can I be your secretary?"

"We'd never get any work done, because I'd be chasing you around the office all the time. Besides, I'm rarely in the office. You might be able to work in Billy Sue's office."

✦ ✦ ✦

Two weeks later, Rosemary started working for Billy Sue. She loved learning her new job and the excitement the airline business, but she wished Catwalk wasn't gone so much. She told her self this was the price that had to be paid for his success. Once they got the passenger airline established, she hoped he'd be home more.

✦ ✦ ✦

On September 7, 1946, Catwalk and Curly sat in the cockpit of a DC-4, going through the pre take-off checklist prior to Aztec Airline's first passenger flight.

From the left seat, Catwalk said, "Battery cart?"

"On."

"Seat belt, no smoking?"

"On."

"Cowl flaps?"

"Open."

"Mixtures?"

"Idle cut off."

"Gear handle down and flaps up?"

"Check."

"Trim tabs set? Parking brakes on? Hydraulic pressure?"

"One thousand pounds."

"Props high RPM? And cross feed valves off?"

"Check."

"Carburetor heat?"

"Cold."

"Main tanks on? I checked the fuel quantity, two thousand gallons. Air speed static selectors saftied?"

"Check."

"Pitot heaters? Anti-icer fluid?"

"Thirty five gallons."

"Generators?"

"Off."

"Fire warning … test." Catwalk pressed a button. An alarm bell clanged behind his head and four red lights glowed in the instrument panel.

"Check list complete."

Curly looked outside and saw the mechanic with a fire bottle, holding up three fingers. He shouted, "Clear on number three."

Catwalk closed the master magneto switch while Curly energized the starter and primed number three engine. He waited twenty seconds then pushed the switch. Catwalk advanced the number three throttle slightly and watched the fuel pressure gauges.

"Switch and boost." The number three engine backfired once and roared to life. The other three engines started equally well and all four settled into an even rumble as the stewardess stuck her head in the door, and said, "Pins aboard and twenty four passengers, Captain."

"Thanks, Jonesy."

Curly checked the free movement of the flaps and the fuel cross feed system as they taxied to the end of the runway. They checked the magnetos and prop feathering mechanisms on all four engines. They set gyros and altimeters, and uncaged the artificial horizon.

Catwalk turned onto the runway and advanced the throttles. At ninety miles an hour a slight back pressure on the yoke lifted the nose off. At one hundred and twenty, Aztec flight One Hundred became airborne.

Catwalk lifted his palm and commanded, "Gear up."

As soon as they heard the knocking of the gear locking up, and saw three green lights, Curly said, "We're back in the airline business, Cat." At five hundred feet, he called back to the cabin and said, "We're turning off the lights, Jonesy. You can pour the complimentary champagne."

◆ ◆ ◆

After Aztec flight One hundred landed in Denver, the crew thanked the passengers for flying with them, Catwalk and Curly took a cab to the hotel where they celebrated over drinks.

"I've got to tell you, Curly, I've been holding my breath since we applied for this route. I was sure someone was going to find a reason to stop us from starting our passenger service."

"Cat, you worry too much,"

Catwalk laughed and said, "With you for a partner, someone has to do the worrying. You have to remember, I've been in this business before and had it all taken away from me."

Curly put an arm around Catwalk's shoulders. "Old buddy, you don't have to worry anymore. We're back in the airline business and nobody can take this away from us."

Catwalk smiled at his friend's confidence. He called Rosemary to tell her he'd be home first thing in the morning, then he and Curly got drunk.

◆ ◆ ◆

In Collinsville Federal Prison, Alton Jones listened intently as another inmate described his escape plan. Over the years, Jones had heard several escape plans, but had ignored them as flights of fancy, destined to be failures. This plan, however, was well enough though out to pique his interest. He smelled the sweet scent of freedom.

# Chapter Fifty

Prior to their inaugural flight, Catwalk had covertly approached several Rocky Mountain employees. He offered them a fifteen percent pay raise, double time for overtime, and stock options. Within a month ten former Rocky Mountain employees reported for work.

Catwalk and Curly hired and nurtured a dedicated work force, just as Barney had taught them when he'd first founded Rocky Mountain. Once the word about the working conditions at Aztec got out, employees from other airlines were applying for employment. The formula worked as well now as it did then, but their growth wasn't without problems, such as the night Catwalk found Curly and a stewardess in a compromising situation.

They'd been late flying back from Denver due to weather. Curly said he'd check on the clean up crew, while Catwalk went inside to do the paperwork. An hour later Catwalk saw the lights were still on in the plane. He worried that a crewman had left them on. When he entered the plane, however, he discovered Curly and a stewardess on the floor of the plane, in various stages of undress.

"Excuse me." He shouted.

They both looked at him, surprised and embarrassed. The stewardess grabbed her blouse and covered up. Curly said, "Aw shit, Cat."

Catwalk said, "Marilyn, I'll talk to you later. Curly, put your pants on and meet me inside."

Marilyn asked sheepishly, "Am I fired?"

"No. I don't think it was your fault."

Curly walked into their office and lit a cigarette. Catwalk didn't wait for his excuses. "There are several reasons why you shouldn't have done that."

Curly became defensive. "What makes you think it was my fault?"

"Because I know you, and I know how you act around women."

"It's not like she's married or anything. We're both single, so what's the problem?"

"For starters, she's an employee, and we're supposed to be a company that treats its employees with respect. Did you ever stop to think of what Billy Sue will say if she finds out?"

"Are you going to tell her?"

"I should, but I won't, not unless she asks me about it. I won't lie for you, not to her."

Catwalk didn't have to lie. Billy Sue found out about Curly's indiscretion through the grapevine. The next time she saw Curly, her voice was filled with venom when she said, "You can still visit your son, but our wedding date has just been pushed back—to the year 2000!"

Catwalk and Curly never mentioned the episode again, but Catwalk was troubled by Curly's lapse of judgment. He went back to his apartment, put on a Duke Ellington record and laid down on the sofa. When Rosemary came home they talked at length about the incident. Rosemary agreed that Curly showed bad judgment, but she also said she thought Catwalk was overreacting to something that was really human nature.

Catwalk agreed, then showed her how pleased he was to have someone with whom he could talk about things like this.

◆ ◆ ◆

A week later he stopped by her office and said, "I'm going home to get a few hours sleep. Curly and I are flying to Salt Lake tonight. We're returning tomorrow on fifty two."

"Have a good flight and call me tonight."

◆ ◆ ◆

The flight to Salt Lake was routine and uneventful. The next morning, however, on the flight back they'd just crossed the four corners area when the navigator said, "Four's running hot. It's been above normal for twenty minutes now, but in the past few seconds, it spiked."

Catwalk looked up from the log book and said, "I'll bet it's that crack in the exhaust stack. It's going to be repaired after this flight."

Curly looked out at the far engine. "Let's shut it down before it gets to red line."

"Good idea." Catwalk pulled back the throttle and adjusted the propeller to zero pitch.

Curly looked at the controls, then back at the engine and said, "Fucking thing didn't feather, Cat. It's wind-milling."

Catwalk had just recycled the controls, when Curly shouted, "It's on fire! Pull the bottle!"

Catwalk punched the red knob that actuated the fire extinguishing system. He then looked out the window, but didn't see the telltale white smoke from the foam.

Curly said, "God damn it! It didn't work. Try it again."

Catwalk punched the knob again. No results.

Watching the engine burn unabated, Curly said, "There's going to be some mechanics fired when we get back."

A stewardess came through the door and said, "The passengers are about to panic. How bad is it?"

Catwalk said, "We're trying to put it out. We might have to set down at an alternate."

After she left, the navigator said, "The only alternate airport that can handle our weight is Gallup. We're just as close to Albuquerque."

"I'm heading to Albuquerque. Call the tower."

While Curly called the tower, Catwalk craned his neck to see the engine. The fire, as he'd feared, was spreading to the wing. Once it got to the wing, it would spread to the number three engine, which they'd lose. Then, running on two engines, they might have trouble maintaining their altitude, which they needed because they were over mountainous terrain until they passed Cabezon Peak. Also, while trying to hold their altitude, they stood a good chance of over heating engines one and two.

Curly read his mind and said, "There ain't even a God damn road we can land on."

The stewardess appeared again and said, "The passengers are very worried. Tell me you can put that fire out."

Catwalk said, "The internal extinguishing system didn't work. Prepare the passengers for an emergency landing."

The fire continued to burn, but didn't spread like they thought it would. On three engines, they were able to hold their altitude and Catwalk thought their chances were good for making it to the airport.

Thirty miles from the airport, however, Curly said, "It's on the wing, burning toward number three. Damn it, we only need eight more minutes."

Catwalk started a gradual descent, wary of giving away their precious altitude that kept them above the unforgiving mountain peaks.

Curly shouted, "Number three's on fire! Feather that son of a bitch."

Catwalk shut down number three and increased power on one and two. Now he was very concerned because two engines burning could collapse the wing. If that happened, they'd tumble into the mountains with no chance of surviving. He turned to the navigator, "Gary, pass our fuel load and passenger count to the tower and keep them advised of our position and altitude."

Curly said, "The extinguisher worked, but it ain't enough. The wing is burning bad. How far out are we?"

The navigator yelled, "Eighteen miles."

Catwalk saw the airport and said, "We'll use Runway Nine so I don't have to turn into the dead engines."

Curly called the tower while he watched for any change in the fire. "Albuquerque Tower, this is Aztec Fifty Two, on an eighteen mile dogleg base for Runway Nine. We're declaring emergency with fires in engines three and four. Say the wind."

"Aztec Fifty Two, Albuquerque Tower, cleared to land Runway Nine. Wind Zero Four Zero at one two. The equipment is standing by."

◆ ◆ ◆

Rosemary heard about the emergency shortly after Curly's first call to the tower. She and Billy Sue ran outside where they could see the runways. She had seen other aircraft land with minor emergencies, but this was the first time she'd heard of an aircraft on fire. Wracked with fear, she wondered, with all the pilots flying for Aztec, why did this have to happen to Catwalk?

She saw the speck that was the plane and the smoke it was trailing. From her vantage point it looked like the whole plane was on fire. She wondered if the fire had spread to engulf the entire plane. Tears streamed down her face as she hugged Billy Sue.

◆ ◆ ◆

Catwalk started a gentle turn to final and saw the emergency vehicles with their lights flashing standing by at mid field. He was glad to see them, but if the wing collapsed before they made the airport, the fire trucks would just be picking up the pieces. He again looked past Curly to see the extent of the fire.

"I think we got it made, Cat."

"That's what we thought at Kodiak too."

"Well, if it makes you feel any better, there ain't any logs on this runway."

Catwalk didn't answer. He was on a half mile final approach. Engines one and two were hot from picking up the load from the bad engines, but the descent had helped cool them. The controls felt good, but he didn't know if he had brakes and he'd be landing faster than normal. He'd have to ground loop if necessary, to get the passengers off as quickly as possible.

The wheels passed over the runway threshold and Catwalk slammed the plane onto the runway in a bone jarring landing. He and Curly stood on the brakes. The left brake grabbed slightly and the mammoth plane went into a slow left turn, careening off the runway into the dirt.

Catwalk had just shut off the fuel selectors when the right wing bent and dug into the ground. This straightened the plane, but it was headed for the emergency trucks. As the trucks scattered all three crewmen unbuckled. There was nothing more they could do.

◆ ◆ ◆

Rosemary watched in horror as the burning plane landed and swerved off the runway. Heavy smoke rose off the right side of the aircraft and when the wing broke, the ruptured fuel tanks spewed high-octane aviation fuel onto the airport. When the fuel ignited, it looked like the entire plane blew up. Tears streamed down her face.

◆ ◆ ◆

Catwalk sent Curly and the navigator out the navigation dome in the ceiling of the cockpit. While they were crawling out, he opened the door to the cabin and saw the last of the passengers deplaning. He followed the last stewardess down the slide. On the ground he landed in heavy smoke, then ran to the nearest fire truck where a fireman gave him oxygen.

He watched them extinguish the fire, which had already done major damage to the aircraft. He began replaying events to see if anything could have been done better. Curly interrupted his thoughts. "I'm going down to the maintenance hangar. Someone's ass is going to fry for this."

As he turned to leave, Billy Sue gave him a hug and kissed him on the cheek. She said, "Are you O.K., Curly?"

Curly said, "I'm fine." He kissed her on the cheek, and then left for the hangar.

As soon he left, Rosemary showed up and threw her arms around Catwalk. "Oh God, you're O.K. I saw the burning plane and knew I was going to lose you."

Catwalk smiled and said, "Honey, it'll take more than a little fire for you to lose me."

On the walk to the truck, she asked, "Be honest now. How often does this happen?"

"Sweetheart, I've got fifteen thousand hours of flying time, in all types of aircraft and this is the first time I've ever had an engine fire."

"I wouldn't mind if it was the last one."

"Honey, most of the time flying is boring. Something like this happens very rarely."

"O.K. How about no more fires for another fifteen thousand hours?"

"You've got a deal."

◆ ◆ ◆

Alton Jones had been debating whether go with the three other inmates who were escaping. His time had been extended twice for inciting fights with other inmates, so he was still looking at ten years in the pen. He finally decided this was his best chance to gain back the freedom he'd lost so long ago.

Bobby Keenland talked in a whisper as he explained the final plan, "In a few weeks they're starting construction at the south entrance of the laundry building. They'll have to ship some laundry to a laundry in town. With the construction, they've got to bring all the laundry in the east door, where there's only two other doors to pass through and you're out. During meal times, there's only one guard and he weighs the carts going out, but the guy that runs the scale is working with us. If you hide on one of the carts, you're out of here in five minutes."

"They'll miss you at meal time."

"Not if you request to go to the infirmary for sick call. Complain of abdominal pains and request some blue bombers. It's an antacid and you can't eat for twenty four hours. That explains not being at the chow hall. You beat it for the laundry and you're home free."

Thought of being a free man flooded Jones' soul like an intoxicating liquor. Any apprehension about being caught, vanished. He saw himself sitting on a beach in Mexico, surrounded by raven haired beauties. And, he knew exactly who was going to fly him to Mexico. Then, revenge would be his.

# Chapter Fifty-One

A week after the fiery emergency, Catwalk set his tray on the table in the employees cafeteria and asked Rosemary and Billy Sue, "Can I join you two?"

Rosemary smiled that smile that still took his breath away, and said. "How was your flight?"

"Boring. What have you two been up to?"

Rosemary said, "Well, I went to the doctor this morning."

Catwalk looked stunned. "What for? Aren't you feeling well?"

She stirred her coffee for a few seconds, then said, "Oh no. I feel fine. In fact, I don't even feel pregnant."

Catwalk dropped his roast beef sandwich into his soup and stared open mouthed. "Honey, are you serious?"

"Very serious. We have to start thinking about names."

"Sweetheart, this is the best news you could have given me. Oh my God." He turned to Billy Sue, "I'm going to be a father."

She kissed him on the cheek and said, "I'm so glad for you two. You guys are going to have a beautiful baby."

Rosemary said, "We have to think about getting married too. I got the papers making my divorce final yesterday."

Catwalk said, "That's wonderful. Just find a date when Curly and I are going to be in town long enough for a wedding."

"I already have one."

❖ ❖ ❖

The escape from Collinsville prison went off like a well planned military operation. Once out, Jones ran through the countryside until he arrived at the rail tracks south of town. He waited next to a creek until he saw a slow freight approaching. Once aboard he sat back and looked at the magazine article from several years ago. Nothing could stop him now.

He hopped off in Dillard County and made his way to Larry Gustafson's house. No one answered the door so he broke a window and entered the house. After a few minutes of searching he found a forty-five automatic and a thirty-two caliber pistol. He then took thirty dollars from a dresser drawer. In the kitchen he ate two pieces of chicken, then threw some leftovers in a bag. He grabbed a bottle of bourbon and a coat, then headed back to the tracks. He wanted to get out of town fast because once the escape was discovered, Dillard County was the first place they'd look for him. Jones hopped another train and dropped off at Midland where he checked into a flop house hotel.

He slept for four hours then walked to the airport. After putting on a hat and sun glasses, he asked a ramp worker, "You know where I can find Catwalk? Him and I used to work together at Rocky Mountain and I want to talk to him about job."

"He only flies in here occasionally. His offices are at Albuquerque Airport now."

"Really? Is that where he runs the airline from?"

"Yeah. He outgrew Midland when he started his passenger service."

Jones grinned and said, "Yeah, that's ol' Catwalk, always looking to get bigger. Thanks." Jones then stole a Pontiac and left for Albuquerque.

✦ ✦ ✦

When he arrived in town, Jones rented a room for a week and then left for the airport, where he watched the terminal entrance for a couple hours. When he didn't see Catwalk, he returned to his room and plotted his plan over dinner.

For the next two days, Jones watched people come and go at the airport terminal. Finally, late the second day he saw Catwalk leaving the terminal. He saw him get into a black Chevy coupe. When Catwalk drove off, he was three cars behind him.

Jones followed Catwalk to his house, then found a parking lot where he could watch the house and get an idea of Catwalk's routine. On the second day, he saw Catwalk leaving with a woman. He couldn't believe his eyes—it was the same woman he'd shot at the farm. He swore out loud, "How the hell can that bitch be alive? I served fourteen fuckin' years for her murder!"

Now, more than ever, Jones was determined that he'd get Jackson to fly him to Mexico. Then he'd get rid of both of them for good, and live out his life as a free man.

✦ ✦ ✦

The next day, Catwalk was driving home from work, when he told Rosemary, "I like Thomas Ray Jackson. It has a good ring to it and my

Daddy would be proud to have his first grandson named after him. I know Mother will like that."

"O.K., then. That settles it. Now we have to redecorate his room."

"How are you so sure it's going to be a boy?"

"Because it's only proper that you have young pilot first, and then we'll have a few girls to even things out."

Catwalk smiled all the way home.

When he arrived home, however, his bliss was shattered by a phone call from his brother Cecil. "Luke, I thought you should know; Alton Jones escaped from prison last week. They're conducting a search for him, but the sheriff thinks he left the area."

"Thank you, Cecil. Let me know if you hear anything else, O.K."

"Sure thing, Luke."

Catwalk thought about Jones being on the loose. Would Jones come after him again? Can one man carry that much hate for so long? He didn't say anything to Rosemary, but he told Curly the next time he saw him.

Curly's advice was, "Watch your back, Cat. Last time he showed up when we least expected it. You should start carrying a gun."

Catwalk thought about Curly's advice, but decided against it. Even if Jones was looking for him, how would he know where to look?

◆ ◆ ◆

Jones spent two days working out his plan and watching the terminal to see if he could pick up a pattern to Jackson's routine. After the second day, he ditched the Pontiac so he didn't get picked up on a stolen car charge. He'd steal another car the night before he put his plan into action. By the time they found it, he'd be south of the border in his own private airliner with his own private pilot.

On the fourth day, Jones decided to put his plan into action. Although he'd told himself to be patient, he was anxious to get out of the country, and to get rid of Jackson and the woman. He waited in a coffee shop where he could watch Jackson's house. After he saw Catwalk leave the house, he waited another forty-five minutes, then walked to the house.

He knocked on the door. When the woman answered the door, he stuck the automatic in her face and said, "Hello honey. You remember me?"

Rosemary looked puzzled, from the gun and his question. She shook her head and backed slowly into the room. Trembling, she said, "Wh-What do you want?"

Now it was his turn to be confused. He said, "You don't remember me, from the farm, back in 1934?"

"No, I ... ."

"Jesus Christ, lady. I shot you. You don't remember that."

It dawned on Rosemary who she was facing. The look on her face turned to one of hatred, and she said, "That was my sister, you bastard! You murdered my sister."

Jones smiled and said, "Oh, now I see. Well, yeah, I guess I did."

He then motioned to a window and said, "Get over by the window."

When Rosemary turned her back on him, he took a sap out of his pocket and knocked her unconscious.

Jones checked her pulse to make sure she was still breathing, then tied her up with a curtain cord. He then went down to the parking lot, hot wired a Hudson and made sure the trunk was unlocked.

Jones wrapped a sheet around Rosemary and carried her out to the car. After putting her in the trunk, he drove to the airport. Wearing a ball cap, dark glasses and a jacket, he went into the administrative offices of Aztec Airways. He looked for Catwalk's office, then waited in the lobby until the secretary went to the restroom. When she was gone he walked into Catwalk's office.

The office was empty so Jones sat down behind Catwalk's desk.

Five minutes later, Catwalk returned. When he saw Jones, Catwalk froze and felt his heart rate shoot up. He said, "What do you want?"

Jones leaned back in the chair and put his feet on the desk. "Well, Mr. Big-shot-pilot, I'll tell you what I want. I want a pilot to fly me to Mexico, so I can take a little vacation."

"And if I refuse?"

Jones grinned. "You ain't gonna refuse, because if you do, I'll just leave that little girl of yours right where she is and by the time they find her, she'll be dead from suffocation."

Catwalk said, "You bastard. You're bluffing."

"Call your house. See if anyone answers."

Jones walked around the desk, wearing the grin of a man who held all the cards.

Catwalk walked behind the desk, dialed the phone and let it ring a long time. Then he hung up and said, "Where is she? What have you done with her?"

"Oh, she's fine for now. And you can get her back. All you have to do is take one of your airplanes and fly me to Mexico."

Catwalk opened the drawer with his spare pistol in it. He looked at the gun, then at Jones. Jones had the gun in his jacket pocket aimed at Catwalk. He shook his head and said, "I wouldn't touch that pistol, or you'll never see your lady alive again."

Catwalk thought this through. If Jones had Rosemary, he had to do whatever Jones wanted. Anything else would jeopardize Rosemary, and Jones had no qualms about killing women. He asked, "If I do this, when will you let her go?"

"Oh, I'll untie her when we get in the plane. See, she's going with us."

Catwalk didn't like that scenario, but he had no bargaining power. He closed the drawer and said, "As soon as I see that she's alive and safe, I'll get an airplane."

The grin left Jones' face. With a scowl he said, "No, you black bastard, that's not what we'll do. You'll get a plane right now and once you tell me there is a plane available, you get to see her. Do you understand?"

Catwalk said, "Yes, I understand." He then dialed flight operations. When an operations clerk answered, he said, "Charley, this is Catwalk. Do you have a DC-3 available? I'm going to take some people for a local flight."

"Thanks, Charley." He hung up the phone and told Jones, "There is a plane available."

"Good. Now we can go see your little lady. I sure hope she's still breathing."

# Chapter Fifty-Two

While Jones and Catwalk walked through the offices, on their way out of the building, Jones laughed and gabbed like they were old friends. No one noticed that Catwalk wasn't laughing, or even smiling.

They walked to Hudson and Jones knocked on the trunk. "You O.K., honey?"

Catwalk heard a muffled voice and figured Jones had her gagged. He said, "Get her out of there."

Jones showed him the gun in his jacket pocket and said, "No so fast, pal. She gets out when we're at the plane."

Jones handed him the keys and said, "You drive. You drive straight to the plane we're going to be taking and no tricks or I fill the trunk with bullets."

Catwalk drove toward the DC-3 that Charley said was all fueled, but not due to be put into service until the next morning. He parked next to the plane and Jones opened the trunk.

Catwalk saw Rosemary, bound, gagged, and very scared. He reached in to lift her out of the trunk and said, "I'm here, honey. Everything is going to be O.K. We're going to take a plane ride."

Jones said, "Shut up and get in the plane."

◆ ◆ ◆

Curly had tried calling Cat's office, but when he got no answer, he walked to it and asked Cat's secretary, "Where's the boss?"

"I'm not sure, Curly. He left a few minutes ago with that old friend of his. He didn't say where they were going."

"O.K., I'll talk to him later." Curly walked a few steps, then stopped and turned. He said, "Maggie, describe this friend of Cat's."

When the secretary described the man she'd seen, Curly knew it was Jones. He said, "Are you sure you don't know where they went? Did Cat say anything?"

"No. They just walked out."

"Which door?"

"Employees parking lot."

Curly ran for the door. Once outside he looked for Cat's car; it was still in his parking space. That meant Jones had a car. They didn't have much of a head start, but if they drove off the airport, they could have gone anywhere and he'd never find them. He walked into the parking lot and looked around the field, looking for anything out of the ordinary. He saw the Hudson, parked near a DC-3, where no cars were allowed. He knew immediately that Jones was making Catwalk fly him somewhere.

He jumped into his car and tore out of the parking lot. He had an idea, but he needed time and he needed to get on the plane. Catwalk wouldn't be able to start taxiing for about five minutes. He hoped that was enough time.

◆ ◆ ◆

Jones herded Catwalk and Rosemary into the plane. He told Catwalk, "All right, fly boy, get this thing off the ground and don't give me any stuff about having to get fuel. I checked and found out that planes are always fueled right after they land."

Catwalk headed for the cockpit and said, "We've got fuel, but these engines have to warm up before I can start taxiing."

"Get 'em started then. As soon as they're warm, we take off. Set your course for Acapulco."

Catwalk started engines, then went through the checklist. While doing this, he frantically thought of how he was going to subdue Jones without getting himself or Rosemary shot.

◆ ◆ ◆

Curly saw the engines turning on the DC-3. He also noticed the door was still open so Catwalk wasn't ready to taxi yet. He prayed that he found Cat in the plane and not some mechanic who was taking the plane for a maintenance test flight.

He parked so Catwalk would see him from the cockpit and walked toward the open door. Once he reached the door he climbed the steps and entered the plane. He threw the parachute he'd picked up into the plane and acted surprised when he saw Jones and Rosemary sitting in the cabin.

Jones pointed the pistol at Curly and said, "Hold it right there."

Curly said, "What the hell are you doing here?"

Jones walked up to Curly and said, "It's been a long time friend." He then punched Curly in the jaw. "That's for bringing the law to my hanging." Curly went down.

Jones kicked him several times and said, "This is your lucky day, friend. You'll get to die with your nigger buddy and his lady."

Rosemary yelled, "Oh, God help us!"

Jones yelled, "Shut up, bitch." He then yelled to the cockpit, "Let's go, you ain't gotta warm them engines all day long."

Catwalk stood up and looked back in the cabin. When he saw Curly, with blood dripping from his jaw, he said, "What brings you to the party?"

"I remembered this plane didn't have any parachutes. I stopped by the parachute loft, but I could only get one, so I dropped one off. It looks like my timing wasn't too good."

Jones said, "Cut the talking." He held the gun on Catwalk, "Close the door and get this thing in the air."

"When I close this door will you untie my wife?"

"She gets untied when we're in the air."

Catwalk closed the door and headed for the cockpit. He thought about what Curly had said. He suspected Curly was trying to tell him something, but what? He thought about the parachute. They didn't normally carry parachutes on the DC-3s, only the older cargo planes. So why had Curly brought a parachute to this plane, and why just one?

As he was tying up Curly, Jones yelled, "What's taking so long, Jackson?"

"I've got to get clearance to taxi."

Jones walked to the cockpit and said, "God damn it, you better not be pulling any of your shit or I'll drill that lady, just like I did her sister."

Catwalk grit his teeth. He saw Sam going down after being shot. The thought that Jones could easily do the same to Rosemary made his blood run cold. It took every ounce of resolve to keep him from grabbing Jones by the neck and pummeling him. Instead he acknowledged ground control by saying, "Roger ground, Aztec three-four-seven is taxiing to runway three-four."

He told Jones, "We're taxiing now."

Jones said, "Good job, Jackson. Next stop Acapulco." He then went back to the cabin where Curly and Rosemary were tied up in their seats.

Catwalk taxied slower than normal to give himself time to think. Once at the runway, he went through his magneto checks twice. What had Curly been trying to tell him?

Finally, he couldn't stall any longer. He called the tower, "Albu-querque Tower, this is Aztec three-four-seven ready to depart runway three four, VFR to the south."

"Aztec three-four-seven, Albuquerque. Wind three-two-zero at seven, runway three-four, cleared for take off. Left turn out of traffic approved."

# Chapter Fifty-Three

Catwalk took off and followed the Rio Grande River southbound until he picked up the El Paso range station. He then crossed El Paso and tracked outbound due south. As he flew he thought of ways to overcome Jones, but most of his plans were flawed. He considered climbing to a higher altitude until Jones passed out from lack of oxygen, but that would affect everyone else and he couldn't tell them to go on oxygen without Jones knowing it.

He thought over and over again about the parachute Curly brought to the plane. Surely there must have been a reason behind it. So what was Curly's plan to put it to use? Why only one chute; their parachute loft had forty or fifty chutes on hand, but Curly brought only one. Who had he planned on using it?

Having Rosemary along complicated things. If it was just him and Curly, he could throw the plane around and they could take their chances of getting shot while jumping Jones. After losing Sam to a wild gun shot, he wasn't going to do anything to jeopardize Rosemary. This made the task of overcoming Jones that much harder, and if they didn't find a way to subdue him, they were goners. He had no doubt when they reached Acapulco, Jones would kill the three of them. Catwalk couldn't envision Jones turning them loose to return and tell the American authorities where he was. He leveled off at eighty five hundred feet with these thoughts racing through his mind.

◆ ◆ ◆

Catwalk unfolded his chart and plotted his course and fuel range. The coast by Acapulco was notorious for storms, so he decided to land short in Guadalajara and refuel. This too could cause problems. Lately, the purity of the Mexican fuel was suspect and cases of contaminated fuel were not unusual. He thought of his forced landing many years ago in Raton Pass. Down here, however, there were stretches of hundreds of miles with nothing but hills, so a flat landing area may be harder to find down here than it was in the pass. And, they only had one parachute, so … .

Then it hit him like a bolt of lightning! He knew why Curly brought only one chute. A plan started to take shape. He had to pray that he and Curly were thinking along the same lines—their lives depended upon it.

◆ ◆ ◆

He looked back in the cabin. Curly was tied up and gagged in a window seat halfway back in the cabin. Rosemary was sitting on the other side of the cabin a few rows behind Curly. It didn't look like she was tied up or gagged, but probably tied to her seat. Jones was three rows further back, where he could keep an eye on both of them. With everyone tied up or bound to their seats, they'd have to outsmart Jones; there would be no overpowering him.

◆ ◆ ◆

Thirty minutes later, after thinking over the plan, that he hoped Curly shared with him, Catwalk gave the control yoke a few quick turns, causing the aircraft to roll to the left and right twice in each direction.

Upon feeling the aircraft roll, Jones stood up and walked up to the cockpit. He said, "What's wrong, fly boy?"

"Nothing, just some clear air turbulence. It's not unusual over these hills and you'll probably feel more of it before we reach Acapulco." Catwalk then created some more turbulence by turning the wheel slightly. While doing so he gave the appearance of fighting the aircraft to keep it straight and level.

He told Jones, "It's getting rough. You'd better sit down and fasten your seat belt."

"You just fly the plane and get us there, Jackson. Don't worry about me."

Catwalk continued his charade of fighting the plane. Finally, Jones turned and walked back to the cabin. As soon as Jones had his back turned on him, Catwalk looked back at Curly and pointed at Jones. He then made the gesture of pulling a parachute ripcord. Curly nodded very slowly. Catwalk sat down and continued to "fight" the aircraft.

Rosemary had been frightened to death ever since Jones walked into her house. Now, after seeing Catwalk's gestures, she had some hope that somehow Cat and Curly would get them out of this. She looked at Curly. Again he nodded almost imperceptibly. Rosemary closed her eyes and said a prayer.

◆ ◆ ◆

Four hours later, Catwalk called Jones. He came up to the cockpit. "There are storms building over the coast. I've got to stop in Guadalajara and refuel, so we'll have enough fuel to hold if we have to wait for the storms to clear. We shouldn't be on the ground for more than thirty minutes. From there it's only an hour and a half to Acapulco, unless the storms delay us."

Jones thought about this for several minutes. Clearly, he was worried that the refueling stop would present Catwalk with a chance to somehow foil his plans. He said, "You listen to me, nigger, and you listen good. While we're refueling, I'm going to have a gun pointed at your lady's head. Your buddy is tied up so he won't cause any trouble. If I see anything funny going on, or if anyone tries to get into the plane, I'll put a bullet in her. You've got to remember, I've got nothing to lose. The worst that can happen to me is, I go right back where I came from. Do you understand?"

"Don't worry." Catwalk insisted, "All we're doing is refueling and no one is going to get on the plane. I guarantee you, no tricks."

Jones went back to the cabin and told Curly and Rosemary. "We're going to land and refuel. While this is going on, I'm going to have a gun pointed at the lady. If anything goes wrong, or anyone tries to pull anything, I will pull the trigger."

Rosemary looked at Jones, silently weighing his words. She had to trust Catwalk to get them out of this, but the odds seemed to be stacked heavily against them.

Curly watched Jones. He'd been praying that he and Catwalk had the same game plan. With the refueling stop, it looked like Catwalk was laying the foundation for their trap, but he still knew, if there was any difference in their unspoken plans, it would be fatal for all of them.

# Chapter Fifty-Four

Catwalk landed at Guadalajara and taxied to the transient refueling ramp. When the ramp attendant walked out to the plane, Catwalk recognized Jorge Velasquez, whom he'd gotten to know and had had lunch with, when they were flying cargo flights down here.

Catwalk opened the cockpit window and said, "Top off both sides, Jorge."

Jorge was overjoyed at seeing his old friend. "Hey, senor Catwalk, how have you been? I haven't seen you for a long time."

Catwalk cursed Jorge's congeniality. He didn't want to do or say anything that Jones could interpret as being suspicious. And, he didn't want Jorge to get the idea that anything was wrong. He said, "I've been fine, Jorge. We don't fly through here anymore."

"That's too bad, I miss seeing you and Mr. Curly. How is he? Is he flying with you today?"

"No, not today, Jorge. I'm running late, can you get us refueled as quickly as possible?"

"Si, senor Catwalk. I'll have you filled up in a jiffy."

Catwalk felt the barrel of the pistol in the back of his neck. Jones had appeared behind him. He said, "What's all this talk about?"

Catwalk slid the window closed, then turned his head and said, "Just an old friend. He'll refuel us and we'll be off the ground in no time."

Jones wasn't convinced. "God damn it, Jackson. I swear if you're trying to get help, your old lady is dead in a second."

"I'm not doing anything except getting the aircraft refueled. We'll be taking off shortly."

Jones said nothing. Catwalk then heard his steps retreating back into the cabin. He breathed a sigh of relief, but only for a second. Jorge's helpful attitude again raised the level of anxiety.

Outside, he was motioning Catwalk to open the window. Catwalk opened the window and Jorge said, "Hey, senor Catwalk, you have much oil spray on your number one engine nacelle. You should let me clean it off and check the level of your oil tank."

"It's O.K., Jorge. The oil pressure is good and we don't have far to go."

Jorge looked at him with questions all over his face. Catwalk knew it was because they both knew any other time, Catwalk would never start the engine until the oil level was checked and brought up to the proper level. Catwalk said, "How's the refueling, Jorge? Are we about ready to go?"

Jorge said, "Is everything O.K., Senor Catwalk?"

Catwalk silently cursed. He expected to hear a gun shot any second. Trying hard to sound convincing, he said, "Everything is fine, Jorge. Couldn't be better, except I'm late with a real important load."

"O.K, Senor. I'll get going. You come back when we can have lunch again."

"I'll do that, Jorge. Thanks."

A few minutes later another ramp attendant appeared next to his engine with a fire bottle. Catwalk yelled, "Clear on number two." He then completed the engine start procedures and sighed a, "Thank God." He saluted the ramp attendant and taxied toward the runway.

◆ ◆ ◆

After departing he set his course for the rugged hills south of Morelia. He'd flown over them many times when they were flying cargo and often thought this would be a terrible area in which to have engine problem, because level places where you could make a forced landing were almost nonexistent. If you lost power around here, your chances of surviving were slim at best.

Once he leveled off, Catwalk again went over the plan in his head, trying, for one last time to find any flaws. Thirty miles south of Guadalajara, he decided it was time to put the final phase of his plan into play. This was the moment when he and Curly would find out if Jones was as predictable as they hoped he was.

He eased back on the fuel mixture until the number two engine started running rough. Then, he yelled out, "Shit! God damned Mexican fuel."

Jones came running to the cockpit. "What's wrong with that engine?"

"I don't know; the gauges are all fine. The only thing I can think of is, we must have got some bad fuel."

"Are you sure?" He pressed the gun barrel against Catwalk's head. "If you're pulling something, I won't hesitate to shoot because there's another pilot in back, who can fly and right after I drill you, your old lady gets it."

Catwalk held up his hands and yelled. "Jesus Christ, man. What could I be doing? Do you think I'm intentionally causing an engine problem down here?"

"What can you do? Can we still fly?"

Catwalk looked at the rugged mountainous terrain below him. "Yes, if this one quits, we can still fly on one engine. The problem is, if we lose both engines. Then, I've got to find somewhere to land, and as you can see, there aren't any places out there that are level enough to land on. If we lose both engines, we're going to crash—period."

Jones ran back to Curly, took his gag off and stuck the gun in his face. "Your pal says we might lose both engines; is he telling it straight?"

"Of course he is. It's not uncommon to get bad fuel down here. If we did, the only direction we're going is down and you're going with us."

While Jones was busy with Curly, Catwalk had adjusted the fuel mixture so the other engine started running rough. He yelled, "Number one is running rough too. We're going to have to find a place to set it down."

Curly said, "There ain't anywhere down here, Cat. You know that." He looked at Jones, "You better prepare for a crash landing."

Jones stood back and broke out in a sly grin. "Like hell I am. You prepare for a crash landing, chump. I've got an ace in the hole and you gave it to me."

Jones went to the back of the cabin and put on the only parachute in the plane.

Curly yelled, "Jesus Christ, Jones. For once in your life, why don't you do the right thing and give the parachute to the woman."

Catwalk heard this and knew the plan was taking shape—but then, he had a sobering thought: it wouldn't be out of character for Jones to shoot everyone before he bailed out? He had to persuade him to hit the silk.

Picking up on Curly's logic, he stood up and yelled, "Give her the parachute, Jones. We've only got a few seconds and we're going in."

Jones grinned and waved his pistol around the cabin.

Catwalk yelled, "We don't have much time, Jones."

Jones said, "You don't have much time, pal!" He then checked the parachute straps and wrestled the door open. Standing in the slipstream, he said, "So long, suckers."

♦ ♦ ♦

Alton Jones jumped into the Mexican sky. For a moment—just a brief moment—he was convinced he'd beaten the odds and would be living an idyllic life on a beach in Mexico.

♦ ♦ ♦

Catwalk looked out the cockpit window and saw his life's nemesis falling toward the hills below. He brought the fuel mixtures back to normal. Soon, both engines began purring like a contented cat. He banked the plane to the north and set the auto pilot.

He went back to the cabin. As he untied Rosemary, he said "Everything is fine, honey and we're going home." He then untied Curly and closed the door.

She asked, "You mean we're not going to crash? I though the gas was dirty."

"No, it's not. Curly knew if we faked having engine problems, Jones would want to save himself. That's why he brought only one parachute."

Rosemary looked at Curly. He was laughing.

Catwalk looked at Curly and began laughing.

She said, "What's so funny?"

Catwalk said, "I'm guessing Deputy Jones got the biggest surprise of his life when he pulled the ripcord and nothing happened."

Rosemary looked at Curly and said, "You mean … .?"

Curly nodded.

She looked at Catwalk, and said, "Curly saved our lives."

"Maybe, but he's still a lousy chicken thief."

## ABOUT THE AUTHOR

Born and raised in northern Illinois, Jeff Egerton was seventeen and broke when he hopped a freight train to travel west. His journeys lasted less than a year, but vivid memories of those adventurous times survive to this day.

Jeff then enlisted and traveled to South Vietnam, courtesy of the US Marine Corps. Following a career in aviation, he began writing international crime novels. Lodged in the back of his mind, however, was a novel about young men riding the rails across America.

He began his research and discovered a time when thousands of young men traveled in boxcars out of necessity—during the Great Depression. When he read about the incredible racial inequities of the era, he knew the story had to be told.

Thus, over forty years, the most intriguing depression era novel since the *Grapes of Wrath,* was born.

Jeff currently resides in Tucson with his wife, Diane.

Printed in the United States
123790LV00004B/334-351/A

9 781596 635661